# *WOLFSTORM*

Ian Pugh was born in Bulawayo, Zimbabwe in 1962. After school he spent time working and hitch-hiking around Europe and North America, before returning to South Africa to complete a Bachelor of Arts degree (English Major) at the University of Cape Town. A few years as a "creative" in the advertising world followed but the travel bug remained and he was soon "going walkabout" again, this time for an extended period around Australia, Asia and the UK. During this time he wrote his film script, *Pawpaw*, which went on to win Best New Screenplay at the Cape Town Film Festival. He now lives in Bulawayo with his wife, Lara, and son, Sam, where they run their own design company. *Wolfstorm* is Ian's first book.


## What young readers are saying about *Wolfstorm*...

I loved *Wolfstorm* <u>so</u> much. It is one of the best books I have ever read!
— *Martine Ilgner, Age 12, Johannesburg, South Africa*


This book has been the best. I've never read anything better or anything that has made me want to finish it all at once. When's the next book coming?
— *Sam Nothnagel, Age 11, Melbourne, Australia*


**IMPOSSIBLE TO PUT DOWN!!** I thought it was an awesome book!
— *Travis Hall, Age 11, Johannesburg, South Africa*


I thought *Wolfstorm* was the best book I have read for ages. I read it in two days as I really wanted to find out what happened at the end and I wasn't disappointed. I would highly recommend it to other readers.
— *Alex Johnson, Age 10, Northumberland, UK*

I strongly recommend it to readers of all ages as the best book I ever have read. And I have read many good books! I can't wait to read the next one!
— *Savannah Plaskett, Age 11, Bulawayo, Zimbabwe*

I have recently read *Wolfstorm* and I absolutely loved it. I couldn't put the book down because it was exciting and I really wanted to find out what would happen next. I can't wait to read the next Danny Piper Adventure. I think it was one of the best books I have ever read.
— *Evie Costa, Age 12, Sydney, Australia*

I really, really, really loved the book and I hope you write another. If you do I'd be honored to read it. Remember that you'll always have me to read your books.
— *Abby Zimmerman, Age 12, Wichita, Kansas, USA*

I really loved this book and will recommend it as one of my best books read! What I liked about the book was it kept moving, it did not slow down and get boring.
— *Ben Randell, Age 11, Bulawayo, Zimbabwe*

Overall, *Wolfstorm* is an incredible book and I would recommend it to anybody. I got into trouble from mum for staying in bed so long and not getting ready for school, because it was such a gripping story. I'm looking forward to reading the next one in the series and hopefully more after that.
— *James Costa, Age 10, Sydney, Australia*

Wow! This book is amazing and is just packed full of action and excitement. I am not really a big reader but I used to be and this book just got me back into the spirit and it showed me what I was missing. I can't wait until the next book comes out. I would rate it 10 out of 10. It was the best book I've ever read.
— *Joshua Nothnagel, Age 13, Melbourne, Australia*

# *WOLFSTORM*

by
**Ian Pugh**

**Illustrated by Adam Truscott**

Grateful acknowledgement is made for the reproduction of the following lyrics:

"Don't wannabe an American Idiot" - Green Day, American Idiot.

Copyright © Reprise Records 2004

"Don't cha wish your girlfriend was hot like me" – The Pussycat Dolls (feat. Buster Rhymes), PCD. Copyright © A & M Records 2005

Order this book online at www.trafford.com
or email orders@trafford.com

Most Trafford titles are also available at major online book retailers.

© Copyright 2010 Ian Pugh.

All rights reserved. No part of this publication may be reproduced, stored in a retrieval system, or transmitted, in any form or by any means, electronic, mechanical, photocopying, recording, or otherwise, without the written prior permission of the author.

Printed in Victoria, BC, Canada.

ISBN: 978-1-4269-0238-3 (sc)
ISBN: 978-1-4269-0239-0 (hc)
ISBN: 978-1-4269-0240-6 (eb)

Our mission is to efficiently provide the world's finest, most comprehensive book publishing service, enabling every author to experience success. To find out how to publish your book, your way, and have it available worldwide, visit us online at www.trafford.com

Trafford rev. 1/26/10

**North America & international**
toll-free: 1 888 232 4444 (USA & Canada)
phone: 250 383 6864 ♦ fax: 812 355 4082

## A note from the author

Many people look at the world today and think, 'Oh dear, what a mess!' We have terrorists bombing, wars raging and a planet experiencing dangerous climate change. But you know what? With every new young generation on earth today there is a growing awareness (through a world connected and sharing information like never before in history!) that things *don't have to be like this*; that we are able to make things better *if* we take some sort of action! It is by looking back into history that we remind ourselves just how badly human beings have treated each other in the past and by looking forward into the future that we know how badly we are treating our planet in the present!

This book will take you on a journey - into the past and into the future. Many of the events that Danny and his friends experience in the past actually happened (the horrors of World War II, the 'Cockleshell Heroes', Otto Skorzeny - google them or visit our website mentioned below and you will see). History is there to remind us how bad things have been (in many ways much worse than today!) so that we, as human beings, make sure that the same mistakes are not repeated. In *Wolfstorm* you will also have a glimpse into the future. Is that what it will be like? Well, that is going to depend on us - *you and me* - *all* of us!

If you would like to read (and discuss) more about any of the subjects raised in this book, whether it has to do with history, the environment or maybe the science behind time travel, then please visit **www.dannypiper.com** After their great adventure Danny and his friends have a *whole lot more* to say on these subjects and they want to hear what you think as well so please visit the website and join the discussion! We hope you enjoy the adventure you are about to go on! I would also love to hear your thoughts so please feel free to drop me a line at **ian@dannypiper.com**

And now it only remains for me to thank all those people who have helped get *Wolfstorm* to where it is today. This was a journey in itself and, like Danny, Spike and Charley, I needed help from others to keep on going until the end. Many of the people listed below read the book while I was still writing it and sent me such great words of encouragement that I just knew I had to complete it! So my most heartfelt thanks goes to:

My wife, Lara, for doing the cover design and book layout – but, most importantly, for your unwavering love, encouragement and patience; my beautiful boy, Sam, for the hope and inspiration you have given me for the future; Sue-Pugh for your "super-positivity" from the word go; Andy, Nicki, Tars and Liesl for always being there; Barry, a friend who has gone "above and beyond", Jeremy, Izzie, Colin, Vicki, Clive, Eileen, Wayne, Becky, Charles, Rhian, Robby, Marcus, Tom, Savannah, Ben, Gray, Tayla, Chris, Di, Carol, Buck, Sara, Nicki G, Sinead, Martine, Dominique, Travis, Marijke, Sam, Joshua, Ant, Dee, Tom, Samuel, Abby, Kiwi, Lee, Matt, Nicky W, Ross, Courtney, Harry, Joey, Alex, Alice, Suzy, Jo, Evie, James, Jamie, Kath, Rachael, Lindsay (for the French), Kevin Wilson (for photography) and Jill Todd (for the editing). And an extra special word of thanks to Adam Truscott who has done all the wonderful illustrations in this book (cover included). Anyone who would like to get hold of this extremely talented man can do so at **adamink@mighty.co.za**

But I dedicate this book to my parents, Alan and Jill, who have always encouraged me to follow my heart and chase those dreams no matter where that took me, and not once did they ever say, "Hey Ian, shouldn't you be getting a real job?!" Our planet could do with more parents like Alan and Jill. I was lucky. Thanks!

*Ian Pugh, Bulawayo, 2009*

For my parents, Alan and Jill

Life is divided into three terms – that which was, which is, and which will be. Let us learn from the past to profit by the present, and from the present to live better in the future.

*- William Wordsworth*

Learn from yesterday, live for today, hope for tomorrow. The important thing is not to stop questioning.

*- Albert Einstein*

Chapter 1

# The Invitation

Daniel Piper-Adams would probably have been just like any other twelve-year-old English schoolboy if it hadn't been for that one horrific day in Australia.

It had already been two years since that day and yet, for Daniel, the memory was as fresh as yesterday.

It should have been the dream holiday - the sleek, white yacht his dad had hired, the thrill and excitement of sailing around the beautiful Whitsunday Islands, the wonder of snorkelling on the Great Barrier Reef.

A dream holiday - that's what it *should* have been!

That day they had moored the yacht near a reef where the snorkelling was said to be particularly spectacular. Daniel and his sister, Caitlin (who was a couple of years younger than him), couldn't wait to go snorkelling.

"Just stay close, all right?" their dad had warned. "There are strong currents around and if you're not careful you'll find yourselves being swept out to sea."

"OK, Dad," Daniel had said before leaping out to join his sister in the turquoise water.

The thing about snorkelling is that you only have to duck your head a few inches under the water to be immediately drawn into a different world. If that happens to be a world as spectacular as the Great Barrier Reef, with its clouds of rainbow-coloured fish swirling around the spongy corals, it doesn't take long to forget about everything above the water, *which is why neither Daniel nor Catie noticed just how quickly the current was taking them away from the yacht!*

When they eventually did look up, the yacht was just a speck in the distance. Daniel tugged his sister's arm.

"Catie, we have to head back."

Now they both set off swimming towards the yacht, but the more they swam the farther away they seemed to be getting! Catie had started to cry.

"Don't cry - we'll get there!" Daniel shouted to her.

"But we're getting farther away!" she shouted back.

She was starting to panic, which Daniel knew was the worst thing that could happen. He could also see that she was getting tired, and he was starting to feel the same way.

"Here, grab on to my shoulders. Dad will see us now and he'll come and get us."

Now they were both getting very tired and Daniel knew he couldn't keep swimming with Catie hanging on to him.

What happened next was not easy to remember. The psychologist he had once been sent to see said that his mind had blocked it out. All Daniel could remember was the splashing, the saltwater, Catie crying and them both going down. Amongst all this chaos, he vaguely remembered his dad suddenly arriving and saying to him:

"Swim, Dan! Swim for the boat!"

And that's what he had done. By then his mum had also leapt into the water. She swam to him with a life ring, which they used to haul themselves back onto the boat.

As Daniel lay on the deck, heaving for breath, his mum rushed to the side to see where his dad and Catie were. That's when he remembers her starting to scream - screaming their names over and over...

They would never see them again.

And, from that day on, Daniel would never be quite the same again.

*

Over the next two years much of Daniel's behaviour was blamed on this terrible incident. Like the day at his school - Barnstaple

## THE INVITATION

Grammar School, to be precise - when Taggert had made the comment he would later live to regret.

Daniel was new at the school, which was not something unusual. They had moved several times in the last two years, mainly because his mother was good at finding new jobs, but not that great at keeping them! So he was used to being 'the new boy' and receiving all the stick that went with it.

At Barnstaple Grammar School it was Taggert (a giant of a boy - in body, not brain!) who had started the usual comments. Stuff like:

"What's wrong Piper-Adams - you too posh for just one surname? You gotta have two?"

Daniel was usually pretty good at ignoring these kinds of jibes. His name and his accent (sometimes also described as 'posh') were usually the first things that most kids noticed were different and, therefore, picked up on. However, there were certain things (as Taggert was to discover on that grey and windy afternoon) that Daniel found impossible to ignore, and these were usually things that had to do with his dad or Catie.

On that day, Daniel was just about to start his walk home to Woodford Lane when he came across Taggert and his mates standing near the school fountain. As usual, Taggert was trying to amuse his mates by making sniping remarks at anyone passing by.

"Hey Piper-Adams!" he crowed. "If you've got two surnames how come you've only got one parent?"

This stopped Daniel dead in his tracks. It also caused a lot of sniggers from Taggert's mates. But when Daniel now turned to face them, he noticed how quickly the sniggers dried up - only to be replaced by ever-so-slightly-nervous glances in the direction of Taggert.

Daniel was an above average sized boy - a bit taller and broader than most. It was probably this (and his unruly blond hair) that drew a lot of the girls' attention to him (not that he ever seemed to notice or do anything about it!). But if Daniel was big for his age then Taggert was enormous - at least another head taller and considerably bigger in build. So there was now genuine surprise when Daniel started walking towards them, and he noticed how Taggert's mates suddenly started to bunch up.

Taggert looked more surprised than anyone (this is not how these situations usually played out!), but at the same time, he knew he had a lot riding on this moment.

"Better be careful, Daniel!" he sneered, stepping out from his mates. "I hear your old man's not around to help!"

Looking back on things, Taggert would later admit to himself that this last comment had probably been a mistake. It was as if Daniel was suddenly transformed into a raging, snorting, charging bull. He launched himself hard and low, catching Taggert right in the stomach and sending him reeling back through his mates, where he then tripped over a low wall and flipped back into the fountain - with Daniel on top of him!

Floundering around in the water, Daniel managed to get in a few good shots before being overwhelmed by the size and strength of Taggert - and that's when the inevitable blows came raining down.

Thankfully, it wasn't long before Mr Preston, the deputy headmaster, arrived on the scene and broke things up.

They received a mountain of punishment, but despite this (and the bruises), the sight of Taggert hauling himself out of the fountain with all his mates collapsing in hysterical laughter around him, seemed to make it all worthwhile.

\*

When Daniel arrived home later that afternoon he was still trying to stem the flow of the Taggert-inflicted nosebleed that had turned the front of his sodden shirt a nice rosy pink! As he squelched down the passage his mum called to him from another room, but he wasn't in the mood to explain so he carried on through to his bedroom and closed the door behind him.

It didn't take long before she came to investigate. There was a gentle knock and then the door slowly opened.

"Daniel? You OK?"

Daniel didn't bother to look up from what he was doing at his desk.

"Homework?" his mum asked.

"No," he replied. "I'm changing my name."

"Oh," his mum said. "I see."

She was trying to sound casual but her eyes had gone into rapid-blink mode.

"It's now Danny Piper - pure and simple," he said. "And please don't argue about it, Mum, because I've made up my mind."

"I'm not arguing!" his mum protested. She had just managed to get her blinking under control. "But… can I at least ask *why?*"

She could now see that he was busy changing his name on all his school books.

Danny had hoped that his mother might leave him alone, but this was obviously not going to happen, so he put his pen down and turned to face her.

That's when she saw his bloody nose and pink shirt-front.

"Ah, no Danny! What's happened now?"

*"Nothing! It's fine!"*

Danny's sharp reply took his mother by surprise. He took a deep breath and decided to say what had been on his mind for some time.

"Look, Mum, I know how different things used to be, OK? Where we lived, where I went to school - our lives, everything! But that's all gone now. Everything changed when..." He still couldn't bring himself to speak of that fateful day in Australia "...when we became poor. That's the truth, and I'm sick and tired of being called a little rich boy just because they say my name sounds posh! So that's why it's now Danny Piper."

Danny went back to changing his books. His mother didn't say anything for a while. She sat as if mulling over what she had just heard and seemed saddened by it.

"That's fine - Daniel, *Danny*, whatever you want to call yourself. As long as you know - you are the most important thing in my life-"

"I know, Mum. I know," Danny said, trying to stop all the soppy stuff before she really got going.

His mother just smiled. She was already starting to get teary.

"I don't care if we're not rich. We get on all right, don't we? Don't we, Danny?"

Danny nodded. He had heard this many times before. Now his mother would talk about them sticking together.

"We've just got to stick together. Am I not right, Dan?"

"Yes, Mum." Danny nodded again, and then he couldn't resist adding, "Pity not everyone in our family sticks together."

His mother obviously knew who this was aimed at.

"Ah yes, good old Uncle Morty."

Danny was now shaking his head like he normally did when they mentioned his Great Uncle Mortimer.

"He lives in that massive house with all that money and what has he ever done for us?"

It was true, and his mother knew it. After his father had died they had discovered that there was very little money left in the bank. He hadn't made any arrangements or provisions for his family should he die. He was not the sort of person to be thinking of death - he was too busy enjoying *life*! Suddenly his mother had had to find a job to pay the bills. It was a tough time and, although she was not looking for charity, it would have helped if someone like Uncle Mortimer had offered a bit of a loan - just to tide them over until her first pay cheque arrived. The offer never came and there was no way she ever would have asked for anything.

"We don't need him - or his money. We're just fine the way we are. Aren't we?"

"Sure, Mum."

Danny often found it a lot easier to just agree. Talking about this stuff never solved anything anyway, so rather just agree that everything was fine then his mother would give him a kiss on the head and leave, which is what she did now.

"Dinner will be ready soon," she said on her way out.

In truth, their money situation didn't really bother Danny *that* much, although he would never forget his so-called 'new soccer ball' exploding when Gary Todd had taken that penalty! He could feel his ears glowing red just thinking about it!

What really did bother him though was how his mother would get sometimes, late in the evenings when she thought he had gone to sleep. That's when he would hear her crying - and he knew what she was crying about. She was yearning for the days when they had been a complete family. At times like this, Danny would feel this uncontrollable anger rising up inside him and he would start to direct it at other people; people like his selfish Uncle Mortimer.

Mortimer was actually Danny's *great*-uncle, in other words, he was the brother of Danny's grandfather. Both Danny's grandparents on that side of the family had passed away, which meant that Uncle Morty (as they called him) was now the most senior surviving member of the Piper-Adams family.

The last time they had seen Uncle Morty had been at his dad and Catie's funeral. There he was in his electric wheelchair - a dishevelled, eccentric-looking man who had lost both his legs from the knees down while fighting the Nazis in World War II. Danny remembered how he had looked across the two coffins at them. It was a look of great sadness and... what else? Pity? Guilt? He couldn't tell.

After the funeral he had come over to them and mumbled his condolences then, without another word, he had left. He had not even bothered to attend the wake. Instead, he had just returned to Bosworth Manor.

Most of what Danny knew about his great-uncle was what he picked up from other people's conversations. His mother would never say very much on the subject, but when other relatives came to visit (especially the likes of Aunt Hatty and Uncle Martin), it usually wasn't long before Uncle Morty's name came up.

"Let's face it, the poor man has gone completely mad," Aunt Hatty would say, helping herself to another biscuit. "He lost more than just his legs in that war I tell you." She would then tap the side of her head to make sure everyone knew what she was talking about. "And then, after the tragedy in Australia - well, that was obviously too much for his fragile mind to bear."

That's when Uncle Martin would lean forwards and speak in almost a whisper.

"He hasn't been seen for nearly a year now. Never leaves the

## THE INVITATION

house. All his shopping is done by Mrs Barnes, the housekeeper. Some people wonder if he's actually still alive!"

"More tea?" Danny's Mum would ask, trying to lighten things up a bit, but it wasn't that easy to get them off the subject.

"Such a shame," Aunt Hatty would continue. "He was apparently a brilliant scientist, you know? They say he may have even been one of the truly *great* scientists, but that's all gone to waste now and, speaking of waste... all that money..."

It seemed that when the subject of Uncle Mortimer's money came up, both Aunt Hatty and Uncle Martin had great difficulty talking about it. Instead, they would both just look down at their teacups and shake their heads. Eventually Aunt Hatty would manage to utter a few words.

"He'll probably leave it all to that wretched Mrs Barnes. If he hasn't already!"

This was always followed by more serious nodding and biscuit eating.

"It's sad," Danny's mother would say later, when the others had gone, "because, before that terrible war and your dad's death, Mortimer had always been such a kind and friendly man. He would often help out members of the family who were in trouble. We must just accept how he is now. There's nothing we can do about it, so we may as well just get on with our lives."

\*

And so it was on that day, when Danny ended up in the fountain with Taggert and subsequently changed his name, that he also decided to stop thinking about how their lives could have been different if *this* hadn't happened or *that* hadn't happened. Unfortunately, all these things *had* happened and they were just going to have to accept it and move on!

But everything that Danny decided on that day would last for only two weeks - because it was exactly two weeks later, on the first day of the school holidays, that the postman slipped a letter through the slot in their front door. Danny, still half-asleep, picked the letter up and took it through to the kitchen where his mother was making breakfast. The letter was addressed to his mother, so he tossed it down onto the kitchen table and poured himself some cereal.

It was only when he was busy munching his Rice Krispies that he glanced at the letter again. He turned it over to see who it was from - and that's when he stopped chewing.

Written on the back, in spidery handwriting, there was a name and address. It read:

*Sender: Mortimer Piper-Adams*
*Bosworth Manor*
*New Forest*
*Hampshire*

\*

"What do you think he wants?" Danny asked for the third time.

"I've no idea," his mother replied, still scrambling eggs on the stove.

"Well, at least we know he's not dead!" Danny said, holding the letter up to the light to see if he could read anything through the envelope. "Unless he scribbled this on his deathbed. Hey, Mum - maybe it's his will and he's left us all his money!"

His mother gave him one of her looks.

"Come on, Mum! Open it!"

"All right! All right!" At last she brought the breakfast to the table and plonked it down in front of him. "You'd think it was a letter from the queen!"

Danny handed her the letter, but she insisted on wiping her hands on a tea towel first before taking it. Finally, miracle of all miracles, she opened it and began to read, and it must have been very short because she had finished it in less than a minute.

"Well?" asked Danny. "What does it say?"

Instead of replying, his mother just handed him the letter.

# THE INVITATION

Danny squinted as he tried to read the handwriting. It looked like a spider had taken an ink bath and then done gymnastics across the page. As best as he could make out, the letter read:

*Bosworth Manor*
*New Forest*
*Hampshire*

*Dear Margaret,*

*You will no doubt be surprised to hear from me after so many years. The lack of contact between us is entirely my fault and for this I sincerely apologise. Perhaps one day you will learn of the reasons behind my strange behaviour over these many years and I pray that there may be some understanding then. Until that day, if indeed it ever comes, I ask for your patience and forgiveness.*

*I realise this is very short notice, but I would like to invite Daniel up to stay at Bosworth Manor for a few weeks. I believe the school holidays begin shortly, so perhaps this would be a convenient time. If there is any chance of this, I would appreciate it if you called Mrs Barnes on 01425 473581 to make the necessary arrangements. If Daniel came up by train Mrs Barnes could pick him up from Ringwood Station.*

*By the way, Mrs Barnes has two children who must be of a similar age to Daniel, so he must not think he will have to spend his entire holiday with an old man!*

*I look forward to hearing your response.*

*With all best wishes to you*
*Mortimer*

While Danny read the letter, his mother stood staring out of the kitchen window, obviously deep in thought. Only when he had finished did she come over and take a seat at the kitchen table. Then she started to dish up eggs as though nothing had happened!

Danny's head was in a spin! He didn't know what to think. Half his brain was saying, 'Why would I want to go and visit some old man in a wheelchair, who is probably mad, and hasn't bothered to contact us in years?', while the other half was thinking, 'A holiday at Bosworth Manor sounds a bit more interesting than a holiday at Woodford Lane, and what on earth has Uncle Morty been up to all these years?'

"Well?" his mother said eventually, as she casually ate her eggs.

"Well what?" Danny replied, also trying to make out it was no big deal.

"Want to go?"

Danny just shrugged.

"Hmm…" His mother was now shaking her head. "I don't think I want you to go."

"Why not?" Danny asked, suddenly concerned that his mother was going to try and make up his mind for him.

"Well, I don't know. We have no idea what's been going on at Bosworth Manor, do we? I'm not sure I'm happy sending you to some place we know very little about."

"Come on, Mum - it's not like Uncle Morty is going to kidnap me or anything!"

"Oh, so you *do* want to go?"

The question caught Danny a little off guard and he retreated back into his scrambled eggs without answering.

\*

For the rest of the day, Danny said nothing at all about going to Bosworth Manor - although he couldn't stop thinking about it!

## THE INVITATION

Even if he had wanted to, it would have been impossible because his mother kept bringing up the subject with comments like:

"You realise it would mean you having your birthday up there?"

Danny hadn't thought about that. It was his thirteenth birthday the following week.

"Hey, Mum," he said, smiling. "Maybe Uncle Morty is inviting me up there to give me a huge birthday present!"

"I wouldn't count on that, my friend," she replied.

A little later, his mother came up with another suggestion.

"I suppose you could go, and if you didn't like it you could hop on the next train and come home again?"

Danny didn't reply. He was pretending to watch a TV programme (even though he had no idea what it was about). But, right then, the one thing he did know for sure was that this was the best idea he had heard so far. When the programme ended, he casually stood up and walked to the door.

"OK, I'll go."

It was only now, as Danny went through to his room and lay on his bed, that he allowed himself to start getting excited. Whatever happened, this school holiday was certainly going to be *different*!

Of course, as Danny lay there staring up at the ceiling, there was no way he could ever have known just *how different* this holiday was going to turn out; no way he could have known that he had just made the most important decision of his life. Not only was it about to change his whole life forever, but also the lives of a great many other people, most of whom he had not even met yet!

Chapter 2

# Bosworth Manor

The train ride to Ringwood (the nearest town to Bosworth Manor) only took a couple of hours. Danny's mother had done her fair share of fussing at the station.

"Have you got your ticket? Have you got your money for food and emergencies? Have you got the phone number in case you want to come home?"

Danny assured her that he had all these things.

"Now, if Uncle Morty turns out to be strange *in any way* I want you to come straight home. Do you understand?"

"Yes, Mum. You've said that twenty times already," Danny groaned.

"Good, then you won't forget," she said, giving him a hug.

Danny climbed aboard the train and found himself a seat. Just as he was storing his case in the luggage rack, the train began to pull out of the station. He opened the window and leaned out to wave to his mother.

"I'll miss you!" she shouted, waving furiously.

"It's only two weeks!" he called back.

Danny continued to wave until his mother drifted out of sight. It was only when he had closed the window and taken a seat that he thought more clearly about what he had just said.

*Only two weeks!*

This might just turn out to be the longest two weeks of his life!

\*

As the train pulled into Ringwood Station, Danny leaned out of the window to see if he could spot Mrs Barnes and her two children, but there were no children on the platform. In fact, there were very few people at all and only one lady, whom he hoped and prayed *wasn't* Mrs Barnes! She was dressed in tweed and looked ultra-strict.

Danny clambered out with his suitcase and, to his horror, the tweedy lady immediately started towards him. He tried to casually look the other way, but soon felt her presence right behind him.

"Daniel Piper-Adams?" she asked.

It crossed Danny's mind that he could say, 'No, sorry', and get back on the train, but he found himself turning to her and nodding.

"How do you do? I'm Mrs Barnes," she said, holding out a black leather-gloved hand for him to shake. Up close, she looked even more serious - like there was a bad smell around and she was trying to sniff out the culprit. "Your train is late," she chirped. "We had better get moving."

And off she went with quick little steps towards the station exit. As Danny picked up his suitcase and followed, all he could think was, *What am I doing here?*

Soon they were travelling along in Mrs Barnes' car. It was a bit like her - very neat and very old-fashioned! Thankfully, she wasn't one for making small talk, so for most of the time they travelled in silence.

Once they had passed through the small town, they headed out into the countryside and were soon entering the New Forest. Now all signs of houses and people began to disappear and soon there was nothing to be seen but trees and a couple of New Forest ponies. Danny had forgotten that Bosworth Manor was situated in such a remote place. He felt like Hansel, disappearing deeper and deeper into the woods - except that in this version the Wicked Witch was at the wheel!

"Here we are!" Mrs Barnes announced suddenly.

Danny peered up ahead, but couldn't see anything. It still looked like thick forest on either side to him.

It was only when Mrs Barnes actually slowed right down

and began to turn the car that he noticed it was the entrance to a driveway. Once upon a time it must have been a very grand entrance, but now the large brick pillars and the wrought iron letters spelling 'BOSWORTH MANOR' were so overgrown with ivy creepers that they were almost impossible to see. Danny later discovered that Uncle Mortimer had forbidden anyone to chop the ivy creepers down. He was apparently quite happy that most people driving past would never even notice the entrance.

Now they were travelling down a long curved driveway, the forest thicker than ever on either side. As Danny looked out into the dark shadowy trees he suddenly, just for the briefest of moments, thought he saw something. It was just a flash as a figure moved between the trees, then disappeared from sight. Danny looked again. *Was he seeing things?*

Now he saw it again - a figure moving quickly through the forest. Danny watched as it darted in and out of the trees, leaping over ditches and bramble bushes as though they weren't there. Danny looked to see if Mrs Barnes had noticed the figure, and it appeared she had.

"Is that your son?" he asked.

The question almost made Mrs Barnes smile.

"If only that was the case," she said, "if only…"

Danny had no idea what she meant by this, but he quickly forgot about it now as the large grey shape of Bosworth Manor loomed up before them.

The house was huge, even bigger than he remembered. Three storeys high with rows of at least twenty windows on each storey, but the thing that struck Danny immediately was that all the windows had their shutters closed. It was a house without any signs of life; a house that most people would presume was deserted.

Mrs Barnes didn't stop the car in front of the manor house, but drove around to the back and parked outside a quaint thatched cottage.

At least this place looks alive, Danny thought.

Now a tall, wiry man wearing a cloth cap was approaching the car.

"This is my husband," Mrs Barnes announced, as they climbed out.

Mr Barnes stood fidgeting nervously with his cap for a moment before coming forwards to shake Danny's hand. He didn't say anything, just nodded a few times, which did strike Danny as a bit odd.

Danny then noticed another figure emerging from the cottage. It was a boy, about his age, but taller and skinnier. He walked directly up to Danny, peering at him through his rather thick glasses.

"*This* is my son," said Mrs Barnes. "Michael, say hello to Daniel."

Michael stuck out his hand and smiled.

"Hello!"

As he shook Michael's hand, Danny couldn't help feeling slightly taken aback by his direct manner. He reminded Danny of one of those boys that other children sometimes like to make fun of - perhaps because of his height or slightly nerdy appearance - yet he simply didn't seem to care. This is how he was - take it or leave it!

"And that is my daughter over there," said Mrs Barnes, pointing to a nearby tree.

Danny looked at the tree then back at Mrs Barnes, clearly confused.

"Not the tree," said Mrs Barnes. "I'm talking about what's *in* the tree!"

Only now did Danny hear a laugh coming from high up in the branches, but he still couldn't see anyone.

"Say hello to Daniel, Charlotte!" called Mrs Barnes.

"Hello!" came a girl's voice from the tree.

"*That's* who you saw in the forest," said Mrs Barnes, turning to go inside. "Our resident little gypsy."

Just as Mrs Barnes was about to disappear inside, something occurred to Danny.

"Um, sorry but... where's my uncle?"

"Mr Piper-Adams will be working for another few hours yet," Mrs Barnes replied. "You are to join him for dinner. Until then, Michael and Charlotte can show you around. I don't have to tell you where to steer clear of, do I Michael?"

"The dungeon!" said Michael, his face lighting up at the thought.

"Don't be silly, Michael," said Mrs Barnes, shaking her head. "How many times must I tell you it is a wine cellar, not a dungeon!"

"Whatever you say, Mother!" said Michael with a big grin on his face.

Mr and Mrs Barnes went inside, leaving the two boys standing rather awkwardly together. As if to break the silence, Michael suddenly shouted at the tree.

"Hey, get down from there, you little gypsy!"

"I will when I feel like it!" came the shouted reply.

Michael shook his head at Danny and rolled his eyes.

"Sorry, she's a bit odd."

The boys walked over and sat on a bench near the tree.

"So, when were you last here?" Michael asked.

"Oh... *years* ago," Danny replied. "When I was small. I can hardly remember it."

They sat for a few moments, looking up towards the big house then Danny couldn't resist the question any longer.

"So... what's this about a dungeon?" he asked.

"It's a secret," said Michael. "Nobody knows what goes on in the dungeon because nobody is allowed to go down there."

"Except Mr Piper-Adams," said Charlotte from above.

"Of course, except Mr Piper-Adams," Michael snapped impatiently. "That's where he works, Einstein!"

"Works?" Danny was surprised. "I didn't realise… What sort of work does he do?"

Michael shrugged.

"Well, actually, that's also something that nobody knows," he said, clearly enjoying the suspense.

The voice in the tree came again.

"Except us."

This really seemed to annoy Michael.

"Shut up, Charles, and get out of the tree will you!" he shouted.

Danny's interest was growing by the second.

"So… you *do* know what he does?"

"Not really," Michael replied, and then as if to change the subject, he suddenly got to his feet. "Come on, I'll show you around."

Danny didn't enjoy being left in the lurch like this, but there was little he could do except follow Michael. They walked off into the gardens then Michael winked at him and signalled back towards the tree. He was predicting movement in the tree and, sure enough, the leaves and branches soon started to rustle and, moments later, a figure dropped down onto the lawn below.

Danny's first thought was that Charlotte *did* look like a little gypsy! She was probably a year younger than Danny and Michael - quite short and very scruffy. She wasn't wearing any shoes and her jet-black hair was wild and tangled, but, as she smiled shyly at Danny, he couldn't help but think that, beneath all the dirt and tomboy looks, there was without a doubt a pretty girl in there somewhere.

"Daniel, meet my sister. Some people call her Charley, but I call her Charles because she should have been a boy."

"Hi," said Danny, adding, "by the way, everyone calls me Danny."

"And everyone calls him Spike," said Charley, nodding towards Michael. "Do you know why?"

Michael rolled his eyes and waited for the explanation.

"Because he's long and pointy!"

Charley erupted into giggles and Michael shook his head and put on his best fake smile.

"Gee, Charles, I think I'm going to bust a gut I'm laughing so much. That is just *so* amusing!"

Charley was nodding as she continued to giggle.

"I know it is!"

Looking at the two of them together, Danny couldn't believe that they were brother and sister. They were just *so different*! Michael (or rather Spike) clearly took after their father while Charley was small and dark like their mother.

"Come on, let's show Danny around," said Charley.

\*

The property was so huge that looking after all the gardens was obviously too much work for one man (namely Mr Barnes), which meant that much of it looked wild and untended. Charley, who seemed to know her way around every nook and cranny, led the way and they soon arrived at an old rundown pavilion overlooking a giant duck pond. The pavilion was barely visible amidst a tangle of vines and creepers, and the pond was so filled with mud and reeds that no self-respecting duck would have gone near the place!

They stood there for a moment surveying this sad sight then Charley came out with something that surprised them all.

"Sorry about your dad and sister," she said suddenly.

It was the last thing Danny was expecting to hear and, for a few seconds, he had no idea how to respond. Spike saw this and gave Charley a dirty look for being so blunt. Charley didn't think she had done anything wrong and they now started a silent war of mouthed words behind Danny's back.

"Just forget about it, all right?" snapped Danny.

The sharpness of his tone stopped the argument immediately, and now a very uncomfortable silence descended over the three of them. Eventually Spike couldn't bear it any longer.

"Come on, let's go and show Danny the monkeys," he suggested.

This seemed to do the trick as Charley suddenly let out an excited scream, 'Eeeeveeeee!' and took off through the undergrowth.

"Excuse my sister," Spike muttered as they started to walk. "She doesn't know the meaning of tact. We saw a photo of you with your sister and your dad in the main house, obviously taken when you were much younger, then our mother told us… you know… what happened."

Again it was clear that Danny didn't want to talk about it and he now changed the subject completely.

"Did you say *monkeys* back there?" he asked.

Spike clearly welcomed the change of subject as well.

"You mean you don't have monkeys where you come from?" he asked, and the grin returned to his face.

\*

Sure enough, a few minutes later they were sitting beside a cage housing a couple of the cutest little monkeys Danny had ever seen. Apparently, Uncle Morty had ordered the monkeys from somewhere overseas and they had suddenly been delivered a few months back. Nobody was exactly sure why he had got them because, as far as Spike and Charley knew, he never came to see them. He had told Mrs Barnes that their names were Adam and Eve, and had given her strict instructions to make sure they were well looked after.

Mrs Barnes thought the monkeys were just another part of Mr

Piper-Adams' strange behaviour, but Spike and Charley were delighted by their arrival. Charley had grown especially close to them and now, as she slipped into the cage, both monkeys immediately leapt up onto her shoulders.

Danny and Spike sat watching Charley playing with the monkeys until Danny could no longer resist bringing up the subject of his uncle again.

"So, come on, guys, you have to tell me - what's Uncle Morty been up to in 'the dungeon'?"

"We're honestly not sure," Spike replied. "For years now he's been working down there. The only people who ever visit here are delivery guys bringing all sorts of equipment and stuff. They take it down into his workshop, but nobody knows what it's for."

"We know a secret way into the dungeon," Charley said suddenly.

Spike flung her a look as if to say '*shut up*!' - but it was too late. Danny couldn't believe his ears.

"*You've been down there?*"

Spike was still giving Charley a dirty look - but eventually he nodded to Danny.

"And?" Danny asked impatiently. "What did you see?"

"A giant washing machine," said Charley with a giggle.

Spike also let out an amused grunt.

"Yeh, Charles thinks the thing he's been building looks like a giant washing machine, but to be honest with you we actually have no idea what it is."

Now the curiosity was getting too much for Danny.

"Can't we go and see it? How do we get down there?"

"Not while he's there!" said Charley.

Spike agreed.

"The only time it's safe to go there is late at night when he's in bed."

"Except sometimes he works all night," added Charley, "and that's when we hear the noise."

"The noise?"

Spike nodded.

"Sometimes late at night we've heard a very loud noise coming from down there."

"Like a plane taking off," said Charley.

"Yeh," agreed Spike. "Like there's a jumbo jet down there winding up its engines."

Danny's mind was racing. This was all sounding more and more bizarre!

"What is it? Surely your parents must know?"

This made both Spike and Charley laugh.

"Try asking our mum," said Spike, putting on a voice just like his mother's. "It's Mr Piper-Adams' project and it's no business of ours! Stay away from there or we will all be without a place to live!"

Danny had to smile at how well Spike could imitate his mother.

"She'd kill us if she knew we'd been down there," added Spike with a grin, glancing at his watch. "Speaking of which, we'd better get back. You don't want to be late for your dinner with Uncle Morty."

Do I even *want* to have dinner with Uncle Morty? was all Danny could think.

*

Walking up to the manor house with Mrs Barnes, Danny felt like he was being escorted to the headmaster's office.

They entered through the back doorway into the most enormous kitchen Danny had ever seen. Their whole house at Woodford Lane could have fitted into this kitchen! From here they went down a long corridor lined with real suits of armour, and Danny suddenly had a vague memory of playing amongst these towering figures when he and Catie were very young.

Finally they arrived at the dining room, which was actually more of a hall than a room. Running down the centre was a massive table, big enough to seat thirty or more people - but this evening it was only set for two, with a place laid at each end.

"Take a seat down there, please," ordered Mrs Barnes, pointing to the far end of the table.

Danny did as he was told. The chair at the end was so heavy he could hardly move it, but he eventually managed to sit.

"Sit quietly and don't touch anything," said Mrs Barnes as she turned to leave. "Mr Piper-Adams will be along shortly."

With that, she disappeared out of the room, leaving Danny feeling very small and alone in the midst of the great hall.

The hall was dimly lit - the only light coming from the candles lining the table. It took a few moments for his eyes to adjust then he began to see faces peering at him out of the gloom. They were portraits (mainly of self-important looking men with big moustaches) decorating the walls of the hall. Like the suits of armour, the paintings seemed to jolt a memory of something from when he was small. He could vaguely remember his dad showing him the portraits and explaining how all these people were his ancestors - the Piper-Adams family dating back for centuries.

What a dreary bunch! Danny thought. They could have at least *smiled*! Mind you, living in this house...

Danny was so busy craning his neck around to look at the portraits behind him that he didn't notice the wheelchair arriving at the entrance to the hall.

"Daniel."

The voice gave him such a fright that he kicked his shin on the table leg. Now he saw the wheelchair coming down the hall towards him. It was one of those electric types that made a light humming sound when moving. As it trundled towards him, he began to make out the hunched figure of Uncle Mortimer.

Although Danny had vague memories of his uncle from the funeral, the figure that now emerged from the gloom was like no one he had ever seen before. To be honest, Uncle Morty looked scary! His white hair was long and straggly. His face was covered in grey stubble. His clothes were crumpled and grimy, but the thing that struck Danny the most was how tired he looked. He looked like he hadn't slept in weeks!

"How do you do, Daniel?" his uncle said. "I'm so pleased to see you again after so long."

As he shook Danny's hand he adjusted the glasses perched on his nose, so that he could take a long hard look at Danny's face. This made him appear sad for a moment, but he quickly recovered and did his best to smile.

"Yes," he said, nodding, "you are certainly your father's son."

Mrs Barnes had now entered the hall with a tray of food. She placed a plate at the end of the table for his uncle then came down with Danny's.

"Eat it while it's hot," she said.

Danny was interested to see that even Uncle Morty listened to Mrs Barnes. Obediently, he retreated in his wheelchair back to his end of the table.

"How old are you now, Daniel?" he asked, parking the chair at the head of the table.

"Twelve," Danny replied.

He thought about mentioning his fast approaching thirteenth birthday, but then decided against it.

With all the silver candlesticks between them, Danny could hardly see his uncle. He had to lean right over to one side, but then found that his uncle was leaning the other way.

"This is ridiculous!" Uncle Morty stormed, suddenly grabbing his plate and reversing his chair away from the table. "I'm going to sit down there, Violet!"

Mrs Barnes, who had just returned with some wine, didn't look too pleased, but there was no arguing as Uncle Morty drove his wheelchair back down the hall and parked beside Danny.

"That's better," he said, giving Danny a smile and starting to eat. "How's your mother, Daniel?" he asked, shovelling in more food and not bothering to wipe the gravy off his chin.

*What do you care?* was Danny's first thought, but the last thing he wanted was to have his uncle feeling sorry for them, so instead he replied:

"She's all right... I suppose."

Now, from deep inside, Danny felt the old feelings of anger rising up again. Suddenly he felt like shouting, *Don't you care about your family?* Again he managed to keep a lid on it and said nothing.

Perhaps his uncle could sense how Danny was feeling because he now moved his chair even closer and checked that Mrs Barnes was not in the hall.

"I know what you must think of me. All these years - me cut off from you and your mother and everybody else, but I'm hoping I can make you understand. I'm hoping that I can help all of us in a way that neither you nor anybody else could possibly imagine. You see, Daniel, over the last... God knows how many years, I've been working on something. Something that has the potential to change all our lives forever."

*Yes, whoopee! A giant washing machine!* thought Danny.

Now his uncle was looking at him very seriously.

"I want to be honest with you right from the start, Daniel. I need your help. The reason I have invited you here is because I badly need your help."

This took Danny by surprise.

"My help? How can I help?" he asked, scowling.

"That's what I'm going to tell you tonight. Tonight I will tell you everything, and I'm going to show you something that no one else has *ever* seen before."

No one except Spike and Charley Barnes, Danny thought. The excitement was growing inside him. But Uncle Mortimer was still looking very serious.

"Now you must listen to me, Daniel. This thing that I am going to ask you to do is not easy. In fact, it will be extremely difficult - and dangerous. Yes, there will be a lot of danger." His uncle was now gripping his arm. "But listen," he said. "Should you not want any part in it, that is fine. The choice is yours. I would never dream of forcing you to do anything. Do you understand?"

Danny nodded.

"All I ask," he continued," is that if you decide not to do it, you won't breathe a word of what you have seen or heard tonight to anyone. Nobody else must ever know about this. Do I have your promise on that, Daniel?"

Danny nodded again.

"Good. Now finish up your food and we'll go down."

Danny looked down at his plate and realised he hadn't touched anything yet. It felt like a million butterflies had just taken flight in his stomach - and he certainly wasn't feeling hungry! He ate a few mouthfuls then put down his knife and fork.

"Done?" his uncle asked.

Danny nodded.

"Right, let's go down."

Danny followed behind Uncle Morty's wheelchair as they made their way out of the hall and down the passage. When they reached the main staircase of the house his uncle removed a bunch of keys from his pocket and began to unlock what appeared to be a wooden wall panel. It was actually a concealed door, which now slid open to reveal a lift. They entered the lift and Uncle Morty pressed a button marked 'CELLAR'. The door closed and the lift began to move slowly downwards.

As the lift slowed, then bumped to a halt at the bottom, Uncle Morty turned to Danny.

"Ready?"

Danny nodded. This was the moment of truth. He could barely breathe with the excitement.

The lift door slid open.

Chapter 3

# TIM

As the lift door opened there was nothing to be seen but darkness, but then the lights flickered on and it was as if Danny had left an old world behind and was entering *a brand new one!*

The room may once have been a wine cellar, but now it resembled something between a space rocket control room and a workshop for mending electronic gadgets. All the way around the room, against every wall, were work benches covered with tools, desks with rows of computer screens and banks of very hi-tech looking machinery and equipment.

Danny stood rooted, gazing around at everything, trying to take in the sight of all this impressive technology, but it was something situated right in the centre of the room that grabbed his attention.

This must have been 'the giant washing machine' Charley had spoken about. He could see why she had described it that way - it was basically square in shape and had a round door in the front, but if this was a washing machine it was without a doubt the *coolest* he had ever seen! It was made from shiny silver chrome and a sleek black material, and it was certainly *huge* - big enough for a grown man to stand inside.

Uncle Morty was clearly enjoying the fact that Danny was so taken with the machine, and he now watched as his nephew walked around it, running his hand along the sides. It was beautifully smooth; no sharp corners, all rounded curves. Once he had been all the way around it, he came back to the door in the front and tried to look in through the glass window, but the glass was tinted and he couldn't really see anything. Now he noticed something painted above the door - three small letters - TIM.

For the first time since he had laid eyes on the machine, Danny

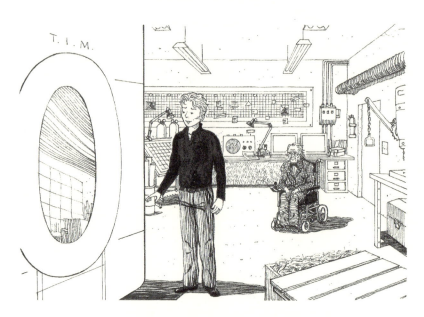

now looked over to see where his uncle was.

"TIM?" he asked.

"Yes." Uncle Morty nodded with a smile. He seemed to be bursting with pride. "It stands for Time Itinerant Module."

Danny's expression remained blank.

"What does that mean?"

Uncle Morty now manoeuvred his wheelchair alongside another chair and indicated that Danny should come and sit. Looking very serious, he started to repeat what he had said earlier about how Danny should never reveal to anyone what he was about to witness.

Danny did his best to listen, but something was distracting him. For some reason, his attention was being drawn up to an old metal grate situated high up on the wall behind his uncle (this, he would discover later, was a chute, leading up to ground level, which had been used in the old days to push boxes of wine down into the cellar). It was behind this grate that Danny thought he had seen something.

Now he saw it again - something was glinting in there. He looked harder, then realised what he was looking at. It was Spike's face! The glint was coming off his glasses, and beside him he could now see another face - Charley was also there! Danny couldn't believe it - they were being spied on by Spike and Charley!

"Daniel!"

Danny snapped his attention back to his uncle. He had to do his best to make sure his facial expression didn't betray what he had just seen.

"It is very important that you listen to this, Daniel," Uncle Morty was saying.

Danny nodded, trying to keep his eyes fixed on his uncle's face.

"As I have already said, I asked you to come here because I need your help, and I can now tell you that this help involves that machine over there. That machine I call TIM."

Danny looked back at the machine. There was something mysterious and special about it, but he didn't know what.

"Daniel," his uncle continued, making sure he still had Danny's full attention, "I need you to travel somewhere in this machine for me."

"Travel?" Danny remembered what Spike and Charley had said about the loud aeroplane sound, but this machine didn't look like it could move. "I don't understand," he said.

Now his uncle cleared his throat, took a deep breath and looked Danny in the eyes. Danny felt a jab of excitement in his belly. He knew that the time had come for him to hear the truth.

"Daniel," Uncle Morty said, his eyes gleaming with excitement, "this machine is designed to travel through time."

Danny carried on staring at his uncle - letting the words seep slowly into his brain.

"Travel through time," he repeated slowly.

"Yes," his uncle said nodding and smiling.

Suddenly there was a cough from behind the grate in the wall. Uncle Morty began to turn around, wondering if he had heard something. Danny had to think quickly.

"What do you mean - 'travel through time'?" he asked loudly, to divert his uncle's attention.

It seemed to do the trick - Uncle Morty turned back to him.

"I mean exactly that. I mean I have discovered a way to travel across time zones."

"Give me a break!" Danny couldn't help smiling. "Are you saying that someone could get into that... thing... and travel into... say, the future?"

Uncle Morty was nodding vigorously.

"Or the past. Yes! That is exactly what I'm saying!"

For a moment Danny felt like bursting into laughter.

"Do you really expect me to believe that?" he asked incredulously.

"No, I don't expect you to believe it," his uncle replied, still smiling, "but it's true. It has taken me countless years of excruciatingly hard work, but finally I have discovered and mastered the secret of time travel."

He *has* gone mad, was all Danny could think.

"But of course I never thought that you or anyone else was just going to believe what I said," his uncle continued. "You're probably thinking the old man has gone completely bonkers!"

*You've got that right!* Danny was thinking.

As he leaned forwards in his wheelchair, Uncle Morty's eyes were still gleaming with excitement (or was it madness? Danny couldn't quite decide).

"I realise it is something quite extraordinary that I am asking you to believe - and that is why I have come up with a demonstration to prove that what I am saying is indeed true." Uncle Morty now manoeuvred himself over to a desk and picked up a video camera.

"By putting this camera inside TIM and sending it to another time I will demonstrate to you that the machine has in fact travelled to another time zone."

Danny was still very reluctant to believe anything.

"How do I know you haven't already filmed something with that camera?"

"The tape is blank," his uncle replied, "but listen, you tell me the period in time and the location that I should send the machine backwards or forwards to. That way, there is no way I could ever have known what to film in order to trick you."

All right, thought Danny. Let's just play along with the old guy. What a laugh I'll have with the others later!

His uncle now manoeuvred his wheelchair over to the machine and pressed a button. The round door slid open, smoothly and silently, and a ramp for the wheelchair slid out. Uncle Morty drove inside and Danny decided to also go in for a look.

Inside, a single black leather chair sat before a flashing control panel. Danny had to admit it looked incredibly impressive. His uncle placed the camera in a specially designed holder, so that it would face out of the glass window situated in the door. Danny noticed that you could see out through the window, but not in. Once the camera was in position he went over to the control panel.

"Right. Give me a date and a location."

"What do you mean?" Danny asked, frowning. "Any date?"

"Any date, any place."

Danny thought about this for a few moments. What had they just been learning about in history at school?

"OK," he said eventually. "I know. The Year - 1066. The place - Hastings."

Uncle Morty looked dubious.

"Hmm, the Battle of Hastings, eh? Hope TIM doesn't end up getting damaged in the middle of a battle... All right. Why not?

If I'm not mistaken, it took place on October 14th, 1066 - so let's put that in." He punched numbers into the control panel. "Now the location - Hastings, England. I punch in the place and the machine will give me the exact longitude and latitude. Then I programme in when I want it to return here. Let's make it a very short time after it leaves. Right. All set."

He now started the camera rolling then they both left the machine.

Moments later, Uncle Morty was positioned at a large control desk, pressing more buttons and studying the various screens in front of him. He was so busy with what he was doing that Danny could now afford to look up at the metal grate. He almost burst out laughing when he saw how large Spike's eyes had grown!

Danny signalled secretly that they should keep quiet, and both Spike and Charley nodded.

"Right! Now move over here please, Daniel," his uncle instructed, and Danny joined him at the control desk. "I suggest you block your ears; this gets very loud."

His uncle made the final preparations and pressed a large green flashing button. Now the noise began. First as a low humming sound that grew louder and louder until it reached a high-pitched screech like a jet engine. Danny blocked his ears. He could see that the machine had now started to vibrate - hardly noticeable at first, but as the whining sound grew, so did the vibrations. Danny could barely stand the noise any more. He expected the whole thing to explode at any moment! And yet his uncle did not seem in the least bit alarmed. He wasn't even blocking his ears. He was either used to it - or it had made him deaf already!

Then the most amazing thing happened.

The machine disappeared.

Suddenly they were staring at an empty space, and there was silence...

Danny stood frozen, his fingers still stuffed into his ears. All he could do was stare at the empty space in amazement. He was about to move forwards for a closer look when his uncle stopped him.

"Stay where you are, Daniel!" barked Uncle Morty.

It was lucky he shouted because seconds later the screeching, vibrating machine suddenly reappeared!

Now Uncle Morty started pushing buttons again, and the noise and vibrations gradually began to subside until, eventually, silence returned.

"Righto, let's see what we've got," said Uncle Morty, grinning. "Fetch me that camera, will you? And be careful - the outside will be hot."

As Danny approached the machine he could feel the heat coming from it. He quickly pushed the button and the door opened to reveal the camera still running. He slid it off its mounting and took it back to his uncle. Uncle Morty then plugged it into a TV monitor and a picture appeared on the screen.

The first bit of footage showed Danny and Uncle Morty standing looking at the machine. As the sound grew louder, the camera began to shake and Danny could see himself blocking his ears.

Suddenly - a blinding flash, and then they were looking at a typical English country scene; green hills, hedgerows, a forest in the distance. It could have been anywhere in England at any time!

Uncle Morty couldn't conceal his disappointment.

"Oh dear. That doesn't look particularly exciting does it?"

What a surprise, Danny thought. It was probably recorded down the road yesterday!

They carried on watching and Uncle Morty was about to press fast-forward when Danny noticed something.

"Hold on! What's that?"

He had seen something moving in the foreground of the

picture. Now he realised it was somebody lifting their head up slowly out of the grass. Then more heads began to appear - some in the grass, some from behind a hedge, a few more from behind a tree. All the people seemed to be looking rather nervously in the direction of the camera. It was as if something had caused them all to dive for cover and they were only now feeling brave enough to take a look.

Danny moved closer to the TV screen. The figures were now getting to their feet and picking something up off the ground. And now he saw what they were picking up – it was swords, shields and helmets. He looked closely at the helmets – they were pointed, with chain mail draped down the sides - just like those worn by the Norman soldiers in his history book.

*Could this be true?* Could these men (who were now getting braver and coming towards the camera) really be soldiers in the army of William the Conqueror, about to engage in the Battle of Hastings? Danny racked his brain, trying to come up with another explanation for what he was seeing!

On the TV, the bravest of the soldiers was now edging closer to the machine, his sword at the ready. He came slowly up to the window and pushed his large hairy face up against the glass.

Suddenly the blinding flash again, followed by footage of Danny and Uncle Morty back in the cellar.

"That will give them something to talk about!" Uncle Morty guffawed.

This was all too much for Danny. He had to sit down again. Uncle Morty moved the wheelchair up beside him, but didn't say anything. Eventually, Danny broke the silence.

"What do you want me to do?" he asked.

"I want you to travel somewhere," Uncle Morty replied. "To a different time, a different place."

"Why don't you go yourself?" Danny asked.

"Oh, believe me I've tried! The place where I had to go and

the things I went there to do... well, let me just say, it was not easy for an old man in a wheelchair. I also collected something that prevents me from travelling again." Uncle Morty now pulled up his sleeve and pointed to a small mark on his forearm. "Something in here."

Danny took a closer look, but could hardly see anything. He looked at his uncle suspiciously.

"There is much to explain, Daniel, and in time you will know everything, but for now, all I ask is that you be patient and listen to my story."

"Is it your legs?" Danny asked suddenly. "Is it about saving your legs?"

Uncle Morty threw his head back and roared with laughter.

"My, my, your mother always said you were a bright boy!" He looked at Danny more seriously. "Yes, son, the legs do have something to do with it, but it's a lot more than that. You see, on the day that I lost my legs, I lost something far more valuable as well - something that made me almost want to stop living."

Uncle Morty could see the confusion written all over Danny's face.

"Look, Daniel, let me just tell you the story and then..."

But he wasn't able to finish his sentence because, right at that moment, there came the most awful crashing sound from across the cellar.

At first they couldn't see what had caused it because there was now a large cloud of dust hanging in the air, but as the dust settled, the sight that greeted them was of a visibly stunned Spike, sitting on the floor surrounded by debris, with the metal grate lying beside him.

Spike looked up at the hole in the wall from which he had just tumbled and saw Charley's face peeking down at him. He looked over at Danny and Uncle Morty. If he could have waved a magic wand and disappeared at that moment, he most definitely would have, but unfortunately his name wasn't Harry, it was Spike! So instead, he stood up, dusted himself off a bit and then, in the most casual voice he could muster, he said:

"Hello!"

## Chapter 4

# Michelle

Some time had passed, but Uncle Morty was still sitting with his head in his hands, sounding extremely upset.

"This changes everything! Now what am I going to do?" he moaned.

Across the cellar, Danny, Spike and Charley were doing their best to clean up the mess caused by Spike's fall. Spike and Charley seemed quite keen on keeping their distance from the distressed Uncle Morty and there was a lot of whispered discussion going on. All three of them appeared to have a different opinion on what should happen next but eventually they seemed to reach some sort of agreement and were ready to put their case to Uncle Morty. As they made their way across towards him, Spike and Charley were happy to let Danny lead the way. Whether he liked it or not, he had been elected spokesperson.

Uncle Morty lifted his head out of his hands and eyed the little peace party that had gathered before him.

"Uncle Mortimer," Danny began, in his most confident-sounding voice, "we have discussed everything and have come to an agreement."

This news appeared to be of no comfort whatsoever to the old man.

"Spike and Charley here, have agreed not to tell anyone about what they have seen and heard tonight."

"Is that so?" his uncle said, folding his arms, seemingly not believing a word of it.

"Yes, but there is one condition."

"One condition? Is there? Really?"

"Yes," Danny said, still trying to act a lot tougher than he was feeling. "The condition is that they be allowed to come on the trip with me."

"The trip?"

Uncle Morty's unruly eyebrows arched quizzically. Danny nodded and gestured towards TIM.

"Yes, on the trip."

Only now did it dawn on Uncle Morty what he was talking about.

"Out of the question!" he boomed, which made Spike and Charley tuck in a little closer behind Danny. "Isn't it bad enough that I am asking *you* to risk great danger to help me? Now you expect me to put two more children at risk as well! Impossible! Out of the question!" Uncle Morty was now glaring directly at Spike. "Do you think this is some sort of game, Michael? Like one of those computer games you like so much. Do you?"

"N-no, Sir," Spike stammered.

"This is my life we are talking about!" Uncle Morty boomed. "This is my whole life's work!"

"And we are willing to risk *our* lives to help you!" Danny blurted out suddenly.

This single sentence had the amazing effect of suddenly taking all the wind out of Uncle Morty's sails. He made as if to say more, but then thought better of it. This gave Spike some confidence.

"Yes, and if there are three of us, we have more chance of succeeding," he volunteered, not very convincingly.

It wasn't clear if Uncle Morty had even heard him. He was now shaking his head again.

"Listen. You are right. I should be grateful that you are all willing to help me, but what you don't realise is that the time and the place that you will have to travel to is one of the most terrible in the history of the world! I am talking about sending you to Europe during the Second World War - when the Nazis were at the height of their power! It is like sending you all back to hell-"

"Uncle Mortimer," interrupted Danny, "can't you at least just tell us your story? Tell us exactly why you want us, or rather *me*, to go back there."

Uncle Morty thought about this for a while then nodded his agreement.

"All right. I will tell you the story, but that doesn't mean I'm agreeing that you should all go. My goodness, your mother would kill me! Which reminds me - shouldn't you all be in bed by now?"

"Mother thinks we *are* in bed," said Charley.

"You're little rascals, you know that?" the old man said, but now at least there was a twinkle in his eyes, which made Spike and Charley relax a little.

"All right, sit down and let me tell you what happened. The year was 1942 and I was serving in a unit called the SOE - the Special Operations Executive or just, 'Special Ops'. Ever heard of them?"

"I have," Spike said, nodding.

"Spike knows everything about war," Charley groaned.

"Good," Uncle Morty continued, "then he will know that at that time the German army, under the command of Adolf Hitler, were busy trying to conquer Europe. They had already defeated France and were occupying the whole country. The Nazis had total control over the country and had even put a government in power that would do everything they told them to do.

Our mission in Special Ops was to parachute into occupied France and cause as much havoc for the Nazis as possible. The prime minister, Winston Churchill, had ordered us to 'set Europe ablaze!', so this is what we tried to do. We blew up bridges and railway lines, ambushed German convoys and reported all troop movements by radio to headquarters in Britain. We were a thorn in the side of the Nazis and they were always trying to find us.

It was a very dangerous time and we often had to rely on the local French people to provide us with food and places to hide.

Of course, most of the French people hated the Nazis and wanted them out of their country, but we had to be careful because the Nazis would reward people for any information leading to the capture of soldiers like ourselves.

Some of the French people took enormous risks to help us. Not just helping us to hide, but also delivering important documents, smuggling radios to us, sometimes even helping to get our soldiers in and out of the country. Anyone caught by the Nazis doing any of these things would be lined up against a wall and shot!

During this time we worked very closely with members of the French Resistance group known as 'the Marquis'. In 1942 our unit and members of the Marquis worked together on an important mission called Operation Josephine. It involved blowing up a power station situated near Bordeaux where a fleet of German U-boats were based."

"U-boats are German submarines," Spike explained to Charley.

"That's right," said Uncle Morty, nodding, "and when we blew up this power station it put the submarines out of action for several months. As you can imagine, this infuriated the Nazis and a massive manhunt was launched in the area to try and find us. Suddenly there were soldiers and Gestapo everywhere. There was a reward put out and we had to be very careful of collaborators.

Two members of the Marquis who helped us during Operation Josephine were a brother and sister called Christian and Michelle Borges. They were dedicated to the cause of ridding their country of Nazis and they risked their lives every day to help us.

After Operation Josephine, the Borges family allowed several of us to hide out in the basement of their house in Bordeaux for a long period of time. This was an incredibly brave thing for them to do; anyone seeing us coming or going could have reported us and that would have spelt disaster.

It was during this time that I got to know Christian and Michelle very well. They were just normal young people. If there had been no war they would probably both have been at university, studying to be doctors. Michelle always said she wanted to be a doctor, so that she could help people, but with the war on she had chosen to help people in a different way.

Michelle and I fell in love. I had never known anyone so brave and so beautiful - so willing to put the lives of others before her own. We would sit in the darkness of her parents' house, listening out for the sound of German army boots, and talk about the future. After the war, she was going to return to England with me and we were going to be married. She was scared of coming back to England because she said her English was so terrible! I would laugh at her and say, 'How can someone be scared of speaking English and yet be brave enough to risk their life helping us every day?'."

As Danny, Spike and Charley waited to hear what happened next, it seemed like Uncle Morty was momentarily lost in his memories.

"What happened to her?" Charley asked in a small voice. "Did she die?"

The question made Uncle Morty look as though his heart might break. He had tears in his eyes and it took a few moments before he was able to speak again.

"In December 1942, we received top secret orders about another mission. British Commandos were launching one of their most daring raids of the whole war. It was called Operation Frankton, and the commandos involved would become known as the 'Cockleshell Heroes'."

At the sound of this name Spike's eyes lit up.

"The soldiers in the canoes!" he said excitedly.

"That's it, Michael. The canoes were called 'cockleshells'. Ten British Commandos were dropped off by a submarine off the coast of France. Their orders were to canoe up the River Gironde to the harbour at Bordeaux. In the harbour they would find a fleet of German merchant ships that had been supplying the German army in France. The commandos were to attach limpet mines to the sides of the ships and blow them all to smithereens. This would cut off a major supply line to the Germans.

Our job was to do anything we could to help. If necessary this would mean creating a diversion, so that the German guards at the harbour did not notice the canoes coming in silently under cover of darkness.

On the night of the 5th of December, six of us (three Special Ops forces and three members of the French Resistance, including Michelle and Christian) left the Borges' house and made our way down to the harbour. We were all dressed as civilians, although we had weapons concealed under our jackets. We left in pairs, which we thought would draw less attention to ourselves. At first Christian and another Special Ops man, Roger Jakes, slipped out looking like two young Frenchmen going out on the town, then the other soldier, Tommy Mitchell, left together with one of Christian's friends. Finally, Michelle and I left together. We always tried to keep one French-speaking person together with an English-speaking person in case anyone ran into a Nazi patrol.

Nobody really knows what happened that night, but what is certain is that the Nazis knew something was up and were on the lookout for us. We suspect a woman named Madame du Pont, who lived across the road from the Borges' house. She was one of those sad people who have nothing better to do than peek out through their lace curtains to spy on the neighbours. We now think that she must have seen us leaving the Borges' house that night and decided there was something suspicious going on. She would have got on the phone to the local Nazi headquarters and reported that she had seen us heading towards the harbour.

Anyway, we were not to know this as we made our way down to the harbour. I remember it so well, walking hand in hand with

Michelle. It was the first time we had ever done that in public and, as it turned out..."

Again, Uncle Morty's voice trailed off and he took a few moments to gather himself before starting to speak again.

"We took a back route into the harbour area through all the warehouses, until we met up with the others on a quayside just across from where the ships were moored. We knew that, if all went according to plan, the ships would be at the bottom of the harbour before the night was out. From where we sat in the shadow of some packing crates we could see a few guards standing at the railings. One of them was talking to his mate on the ship next door. They didn't seem to be keeping a close lookout, which suited us fine.

We hadn't been sitting there long when Christian suddenly nudged me and pointed into the harbour. At first I could see nothing then I spotted them - two dark shapes moving silently through the waters. Our hearts leapt - they had arrived exactly according to plan! There were two men in each canoe, but we could hardly make them out with their black clothes and blackened faces.

We held our breath as the canoes glided silently towards the ships. We could still hear the one guard chatting to his mate, but all of a sudden, in mid-sentence, he stopped talking! It was as if he had seen or heard something. The commandos immediately stopped paddling - hoping and praying that they couldn't be seen in the inky darkness. Now the guard seemed to be asking his mate if he had seen something down in the water. It was a crucial time as they both stared out into the darkness then one of them went off to get a torch! We knew we had to do something *and fast*!

It was Michelle who acted first. Quick as a flash she was up and running along the quayside towards the ships. I ran after her and, to my surprise, she suddenly turned on me and started to shout at me in French! I realised what she was playing at - she was pretending we were lovers having a quarrel. I joined in, shouting back at her in my very bad French. It seemed to be working, as we now had the guard's attention. This meant the commandos could start paddling again, and they pulled their canoes right in close to the ships and began to attach their mines.

Meanwhile, Michelle (who was still shouting at me) now walked straight up the gangplank of one of the ships. Of course the guard immediately came over and tried to stop her, but when she asked for a cigarette and he saw what a beautiful young woman she was, he was only too happy to oblige. All I could think about was the commandos below, placing their mines. I had to get her off the ship! I now also went aboard and implored her to come with me, but she wanted to keep the guard's attention, so she shouted at me to leave her alone, all the time smiling at the guard - making him feel important.

Suddenly - *disaster*! There were soldiers running down the road towards the harbour, and we could tell they were looking for something. This was not a routine patrol - they had definitely been tipped off! The soldiers started to shout at the guard, asking him

who we were. Suddenly it felt like we were trapped and now the guard started to scream at us to get off the ship. We had no choice and we were about to go down the gangplank into the hands of the soldiers when suddenly Christian and the others opened fire and all hell broke loose!

With all the gunfire we had to retreat back onto the ship. Now the guard started firing at us and we had to duck and dive, and take cover. All the time I was thinking, We need to get off this ship! It could blow at any moment!

Now soldiers were also coming onto the ship and we were forced to retreat farther down the deck. The soldiers were being led by a captain who was screaming orders and driving them forwards. We fired our revolvers, but they were no match for the soldiers' machine guns. We kept retreating, but were now running out of deck! Soon we were at the bow of the ship and there was nowhere left to go! We reached the railing and looked over - we were going to have to jump! I happened to glance over my shoulder and, to my horror, I saw the captain hoisting a bazooka onto his shoulder! One blast from that thing and I knew we would both be history!

'Jump!' I screamed at Michelle.

We both climbed up onto the railing and were just about to jump when there was suddenly a deafening blast. The next thing I knew I was in the water - floundering around - screaming for Michelle! I couldn't see her anywhere! I then felt hands grabbing me and men with blackened faces were hauling me into their canoe. I was still screaming out Michelle's name - looking for her everywhere - but that's when one of the commandos put a hand over my mouth to gag me, so that I wouldn't attract the soldiers' attention.

I looked up and... it is a sight that will forever haunt me. I saw the figure of Michelle, standing on the deck. She had her hands in the air and there were soldiers all around her. The bazooka shell had exploded at my feet, shattering my legs and blowing me overboard, but the blast had obviously blown Michelle sideways onto the deck and, by the time she had recovered, it was too late - the soldiers had her.

Again I tried to call to her to get off the ship - but again the commando smothered my screams…and then…"

The tears were now rolling down Uncle Morty's cheeks. It was as if he was back in the icy darkness of Bordeaux harbour. His next words were barely audible.

"… and then… the ship exploded."

Chapter 5

# The Pact

After Uncle Morty's story, a horrible silence, punctuated only by the odd sniff from Charley, descended over the cellar.

Eventually, he looked up at them through watery eyes and nodded his head towards the lift.

"Why don't you all run along, eh? We'll talk again tomorrow."

There was still *so* much to talk about, but Danny knew it was time to leave his uncle alone with his thoughts.

They all said goodnight and took the lift back up to ground level.

\*

Once outside, they quickly walked back towards the Barnes' cottage, barely able to contain their excitement. What a night it had been! They had seen and heard so much!

"Poor Uncle Morty," said Charley. "We have to help him."

Danny was just about to reply when a figure suddenly stepped out of the shadows in front of them.

"And what, may I ask, are you all doing out of bed at this hour?"

It was Mrs Barnes, and she did *not* sound amused!

"Uh… we've been with my uncle," Danny said quickly.

"All of you!" she exclaimed, turning on Spike and Charley. "What on earth were the two of you doing there?"

Spike had to think quickly.

"We went for a walk, and Mr Piper-Adams saw us and invited us in."

"For a cup of tea," Charley added quickly.

"Oh, you went for a walk, did you?"

Spike and Charley nodded.

"What, just out to get some fresh air, were you?"

Spike and Charley nodded some more.

"Yes, *and my name is Madonna*! What do you take me for? You were snooping around the wine cellar weren't you?"

Spike and Charley swapped glances, but didn't reply.

"Get to bed all of you! We'll talk about this tomorrow!"

\*

The lights were out in Spike's bedroom and the three of them had gathered around the computer on his desk. On the screen was a big picture of Adolf Hitler - an evil-looking man with dark, slicked-down hair and a large bushy moustache.

"The Wolf," said Spike. "That's what he liked to call himself. He even named one of his headquarters 'The Wolf's Lair'. In his early days he would go out on the streets in disguise and actually call himself 'Mr Wolf'. One of the most evil men in history. You wouldn't believe some of the terrible things he ordered his Nazis storm troopers to do during the war."

"Like what?" asked Charley.

"Like killing six million people just because of their religion."

Danny was looking worried.

"Uncle Morty's right you know. It's far too dangerous for us all to go. I think I should just go myself."

Spike wasn't interested.

"Are you mad? We have three times the chance of succeeding if we all go."

"Or three times the chance of something going wrong! Like Uncle Morty said, this is not a game. Going back to those times is going to be incredibly dangerous."

Spike wasn't paying much attention to Danny. It seemed like he had already made up his mind.

"I'll tell you what's also dangerous," he said, "our mother! If she even gets a whiff of what's going on here we'll all be locked up so fast - and not let out until Mr Piper-Adams is safely tucked away in a mental hospital!"

"We'll have to be careful when we discuss it," said Charley in a whisper.

Danny nodded his agreement.

"From now on we should never talk about it if there's any chance of us being overheard."

"We should have a code name," suggested Spike, "so no one knows what we're talking about. We could call it…"

Charley was still looking at a picture on the screen of 'Mr Wolf' (Hitler) standing beside his storm troopers.

"How about *Wolfstorm*?" she said suddenly.

The boys looked at each other. They seemed to like it.

"Why not?" said Spike. "No one's going to know what we're talking about if we say '*Wolfstorm*'."

"All right," agreed Danny. "We can call it that, but I still think I should go alone."

"Danny, do you really think Charley and I are going to let you leave us here while you go off on the adventure of a lifetime?"

"Dream on!" said Charley with a smile, and Danny could see by the looks on their faces that there was no argument.

"All right then," said Danny. "Let's make a pact right here and now. We must all swear that we will never tell another soul about what we have seen tonight - about Uncle Morty and TIM, and about *Wolfstorm*."

And so it was, in Spike's darkened room, with only the light from the computer screen, that they all joined hands and, one by one said:

"I swear."

\*

The next day was gloriously sunny. In fact, the only slightly frosty thing about it was the looks the children were getting from Mrs Barnes. Mr Piper-Adams had announced to her at breakfast that he would like to go outside today and he would be very pleased if all three children could join him. To say this surprised Mrs Barnes somewhat was an understatement. Firstly, Mr Piper-Adams very rarely ventured outside and secondly he had never before shown the remotest bit of interest in her children, or anybody else's for that matter!

As Mr and Mrs Barnes cleared up after Mr Piper-Adams' breakfast, they looked out of the dining room window at the strange sight of the old man buzzing down the garden path in his wheelchair with the three children in tow.

"Something funny is going on," Mrs Barnes muttered under her breath, "and I'm going to find out what it is."

*

Uncle Mortimer and his three young companions had now arrived at the overgrown and rundown summer house.

"What a mess," the old man said, looking all around him. "I've neglected so much."

## THE PACT

Danny felt a nudge from Spike - a not-so-subtle reminder that he had been elected to break the news to his uncle.

"Uncle Mortimer," he said. "We've made up our minds. We all want to take the trip on TIM and we've all sworn ourselves to secrecy."

As expected, his uncle did not look at all happy with this news and he now viewed the three of them with a very serious expression.

"Hold on," he said. "Before you make any rash decisions I need to tell you more about the incredible dangers that surround a journey of this nature. And I'm not even talking about the obvious dangers of returning to wartime France."

Uncle Morty pulled up his sleeve and once again revealed the strange mark on his forearm. It was the first time Spike and Charley had been able to see it properly and they both leaned forwards for a closer look.

"What is it?" asked Spike.

"Inside here, just under my skin, a small computer chip has been inserted. It is called a 'Body and Mind' (or BAM) chip," explained Uncle Morty. "On this chip a computer program has been loaded, called *Attila*. It stands for something like Anti Time Travel Alert. Its function is to send out alert signals should I ever again attempt another trip on TIM."

"Alert signals to whom?" asked Danny.

"That is what I need to explain to you. You see, time travel brings with it another danger far greater than you could ever imagine, but, for you to fully understand, I need to explain something about the enormous effects that time travel can have on everything. What you have to understand is that if anyone goes back in time and changes something, those changes will have a ripple effect all the way through time."

Uncle Mortimer realised that what he was explaining was difficult to grasp, so he thought for a moment about how he could make it easier to understand.

"All right, let me give you an example. If, let's say, by some miracle you did manage to go back to France and change what happened on that terrible night, it would literally change everything about my life. I mean, just think about it - if Michelle had not died that night, she and I would probably have got married. We may have even had children. My whole life would have been different. Do you follow?"

The children all nodded.

"Now, here's the bit that will sound strange. If Michelle and I were married and everything was different in my life, I would probably have had no desire to travel back in time. If that was the case, it is extremely unlikely that I would have built TIM."

Charley looked thoroughly confused, but the cogs in Spike's brain were obviously turning furiously.

"So, you're saying that if we went back and saved Michelle's life, everything here would change and TIM would cease to exist?"

"Exactly!" said Uncle Morty, snapping his fingers and pointing at Spike. "You've got it, Michael."

This had thrown up other questions for Spike.

"But if we *do* go back and help save Michelle's life, and TIM disappears, how are we going to get back from 1942? Won't that mean we'll be stuck there?"

Uncle Morty smiled.

"Well done, Michael, you're thinking, but take that thought one step farther. If Michelle lived and TIM never existed then you would not have gone on that trip. Once the major change takes place everything will alter and you will find yourselves back here in the present time with perhaps no knowledge of what you have done because, as far as we will all be concerned, none of it ever happened!" Uncle Morty laughed when he saw the expressions on the faces of Danny and the others. "I know it's confusing," he said, "but the more you think about it, the more it makes sense."

"It doesn't make sense to me," said Charley.

"Yes, and I'm not surprised," Uncle Morty continued. "It is a very strange thing to grasp. What you have to try and understand is that if you all go back in time and alter anything then things will change in our lives in ways we cannot predict. Perhaps you'll be living somewhere else. Perhaps, with Michelle as my wife, I may not have employed Mrs Barnes as a housekeeper. Who knows, there's a chance that I still may have. We cannot predict what will happen when we start changing the past, and that is what makes it such a dangerous thing to play with." He revealed his forearm again. "Which leads me back to this. You see, because going back in time and changing things has such a profound effect on everything throughout the rest of time, it will one day become *illegal* to travel through time. I have seen this for myself - in the future."

"You've been into the future?" Spike gasped.

"Yes," Uncle Morty nodded, "and into the past - back to wartime France in fact. That proved to be my final trip and, unfortunately, it ended before I had a chance to achieve anything."

"What happened?" asked Spike impatiently.

"I'll tell you now, Michael," Uncle Morty continued. "For my first test trip on TIM I decided to go into the future in search of technology that I thought might help me on my next trip. I decided to go forwards to the Year 2200, but I had no way of knowing what currency I would need to buy anything. I knew that if I took money from today it would probably have no value in two hundred years time, so I ended up taking diamonds in the hope that they would still be valuable in the future. As it turned out they were useless. In the course of the next century there are going to be so many discoveries of diamonds that the value is going to fall to almost nothing. Anyway, I did learn what will be of value in 2200 - and I also did a lot of window shopping while

I was there - so I have some good ideas of what to buy."

Spike's eyes had grown enormous.

"Are we also going to the future?" he asked, breathless with excitement.

"Not so fast, Michael," Uncle Mortimer replied sternly. "I haven't even told you about the real dangers yet." Now the old man looked down at his forearm again. "It was only when I arrived in 2200 that I discovered time travel had been made strictly illegal. The first hint I got was when I saw a computer program for sale, which I was told would prevent time travellers from being traced and caught. It was a real shock because, at that moment, I suddenly realised that I was breaking the law! The program was called *Attila Killer* and, if I could have afforded it, I would have bought it. If that had happened… well, I probably wouldn't be asking for your help now."

"But who gave you the chip," asked Danny, "and that *Attila* program?"

Uncle Morty smiled.

"Who do you think? Some things don't change!"

"The police?" Danny ventured.

Uncle Morty nodded.

"That's right, but these are not your average coppers. They are the Time Crime Police or 'Timecops' as they are called in 2200. They have sophisticated equipment that detects anyone time travelling. From 2200 I decided to go back to 1942. I was going to try and change the events that led to Michelle's death, but I had only been there for an hour when the Timecops suddenly turned up. They had traced me with their equipment, and that's when they put this chip into my arm and the *Attila* program, and sent me back to the year from where I had come. *Attila* was programmed to activate as soon as I got back here, making it impossible for me to time travel anywhere else. The Timecops told me they were installing *Attila* because it was my first offence. If they ever caught me again, I would be arrested and detained for life.

The Timecops also told me about an even greater danger. They are called Time Hogs and, by all accounts, they are the scum of the universe. They are bounty hunters - ruthless killers that patrol through time looking for time travellers like myself. They don't bother with *Attila* or arrests. They kill on sight. Apparently they come from a time farther in the future when time travel is considered an even greater offence. These Hogs are paid handsomely for each time traveller they eradicate. Thankfully I have never laid eyes on one of these creatures and I pray that none of us ever will. They say that a genuine *Attila Killer* program should prevent these Hogs from detecting a time traveller - which is why it is so expensive."

Uncle Morty looked over at the three youngsters, who were all trying to absorb what they had just heard.

"So now you see why I am so reluctant to send you all off into such danger. Believe me, if it wasn't for this blasted thing in my arm, I would go again myself! I have spent so long on this project, and when they put this thing into me it seemed like all my efforts were in vain. You must know that it was only as a very last resort that I asked you to come here, Daniel. I'm getting very old now and I know that if I don't do something soon it will be too late. I thought if I could plan everything, right down to the smallest detail, it would hopefully minimise the risks involved. Maybe, just maybe, there would be a good chance of you succeeding."

Now Uncle Mortimer began to speak directly to Danny.

"But, listen to me, my boy. I will fully understand if you are reluctant to go. I would never force you or-"

"When do we leave?" asked Danny.

If his mother had been there, she would have recognised the expression on his face. It was the expression he got when he had made up his mind to do something and nothing, *but nothing*, was going to stand in his way.

\*

Just as Danny was making his big decision, Mrs Barnes (still hovering in the manor house dining room) was busy trying to make a decision of her own. Her husband had just suggested something to her and his eyes were now darting around excitedly as he awaited her reply. Whatever it was, Mrs Barnes was clearly in two minds about it, but eventually she nodded and said:

"All right then. I'll keep an eye out. You go and take a quick look."

It was the answer Mr Barnes had been hoping for. He scurried out of the dining room and down the long passage lined with the suits of armour. When he reached the wooden wall panel that concealed the secret lift to the cellar he came to an abrupt halt. From out of his jacket pocket, he removed a bunch of keys.

Chapter 6

# The Great Escape

On his fifth attempt Mr Barnes found the key that slid smoothly into the keyhole of the secret door. His hand was trembling with excitement as he turned it. The wooden panel clicked open.

He had ended up with the keys quite by chance. Normally they would have been safely in Mr Piper-Adam's pocket, but since the night before, the daily routine seemed to have been turned on its head. That morning Mr Piper-Adams had been so intent on going out with the children that he had left his keys on the table beside his bed. Mr Barnes had noticed them while he was making the bed, and the temptation had been too much. Of course, he had had to run the idea past his wife, who would normally have said a flat, 'No!', but with all the strange things going on at the moment, even Mrs Barnes' curiosity had got the better of her.

Now he was stepping into the lift. He saw the button marked 'CELLAR' and pressed it.

\*

"What do you say we go and see the monkeys?" suggested Uncle Morty, and Charley's face immediately lit up. "How are they doing these days, Charlotte?"

"Fine! Except they haven't had nuts for about two weeks now," Charley replied. "They love nuts, but Mum keeps forgetting to buy them."

"Oh, we'll buy them nuts," Uncle Morty said, grinning as he pointed his wheelchair in the direction of the monkey cages. "We'll buy them plenty of nuts!"

\*

For ten long years Mr Barnes had wanted to see what was going on in the cellar, and now, at long last, he would get the opportunity. The lift stopped at the bottom and the door slid open.

Even though Mr Barnes knew that Mr Piper-Adams was outside he still stuck his head out of the lift and had a good look around before stepping out. He had seen all sorts of equipment being delivered to Bosworth Manor, but it was quite mind-boggling to see it altogether in one room like this. Apart from the TV and the video machine, he had no idea what half of the equipment was - but it certainly looked very impressive!

Then his eyes fixed on the large shiny machine in the centre of the room. Was this the machine that made all the noise; the machine that had consumed Mr Piper-Adams' every waking hour for the past ten years?

He moved over for a closer look and soon had his face pushed right up against the little window in the front, but frustratingly he couldn't see through it. He noticed the button beside the door. He gave it a little prod and jumped back as the door slid open. Not knowing what to expect, he cautiously stuck his head through the doorway and looked around.

"What on God's earth...?" he muttered, when he saw the control panel with all its screens and dials.

\*

It was the first time Uncle Mortimer had been to the monkey cage with Spike and Charley, and he seemed to be really enjoying the experience. He watched as Charley went into the cage and the monkeys leapt up onto her shoulders.

"They love you, Charlotte!" the old man said, beaming.

"They think she's part of the family," said Spike with a grin.

\*

In his search for more clues about the strange machine (and because it was the only bit of equipment in the cellar that he could identify!) Mr Barnes had decided to take a look at the tape in the video camera. The first bit of footage showed Mr Piper-Adams and Daniel standing in the cellar. This was followed by a sudden flash - then there were people dressed up as Norman soldiers crawling around in a field. Next it was back to Mr Piper-Adams and Daniel in the cellar.

Mr Barnes scratched his chin. He had a strong feeling that this strange video held an important clue. He just couldn't quite put his finger on it!

\*

"I can't believe I've never done this before," Uncle Morty said, chortling to himself.

Adam the monkey was now perched on top of Charley's head! Uncle Morty now turned to Danny.

"Perhaps you *will* need a couple of assistants on your trip?" he said.

Danny was pleased to hear Uncle Morty saying this, as it sounded like he was coming around to the idea of Spike and Charley joining him on the trip. He went over and sat beside his uncle.

"In fact, it looks like there could be five of you going," Uncle Morty continued.

"Five?" Danny shook his head, not understanding. "Who else is coming?" he asked.

Uncle Morty gestured over towards the monkey cage.

"There are your passengers," he said, smiling.

Danny looked at the monkey cage then back at his uncle.

"What... the monkeys? The monkeys are coming as well?"

"I recruited them especially for the trip."

"Yay!" Charley shouted suddenly, causing Adam to leap off her head. "You're coming on a trip with us, Evie!" she screeched.

Uncle Morty could see the confusion on Danny's face.

"Daniel, do you remember me saying that I had discovered something you could take to the future; something of value that could be used as currency?"

Danny nodded.

"Well, *there* is your currency," he said, nodding towards the cage.

It took Danny a few moments to get what he was saying.

"We're going to sell the monkeys!" he exclaimed.

"Oh, yes." Uncle Morty smiled. "You see, I discovered that in the Year 2200 the capuchin monkey no longer exists. It is extinct. Can you imagine the value of an animal that has been extinct for nearly two hundred years? I'm afraid the world of the future is a very sad place indeed. When I did my research in the Year 2200 I unfortunately discovered that there are hundreds of extinct animals. The black rhino, the cheetah, the giant panda, the Bengal tiger, the Arctic wolf - the list goes on and on. I chose the monkeys because they would be easier to transport. I didn't think having two baby rhino on board TIM would be such a good idea!"

Charley's initial excitement was now turning to dismay.

"Do you mean we're going to take them to the future and leave them there?" she asked.

"Yes, Charlotte," said Uncle Morty, nodding. "That's exactly what I mean, but don't be sad. Adam and Eve here are hopefully going to bring a whole new generation of capuchin monkeys back onto this planet. By selling them there, you should get enough money to buy everything you need." For a moment Uncle Morty appeared to be temporarily lost in his thoughts, as if remembering what he had seen in 2200. "Yes," he said quietly, "the world of the future is a sad place indeed." He snapped himself out of it and looked at his watch. "We had better get back," he said. "There's still a lot to do."

\*

Up at the manor house, Mrs Barnes was keeping a sharp eye out for any signs of Mr Piper-Adams and the children, when her husband came bounding through the doorway.

"What's taken you so long?" she snapped.

"Violet, I think there's s-something you should come and

t-take a look at," stammered Mr Barnes.

"What is it?"

"Um… well, it's… I think you should just come and take a look."

Mrs Barnes did not like the idea one little bit. She took another look out of the window. There was still no sign of the others.

"Well, it had better be quick," she said as she herded Mr Barnes back out through the doorway.

*

A couple of moments later, Uncle Mortimer and the children emerged from the trees near the summer house and started up the path towards the manor.

"Right, Michael and Charlotte, I think you had better get home before your mother starts to worry," said Uncle Morty. "Daniel, I would like you to come to my study please. There is something I have to show you."

"OK, see you later," said Spike, and he and Charley ran off towards their cottage.

Danny helped his uncle manoeuvre the wheelchair up the ramp beside the steps and in through the front door of the manor house.

Uncle Morty had half-expected to find Mrs Barnes waiting for them, but surprisingly, there was no sign of her. He trundled down the passage and turned into a room opposite the secret lift. This was his study - a chaotic room, cluttered with old furniture and piled high with books and papers.

"Close the door, will you, son? What I'm about to tell you is definitely for your ears only."

What now? thought Danny. His head was already bursting with all he had heard today!

Uncle Morty buzzed around behind his large messy desk and Danny noticed how serious he was looking.

"Daniel," he began, "there is something of great

importance that I haven't mentioned to you yet. Apart from the death of Michelle, there has been another great tragedy in my life - and it is one that I share with you. Of course, I am talking about the death of your father and sister." Now Uncle Morty hesitated, as though trying to decide how best to say what he had to say next. "I realise what I am about to say will weigh heavily on your mind," he continued, "but I have thought long and hard about it, and have come to the conclusion that it is something we just have to try and achieve. Daniel, can you imagine how different your life would be if your father and little Catie had not died that day in Australia?"

Danny stared at his uncle, his mind racing.

"Yes, Daniel - I'm talking about the possibility of one day going back in time and trying to save their lives as well. Not on this first trip, but on the next one."

Danny sat motionless - completely stunned. It was something that had crossed his mind the night before when he had first realised the potential of TIM, but when Uncle Mortimer had explained that once the change had taken place TIM would no longer exist, he had put it out of his mind.

"But you said yourself that after this trip TIM will no longer exist and we'll all end up back here with no knowledge of what has happened."

"That's right," said Uncle Morty, nodding, "which is why we have to somehow come up with a way of keeping that knowledge."

"But how?" Danny shook his head. It was still not making sense to him. "You said that everything about TIM will disappear when the change takes place."

"True, which is why we need a way to somehow hold on to the information about TIM."

"But how?" Danny repeated.

"We do it with this," Uncle Morty replied, trying to open one of his drawers, but finding it locked. He began to dig around in his pockets for his keys, but couldn't find them. "That's strange," he remarked, frowning, "I must have left my keys somewhere."

Danny could tell that Uncle Morty was worrying about his keys, but he tried to push the matter to one side.

"Anyway," he continued, "what I have locked in this drawer is a detailed book of instructions on everything I did to create TIM. Basically, it is a manual explaining *exactly* how to build a time machine."

"But... when we make the big change, won't that book cease to exist as well?" Danny asked.

"You're right. It would *if* the book stayed where it is now - in this time period. However, if we take the book to a point in time *before* the change takes place then it will not be affected. You have to understand that when something is changed, everything *after* it is affected, but something that has already happened will not be affected."

Danny was still battling to make sense of everything he was hearing.

"What I am saying, Daniel, is that I need you to give me the manual *before* the change takes place; before you try to save Michelle. That way, no matter what happens, I will have the knowledge with me of how to build another TIM. I have also included in the book a letter to myself explaining everything that has happened."

Danny could see that his uncle was getting increasingly frustrated at not being able to unlock his drawer.

"*Blast it*! Where could those keys be?" he fumed, but again he tried to put the matter to one side. "Anyway, the note I have written to myself in the book says that I should ignore the contents of the book until your thirteenth birthday. On that day, we are to look at the book together and discuss the idea of building a second TIM. Then, God willing, you can go back on another trip to try and save the lives of your father and sister."

Danny couldn't believe he was hearing those words. It still seemed a long way off (with *so many* things to achieve before then!), but at least there was a chance - and this was enough to make his heart soar!

"Of course," Uncle Morty continued, "I have considered the possibility of you travelling to the time of that terrible accident on *this* trip, but I've decided it may backfire on us. You would obviously have to go there before going back to wartime France, and I'm worried that saving your father's life now may, in some way, endanger the invention of TIM. Your father and Catie's deaths were another major reason why I never gave up on TIM. It is possible that if he had lived, TIM may never have been invented. If that is true then saving their lives now may cause TIM to disappear before you've had the chance to go back to 1942, so I think this is the best way to do it, Daniel."

Danny nodded his agreement. He was busy thinking that it was only a few days until his thirteenth birthday. How odd it was to think that, if all went according to plan, he would arrive at his thirteenth birthday with no knowledge whatsoever of any of this then his Great Uncle Morty would visit him with a plan to build a time machine!

Uncle Morty was now rummaging through his pockets for the umpteenth time, but was still coming up empty-handed.

"Right, that's it!" he said. "I've got to go and look for those keys! If you'll excuse me, Daniel - it's very important I find them. I have to give you that book!"

With that, Uncle Morty buzzed out of the room, and Danny listened as his wheelchair disappeared down the passage.

Soon there was silence. It was the first time all day that Danny had had any time to reflect on what was happening. He went over to the window and looked out across the grounds. Was all this really happening, or was it all just an incredible dream - and he would soon wake up at Woodford Lane?

Now his thoughts were suddenly interrupted. There was a sound coming from out in the passage and, if he was not mistaken, it was the sound of the lift coming up from the cellar!

That's strange, he thought. Who on earth could be in the lift?

His first impulse was to go out into the passage to see for himself, but something stopped him and, instead, he went behind the study door, from where he could see out into the passage through the crack.

The lift arrived at the top and, seconds later, the wooden panel slid to one side.

When Danny saw who it was, he gasped and pushed himself back against the wall.

*

Mrs Barnes looked troubled as she stepped out of the lift with her husband. Like her husband, she had not fully grasped everything she had just seen down in the cellar, but she knew that there was something funny going on and she was determined to find out exactly what it was! If Mr Piper-Adams was tinkering with his inventions on his own that was one thing, but when he started to involve children (especially her own!) - well, that was an entirely different matter all together!

She felt like she needed help getting to the bottom of all this, and somebody had sprung to mind. He was probably the most sensible man in the nearby town - someone she admired very much and was proud to be able to call a friend. He would know what to do.

"Keep a lookout for them while I make a call," Mrs Barnes said to her husband, and he obediently posted himself at a window while she went to the telephone in the hallway and dialled.

"Good morning, is that Ringwood Police Station? Could I speak to Inspector Keegan please?" she asked, then a few moments later, "hello, Tom, it's Violet Barnes. I'm terribly sorry to bother you, but there are some rather odd things going on here at the manor and I was wondering if you wouldn't mind coming out to take a look... As soon as you can if possible... Oh, wonderful. Thank you very much, Tom. Goodbye."

Mrs Barnes replaced the handset.

"What did he say?" asked Mr Barnes.

"He's coming straight over, of course," she replied. "Tom Keegan is a man of action."

*

Danny had heard every word of the telephone conversation and he now remained frozen, pinned against the study wall, too terrified to move in case a squeaky floorboard gave him away.

Now he heard something else - an electric buzz, growing steadily louder. It was Uncle Morty's wheelchair. He was on his way back!

Mr and Mrs Barnes must have heard it as well because suddenly she was issuing instructions to her husband.

"Put the keys in the study!" she hissed.

That's it, thought Danny. I'm finished!

Mr Barnes came rushing into the study, slapped the keys on the desk and scurried out again. Had he glanced up to his right he would have seen Danny behind the door, but thankfully he was in too much of a rush.

Only when Danny heard their footsteps disappearing towards the kitchen was he able to breathe again. Next moment, Uncle Mortimer came in cursing.

"Still can't find those confounded keys!" he stormed. He then saw the expression on Danny's face. "What is it, son? You look like you've seen the Devil!"

"Mrs B-Barnes," Danny stammered.

"Yes, what about her?"

"She's been down in the cellar, and she's called the police!"

Uncle Mortimer took a few moments to digest this information before starting to shake his head.

"No! I will not let that woman disrupt my plans! Not after ten long years! Not when we are getting so close!"

Danny noticed how the veins had started to bulge on his uncle's forehead. He looked like he could use some good news.

"Your keys," said Danny, pointing at the desk.

"Right!"

Uncle Morty frowned - there was no time to even ask how they had got there - rapid organised action was required! He snatched the keys up off the desk and sped around to the other side where he now started to unlock the drawer.

"Daniel, we have no choice. Your expected time of departure has just been moved forwards. We have to act fast, and I'm going to need your undivided attention!"

Uncle Morty now removed a book from the drawer. It was not large, but quite thick, with very worn-looking pages. He flicked through it briefly and Danny could see that it was filled with tremendously detailed figures and diagrams.

"I don't have to tell you the importance of this book," Uncle Morty said, his expression deadly serious. "You know as well as I do that the key to saving the lives of your father and sister may lie within these pages. You must make sure you give it to me *before* the change takes place. Do you understand?"

Danny nodded and took the book from his uncle. As he placed it in his rucksack he couldn't help wondering how things would be the next time this precious book passed between them.

"Right! Next!" Uncle Morty was now holding a strange-looking circular object, with a button in the centre. "When you get to the future, press the button on this and a taxi belonging to a man named Reg will arrive to pick you up. This is how you call taxis in the future. He will know where to find you. OK?"

Danny took the disc. He had questions, but there was no time. Uncle Morty had already moved on to the next item.

"All right, next I have a list of things you must buy in the future. I don't have time to explain what each thing is now, but if you go to the addresses written on this paper you will find the shops that sell the items. Top of the list is the *Attila Killer* program. It is very important that you have a BAM chip inserted and this program loaded on to it. Otherwise the police or, God forbid, the Hogs, will track you down! *Do you understand?*"

"Yes," Danny said, nodding.

Uncle Morty handed him the piece of paper.

"The place to sell the monkeys is also on there" he added. "When you sell the monkeys they will put the money on to this thing - a moneycard." He now passed Danny a card the size of a bank card, but paper-thin with a colour display screen. "It has twenty-five WDs on it," he said, "enough for your taxi ride into London."

"WDs?" Danny queried.

"World Dollars," replied Uncle Morty. "The world only has one currency by the Year 2200. You will use this card for all your financial transactions. Is that clear?"

Danny wasn't sure, but he nodded anyway and placed the card in the rucksack.

"All right, Daniel. Now, the last thing we have to do is to get the monkeys."

"But what about Spike and Charley?" Danny cried.

"I'm sorry," he said, shaking his head. "It's too late. We can't risk going to find them! Not with Mr and Mrs Barnes around!"

Danny couldn't believe what he was hearing.

"I can't leave them! I promised! We made a pact!"

"Please, son," Uncle Morty pleaded, "just go and get the monkeys."

But Danny had other ideas.

"I'll see you down in the cellar!" he shouted suddenly, and before his uncle could say another word he had darted out of the study.

"Daniel! Please!" Uncle Morty shouted after him.

*

Danny decided it would be safest to approach the Barnes' cottage from the back. That way he was hoping he could talk to Spike and Charley through their bedroom windows, without being seen by Mr and Mrs Barnes.

He approached cautiously, picking his way from one tree to the next. Soon, only Mr Barnes' veggie garden lay between him and the cottage. Crouching down low, he quickly scampered through the veggies and pressed himself up against the back wall of the cottage. Spike's bedroom window was right beside him. He slowly shuffled sideways and tried to peer in through the window. It was difficult to see inside and he was forced to push his face up against the glass and cup his hands around his eyes. As his eyes grew accustomed to the gloom he noticed a figure standing in the middle of the room.

"Can I help you, Daniel?" said the figure.

*It was Mrs Barnes*!

"Oh… er… not to worry, thanks," Danny replied, trying to sound casual. "I was just looking for Spike."

"Michael and Charlotte are right here," she replied sharply, "and I would suggest you also come inside. I am about to phone your mother to make arrangements for your return home."

Danny had noticed some movement behind Mrs Barnes and he now saw that it was Spike, standing by the bedroom door. He was trying to communicate something to Danny using sign language, but it was difficult to make out what he was trying to say. Spike then had to stop quickly when his mother turned towards him.

With Mrs Barnes now facing the other way, Danny grabbed the opportunity to try and communicate with Spike. He pointed towards the monkey cages, made a monkey face and started to scratch himself under the arms like an ape.

The sight of Danny 'aping' outside the window was too much for Spike - he couldn't stop himself from smiling. Mrs Barnes swung around to see what was so funny - and caught Danny in 'mid-ape'!

"Oh, so now we're playing the fool and being rude are we?"

"Er... no, Mrs Barnes."

"I suggest you get in here this instant, young man," she uttered fiercely.

Suddenly there was another voice, right beside Danny, which made him jump.

"I think that's a good idea, don't you, Daniel?" said the voice.

It was Mr Barnes, standing amongst his tomato bushes, just a few yards away. He had a threatening look about him, as if he was about to pounce.

"Mr Barnes!" said Danny, quickly trying to weigh up his options.

"Let's go in, shall we? There's a good lad," said Mr Barnes, taking a step closer.

Danny knew it was now or never. As he began to move, Mr Barnes lunged at him with outstretched arms. Danny ducked at the last moment, causing Mr Barnes to stumble forwards into his veggies. Now Danny ran! He knew that Mr Barnes would be right behind him. He had to get to the wine cellar - *fast*! He rushed through the back door of the manor house, skidded through the kitchen, out into the passage and straight into the large burly figure of Inspector Tom Keegan!

Danny bounced off Inspector Keegan like a ball off a wall - and ended up flat on his back on the floor. The policeman reached down and hauled him to his feet.

"So, what's the big rush then?" he asked.

Danny could hear Mr Barnes coming through the kitchen. He had to think quickly.

# THE GREAT ESCAPE 73

"Inspector, please help me!" he said, trying to sound terrified.

"What? Help you? How, lad?"

"It's... it's... Mr Barnes!" said Danny. "He's gone a bit strange!"

"A bit strange?" the inspector repeated, shaking his head, but before he could find out more, Mr Barnes came flying around the corner.

Danny took cover behind the policeman.

"Help me, *please*!" he shouted.

When Mr Barnes saw the inspector he did his best to try and compose himself. The fact that he had squashed tomatoes down his front was not helping.

"Hello, Bill!" said the inspector. "So - what's going on here then?"

"Oh, hello, Tom - um... just trying to er... catch this young fellow actually. That's all. For his own good, you understand?"

"Why? What have I done?" Danny shouted from behind the inspector.

He now realised that his back was up against the sliding wooden panel.

"Yes, Bill, what exactly *has* the boy done?"

"Done? Oh, er... well, nothing really... it's just, you see, old man Piper-Adams seems to be up to something and well... we think there's something fishy going on."

"What's that got to do with the boy, Bill?" the inspector asked, taking a few steps towards Mr Barnes.

"Oh. We're not sure, but... well, perhaps it would be best if you spoke to Violet!"

"Yes, and where is that lovely wife of yours, hmm? Why don't we all sit down, have a nice cup of tea and talk about what's going on?"

Now the inspector rested a hand on Mr Barnes' shoulder and began to guide him back towards the kitchen. Danny acted as though he was following along behind them, but as soon as they rounded the corner in the passage, he ducked back to the sliding panel. He pushed it aside as quietly as possible and pressed the button for the lift. Thankfully, the lift was there and the door opened immediately. He jumped in and pressed the 'CELLAR' button. He then heard Mr Barnes roar.

"He's going down in the lift!"

Now there came the thunder of footsteps. Danny pressed himself up against the back of the lift as Mr Barnes came lumbering towards the closing doors. For a second, his gnarly fingers tried to keep the doors open, but then they slammed shut and the lift was going down.

\*

Uncle Morty had heard the commotion upstairs and was now waiting outside the lift with a chair at the ready.

"Here!" he shouted, sliding the chair over to Danny. "Lodge it in the lift door to stop it going up again!"

Danny grabbed the chair and jammed it in the lift. When the door tried to close it crunched up against the chair and sprung open again.

"Where are the others?" Uncle Morty asked.

Danny shook his head.

"I don't know. I tried to tell them to get the monkeys, but I don't think she'll let them leave the cottage!"

"Blast that confounded woman!" the old man roared. He gestured towards TIM. "We have no choice. I'm sorry, my boy. If you don't go now it'll be too late!"

As much as Danny hated to admit it, he knew his uncle was right.

\*

Inside TIM, Uncle Mortimer made sure Danny was strapped into the seat before shifting his attention to the controls.

"Now please concentrate!" he said. "I have already programmed the machine where to go. Look here - Trip 1: England, 2200. Trip 2: France, 1942. All you have to do is select 'Trip 1' or 'Trip 2' and press 'ACTIVATE'. Do you understand?"

"Yes," Danny said, nodding.

There was another crash as the lift door slammed into the chair again. Uncle Morty handed Danny his rucksack.

"Look after the book!" he pleaded.

The lift door crashed again - the chair was now buckling under the barrage.

"We can't wait any longer, son," his uncle muttered. "Press 'ACTIVATE'!"

Danny knew what this meant. By pressing 'ACTIVATE', TIM would begin the process of departure and there would be no going back. His finger hovered over the button.

The lift door crashed again.

"*Press it!*" roared Uncle Morty.

Danny couldn't believe how *wrong* everything had gone already! He pressed the button and TIM's low whine began. Uncle Morty pulled out a small box, which he thrust into Danny's hand.

"The monkeys haven't made it, but you can try and trade these."

"What are they?" asked Danny.

"Just a little something that will hopefully have some value in the future. If you can afford nothing else make sure you buy the *Attila Killer* program! Do you understand?"

Danny nodded. Everything was happening so fast and the noise was growing so loud. Uncle Morty had laid a hand on his shoulder and was saying something - but he couldn't hear what it was. He leaned closer.

"The best of luck, my boy!" his uncle roared. He was trying to smile, but Danny could see the tears welling up in his eyes. "I'll see you soon!"

Uncle Morty turned his wheelchair around and headed down the ramp. Once outside, he pressed the button and the door slid closed.

Inside, Danny could see the countdown on the control panel - numbers spinning around at an incredible rate.

*400 seconds... 350 seconds... 300 seconds...*

Through the window he could see Uncle Morty turning his wheelchair around to face TIM.

*250 seconds... 200 seconds...*

Now TIM had started to vibrate, causing Danny to clutch on to the armrests of the seat. The window was now vibrating so much that he could only just make out Uncle Morty, but what was his uncle doing? He was suddenly waving his arms and motoring forwards in his wheelchair! What was wrong now?

In the violently vibrating capsule Danny managed to unbuckle himself and get to his feet. Unsteadily, he moved towards the window to try and see what was going on. He pushed his face up against the window and the sight that greeted him now made his heart leap!

Charley had just jumped down from the wine chute onto the cellar floor, and behind her, clutching on to a monkey cage, was Spike, also getting ready to jump.

*150 seconds... 100 seconds...*

Spike jumped and landed badly, taking a tumble across the floor. His bag went flying in one direction and the monkey cage in the other.

*80 seconds... 70 seconds...*

Charley now rushed to his assistance, picked up the monkey cage and started to scream at Spike.

*60 seconds... 50 seconds...*

Spike was now on his feet, but obviously disoriented, he began to stagger off towards Uncle Morty.

*40 seconds... 30 seconds...*

# The Great Escape

Danny couldn't stand it any longer. He hit the 'DOOR OPEN' button and leapt out. First, he bundled Charley and the monkey cage inside then he went over, grabbed hold of Spike and dragged him in as well.

*20 seconds… 10 seconds…*

Danny scrambled in after Spike and pressed the 'DOOR CLOSE' button. As the door closed, the screeching of TIM outside gave way to the screeching of the monkeys inside. The vibrations were now so strong that they all just had to hold on to anything they could.

The last thing Danny saw was Uncle Morty's smiling face, his one hand raised in a gesture of farewell - then there was a blinding flash.

At almost the exact moment that TIM disappeared, the chair in the lift disintegrated and the lift door closed and headed for the top, but Uncle Morty didn't seem to mind at all.

\*

Moments later, the lift door opened again and the angry trio of Mr and Mrs Barnes, and the inspector emerged. Mr and Mrs Barnes both rushed to the spot in the cellar where TIM had stood.

"It was *here*! It was right here!" Mr Barnes shouted.

"What have you done? Where are the children?" Mrs Barnes screamed.

Uncle Morty seemed quite content to just sit back casually in his chair.

"If I were to tell you, my good lady, you wouldn't believe me anyway," he said, smiling.

Now the large inspector came over to Uncle Morty.

"I think you had better come down to the station with me, Sir."

"Lead the way, Inspector," said Uncle Morty, whose serene smile was sending Mrs Barnes into even more of a rage. "Lead the way!"

Chapter 7

# Monkey Business

The vibrations inside TIM grew so violent that everyone was shaken to the floor. It was utter chaos - screeching monkeys, rattling equipment and a light so blinding that they were all forced to shield their eyes. Now, to add to everything, they could feel an intense heat coming through the floor!

Great! thought Danny. We're going to cook in here like baked beans in a can!

Although she was trying not to show it, Charley was finding the whole experience terrifying beyond belief. She had her head right beside the monkey cage and was trying to take her mind off her own fear by talking to the monkeys.

"It's all right, Evie. It's all right, girl. Everything's going to be OK," she was muttering unconvincingly.

Then suddenly it stopped.

No more vibrations.

No more blinding light.

They all lay there for a few seconds. Was that it? Was it over? Even the monkeys started to calm down.

It was the heat from the floor that forced Danny up onto his feet. He staggered over to the window for a look and that's when he suddenly recoiled in horror. At the window, a creature with massive eyes and a great curling tongue stared in!

"*Get back!*" shouted Danny.

"What is it?" cried Spike, diving for cover behind the chair.

The boys braced themselves for an attack, expecting the door to be ripped open at any second. Instead, there came a strange noise. It sounded like… Charley giggling?

"What's so funny?" Spike growled angrily.

"Look," said Charley, gesturing towards the window.

When Danny and Spike looked again, they were able to see the creature's head more clearly. It was a cow.

"Ooh, a big scary cow!" said Charley, still giggling.

Even when they had all climbed out of TIM, Charley was still smirking at the boys' reaction.

"Ah, give it a break, Charles!" whined Spike. "We've got to be careful. We don't know what's changed in the last two hundred years!"

"You're right, Spike," said Charley, pretending to look serious. "Those evil-looking cows could be man-eaters."

Spike gave her a withering look and went off to join Danny.

\*

Danny was taking a look around. Apart from the cows, the meadow and surrounding farmland seemed deserted. Thankfully, it appeared as though no one had witnessed their arrival. Nearby was a haystack, which had given him an idea.

"Come on," he said to the others. "We'd better cover TIM up."

As they began to pile the hay on top of TIM, Spike was looking around at their surroundings.

"Do you really think this is 2200? It all looks the same."

"We'll soon find out," said Danny.

He dug around in his rucksack until he found the small taxi-caller disc that Uncle Morty had given him. He pressed the button on it.

"Now what?" asked Charley.

Danny shrugged.

"I suppose we just wait and see."

Once TIM had been completely disguised as a haystack they all walked up to the top of a rise from where they had a good view all around them. They could see the farmland stretching to the horizon in every direction. There were plenty of cows and sheep grazing in the meadows, and the fields were thick with tall green crops. Uncle Morty had said the Earth was a sad place in 2200 and yet, as far as they could see, it was not looking too bad at all! The only thing that did strike them as a bit odd was the colour of the sky. It was a strange, dark purple colour.

\*

The monkeys seemed to sense it first. They both looked up from the game they were playing with Charley and began to scan the horizon with their beady little eyes.

Then Charley spotted it - a small black speck in the sky.

"Look!" she said, pointing.

Whatever it was, it appeared to be heading in their direction.

"Must be a plane," said Spike, squinting.

As the object drew nearer, they realised this was no plane. Firstly, it was silent and secondly, it looked more like a car than a plane. In fact, it looked very much like one of those black London taxicabs - except it had no wheels and it was flying!

The cab swooped down and came skimming across the meadow towards them. As they all stood gawking, it pulled up right in front of them, still hovering about a foot off the ground. Next thing, the back door popped open and a voice inside shouted:

"Hop in then!"

Hesitantly, they collected up the monkey cage and their bags, and clambered in.

"Where to?" asked the cabbie.

He was a fairly normal-looking bloke, except for his incredibly pale skin, which looked like it had never seen the sun - *ever*!

"Are you Reg?" asked Danny.

"That's right."

"My uncle said you would know where to take us if I gave you this address."

Danny handed him the piece of paper and when Reg read it he seemed to remember Uncle Morty.

"Oh, yes! The funny old bloke in the ancient wheelchair?

Could have got an absolute fortune at any antique shop for that wheelchair!"

Once Reg had taken note of the address he handed the piece of paper back to Danny, put 'the car' into gear and suddenly pulled away! It took them all by surprise and Charley instinctively grabbed hold of Danny's arm and held on tight as the car climbed rapidly up and away. It was only when they had levelled out and were cruising along smoothly that Charley realised her fingernails were still digging into Danny.

"Sorry," she mumbled, releasing her grip and quickly looking out of the window.

"So, how is that old uncle of yours anyway?" Reg asked. "He must have been the most clueless passenger I've ever met! He didn't know *anything* about *anything*! Well, except for history, which he seemed quite clued up on, but he sure wanted to learn! Didn't stop asking questions!"

Although they were listening to Reg, Danny and the others couldn't stop peering out of the windows. The views were amazing - miles and miles of beautiful green farmland - and here they were, cruising above it all - in a car!

"I don't think your uncle had ever been off the farm!" Reg continued. "He didn't know about moneycards or anything. It was like he'd come from another planet! Speaking of which, I hope you kids have a moneycard with you?"

Danny pulled out his card to show Reg. He took a quick look at it, nodded and looked back at the three of them again.

"I don't mean to be rude but... where on earth did you get those outfits? You shop at the same place as your uncle?"

Danny and the others looked down at their clothes then leaned forwards to see what Reg was wearing. He had something on that looked like a shiny satin tracksuit. If everyone was dressed like Reg they were definitely going to stand out in the crowd!

"Right, we're leaving the farm atmosphere now," Reg

announced suddenly.

They had no idea what he was talking about, but all of a sudden they were passing through some kind of strange mist - then they emerged into grey skies and drizzle! The sudden transformation was bizarre!

And now, when they looked again at the view below, they were shocked to see a grey waterlogged landscape. It was so wet that most of the land was flooded and only those structures built on higher ground were out of the reach of the floodwaters. Elsewhere, tall grey buildings rose up out of the waters and, instead of car parks, they had marinas full of boats beside them. Another thing they noticed was that it had suddenly become very warm and muggy - so much so that Reg now switched on the air conditioning. Danny had once been to India with his parents during the hot, wet monsoon season and this is exactly what it reminded him of.

"Is this England?" he asked.

"Of course!" Reg laughed. "Where do you think it is?"

"But..." Spike pointed back, from where they had just come. "Why the sudden change?"

Reg shook his head.

"Don't tell me you guys have never left the farm either! Surely you know that farms have their own artificial atmospheres where the climate can be controlled? Otherwise nothing would grow. What do you think is going to survive out here where it rains all day, every day?"

They all peered out at the flooded grey wasteland. It was almost impossible to imagine that these were once the rolling green hills of England. Now it looked more like the murky grey sludge of England!

"Is the whole country like this?" Danny asked.

Reg nodded.

"Except for the farms and some of the cities that can afford their own atmospheres. It's an expensive business creating mini-climates."

They now noticed what looked like rows of big red balloons stretching out in lines in the sky on either side of them. Reg guided his car between the balloons. It was like they were lanes in the sky because they could now see other skycars moving in the opposite direction in lanes with large green balloons. Suddenly a very sleek-looking skycar flashed past them, causing the cab to wobble a bit.

"*Skyhog!*" roared Reg.

Now the sky was filling up with skycars and Danny could see why they needed lanes. He also noticed that there were lanes above and below them.

The landscape way down below remained flooded, but up ahead they could now see what looked like a giant dome of mist rising up out of the floodwaters.

"What's that?" Danny asked.

"London One, of course," replied Reg.

"London One? How many Londons are there?"

Reg shot Danny a look, as if to say, 'Are you having me on?'.

"You're sounding worse than your uncle," he said with a smile.

With London approaching below and all the sky traffic around them, it was difficult to know where to look.

"Reg, would it be possible to fly lower over London?" Spike asked.

"Yeah, we can go a bit lower," Reg said, nodding, "but we can't go into London One's atmosphere."

Spike now spotted something else in the sky up in front of them. It looked like a huge city floating in mid-air.

"What's that?" he asked in amazement.

Once again Reg gave them a strange look.

"You guys really need to get off the farm more! That's LA of course!"

"LA? You mean like... Los Angeles?"

"Not Los Angeles! *London Air!* Where all the rich people live! You never heard of London Air? They live above the clouds. You can always tell someone from London Air because they always have a suntan! That's why it's so expensive to live up there."

Danny nodded, trying to make out that he had heard of it before.

"Of course... London Air."

Reg was now taking a lane that seemed to dip down to a slightly lower altitude.

"This is as low as we're allowed to go over L1," he explained.

They all looked out and the first thing they saw was that a giant flood barrier had been built all the way around the centre of London, making it a dry island in the midst of all the floodwater. Anything too far out of the city centre was now underwater. It was above this 'dry island' that the dome of mist arose, creating an atmosphere for the city and shielding it from the awful weather outside. From what they could see through the mist, the city centre was looking very much like it looks today, except for one thing - there were no cars on the streets. In fact, all the streets looked empty.

"Where is everyone?" asked Charley.

"What do you mean?" replied Reg, looking confused.

"Where's all the traffic? The people?"

"Can't you see the buses?" said Reg.

Now, when they looked more closely, they did notice some large red double-decker buses hovering sedately around the city.

"Bus-loads full of tourists," said Reg. "Only the wealthiest tourists can afford to visit L1."

"You mean no one lives down there?"

"Blimey! You lot *are* worse than your uncle! Of course people live there! The royal family lives there. The prime minister lives there. Anyone else who is considered a celebrity or a tourist attraction lives there, but that's it; if you don't pull the crowds you're out! Heard the queen is now charging a thousand WDs for a five-minute audience. Must be very boring shaking hands with tourists all day long, but she has to earn her keep I suppose."

"So you mean to say we can't just go down and land there?" Danny asked.

Reg threw his head back and roared with laughter.

"Land in L1! That's a good one! You feeling rich? Listen, L1 is booked up for the next ten years. It's one of the world's biggest tourist attractions. People save up their whole lives for a two-week stay in L1. You know - do the historical sites, catch a few shows, meet the queen. It's the holiday of a lifetime!"

Spike looked over at Danny. They had a lot to learn, but perhaps this wasn't the time for too many questions.

Now they moved into a great shadow and, looking up, they realised they were passing under the monumental structure of London Air. It looked like a platform the size of a hundred football fields, which was somehow suspended in mid-air!

Moments later, they had forgotten about LA because up ahead they now spotted something even more mind-boggling! At first it just appeared to be a place on the ground where all the skylanes converged, but as they drew closer they realised that this wasn't just a place on the ground - it was a gigantic *hole* in the ground!

If LA above was bigger than a hundred football fields then this enormous opening must have been at least ten times as big again. It was also surrounded by a giant flood barrier that was keeping the water back, and there were literally thousands of skycars descending into it on the one side and rising up out of it on the other. As Reg came over the top of it, they all looked down into the giant opening and it was a sight that took their breath away. It seemed like it went down forever, as far as they could see!

"Wow!" said Spike.

He couldn't believe his eyes!

"Welcome to the Grand Passage," said Reg with a smile. "Going down!"

He pressed some buttons on the control panel of the skycar and it began to descend like a helicopter.

"Right, where did you say that shop was? L15?"

Danny looked at the paper again and read it out aloud.

"L15. SW19."

"Righto."

As they entered the giant opening the sights all around became more and more astounding. It was as if there was a multitude of storeys built beneath the surface. At each level there were brightly lit signs with the names of the different levels - L2, L3, L4 - but each level was equal to about ten storeys of a normal building. At each level there were docking bays where skycars (mainly skytaxis and skybuses) could dock and drop off their

passengers. The first few storeys seemed to be mainly shopping malls, with huge windows facing out into the Grand Passage and flashy advertising signs. Then they were passing by what seemed like many storeys of offices and banks.

... L5... L6... L7...

Now they were passing a series of gyms where they could see aerobics classes and people exercising on machines, then it seemed like they were looking into school classrooms. Below the classrooms were floodlit fields with a whole lot of schoolchildren playing football.

... L8... L9... L10...

Of course, Danny thought, everything is flooded above ground, so everyone's moved underground!

"Wow!" said Spike again. "How far does this go down?"

"How far? Well, I heard they were building L150," Reg replied, "but you wouldn't catch me going down there. In fact, if I can help it, I try not to go below L80. Anything below L100 is definitely not recommended. They don't call it *The Devil's Dungeon* for nothing! So do yourselves a favour and don't venture down there, OK?"

"Why?" Danny asked. "What's down there?"

"Well, let's just say, the scum of the earth usually settles at the bottom. They have been having terrible problems getting the police to work down below L100 - so the people who live down there are pretty much a law unto themselves. They are welcome to it! As long as they don't bring their crime and trouble up to where the decent folk live, it suits me. You see, law enforcement costs money and the closer you are to L1 the more money you have."

Right on cue they passed a police skycar hovering in a stationary position right beside the descent lane. They were so close that they were able to see the two serious-looking officers in the car. They were wearing black helmets and black sunglasses, and seemed to stare into Reg's cab as they went by. Danny and the others sunk back in their seats. Danny just hoped they weren't Timecops. He even glanced back up to make sure they hadn't started to follow them, but the police car remained where it was.

Danny now looked at Uncle Morty's list again. He knew their first priority must be to get the computer chips and the *Attila Killer* program. The address to buy *Attila Killer* was on L86, which gave him a slightly uneasy feeling. The other items on the list looked like they could also be computer programs.

*Attila Killer*
*Combat X*
*Go Ape!*
*Minderbender*
*Translatormates*
*Immobilasers*

"Righto - here we are!" said Reg suddenly. He waited for a couple of skycars to pass by then pulled over towards a docking bay. As the cab approached the docking bay it seemed to get sucked onto the end of a gangway. "Fifteen WDs thank you very much," Reg said, smiling.

Danny passed him the moneycard and watched as Reg stuck it into a slot on his dashboard. A couple of seconds later there was a beep and the card came out again. Reg handed it back to Danny, who had a look at the screen. It read 10 WDs. That was all the money they had left.

"Thanks, Reg," they all said as they climbed out.

"Righto, be careful out there and remember what I said about going down too low. If you need another lift you know how to get hold of me."

Danny had one more question.

"Reg, how do we find this shop in SW19?" he asked.

"You take the Tube of course," Reg replied. "How else?"

Reg pointed towards some doors bearing the London

Underground insignia then he closed the back door of the cab, gave them a smile and a wave, and pulled away from the docking bay.

As they watched the cab rising up out of the Grand Passage it felt like their only friend in the world was leaving them behind. Danny knew this would be a good time to put on a brave face.

"Come on," he said, trying to sound casually confident. "Let's go and catch the Tube."

*

Minutes later, the three of them were standing transfixed, staring up at a vast tower of giant transparent tubes. In these tubes they could see sleek-looking trains arriving in a blur, waiting briefly for people to get on and off then disappearing again in a flash. Every now and again a train would pass through the station without stopping - just a split-second flash then it was gone.

There were also huge amounts of people on the move. People who (unlike them!) seemed to know where they were going. They noticed all sorts of outlandish styles of clothing going by (all made from the same shiny material as Reg's outfit) and some truly bizarre hairstyles. They also couldn't help noticing how pale everyone looked.

"Now where do we go?" Charley muttered, gawking up at the tower of tubes.

Spike was doing his best to make sense of a large electronic sign saying 'VERTICAL TRAVEL' with an arrow pointing in one direction and 'HORIZONTAL TRAVEL' with an arrow pointing in the other direction.

Standing there in their funny clothes, with their monkey cage, trying to work out which direction to go in, they must have looked very out of place. They were certainly receiving some odd looks.

Then they were surprised by a voice behind them.

"You look lost," said the voice.

They turned to find a young girl, about their age. She was wearing a small, pink shiny dress with large black boots, and her long unruly hair was streaked in black and blonde.

"Where you going?" she asked.

"SW19," replied Danny, showing her the address on the piece of paper.

The girl read the address then beamed a smile.

"Wilson's Wildlife! Coolatious! I'm going near there. I can show you if you like?"

"That would be great, thanks," said Danny, looking relieved.

Now Charley noticed how the girl was looking at their clothes.

"Where you fellowchies from?" she asked.

"Uh... long story," said Danny.

The girl cast another critical eye over them and nodded. "I bet it is!" Then she turned on one of her huge heels and headed towards the escalators. "This way!"

They took off after her and Danny ran to catch up.

"Thanks, we appreciate the help," he said.

"No probs," she replied.

"By the way, I'm Danny and these are my friends Spike and Charley."

"Hi, I'm Soro."

Sorrow? thought Danny. Interesting name!

Soro glanced back at Charley and Spike, who were carrying the monkey cage.

"What you got in the cage?" she asked.

"Oh... er... monkeys," Danny replied.

"Monkeys!" Soro chuckled. "Coolatious! That why you going to Wilson's Wildlife?"

"That's right," Danny replied, nodding. "To sell them."

They were approaching a row of gates and Danny was amazed to see that everyone was just placing their hands on green pads and the gates were opening automatically for them. Soro did this as well, the gate opened up for her and she went through. Danny tried to do the same, but nothing happened. Soro looked back at him quizzically from the other side of the gate.

"Oh... we don't... um..." Danny held up his hand sheepishly. "We can't..."

"You got no money on your chip?" Soro asked.

"Uh, we don't have chips," Danny mumbled.

Soro couldn't believe what she was hearing.

"*You don't have chips?*"

Danny shook his head. It was getting embarrassing with all the people streaming past.

"How about a moneycard?" Soro asked.

"Yes, we have one of those!" Danny said, grabbing it out of his pocket.

"Whoopee for that," Soro muttered.

She now had her arms folded and was eyeing the three of them with a growing sense of disbelief. She pointed to the place where Danny should slot in his moneycard. He did this twice, so that Charley and Spike could get through, but when he tried for himself the machine just made a funny beeping sound and spat the card back out. Danny looked at the screen on the card - it read, 'INSUFFICIENT FUNDS'.

"What's the matter?" Charley asked, from the other side of the gate.

"The card has run out of money," Danny replied.

Soro rolled her eyes and shook her head. She swiped her hand over a pad and the gate opened for Danny.

"Thanks," Danny said rather sheepishly as he came through. "I don't know how we can repay you."

"No probs," she replied. "You can pay me back when you sell your monkeys."

"No probs," Danny said with a grin.

Now it was Charley's turn to roll her eyes.

\*

A short train trip later and they found themselves approaching the most amazing shop front they had ever seen in their lives! It was an enormous place with huge windows and a giant neon green sign stretching right across the top, which read, 'WILDMAN WILSON'S WILDLIFE EMPORIUM'.

It was only now, as they drew closer, that they saw exactly what was in the giant shop windows. One window was designed to look like the African bush and had a full-grown lioness with three cubs in it. Another was a mini-rainforest filled with an array of beautiful birds, whilst a third window was a giant fish tank teeming with all sorts of colourful fish, including eels and stingrays.

Hanging beside the grand shop entrance was an enormous poster of an elderly man with long white hair and a beard. He was dressed in safari gear, including a bush hat, and was surrounded by animals of all descriptions. The message below the picture read, 'WELCOME TO WILSON'S WILDLIFE!'.

"That's Wildman Wilson," said Soro. "You must have seen him on TV. They say he's seen every type of animal on earth!"

Looking up at the giant image, Spike thought that Wildman Wilson looked like Father Christmas on safari!

As they entered the shop the first thing that struck them was the incredible noise! This was not surprising when they saw just how many animals were housed in this massive building. It was set out like a giant supermarket, but instead of walking down aisles of groceries they found themselves walking down aisles of wild animals in cages!

Everything was in its own department. Above them now was a large sign saying 'CATS' (with a picture of Wildman Wilson holding a baby leopard) and suddenly on either side of them were lions, leopards, panthers and every other species of wild cat you could imagine.

At least these animals still exist on Earth, Danny thought. He just wondered how many were still left in the wild!

Next they were passing under a sign saying 'SNAKES' with a picture of Wildman Wilson with a large python draped around his neck. As they passed through this department Charley kept looking straight ahead! Eventually they reached some offices at the back of the shop and here they found a receptionist, also dressed in safari gear.

"Welcome to Wilson's Wildlife," she said with a polite smile. "How may I help you?"

"We would like to see Mr Wilson please," said Danny.

"I'm afraid that's impossible. Mr Wilson is a very busy man."

"I have some monkeys I would like to sell to him."

"I'm afraid buying is only on Mondays and Fridays," said the receptionist, pointing to a sign.

Danny could feel his anger rising.

"Please can you give Mr Wilson a message?" he said, trying to stay calm. "Please tell him that I have two capuchin monkeys for sale."

"Like I said - you'll have to come back on Monday-"

"Capuchin monkeys!" Danny said in a firm voice. "I think if you tell Mr Wilson they are capuchin monkeys he will be very interested."

The receptionist and Danny stood staring at each other. Eventually, sensing that Danny was not going to budge, she picked up the phone.

"Excuse me, Sir, we have some people here who say they have some cappuccino monkeys."

"*Capuchin!*" said Danny, Spike and Charley in chorus.

"Er, sorry. They say they are *capuchin* monkeys." As the receptionist listened to the response on the phone, a wry smile appeared on her face. "Sorry, Mr Wilson says you must be mistaken. The capuchin monkey has been extinct for over a century."

"Tell him he's wrong!" said Spike.

"Excuse me! When it comes to wildlife, Mr Wilson is never wrong!"

"Well, this time he is!" Charley chirped from the back.

Once again the receptionist had no choice but to get back on the phone.

"Sir, I'm terribly sorry, but they say you are... wrong." This must have caused an outburst on the other end because she had to hold the phone away from her ear. She listened for a moment longer then put the phone down. "Now you've upset him. Mr Wilson is coming through."

Moments later, the door behind the receptionist opened and Wildman Wilson (looking a lot smaller than he did in his posters) came striding out of his office.

"All right, who's the monkey who doesn't know his monkeys?" he fumed.

As Mr Wilson approached, Charley placed the monkey cage on the reception desk and Danny pulled the cover off. Mr Wilson certainly must have known his animals because it only took him a split second to recognise the monkeys. He faltered momentarily in his stride and blinked as if his eyes were deceiving him. When he reached the desk he crouched down for a closer look and then, after a long moment of staring in silence, he lifted his eyes to Danny.

"Where on God's Earth did you find these?" he asked.

"I'm afraid we can't tell you that," said Danny, "but if you would like to buy them we are offering you first choice. We do have a figure in mind."

Danny now handed Mr Wilson the paper on which Uncle Morty had written his suggested sale price. Mr Wilson glanced at it and blinked a few more times.

"Not cheap," he said, "but then I suppose they wouldn't be. All right, come into my office."

*

A short time later, Mr Wilson escorted them out again. Danny was staring at the moneycard. He couldn't believe how much money was on it! Charley, on the other hand, was wiping her eyes; having just said a very sad farewell to Adam and Eve. Mr Wilson had made her feel slightly better by saying he would never sell the monkeys. He planned to let them start a family, and he assured Charley that they would be given very comfortable accommodation with lots of room to play. Charley believed him because, as they all said goodbye, she could see that he had very kind eyes - especially when it came to animals.

Danny went over to where Soro was waiting.

"We can pay you back now," he said, brandishing the moneycard.

"No probs," said Soro. "You know it might be an idea for you fellowchies to get some chips inserted. Like the rest of the planet!"

Danny nodded and pulled out Uncle Morty's list of things to buy and where to find them.

"We were going to this shop next," he said. "We have to buy this stuff."

Soro looked at the list then at Danny in amazement.

"*BAM*? You're going to *BAM* to buy… *all this stuff*?"

Danny nodded.

"Can we get chips inserted there as well?" he asked.

This made Soro laugh.

"At *BAM!* Oh, don't you worry about that! *BAM* do chips and a *whole* lot more!"

"Excellent," said Danny, looking pleased.

Soro was still shaking her head in amazement.

"Hey, do you fellowchies have any idea how much money

you're going to need for this stuff?" she asked.

"We know," Danny nodded, holding up the moneycard.

Soro looked surprised then after a few moments consideration, she said:

"Hey, I've got to see this! Do you guys mind if I come along? I can show you where *BAM* is."

Danny and Spike seemed happy with the idea, and even Charley had to admit that it helped having someone who knew where they were going.

Meanwhile, Soro was still raving.

"If you guys think *this* shop is amazing - wait until you see *BAM!*"

\*

According to Soro, *BAM* wasn't too far away. They had to first catch a huge super-fast lift to a different level. This took them up five levels in a matter of seconds then they found themselves walking through a shopping mall that never seemed to end.

Along the way, Charley had noticed how Soro kept glancing at them sideways. It was as if she wanted to say something. Eventually she couldn't hold it in any more.

"Hey, fellowchies, I don't mean to be rude but... those clothes! Have you thought about getting some new gear? You look like a bunch of palwaddies!"

"A bunch of *what?*" asked Spike, who then wondered why the others were looking at him.

"Look - one of my *other* favourite shops is just over there," said Soro, pointing. "Why don't we just go and have a quick look?"

Danny started to protest, but Soro was already heading off in that direction.

"Come on. Just have a look!" she shouted back at them.

Danny looked at the others and shrugged.

"I guess it will help us to blend in?" he said.

No one seemed too enthusiastic about the idea, but Soro was now standing at the entrance of the shop, waving at them to join her. Somewhat begrudgingly, Danny and the others went over and followed her inside.

It was easy to see why it was one of Soro's favourite shops; it was like her - young and loud with plenty of attitude! Soro obviously knew her way around and she immediately began picking out clothes. The others hovered nearby looking unsure, but every time they tried to say anything Soro would chivvy them along, saying things like:

"Don't argue. Trust me!"

The result was that in less than ten minutes Danny and Charley found themselves completely transformed - dressed in clothing they might only have ever imagined wearing to a Gothic-Aliens party! Everything was long and shiny, and even their hair had been primped and preened to look more like everyone else's in the shop. While Soro fluttered around them making last-minute adjustments Danny and Charley could do nothing but stare at each other in shock. Suddenly they both burst out laughing. It was the sight of Spike - with his long black and red jacket, and spiked up hair he looked like the King of the Goth-Punks!

Spike put on his best false smile.

"Hey, have you space bunnies looked at yourselves lately?"

Soro was clearly pleased with her work.

"Well, I think you're all looking seriously coolatious!" she exclaimed as she went over to what looked like a large computer screen near the exit.

"Moneycard please!" she said, and Danny handed her the card.

A list of all the garments they were taking was already on the screen and all she did was slot in the moneycard. Once the payment was made she removed the moneycard and handed it back to Danny. She then remembered that they still owed her for the Tube ticket.

"Can I take for the Tube ticket as well?" she asked.

"Of course," Danny said, and he was intrigued by how Soro pressed a few buttons on the moneycard then swiped it over her hand. "Done?" he asked.

"Done!" Soro smiled, giving him back the card. She then herded them all out of the shop. "*BAM,* here we come!"

\*

Ten minutes later they were walking into the extremely modern, ultra hi-tech shop called *BAM*. '*THE ORIGINAL BODY AND MIND ENHANCEMENT CENTRE*!' was the message flashing above the entrance.

Soro had obviously been there many times before.

"Right, the first thing we'll have to do is get the chips inserted," she said, leading them to a booth where a sign said, 'FREE *BAM* CHIP INSERTION'.

In the booth they found a female shop assistant wielding a strange-looking laser-gun contraption. Soro explained that her three friends needed chips inserted, and the shop assistant asked them each to present their hands. She then went to each of them in turn, placing the gun on the palm of their hands and pulling the trigger. When it came to Charley's turn she braced herself for the pain, but it turned out to be barely more than a tickle.

"Is that it?" she asked.

"That's it," said the smiling shop assistant.

"We now have chips inside us?" Charley asked, staring at her hand.

"You do."

"Right, let's go and have some fun!" said Soro as she led them out of the booth. She still had Uncle Morty's list and she now read the first item. "*Combat X*! Coolatious! Right - we should find that over here."

The department she led them to was called 'BATTLE

STATIONS' and the shop assistant who now approached them looked like he belonged in the army. He had huge bulging biceps and a shaved head.

"Good afternoon. My name is Sarge. How may I help you?"

"My friend here is interested in *Combat X*," said Soro, pointing at Danny.

"Yes, Ma'am! Fine choice if I may say so myself!" said Sarge, before turning to Danny. "Will you be wanting to test a trial version, Sir?"

Danny looked to Soro for guidance and she gave a big smile.

"Yes, Sarge, I think he will!"

"In the testing arena?"

Soro's smile grew even larger.

"Yes please - in the testing arena!"

"Excellent!" said Sarge, "This way please, Sir!"

Before Danny knew it, he was being led away from the others.

"See you soon." Soro waved. "Have fun!"

Now Soro beckoned to the others to follow her up an escalator that had a large electronic sign flashing above it, 'SPECTATOR SEATING FOR TESTING ARENA'.

"Come, fellowchies," she said excitedly, "we have to get a good seat for this!"

\*

Sarge led Danny to another booth and asked him to place his hand onto a hand-shaped pad.

"Thank you, Sir. This will just take a few moments." He punched a few buttons and some lights began to flash. "Just hold still please, Sir." Now, as the machine began to hum, Sarge spoke to Danny with great enthusiasm. "*Combat X* - a really excellent choice, Sir! Straight out of the *BAM* top drawer! In fact, I would go as far as to say it is probably one of the finest bits of software ever written. Bit on the pricey side, but in my book worth every

WD."

Danny had not the faintest idea what Sarge was talking about and, before he could ask anything, the machine stopped humming.

"That's it. Let's go and test this baby out! I have loaded the trial version that will only last a few minutes - so let's get started!"

Sarge led Danny towards the back of the shop where they passed through a series of sliding doors then found themselves walking down a long corridor. At the end of the corridor they could hear what sounded like the noise of a crowd - applause punctuated with plenty of oohs and aahs!

Danny was wondering what *on earth* he had got himself into! And the feeling was reinforced when a voice suddenly came over the public address system.

"Attention, shoppers! For anyone interested - the latest version of *Combat X* is about to be tested in the testing arena. Anyone wishing to view this display is welcome. Please remember that the latest version of *Combat X* is on special for this week only!"

As they reached the final sliding door marked 'TESTING ARENA' Sarge turned to Danny with a grin.

"Ready for action, Sir?"

"What am I meant to do?" Danny asked.

"Don't worry, Sir. The program will guide you. I have given you the maximum capability on all disciplines, so you are not going to have any problem with these dudes."

"Which dudes?" asked Danny.

Sarge pressed a button and another door slid open to reveal two of the largest, scariest-looking men he had ever seen! They were built like those wrestlers on TV and were both staring at Danny with demonic eyes. Suddenly it dawned on him that these were the men he was about to challenge! He looked at Sarge as if to say, '*You have got to be joking*!'.

As usual Sarge was grinning.

"Don't worry about a thing, Sir. Just trust in the program. Remember *Combat X* is primarily a self-defence program. It will activate automatically when it perceives your safety is being threatened."

"But what does the program do?" Danny pleaded, trying his best not to sound too exasperated.

"Well, Sir, I think you're about to find that out!" Sarge said, smiling.

He pressed a button and the door marked 'TESTING ARENA' slid open.

\*

As Soro, Spike and Charley took their seats the crowd was still buzzing from the action that had obviously just taken place in the arena. Now there were vendors circulating, selling *BAM* T-shirts, *BAM* burgers and *BAM* popcorn.

They were in a mini-stadium, looking down on an arena. The arena was surrounded by a thick transparent wall and the only way in or out was through a door that was now sliding open. They also noticed various weapons scattered around the arena - an axe, a spiked ball attached to a chain, a sword.

Into this arena, a lone figure now emerged. At the sight of him the crowd erupted and Soro squealed.

"There he is!"

Sure enough, it was Danny walking tentatively out into the arena, still looking like he wanted to be somewhere else. Sarge was down on the sidelines giving him words of encouragement.

Another roar went up as two, enormous unsavoury-looking characters came trotting out into the arena.

Spike and Charley were surprised by the sight of these two giants, but the real shock came when they both began to circle Danny menacingly!

"They're going to kill him!" whispered Spike.

Charley couldn't bear to watch, but Soro was all smiles, having a great time.

"Don't worry, they're only Fish-heads."

Spike gave her a quizzical look.

"Fish-heads?"

"Of course, *Artificials* are perfect for the job - they don't feel any pain and they can be programmed to whatever strength is needed."

Spike took another look at the two giants in the ring. *Artificials! Were these two giants not real people?*

When Soro glanced at him again, he quickly nodded in agreement.

"Of course! Fish-heads!"

\*

Down in the arena, as far as Danny was concerned he was about to be ripped apart by two *very real* monsters! He kept looking to Sarge for assistance - but all Sarge did was encourage him to adopt a fighting stance by raising his fists.

"*How's that going to help?*" Danny muttered, reluctantly taking up the stance.

The giants had now started to grin! One of them made a huge lunge at Danny, which caught him completely off-guard. Before he could react, the man had lifted him clean off the ground. Again Danny looked to Sarge for help.

"What am I meant to do?" he shouted.

"Try something!"

"Like what?"

"Anything you like," Sarge replied with a shrug.

He was looking far too relaxed for Danny's liking! It was all right for him; he wasn't getting swung around by the scruff of the neck. Now Danny felt the other heavy trying to grab him by the feet.

"No way!" he muttered, as he kicked out.

Incredibly, the first kick caught the man under the jaw and

actually lifted him clean off the ground! While the man was still airborne, Danny planted a huge double-footed kick into his stomach, which sent him reeling across the arena, smack into the barrier, where he crumpled in a heap on the floor.

"*BAM!*" the crowd roared.

"Wow!" screamed Spike. "Did you see that?"

"You ain't seen nothing yet!" said a smiling Soro.

Danny hadn't really seen the full effect of his kick because he was still too busy getting swung around by the neck.

"Could you let go of me please?" Danny asked politely.

The ogre just laughed.

"Right, that's it!" Danny said, fuming. "Don't say I didn't ask!"

With that he struck out at the man. In a sudden blur of movement Danny pummelled the giant with a dozen punches - the last of which knocked him clean off his feet. Danny looked at his fists then at the giant lying spread-eagled at his feet.

"Was that me?" he muttered to himself.

"*BAM!*" screamed Spike and Charley, who were now both on their feet. Suddenly they both started to shout and point. "Danny! Behind you! Watch out!"

Sure enough, the other ogre was now rushing at Danny from behind and, what's more, he was wielding a dirty great axe and looking seriously angry! In one smooth movement, Danny grabbed the arm holding the axe then, dropping down onto his back with a foot in the man's stomach, he used his momentum to send him sailing overhead into the barrier, head first!

"*BAM!*"

The force of the crash made Danny wince. He was worried he might have killed the man, but there was no time to dwell on this because the other giant was now grabbing him from behind. Again, it was as if Danny knew exactly what to do. A sharp elbow in the ribs made the man buckle, followed by a fantastically aerobatic kick in which Danny swung around in the air and connected with such a heavy blow that the man went down, and wasn't getting up again either.

Danny stood there looking at the two figures lying in the arena. Only now did he notice the crowd on their feet, roaring their approval.

Sarge entered the arena.

"Good work, Sir! Not everyone is suited to *Combat X,* but you look like you were made for it!"

"Are they all right?" Danny asked, indicating the two men, who still hadn't moved.

This made Sarge smile.

"Of course, Sir, but you've given our Fish-mechanics something to do."

Danny frowned, looking at the men again.

"Fish-mechanics?"

*

Back in the shop, Sarge was explaining a bit more about *Combat X* to Danny when the others came rushing in.

"Hey, nice one, mate!" said Spike, laughing and giving Danny a slap on the back.

Soro had to go one better.

"You were *amazing!*" she said, giving Danny a peck on the cheek.

This was too much for Charley, who just stood back and rolled her eyes.

Sarge, meanwhile, was showing something to Danny on a computer screen.

"You see, Sir, I had it programmed for all the disciplines. Here are the options available."

Danny looked at the list on the screen.

*Karate*

*Judo*

*Tai-kwon-do*
*Kick-boxing*
*Boxing*
*Wrestling*
*Kung-fu*
*Street-fighting*
*Stick-fighting*

Danny was gobsmacked.

"I can do all that?"

"With *Combat X* - yes, Sir! *Combat X* transforms you into the ultimate fighting machine, but, as I mentioned, it is programmed to only activate in self-defence. In other words it can't be used for any purpose other than self-defence, otherwise we'd have every bad guy in town getting *Combat X*ed!" Sarge could tell that Danny had really enjoyed the experience. "Interested in buying it, Sir?"

"Yes, definitely."

"Excellent decision, Sir! Thank you, Sir! Will you be buying anything else?"

"Yes, we will," said Soro, "but we need to go to another department. Can we pay for everything at the end, Sarge?"

"Yes, Ma'am! No problem, Ma'am!" Sarge roared.

\*

The next department Soro led them to was called 'I SPY', and the shop assistant who now approached them was dressed in a tuxedo and black bowtie. This would not have appeared too unusual except that she was a woman.

"Good afternoon," she said, "the name is Bond, Jane Bond. How may I help you?"

"We'd like to look at these items, please Jane," said Soro, handing her the list.

Jane quickly scanned the list before disappearing into the back. It wasn't long before she returned with an armful of boxes that she put on the counter.

"Right, the first item is the *Immobilaser*," said Jane as she pulled out what looked like a small remote control. "Anyone like to demonstrate this?"

"I will!" said Spike quickly.

He had secretly been wanting to try the *Combat X* as well.

"All right," said Jane, pressing a couple of buttons on the remote control. "We can adjust the strength of the *Immobilaser* here." When she was satisfied she looked up at Spike and asked, "Right, you wanted to test it?"

"Yes, please!" Spike replied, stepping forwards enthusiastically.

"OK."

Jane now pointed the remote at Spike and pressed a button. Suddenly he froze in the position he was in - absolutely still - even his eyes stopped blinking. The others couldn't believe it. Charley walked around Spike and looked directly into his eyes. There was clearly nobody home!

"I have put it on the lowest strength, so it should only last a minute or so. We can use this other button here to unfreeze him. The most impressive thing about the *Immobilaser* is that it freezes all brain activity as well, so when we mobilise him again he will not even be aware that this has happened."

To illustrate, she pressed the remote again and Spike suddenly returned.

"All right, go on then," he said to Jane, looking expectantly at the remote. Much to his surprise the others all burst out laughing. "What's so funny?" he demanded.

"You've tested it already, Spike," explained Charley, laughing.

"What do you mean? That's not fair! Nothing happened!"

"Oh yes it did," Charley assured him.

Spike was totally confused, but there was no time to explain because Soro had now drawn everyone's attention back to the list.

"OK, this is my favourite!" she said, squealing enthusiastically. "*Translatormate*! I want to try it out with Danny!"

"Of course you do," Charley mumbled to herself.

Jane instructed Soro and Danny to place their hands onto a couple of programming hand-pads. A machine then started to hum and she drew their attention to a computer screen.

"OK, so this is the advanced version of *Translatormate*, which includes most of the world's languages."

The humming stopped and they removed their hands. Soro was bubbling over with excitement. Danny didn't know what to expect.

"OK, are you ready to chat?" Soro asked Danny.

"Chat?"

"*Oui*, in French. It's so romantic!"

"Er… French?" Danny shook his head. "I don't think so."

Soro was insistent.

"Come on, *mon cheri*. Concentrate. Focus your mind on the French language."

Danny looked extremely dubious. His French was almost non-existent.

"*Alors, je n'ai pas su que vous parliez français?*" asked Soro.

Danny couldn't help chuckling at this. He opened his mouth to speak.

"*Je ne parle pas français,*" he said.

Danny was shocked. *Had that come out of his mouth?*

Soro smiled.

"*Mais on aurait dit que vous parliez français!*" she replied.

Danny spoke again.

"*C'est incroyable! Je n'ai parlé français jamais de ma vie!*"

He couldn't believe it!

"What are they saying?" Charley asked Spike.

"I don't know," Spike replied. "I failed French, remember?"

A few moments later it sounded like Soro and Danny had switched and were now talking in Russian!

"With *Translatormate* you are able to understand and speak fluently in sixty-eight different languages," Jane explained.

Charley was now finding all this chatter in languages she couldn't understand quite tedious - especially because Danny looked like he was enjoying it so much!

"OK, let's try Chinese?" Soro now suggested.

Charley had to step in.

"Hold on! What's next on the list?"

Spike took a look at Uncle Morty's list.

"Just two more items on the list - *Go Ape!* and *Mindbender*."

"OK, let's go and try those," said Charley.

Danny tore himself away from Soro (who was now talking Italian!).

"Jane," he said, "would it be OK for us to pay for this stuff first and the *Combat X,* so that we can see how much money we have left?"

"Of course, Sir."

She started to tally things up on her computer. Danny could tell that Charley and Spike were looking at him as though he was being a spoilsport, but he still had Uncle Morty's instructions ringing in his ears about how important it was to buy the *Attila Killer* programs, and he wanted to make sure they had enough money left.

Now Soro suddenly stepped forwards.

"OK, fellowchies - it's been a lot of fun, but I've got to dash! My folks will be wondering where I am. We'll see you around, OK?"

"Thanks for everything," said Danny. "You've helped us a lot."

"No probs," Soro said, smiling. "Anytime!" She gave them all a final wave before leaving. "*Au revoir,* fellowchies!"

Jane now had a total on her computer.

"Will you be paying by chip or moneycard, Sir?" she asked Danny.

"Moneycard, please," Danny replied, handing her the card.

Jane placed the card into a slot on her computer, but the machine beeped and the card came out again.

"I'm sorry, Sir," Jane said, "but there doesn't appear to be enough money on this card."

"That's impossible," said Danny, with a smile. "Please try it again."

Jane put the card in again, but the same thing happened. Now Danny's smile began to fade. He took the card back from Jane and had a look at the amount showing on the screen. To his amazement the amount was significantly less than when they had left Wilson's Wildlife.

"How can that be?"

Charley and Spike had now gathered around to take a look.

"There's a whole lot missing," said Danny, showing them the card.

Spike was shocked when he saw the amount.

"*It's half of what we had!*" he exclaimed.

They all stood in stunned silence, trying to comprehend what had happened. Eventually it was Jane who spoke up.

"Has anyone else handled your card?" she asked.

They all looked at Jane - then they looked at each other. The same thought had just occurred to all of them.

"*Soro!*" said Charley.

Chapter 8

# The Devil's Dungeon

"Which way did she go?" Danny shouted.

"I didn't see!" Spike shouted back.

They had rushed out of the shop in pursuit of Soro. She couldn't have gone far in such a short time, but outside they found themselves in the midst of a throng of people, streaming in both directions.

"OK, you go that way! I'll go this way!" Danny instructed, then he remembered Charley. "Charley, wait for us here!" he said emphatically, before taking off through the crowd.

Danny's only hope was that Soro's little pink dress would stand out in the sea of people. He darted in and out of the crowd, looking in all directions, knowing that every second was vital! He reached an intersection and suddenly the mall was heading off left and right as well. *Now which way?* He clambered up onto a bench, so that he could at least see over everyone's heads. There were masses of people in every direction, but no sign of a pink dress anywhere.

\*

It was an angry, dejected-looking Danny who rejoined the others by the shop entrance. Spike had also just returned empty-handed and he was now shaking his head unhappily.

"She could have gone into any one of a hundred shops around here," he said.

Charley had been thinking about what must have happened.

"It must have been when she took the moneycard in the clothes shop. Remember, she swiped the card over her hand, and we never checked the balance after that."

"Great!" Spike scowled. "So we've basically got half the money we had an hour ago. What are we going to buy with it?"

All Danny could think now was that they should get the *Attila Killer* programs. The last thing they needed was a visit from the Timecops, or worse still - the Hogs!

Through the entrance to *BAM* Danny could see Jane still hovering by the counter.

"Wait here," he said to the others.

*

Inside the shop, Jane looked up as Danny came over.

"Any luck?" she asked.

"No," Danny replied, shaking his head. "I'm sorry... it seems like we no longer have enough money to buy all the things we wanted. There is one program I wanted to ask you about..."

"Yes?"

Danny hesitated. He knew he was now entering dangerous waters.

"Um... I believe the program is called... *Attila Killer*."

Anyone watching from afar would have thought that Danny had just sworn at Jane. She blinked several times before managing to get any words out.

"May I remind you, young man, that *BAM* is an extremely reputable store that does not deal in illegal goods."

Danny held up his hands, apologetically. This was exactly the reaction he had been dreading. Now he could see that Jane was eyeing the red security phone on her desk.

"I think it would be best if you left immediately," she said sternly, "or I may be forced to call the police."

"Fine," Danny mumbled. "Sorry..."

He was already retreating. Now he spun around and headed straight out of the exit.

*

"What's wrong?" Charley asked when she saw Danny's expression.

Danny just indicated that they should *move*! He headed off

down the mall and the others were forced to trot after him.

"I'm guessing that didn't go too well?" said Spike as he caught up.

"You could say that."

Danny glanced back over his shoulder to make sure they weren't being followed. That's when something caught his eye. There was a man - walking not too far behind them. He was wearing a long coat and a hat, and he seemed to be looking directly at him!

Danny picked up the pace.

Charley could hardly keep up.

"What's the rush?" she asked.

"Just keep walking!" Danny muttered under his breath.

They were now rounding a corner and Danny took the opportunity to glance back again. The man was still there - but now he was even closer!

Oh, great! *An undercover Timecop!* thought Danny. He probably heard me in the shop! Now Danny's mind was rushing. *What should they do? Make a run for it? Duck into one of the shops?* Before he could make a decision, the man suddenly appeared right beside them!

"Excuse me!" he said. "Can I have a word?"

*That's it!* thought Danny. *We're done! We're nicked!* He tried to keep walking, but the man now placed a hand firmly on his shoulder and they were forced to stop.

The man saw how tense Danny was looking.

"Hey, relax!" he said. "I'm not a cop!"

The relief on Danny's face made the man smile.

"Apologies for eavesdropping," he said, "but I overheard you in the shop - asking for a certain program? I can help you."

Danny did not feel comfortable discussing such things in public with a stranger. He shook his head and tried to take off again.

"Thanks, we're fine."

"Hold on," the man said, stopping Danny again. "Not only can I help you with *Attila Killer,* but also those other items you were testing today."

"I'm sorry," said Danny, "but we can't afford-"

"Listen!" The man spoke forcefully, but continued to smile. "This is L5. In L5 you're going to pay L5 prices! I can get you everything - exactly the same products - at *much* cheaper prices!"

Suddenly, what the man was saying began to hit home. Spike and Charley had also moved in closer to hear more. Now the man was extending his hand.

"How do you do?" He smiled as he shook hands with each of them. "They call me Johnny - *'Johnny the Finder'* - because if you need it, I will find it!"

*

A short time later, Danny, Spike and Charley were huddled together having a serious discussion amongst themselves. Johnny was hovering nearby.

"What have we got to lose?" Spike was saying. "We can't afford half the stuff here anyway, and he said he can get us everything - as well as… you know… *that program*!"

"But can we trust him?" Charley asked, eyeing Johnny suspiciously. "Look what happened with Soro!"

"He says we can test everything, Charles!" Spike said impatiently. "He's talking about genuine *BAM* products, but not at L5 prices!"

Charley was still not looking totally convinced.

"What do *you* think, Danny?"

"I don't think we have much choice," Danny replied.

Before he could say more, he noticed Johnny coming over.

"Look, I don't want to rush you or anything," said Johnny, "but, a word of advice - if you're travelling without *Attila Killer*

I would suggest we get moving. Otherwise we're going to have company - and, believe me, that is something that *none of us want!*"

This seemed to do the trick. The thought of a Hog or a Cop arriving at any moment quickly overshadowed any of their other concerns.

"All right," Danny said, "let's do it."

\*

Once again the sheer magnitude of the Grand Passage was enough to take their breath away. Johnny had asked them to wait at a docking bay while he went to fetch his vehicle. Now, as they stood waiting, they could only look on in awe at the thousands of sky vehicles entering and leaving the vast abyss.

The sound of a hooter drew their attention to an approaching skycar. It was a rather tatty-looking vehicle with a dented exterior and a peeling paint job, so it came as a bit of a shock when they saw Johnny waving to them from the driver's seat! He drew up alongside the docking bay and the doors popped open.

"Is he serious?" Charley muttered. "Are we meant to get into *that*?"

There was no arguing.

"Let's go!" Johnny shouted.

They climbed in - Danny in the front and the other two in the back. The interior was also in need of an extreme makeover. Charley looked like she didn't want to touch anything!

As he pulled out into the Grand Passage Johnny seemed to sense their concerns about the vehicle.

"I wouldn't dream of taking one of my good cars to where we're going," he said. "Much safer in this old thing!"

"Oh, right," Danny said, nodding. The alarm bells were starting to go off in his head. "And, uh... where exactly *are* we going?" he enquired.

"L122," Johnny replied casually.

If they hadn't already been in mid-air Charley would probably have climbed straight out again. What was it Reg had said? *'Don't go below L80, and definitely not below L100!'*

Johnny could see the concern on her face in the rearview mirror.

"Hey," he said, grinning. "That's where all the best deals are!"

*

It wasn't long before they started to notice a change in their surroundings. Probably the most noticeable was that everything seemed to be getting darker. The higher levels had been a blaze of colourful, flashy advertising signs and brightly lit shopping malls, but by the time they reached L20, everything had become a lot duller and the advertising boards had all but disappeared.

By the time they got to L40 the sides of the Grand Passage had started to resemble a gigantic block of flats. The only light now came from the thousands of small windows they were passing, and they noticed how Johnny switched on a couple of spotlights he could control from inside the vehicle.

As they passed the L80 sign they all remembered Reg's warning. Everything around them was looking more and more rundown, and it was starting to get very warm. There was also a foul smell in the air that Danny suspected had something to do with the dirty water they could now see spewing out of pipes into the Grand Passage.

Now, as they approached L100, there were suddenly a lot of flashing lights below them and the sky-traffic was becoming increasingly congested. Danny peered down, trying to work out what was going on, then a brightly illuminated flashing sign came into view: 'REDUCE SPEED NOW! POLICE SKYBLOCK BELOW'!

"This is as far down as the cops go," said Johnny. "After this skyblock we're on our own!"

The police officers manning the skyblock were standing on platforms suspended in mid-air by rows of large orange balloons. These platforms stretched right across the Grand Passage with gaps between them just large enough to let the sky vehicles through. Some vehicles were being stopped and the drivers questioned, others were being waved through.

As Johnny's vehicle descended into the glare of the brightly lit skyblock several police officers (all wearing sunglasses) stepped up to the railing to get a better look at them. Being scrutinised like this under such bright lights was horribly intimidating, and they all sat back in their seats. Danny just prayed there were no Timecops amongst them. When one of the cops came right up to the window he dared not look. Eventually the cop stepped back and nodded, and suddenly they were descending again.

This should have been the time for them to catch their breath, but as the bright lights faded they sensed that Johnny was preparing for action. The first thing he did was place what looked like a sawn-off shotgun on the dashboard for easy access.

"Now the fun begins!" he said with a grin.

He began to vigilantly shine the spotlights all around, and as the beams cut through the darkness they now started to see dark shapes coming towards them!

"What are those?" asked Charley, moving away from the window.

"You'll see!" was all Johnny replied.

Sure enough, moments later, one of these dark shapes appeared out of the gloom. Johnny trained a spotlight on it, but it kept on coming. He grabbed his weapon, aimed it out of the window and only then did the object slow down. In the spotlights, they saw that it was a balloon with a small pontoon attached beneath it. Standing on the pontoon was a man in a hooded waterproof poncho. He was clutching on to a very rudimentary-looking rudder that appeared to be attached to a large fan at the back. This is how the balloon was being propelled towards them.

As this strange craft approached Johnny brandished his weapon again and the man quickly turned off his propeller fan and stopped a little way off. He then pulled back a cover on the pontoon and revealed some kind of display stand.

"Afternoon all!" the man shouted across to them. "Can I interest you in some quality merchandise?"

It was only then that Danny and the others realised they were looking at some kind of floating market stand. The hawker was now releasing air from his balloon, so that he could descend at the same steady speed as Johnny's vehicle.

"Come on, gents, and... excuse me - lady. I've got some top quality stuff here. Genuine, out of the box *BAM* programs."

This caused Johnny to smile.

"I'm sure you have. Nothing today thank you!"

Still the hawker edged closer as he tried to show them his wares. Johnny pointed the weapon again, this time directly at the man's balloon.

"I said nothing today thank you. Now back off!"

"All right, all right."

The disgruntled hawker put his propeller in reverse and moved off a bit.

All sorts of other balloon hawkers had now started to arrive on the scene and each of them seemed to be selling something different.

"Best music prices in London!" claimed one.

"Tickets to the big match!" shouted another.

Johnny kept them all at bay by pointing his weapon at anyone who strayed too close.

"Don't be fooled," he said. "They may look like innocent hawkers, but given half a chance they would take this vehicle in a heartbeat."

On hearing this information Spike began to view the hawkers

in an entirely different light! Suddenly he felt the need to assist Johnny in spotting anyone straying too close.

"There! Watch that guy!" he shouted, tapping Johnny's shoulder and pointing.

\*

It came as a huge relief when they eventually saw the flickering L122 sign. They had been harassed by hawkers all the way down and now they just wanted to get out of the vehicle. Johnny steered it towards a rather dilapidated-looking docking bay, but as they approached they could see a lot of movement in the darkness. Shadowy figures had begun to scurry forwards, causing Charley to move away from the window again.

Johnny didn't seem too worried. He merely pointed his weapon and fired off a single loud blast. There was an explosion near the bay, and when the smoke cleared, the shadowy figures had evaporated once more into the darkness.

"Welcome to the *Devil's Dungeon!*" said Johnny with a grin as he docked the vehicle.

Minutes later they found themselves following Johnny down a dark, dripping alley with only a handheld spotlight to illuminate the way.

Every now and again they heard noises in the darkness behind them and Johnny would swing his spotlight around just in time to catch glimpses of figures quickly melting away into the shadows. Charley was sticking *very close* to the others!

Johnny led them down a shuddering, groaning escalator then, after a few more twists and turns, they arrived at a nondescript doorway. He pressed a button and immediately a camera above the door hummed around to check them out.

Johnny nodded to the camera and the door clicked open.

"Welcome to *Frankie and Glide's Shop of Shops!*" announced Johnny, as he held the door open for them.

Whatever Danny and the others had been expecting, the *'Shop of Shops'* turned out to be something of an anticlimax. It was a drab, poorly lit place with an old shop counter, behind which rose a large wall full of shelves. On the shelves were a scattering of items that looked like they had been gathering dust there for some time.

From the back came two men - one short and the other tall. They both wore hats pulled down low over their eyes, making it difficult to see their faces.

"Hello, I'm Frankie," said the shorter of the men.

"And I'm Glide," said the taller man.

"Hello, Finder," Frankie said to Johnny. "What can we do for you today?"

Johnny now took Uncle Morty's list from Danny and handed it over to Frankie at the counter. As soon as Frankie read the first item on the list he looked up at Johnny.

"Oh no, Finder!" he groaned. "Not unprotected time-felons again?"

Johnny grinned like he had heard it all before.

"So sorry, Frankie. I know you just hate to accept money for time-travel protection programs."

Frankie ignored him. He was now looking over at the others.

"I sincerely hope you time-felons have no one on your tail?"

Danny and the others didn't know how to respond, but Johnny stepped in.

"Hey, Frankie," he said. "The quicker we get down to business, the quicker we can stop worrying about that problem. What do you say?"

"Yes, yes, Finder - patience please!" Frankie snapped. He turned to his partner. "So, what do you think, Glide? Do you think we should open up shop for these young time-felons?"

"Hmm…" Glide nodded. "I suppose we could, Frankie."

"Yes, I suppose we could," Frankie agreed, and then surprised them all by suddenly bellowing, "*Open shop!*"

# The Devil's Dungeon

With that command, everything began to change. The lights came up. The whole back wall (dusty shelves and all!) slid aside to reveal the most remarkable hi-tech display they had ever seen. Suddenly they were staring at giant, colourful 3-D images that appeared to be suspended in mid-air all around them. They all seemed to be promoting one *BAM* program or another. Danny could see a figure in mid-air demonstrating *Combat X*.

"Become the ultimate fighting machine!" a voice boomed.

Elsewhere, the image of a giant human brain floated in mid-air with a mass of words and mathematical formulae rotating around it.

"*Mindbender* - unleash the power of your mind!" a voice proclaimed.

It was an overwhelming cacophony of sounds and images – and all Danny and the others could do was stand in the middle, wide-eyed, trying to take it all in! In the bright lights they could also see Frankie and Glide properly for the first time. They were both impeccably dressed in rather brightly coloured suits - Frankie in shiny green and Glide in shocking pink! Beneath their smart black hats, they both had identical features, including finely groomed pencil moustaches. They just had to be brothers!

The old shop counter had transformed into what looked like a giant black and chrome computer, and on top of it was a whole row of programming hand-pads (like the ones at the *BAM* shop). A large screen behind the counter read, 'WELCOME TO FRANKIE & GLIDE'S SHOP OF SHOPS'!

Frankie suddenly shouted again.

"*Shop! Be still!*"

In that instant everything froze - suddenly there was silence.

Frankie and Glide chuckled at the stunned expressions on the faces of Danny and the others.

"We may not be the *BAM!*" shouted Frankie.

"But we've certainly got the *BOOM!*" shouted Glide.

Johnny looked as though he had seen this little show a hundred times before.

"Can we do some business now?" he asked impatiently.

"All right, Finder, all right," said Frankie. "I think we'd better deal with the time-felon problem first, don't you? *Attila Killer* times three, I presume?"

Danny stepped forwards.

"Excuse me," he interrupted. "Before we buy anything we need to know how much it's all going to cost. We don't know what we can afford."

Frankie walked up to Danny. They were almost exactly the same height.

"All right, small man," he said, "and how much were you thinking about spending?"

Danny pulled out their moneycard, but after the Soro experience he was reluctant to hand it over. It was only when Johnny gave him a nod of assurance that he handed it to Frankie. Frankie slipped the moneycard into the computer and, moments later, a figure appeared on the large screen behind them:

12,500 WORLD DOLLARS (W$)

The brothers looked at the figure then took another look at the list of programs. Eventually Frankie shrugged.

"Hmm... well, we'll see what we can do."

"Shop! *Attila Killer* times three!" he called out. He then beckoned Danny and the others over. "Bring your hands here time-felons!"

They placed their hands onto the hand-pads and soon the computer began to hum.

While they were waiting Spike turned to the brothers.

"What exactly does this *Attila Killer* do?" he asked.

"What does it do?" Frankie chuckled at the question. "Well, basically it prevents you from becoming Hog-snacks!"

Both the brothers had a good laugh at this.

"Yes, little Hoggie tasty treats!" said Glide, and he now made little munching sounds, which caused more laughter between them.

Charley looked horrified.

"Is it true that Hogs kill people?" she asked.

"Oh no, not people," said Frankie, leaning closer and putting on his scariest, throaty whisper. "Only time-felons!"

The brothers started their giggling again, but it quickly dried up when Johnny stepped forwards.

"Is this really necessary?" he asked.

"Are we lying, Finder?" Frankie snapped impatiently. Now he glared at the others with a scary intensity. "I hope you had a very good reason to take this little time journey of yours. Hogs only have one mission in life – and that's to get rid of people like you." He let this statement hang over them for a few uncomfortable moments then he smiled suddenly and put on a bright, positive voice. "But don't worry, small ones! That's why we have *Attila Killer*!"

The hum of the computer now began to wind down until it eventually stopped.

"Right, remove your hands please!" Frankie instructed. "You are now officially Attila Killers."

"But how do we know you've programmed us with anything?" Danny asked.

Frankie smiled at this.

"Not very trusting, is he Glide?"

"Not very trusting at all," agreed Glide. "Perhaps a little demonstration is in order?"

"Yes, good idea."

Glide now picked up a strange-looking electronic device that he pointed towards Danny and the others.

"What I have here," he explained, "is an Attila sensor. This is exactly what the Timecops and the Hogs use to detect the giveaway time travel signals that you time-felons will be giving off. Now imagine I am a Timecop or a Hog. When I turn the sensor on - look what happens."

Glide flicked a switch and they all braced themselves for something dramatic to happen, but as the seconds ticked by, they all began to glance at each other. Danny looked questioningly at Frankie, who immediately held up a hand to silence him.

"One moment please!" he hissed.

Then they did start to notice something. They were all starting to feel a little uneasy. It was as if they knew something was wrong, but they weren't quite sure what it was. This feeling of worry continued to get worse until all three of them were glancing around anxiously.

"What's happening to us?" Spike muttered.

He could barely get the words out.

Now they were all visibly trembling and their breathing had become fast and shallow. Danny looked at Charley and was shocked to see the terror in her eyes. He looked at the brothers and saw that they were smiling. They were enjoying this little show!

"*Make it stop!*" Danny roared - and he started towards them.

Frankie quickly retreated behind the computer and Glide switched off the machine. The effect on them all was instantaneous. Their breathing began to slow, their bodies began to relax and, much to their relief, the horrible feeling began to ease.

Frankie was sizing up Danny's mood before deciding whether it was safe to come out from behind the computer. Only when Danny turned away was he able to regain his confident swagger and emerge as though nothing had happened.

"What you have just experienced," he explained, "is the best self-defence mechanism known to man. It's called *fear!*"

"It is another feature of the *Attila Killer* program," Glide continued. "Not only does it scramble the *Attila* sensors, making it difficult for them to find you, but it also warns you when they are around. When you feel that fear you will know that the Timecops or the Hogs are nearby."

"Just pray it's only the Timecops," added Frankie, before suddenly smiling. "Right, let's move on shall we? First let's see what you've spent so far." He now turned to the computer screen and shouted, "Shop! Update!"

Immediately some information appeared on the large screen. It read:

ATTILA KILLER x 3 = W$1,500 each = W$4,500

TOTAL SPENT - W$4,500

A large chunk of their money had just been spent, but Danny knew how important these programs could prove to be.

Meanwhile Frankie was consulting Uncle Morty's list once more. He looked thoughtfully at Danny and the others for a few moments then seemed to make a decision.

"Right," he said, beckoning the three of them forward. "The most important thing to remember when engaging in any Body and Mind enhancing program is to only choose a program that suits you. For a program to be effective it has got to like the body *and the mind* that it is in".

"So, no offence to you," Glide said, pointing at Spike, "but I don't think you and *Combat X* would be well suited. Now *Mindbender* - that could be a different story."

Spike seemed disappointed. He had liked the look of *Combat X*.

"What is this *Mindbender* anyway?" he asked sulkily.

"Well, let's find out, shall we?" said Frankie excitedly. "In my opinion it should be *Combat X* for you," he said, pointing at Danny. "*Mindbender* for you," he said, indicating Spike "and yes, I think *Go Ape!* for you," he said, nodding at Charley.

Once again they were all summoned over to the machine and instructed to place their hands on the hand-pads. Frankie told the computer what to do.

"Port One - *Combat X*. Port Two - *Mindbender*. Port Three - *Go Ape!*"

The computer took a few seconds to process this information then began to hum again. When it was finished the brothers indicated that they could remove their hands.

"Right!" Frankie said, rubbing his hands together excitedly. "Now I presume you'll want to do some testing? How about we start with *Mindbender*?"

Suddenly Spike found everyone staring at him.

"What?" he asked, shrugging. "What am I meant to do?"

Frankie and Glide chuckled at this. Glide came over to explain.

"OK, all we want you to do is concentrate on getting somebody here to do something."

Spike still looked confused.

"What do you mean 'do something'?"

"I mean we want you to *really* concentrate - to focus your mind - on getting somebody here to perform some sort of action."

"Are you serious?" Spike looked dubious. "Any sort of action?"

"Well, anything within reason."

Spike looked around at everyone. He then seemed to make up his mind. He closed his eyes and began to concentrate hard on something. A few moments later Charley walked over to Danny and gave him a kiss on the cheek.

It took Charley a few seconds to register what she had just done - then suddenly, the shock! *Had she really just done that*? She felt the colour rushing to her face! She buried her face in her hands and quickly retreated behind Johnny.

Danny stood blinking, still trying to work out what had just happened then everyone started to laugh and no one was laughing harder than Spike! He couldn't believe it! He had concentrated hard on trying to make Charley kiss Danny and that is exactly what had happened! Now it began to dawn on him - the full potential of the power he suddenly seemed to possess!

"Do you mean I can get people to do *anything* just by thinking about it?" Spike asked, incredulous.

"Well, not *anything*," Glide replied. "The creators of *Mindbender* obviously had to put in *some* restrictions! You won't be able to get anyone to do anything nasty or cruel, but anything that won't cause too much harm usually works."

"And you're in luck," added Frankie, "because with this version of *Mindbender* you get *Encyclopaedia* free."

"What's *Encyclopaedia*?" Spike asked.

"What does it sound like, Genius?" Frankie asked, rolling his eyes. "Tell me something, what is another name for sleeping sickness?"

"Trypanasomiasis," Spike said without hesitation – and then immediately cupped a hand to his mouth.

*How on earth did he know that?*

"OK," continued Frankie, "and where are the Faeroe Islands?"

"In the North Atlantic, between Iceland and Shetland," Spike answered without hesitation. This was too much for him! "I can't believe it," he said, shaking his head. "Do I know *everything*?"

Frankie smiled at this.

"Hey, hold on, Genius, let's not get too carried away. You don't know *everything*, but you probably know as much as is in your average set of *Encyclopaedia*."

Spike looked like all his Christmases had arrived on the same day! If only he had had this program before his exams!

Frankie, meanwhile, was trying to coax Charley out from behind Johnny.

"Time to *Go Ape!* I think? Come over here with me," he said.

Charley reluctantly followed him to the back of the shop.

"For you, we are going to need some height," said Frankie. He suddenly shouted, "Open warehouse!"

On that order a large section of the back wall slid aside to reveal a warehouse filled with rows of extremely high shelves. These shelves were so high that they could only be reached by large automated cranes.

"All right," Frankie said to Charley. "I need you to collect something for me. You see that top shelf right up there?" He pointed up to one of the highest shelves in the warehouse. "I want you to bring me something from that shelf."

Charley looked at him as though he was mad.

"How am I meant to get up there?"

Frankie shrugged.

"You figure it out. Come on - one item from the top shelf, as quickly as you can, please."

Charley was looking very doubtful as she walked over to the base of the shelves. She had an uncomfortable feeling that she was about to be made a fool of again.

"Right, are you ready?" asked Frankie.

"No," replied Charley, bluntly. "How do you expect me to get up there?"

"Just give it a try," he replied, smiling.

Charley looked up at the shelves towering above her. She took a deep breath and tentatively reached up for the shelf above her head. As she pulled herself up, she made an amazing discovery - with just one arm she easily had enough strength. She reached up for the next shelf and did the same again. She didn't even need to use her legs! One shelf after the other, she climbed rapidly up to the top. When she reached the top shelf she grabbed a small box of something then came skidding all the way down like she was coming down a fireman's pole. When she was still more than ten shelves from the bottom she casually jumped off and landed lightly beside Frankie.

As she straightened up Charley held out the box for Frankie, but he didn't take it. Instead, he just grinned.

"Now put it back, please."

With new found confidence, Charley scurried up and down the shelves in no time at all. She could not hide the absolute delight she was feeling, especially when she looked over at Spike and Danny, and saw their wide-eyed expressions.

Frankie nodded, clearly pleased with his choice.

"Just as I suspected - we have a little ape on our hands here. As you have just witnessed, *Go Ape!* gives you the agility and the climbing ability of our closest relatives."

"Just right for her!" said Spike with a grin.

Now Frankie turned back to the computer.

"Shop! Total spending so far?"

Once again the information flashed up on the large screen.

ATTILA KILLER x 3 = W$1,500 each = W$4,500
COMBAT X = W$2,000
MINDBENDER = W$1,500
GO APE! = W$1,500
TOTAL SPENT – W$9,500

Frankie now consulted the list again.

"OK, next! *Translatormate* for all?"

Once again they were summoned over to the hand-pads and the computer was instructed to give them *Translatormate*. When it was done the information flashed up on the screen again.

TRANSLATORMATE x 3 = W$500 each = W$1,500
TOTAL SPENT - W$11,000

Danny was now very aware that there was not much money left on the card.

"Right, and the last thing on your list is *Immobilasers*," Frankie called out to the computer again, "Shop! *Immobilasers* times three!"

Almost immediately three small boxes appeared on a shelf

behind them, and the information flashed up onto the big screen

IMMOBILASERS x 3 = W$750 each = W$2,250

TOTAL SPENT - W$13,250

Now an alarm sounded and a caption began to flash on the screen in large red writing.

INSUFFICIENT FUNDS!

"Oh well." Frankie shrugged. "It looks like you'll only be able to afford two of those." He handed Danny the *Immobilasers* then removed the moneycard from the machine and handed that back as well. "Thank you for shopping at *Frankie and Glide's Shop of Shops*," he said, looking very pleased with the day's business.

Danny was just putting the moneycard away when he was suddenly startled by the sound of a fierce roar. He looked up and was shocked to see a huge man charging aggressively towards him.

"Watch out! A thief!" Frankie screamed.

Without a moment's hesitation Danny moved deftly to one side and in seconds had delivered two punches and a kick to the man,

who went sprawling across the shop floor. It had happened so fast that it took Danny a few seconds to realise what he had just done. He then heard the sound of the brothers' laughter again.

"Well, I guess the *Combat X* is also working, hey Glide?"

"Yes, I think our fishy friend over there would certainly agree!" replied Glide, indicating the man still sprawled on the floor.

\*

The two brothers stood by the door and shook hands with each of them as they left.

"Remember to use your *BAM* programs responsibly," said Frankie.

"And good luck on your travels!" said Glide.

Once everyone had left the shop Frankie closed the door and locked it, and then suddenly bellowed:

"Coffee Shop!"

One of the shop walls was instantly transformed into a coffee bar with stools and a coffee machine. The brothers took a seat and poured themselves some coffee.

"Not a bad day's work, hey Glide?" said Frankie.

"Not bad at all."

"Of course, they probably won't be *as pleased* with their programs in a few days time," said Frankie.

"Well, what do they expect?" said Glide. "At prices half those of genuine *BAM* products of course they're not going to be *perfect!*"

"Anyway, I'm sure they'll be *far away* before they experience their first glitches."

"Perhaps a whole century away?" said Glide, smiling.

With that, they chuckled and raised their coffee cups in a toast.

\*

Johnny insisted on dropping the others off at L80. He had suddenly announced that he had an urgent meeting somewhere and that L80 was the best he could do. As he deposited them at a docking bay, Danny asked if there was no way he could take them to a higher level, but Johnny could not be persuaded.

"I'm really sorry!" he shouted as he closed the doors and waved.

The next thing they knew, the old banger was disappearing off into the Grand Passage.

"That was odd," remarked Spike. "He suddenly couldn't wait to get rid of us."

"What now?" asked Charley.

"We could call Reg," suggested Spike. "Where's the taxi-caller?"

"We don't have any money left, Genius!" said Charley.

It was a good point. They should have kept some money on the moneycard. Now they all stood around, pondering their next move. Danny appeared to remember something. He unzipped his rucksack and started to rummage around inside.

"What are you looking for?" asked Charley.

"Something Uncle Morty gave me," Danny replied. "He said it was for emergencies."

He removed the small box his uncle had handed him shortly before their departure. He hadn't even had a chance to look inside it yet. The others gathered around as he opened it up. Inside were two items - a very old-looking compass and some kind of military medal.

"Oh great, a medal," said Charley, clearly disappointed.

Spike was now studying the medal more closely.

"Hold on," he said, "this is a Victoria Cross - the highest award for bravery in the British Military. If this belonged to Uncle Morty he must have been quite the soldier in his day!"

"It's got to be worth something, eh?" said Danny. "I mean - it must be from the Second World War."

"Definitely," agreed Spike.

"Maybe Reg will be interested?" said Danny.

It was a worth a try. They pressed the taxi-caller and Reg sent back a message saying he was on his way.

\*

When Reg saw the medal he couldn't believe his eyes.

"Where *on earth* did you get this?" he asked Danny.

"My uncle," Danny replied.

"And where did he get it from?" asked Reg.

"He was awarded it," Spike blurted out - then quickly shut up when he saw how Danny and Charley were looking at him.

Reg, however, had already noticed the inscription on the medal.

"But hold on - this says 1943. The Second World War... your uncle fought in the Second World War?"

Suddenly there was a mild sense of panic as all three of them glanced at each other.

"It was my great, great, great... great-uncle," said Danny quickly.

"Really?" said Reg. "Your great, great, great, great-uncle, eh?"

He wasn't sounding very convinced. Danny knew the conversation needed to be moved on *and fast*!

"Anyway, Reg," he said, "we were wondering if we could do a trade with you? You take us back to where you found us on the farm... and we'll give you the medal."

Reg blinked a few times - unsure if he had heard correctly.

"Sorry? You're going to give me a two hundred and fifty-year-old Victoria Cross for a ride to the farm?"

All three of them nodded in reply.

"Well," said Reg, "what else can I say but... hop in!"

\*

From the moment they climbed into the cab Danny sensed that Reg was now looking at them all with renewed interest. It was as if something in the conversation about the medal hadn't quite rung true and he was now starting to put all the pieces together. Danny had ended up in the front seat beside Reg and, as the cab ascended out of the Grand Passage, he could feel Reg constantly glancing across at him.

"Sell your monkeys?" he asked.

"Yup," Danny replied.

"And I see you bought some new clothes?"

Danny nodded. He was feeling like the less he said the better.

"Got rid of those old clothes, eh? The ones that looked like they had come from *another time*?"

Danny was now convinced that Reg had guessed their story, so he decided to look out of the window. Perhaps if he ignored him he would stop asking questions!

Outside the grey drizzle was coming down and the depressing flooded landscape spread out for as far as he could see. *Is the whole world like this?* Danny wondered.

It was as if Reg was reading his mind.

"The Earth must have been a beautiful place a few hundred years ago?" he mused.

Now Danny *knew* that Reg was on to them. He continued to look out of the window. This was one conversation he was not going to be drawn into!

"I bet England wasn't like this back then," Reg continued, "with all the floods and the monsoon climate. Anyway, I suppose it's better for us in the northern hemisphere. Not like in the south where they've barely got any water at all! Decades of drought, wars over water. What a mess!"

Listening to Reg made them all want to start asking questions about the state of the world. Spike even opened his mouth to say something, but Charley quickly tapped his leg and gave him a fierce look.

Reg seemed to have accepted that he wasn't going to get a

response out of them, but he did have one final thing to say.

"It's just a pity that people didn't start doing something to avoid this mess a couple of hundred years ago!" he said, sounding almost angry. "You know, if they had *really acted* back then it would have made all the difference now. I mean look at the state of this place!"

With that, he decided to leave the subject alone, and they flew on in silence.

\*

As they swooped down on the meadow Danny was pleased to see the haystack covering TIM was still there. Reg landed the cab and they all clambered out and went around to his window.

"Thanks, Reg," Danny said, handing him the medal.

But Reg shook his head.

"No," he said. "Someone else deserves that a lot more than I do."

"Are you sure?" asked Danny.

"Yes." Reg smiled then added with a twinkle in his eye, "And give my regards to that old uncle of yours!"

Danny also smiled.

"I will."

Reg put the cab into gear and looked out at the three of them one last time.

"Listen," he said, his expression now serious. "I'm not sure where you've come from or where you're going, but I'll just say this - be *very, very* careful out there, all right?" He then gave them a last smile and shouted, "Now get out of here!"

Suddenly he had gone and they watched as the cab climbed up and away into the purple sky.

\*

They had to shoo a few cows out of the way to get to the haystack. It was then a case of pushing all the hay to one side until TIM's sleek metallic exterior was once again glinting in the strange purple light.

Danny was glad to be back with TIM. It felt like the first half of their mission was out of the way. He pressed the button and the door slid open.

"Round two," he muttered, as he waved the others in.

Once they were all inside with the door closed, Danny took a seat in the chair and studied the control panel. Behind him Charley and Spike were trying to find enough space on the floor to sit down.

"Give us a bit of room, Charles!" Spike complained.

"Where would you like me to go?" Charley asked, her legs already scrunched right up.

Danny flicked the power switch on and the control panel lit up around him. Now he had to remember Uncle Morty's instructions. He pressed a button to select *Trip 2 - France, 1942* then with his hand hovering over the 'ACTIVATE' button, he turned to the others.

"Everybody ready?" he asked.

That's when he saw Charley's face. She was staring up at the small window in the door, on her face an expression of *utter horror!*

"What's the matter, Charley?" Danny asked.

Spike, who still hadn't sat down, also looked at her, but shook his head immediately.

"Yes, Charles," he said with a smile. "What is it - a big scary cow again?"

Charley opened her mouth to try and say something, but no words came out.

"Give it a break, Charles!" said Spike. "You're not fooling anyone this time!"

Then Spike glanced at Danny - and he had the same shocked expression! He decided to look for himself and when he turned around, the sight at the window made him recoil in horror.

"*Aaah!*" he screamed, stumbling back and falling over Charley.

At the window was the most repulsive grotesque face they had ever seen. It was possibly human, but it was so scarred and deformed that you would have been forgiven for thinking otherwise. It was a face that looked like it had weathered many battles. It was covered in scars - one so large that most of the hair on one side was missing.

And it wasn't the only one out there! Now a second equally revolting face appeared at the window, except this one was grinning grotesquely, revealing a mouthful of teeth that were either missing or half-rotten.

Although Danny had never seen *anything* like these creatures before, he had a horrible feeling he knew what he was looking at. Something told him that these were what Uncle Morty had described as 'the scum of the universe' - the ruthless, time-travelling bounty hunters known as Hogs.

A banging sound began on the side of TIM and the whole machine started to rock.

Danny leapt for the controls...

## Chapter 9

# 1942

The heat was so intense and the shuddering so violent that Danny really thought TIM was going to fall to pieces this time. Once again, the incredible blinding light left them no choice but to shield their eyes.

Then suddenly... darkness.

They lay in a tangle on the floor - no one really wanting to move, no one sure what to expect next. As the whine of TIM faded, an eerie silence descended until all they could hear was their own breathing.

Eventually it was Charley who broke the silence.

"Spike," she muttered.

"What?"

"Get off me."

"Oh, sorry."

Spike lifted himself up, so that Charley could wriggle out from underneath him.

Danny was lying on his back beside the control panel. As he stared up into the darkness all he could think about were the two disgusting-looking creatures they had just seen at the window.

"Were those what I think they were?" he asked.

"Hogs," said Charley in a breathless whisper.

"They had to be," agreed Spike.

Now, as the silence returned, their thoughts all started to follow the same lines. It was Spike who voiced what the others were already thinking.

"I thought these *Attila Killer* programs were meant to make it difficult for them to find us? They didn't seem to have too much of a problem!"

Danny couldn't argue. He was now also starting to wonder

about the other so-called amazing programs they had bought! Charley had a more immediate concern.

"Those revolting creatures can travel through time, right? Well, doesn't that mean they could follow us here *right now*?"

These words had barely left Charley's mouth when there was suddenly a noise from outside TIM.

They all froze.

They noticed a flickering light coming in through the window.

"It's *them*!" said Charley in a hoarse whisper.

"*Ssshh*!"

They all listened for the slightest of sounds.

At first… nothing… then… well then they heard something that sounded like the clucking of chickens!

"Chickens?" whispered Spike.

"*Ssshh*!"

Suddenly a knock on the window made them all jump - then a voice.

"*Bonjour?*"

It sounded like the voice of a man, right outside the door. It came again.

"*Bonjour. Est-ce qu'il y a quelqu'un là dedans?*"

French?

Danny was the first one to his feet. He peered out through the window. It was dark, but in the glow of a paraffin lamp he could now make out the face of an old man.

"Who is it?" asked Charley from the floor.

"Well, it doesn't look like a Hog," Danny replied.

He lifted the handle and pushed open the door.

"Hello," he said to the old man.

The old man was just about to reply when he noticed Charley and Spike behind Danny. He seemed surprised by this.

"*Est-ce qu'il-y-a quelqu'un ici qui s'appelle Daniel?*" he

asked.

"What's he saying?" asked Spike.

Charley then surprised them all, including herself.

"He's asking if one of us is Daniel," said Charley. She replied to the old man. "*Voilà Daniel*," she said, nodding at Danny.

Spike was looking at Charley in amazement.

"How did you do that?"

"It must be the *Translatormate* program," she said, shrugging. "Just concentrate on speaking French."

"I am," protested Spike, "but nothing's happening!"

Now Danny tried and, sure enough, the words he started to speak were also French.

"How did you know my name?" Danny asked.

"Mortimer told me to expect only one person. He said there was a chance it would be a boy named Daniel."

Even though the old man spoke very quickly Danny could (to his astonishment!) understand every word. At least *this* program was working!

"You know my uncle?" Danny asked.

"Yes, I will explain everything, but we must get inside. It is not safe here."

The old man now began to shepherd them out of TIM. Danny introduced him to the others.

"These are my friends - Spike and Charley."

Charley greeted the old man.

"*Bonjour. Ça va?*"

"Allo. How do you do?" said Spike, then he looked to Charley. "Was that French?"

"No, Spike." Charley giggled. "That was English with a silly French accent!"

"My name is Maurice," said the old man, in French. "Come on, let's go inside quickly."

Looking around, they now realised they were inside a barn.

There was a large pile of hay beside them and several chickens clucking around their feet. Uncle Morty had clearly chosen TIM's point of arrival carefully, as this was an ideal hiding place.

Maurice opened the barn door and made sure the coast was clear before leading them out across a paddock and into a small farmhouse. Once they were all inside he shut the front door and bolted it. He took them through to a cosy little kitchen. It had been cold outside and Charley was pleased to see a large wood-burning stove in the corner of the kitchen. However, her hopes of warming up beside the stove were dashed, as Maurice now pushed the kitchen table to one side and opened up a trapdoor in the floor.

"This way," he said, leading them down some stairs.

At the bottom of the stairs they found themselves in a cellar. While Maurice moved around lighting candles, they saw that he had made up a small bed in one corner and on a low table he had laid out a meal of bread, cheese and salami. He had definitely been expecting somebody.

"Eat," said Maurice. "It may be the last decent meal you see in a while. I haven't seen salami like this in years. I was only able to buy it through Mortimer's generosity."

It didn't look particularly appetising, but none of them wanted to disappoint Maurice, so they moved over to the table and began to help themselves. Charley could smell the cheese from where she was standing and decided to stick to the salami.

"I hope you have not brought any police with you, like your uncle?" Maurice was saying.

Again it was only Danny and Charley who seemed to understand him. Spike was concentrating hard, but was only succeeding in becoming more and more frustrated!

It took Danny a few moments to fully grasp what Maurice had just said about the police. He realised it must be the Timecops to whom Maurice was referring. He remembered Uncle Morty saying that on his journey aboard TIM it was here in wartime France that the Timecops had caught up with him. That's when they had programmed him with *Attila* and sent him back to where he had come from.

"When was my uncle here?" Danny asked.

"Two days ago," Maurice replied.

Danny and Charley looked at each other in amazement. *Two days ago! How could that be possible?* Spike continued to look lost.

"What was that? What are you talking about?"

While Charley translated for Spike, Danny thought about it more, and it now dawned on him that, of course, it was possible that Uncle Morty had been here just two days ago. It just meant that he had programmed TIM to arrive with them aboard a few days after he had been sent packing by the Time police.

It was not a comfortable thought knowing that either the Timecops or those unbelievably horrendous-looking Hogs could arrive at any moment, but there was no time to dwell on that now. Danny knew that the best thing they could do was to put their plan into action as quickly as possible.

"What date is it?" Danny asked in French.

"December 3rd, 1942," replied Maurice.

"OK," said Danny, nodding.

He remembered that Michelle had died on the night of December 5th. That meant that they had tomorrow and the next day to find the young Mortimer, give him the journal then put together a plan to save Michelle.

"How far away is Bordeaux?" asked Danny.

"It's not that far," Maurice replied, "but you have to be very careful. There are German soldiers *everywhere*!"

Now they noticed that Maurice was looking at the clothes they were wearing. How strange their bizarre Year 2200 fashion must have looked to him!

"I will have to see if I can find you some clothes," Maurice muttered.

"Do you have family, Maurice?" asked Danny.

It was a question they could see Maurice did not welcome and did not want to answer. He got to his feet and went over to the bottom of the stairs.

"Not any more…" was all he said before climbing back up the stairs.

"What was that? What did he say?" asked Spike, still looking as confused as ever.

*

A short time later Maurice returned with some clothes. They could tell by the way the clothes were so beautifully washed and folded that they obviously meant a lot to him. He handed them the neat piles, along with some more blankets.

"Thank you," said Charley.

"Now get some rest," said Maurice. "I'll see you in the morning. You must get an early start."

Maurice climbed the stairs and closed the trapdoor behind him. They could hear him dragging the kitchen table over the trapdoor then the soft pad of his footsteps as he went off to his bedroom. It was time for them to consider their own sleeping arrangements. Basically there were two options - the bed or the cold, stone floor.

"You two share the bed," Danny said to the others.

Both Charley and Spike immediately began to protest (Charley wasn't sure she liked the idea of sharing a bed with her brother!), but Danny was already laying some blankets on the floor.

"Just sleep feet to feet," he said. "Come on, let's not argue. We need to get some rest."

The others knew he was right. They both clambered into the bed from opposite ends while Danny tried to get comfortable on the floor.

"Are you all right down there?" Charley asked.

"Yes, I'm fine," lied Danny.

"All right, all right - enough of the French!" moaned Spike.

It was only then that Danny and Charley realised they had indeed been speaking French to each other. Charley couldn't resist a last little dig.

"Good night, sleep well," she said to Danny in French.

"Very funny," grunted Spike, unhappily.

Why was it only *his* translator program that wasn't working?

\*

They awoke the next morning to the sound of Maurice tapping on the trapdoor.

"It's time to get up," he was saying.

Danny sat up feeling stiff from the cold hard floor. Charley and Spike lay in the bed for a few moments, blinking and rubbing their eyes, trying to remember where exactly they were. Eventually Spike climbed out of the bed.

Danny was busy looking through the clothes that Maurice had given them. He handed Spike a few of the items that he thought would fit him best.

"All right, men changing here!" said Spike to Charley. "Let's have you looking the other way, please!"

Charley smiled and obediently rolled over to face the wall. When the boys had finished changing she turned back to look and immediately burst out laughing. They looked like a couple of street urchins - and Spike's trousers were way too short!

Danny was finding the clothes a bit on the scratchy side, but at least it meant they were going to be able to blend in.

"I wouldn't laugh too much if I was you, Charles," said Spike with a smile. "It's your turn now!"

"Well, you'd better get out of here then," said Charley, who did not look ready to leave the warmth of her bed.

"Come on," Danny said to Spike, "let's go up."

\*

Upstairs they found Maurice in the kitchen making coffee. On the table was a meal that looked identical to the one they had had the night before. Maurice told them to help themselves, and again they did their best to eat something. The old man showed Danny a rough map he had drawn with directions on how to get to Bordeaux. As Maurice explained the map to Danny in French, Spike could only sit there grumpily, not understanding a word. Unfortunately the night's sleep had not made any difference to his useless translator program!

They were interrupted by a noise. It was Charley coming up through the trapdoor from downstairs. When Maurice looked up and saw her, he immediately became choked up, his eyes filling with tears.

Charley was amazed that the sight of her in this old dress had caused such a strong reaction. She came over to Maurice, who was now wiping away the tears, and laid a hand on his shoulder.

"What's the matter?" she asked him in French.

"I'm sorry," said Maurice, doing his best to give her a smile. "It's just that when I saw you... you reminded me so much of our little Amelie. She was not much older than you."

Charley took a seat beside Maurice at the kitchen table.

"What happened to Amelie?" she asked.

Maurice still looked reluctant to talk about his family, but eventually he took a deep breath and told them the story.

"It was two years ago now. A morning just like any other morning. I was out in the milking shed. All night we had heard the big guns of the German artillery. Boom, boom, boom! They were far away and we were quite used to the sound of these guns, so we didn't expect anything. Suddenly... out of the blue... from nowhere... a shell, way off target, landed directly on our house. I lost my whole family - my wife, my son, his wife and their two children, Julian and little Amelie. All gone in an instant. *Why?*

Why could that shell not have landed on the milking shed instead? Why not rather take the life of an old man and a few cows instead of those young people who still had so much life to live?"

The others sat in silence. Even though Spike had not understood Maurice he could tell that this was not the right time to ask what was going on.

"War," continued Maurice, his voice filled with bitterness and regret. "Do these tyrants, these war-makers like Adolf Hitler - do they ever think about the innocents? About beautiful, innocent children like Amelie - whose only care in life was for her lamb and her piglets? So much pain I tell you! More pain than one old man can bear!"

\*

The sun was just beginning to rise as the three of them trudged down the muddy track that led away from Maurice's farmhouse.

They walked all morning, following Maurice's map. There were very few people on the road. In fact, there was very little of *anything* on the road! They were passing through farmland most of the time, yet the whole morning they did not see a single farm animal! The only thing they did see plenty of, was the burned-out remnants of old tanks and armoured cars, all destroyed in battles and now lying derelict, overgrown with weeds.

They could tell when they were nearing the town of Bordeaux, as the road started getting busier. One elderly couple passed them pulling a cart filled with vegetables, which they were presumably taking to the market. Danny wondered if they had once had a horse or a donkey to pull the cart. Now they were pulling it themselves! As they went by, the old couple did not even look up at them. The hardship of life in a time of war was deeply etched into their faces.

It wasn't long after the couple had passed that they saw their first German soldiers. They heard a truck labouring up the hill behind them and got off the road to let it pass. As it went by, they could see the soldiers sitting in the back in their grey uniforms and metal helmets, their upright rifles swaying from side to side. What struck Danny immediately was how *young* the soldiers looked. Some of them did not look that much older than himself!

Soon they reached the outskirts of the town and it was here, as they rounded a corner, that something made them stop dead in their tracks. Up ahead was a roadblock manned by German soldiers. Danny knew how suspicious they must have looked just stopping in the middle of the road, so he bent down and pretended to be doing up his shoelaces.

"What do we do now?" muttered Charley.

Spike was taking a good look at the soldiers. These were not young soldiers like the ones in the truck. They were older, harder-looking men, wearing long, black leather coats and gloves. They also wore armbands bearing the Nazi symbol - the red and black jagged cross known as the 'swastika'.

"Gestapo," said Spike, not sounding at all happy about it.

"What does that mean?" asked Charley.

"Bad news," was all Spike said in reply.

What Spike did not have time to explain was that the Gestapo was the name of Hitler's Secret State Police. They had the power to arrest anyone, and were amongst the most feared units in all of Europe.

"Well, we can't just stop here," said Danny, re-tying his shoelace for the third time. "Come on. If anybody asks, we are Maurice's grandchildren. OK, Amelie?"

Charley nodded.

"Let's just hope they don't ask Spike anything in French!"

As they approached they could see the Gestapo officers had pulled aside the old couple with the vegetable cart and were talking to them in German. The couple probably didn't understand a word they were saying and continued to stare at the ground.

Danny noticed they weren't stopping everybody.

"Just keep walking," he muttered.

As they passed the roadblock they felt the eyes of the Gestapo officers' glance over them. They kept walking, staring straight ahead. Thankfully, the officers appeared to be more interested in the old couple.

It seemed they were in the clear - and they were just picking up their pace when one of the officers suddenly shouted across to them.

"Hey, you three! Where are you off to in such a hurry?"

The officer had spoken in German, which Danny had understood perfectly. Without even thinking, Danny shouted a reply.

"We are going to the market!"

It was only after the words had come out that Danny realised he had just spoken in perfect German. The Gestapo officers had noticed because they were now all looking up at him!

"What are you doing?" Charley muttered under her breath.

"I couldn't help it. It just came out," Danny replied.

The officer who had shouted was now coming over.

"Where did you learn to speak such good German?" he asked Danny.

"My uncle," Danny blurted out. "He was German."

"Really? That is good." He turned his attention to Spike and Charley. "And what about you two? Do you also speak German?"

The officer was looking directly at Spike. Moments earlier, Spike had been relieved to discover that he was able to understand the Gestapo officer. Now he felt confident enough to reply in German.

"The bear and the rabbit prefer the ballet to watching football," said Spike.

The officer stared at Spike, blinked a few times - had he heard correctly?

Spike cleared his throat and spoke again.

"The policeman on the scooter plays marbles with his aunt."

The officer didn't know how to react to this. At first he thought that Spike might be mocking him, or perhaps making fun of his language. He looked at Danny.

"What is your friend saying?"

"Oh, sorry," explained Danny. "He is still learning German. I am trying to teach him."

As far as Spike was concerned, he was speaking perfect German and making complete sense. He spoke again.

"If a dog lives on the moon it must eat cheese."

Now both Danny and Charley turned on him with such filthy looks that he decided he had better shut up.

"Yes," nodded the officer, "he definitely needs to practise, but at least he has started to learn. This is important because one day all Europe will be speaking German!"

Danny felt like replying, 'You want to bet?', but instead he just nodded in agreement. This seemed to do the trick because, thankfully, the officer now indicated that they could go.

\*

Charley waited until they were a little way down the road before turning on Spike.

"Spike! What is your problem?"

"I could understand everything," Spike protested, "but when I tried to speak... was it not making sense?"

"It was the biggest load of rubbish we've ever heard!" shrieked Charley. The whole experience had clearly disturbed her. Now she turned to Danny. "And why did you start speaking German in the first place?"

"I couldn't help it," Danny replied. "As soon as I was asked the question in German I had no choice but to reply in German."

Charley was shaking her head.

"I don't think either of your programs are working very well." They walked a bit more before she added, "From now on, how about Spike pretends he can't speak at all? Just don't say *anything*! OK, Spike?"

"Listen to her!" snorted Spike. "Just because *her* translator program is the only one that seems to be working properly…"

\*

Once they reached the town they knew their first priority was to find Michelle - not only to warn her about the dangers that lay ahead, but also because she would hopefully be able to take them to the young Uncle Morty.

Maurice had told them roughly where he thought the Borges' house was and Danny also had the address from Uncle Morty, so they were able to ask people directions along the way.

\*

Soon they were standing on the corner of *Rue des Fleurs*.

"That must be it there," said Danny. "Number five, *Rue des Fleurs*."

From here they could see the neatly painted house with a brass number five on the front door. The question now was whether or not they should just walk up to the house and knock on the door.

"But what if that nosy neighbour sees us?" said Charley. "What was her name?"

"Madame du Pont," Danny replied.

He had been thinking the same thing. They all remembered that it was this Madame du Pont whom Uncle Morty blamed for alerting the German soldiers on the night of the Bordeaux harbour raid. They weren't sure which house she lived in, but she was probably sitting behind her lace curtains now, looking out for any unusual activity.

"We could just pretend to be friends visiting," suggested Spike.

"We look more like urchins who should be begging," said Charley.

She still hadn't got used to the old clothes they were wearing.

The decision was taken out of their hands when suddenly the front door of the Borges' house opened and a very pretty young woman stepped out. She called goodbye to someone in the house then, before they knew it, she was heading up the road directly towards them, swinging her shopping basket and humming a tune.

"Bonjour!" she said brightly as she breezed past them.

They all mumbled 'bonjour' then looked at each other.

"Michelle?" whispered Spike to the others.

"It's got to be," said Danny.

"She's beautiful!" said Charley.

With that, they all took off down the road after her, trying to appear as casual as possible.

Michelle (if indeed it was Michelle!) was such a fast walker that they had trouble keeping up with her. She also seemed to know almost everyone in town because there was barely a person she passed whom she didn't greet.

Eventually they arrived at the marketplace and Danny and the others hovered at a safe distance while Michelle began to move from one stall to the next, chatting with the stall-owners as she selected her produce.

Danny knew that sooner or later they were going to have to just take the bull by the horns and approach her. The problem was she never stayed still for long enough!

Then the opportunity presented itself. For just a few seconds she hesitated in one spot while checking her shopping list.

"Come on," said Danny to the others.

As they approached the pretty lady from behind they were all *really* hoping that is was Michelle! She still hadn't noticed them and Charley was now nodding at Danny as if to say, 'Go on! Say something!'.

Eventually Danny cleared his throat and spoke in French.

"Excuse me," he said, "are you Michelle Borges?"

The lady turned and looked more than a little surprised to find the three of them standing there.

"Yes," she said, nodding hesitantly. "Who wants to know?"

"Um... my name is Daniel and these are my friends Charley and Spike. We need to talk to you about something... um... something really important."

"Yes?" said Michelle. "And what is this important matter?"

"Um... well..." Danny looked around to make sure there was no one in earshot. "Well, actually it's got to do with..." Now Danny lowered his voice. "Mortimer Piper-Adams."

At the mention of this name a look of extreme distress flashed across Michelle's face and she immediately started to move off.

"I'm sorry," she said, "I don't know what you're talking about."

Danny stopped her.

"Please... Michelle. Don't worry, we are here to help."

Michelle had no interest in continuing the conversation.

"I have to go," she said emphatically, and with that she took off through the market.

Danny followed behind her.

"Michelle! Please, just listen to what we have to say," he pleaded.

"Leave me alone!" she replied angrily.

Danny stuck with her and eventually she stopped again on the edge of the marketplace and turned on him fiercely.

"Don't you understand? I can't help you!"

"Michelle," Danny said, lowering his voice again. "We are English. Mortimer has told us about you."

Michelle looked shocked. She glanced around to make sure there was no one standing nearby.

"English? What do you mean? What are you doing here?"

"Um... that's a bit of a tough one to explain at the moment," said Danny, "but... we *really* do need to see Mortimer."

"*What?*" Michelle shook her head. "That's impossible!"

She was struggling to make sense of everything and, for a moment, Danny thought she might bolt again.

"Please…" Danny tried again. "It is *very* important. In fact, I can tell you quite honestly that it is a matter of life and death."

Michelle continued to stare at Danny, looking for any clues that this might be some sort of trap. Spike and Charley then caught up with them as well and this only added to her confusion.

"Let me show you something," said Danny, removing Uncle Morty's journal from his rucksack. "Look, this journal is actually written by Mortimer."

Michelle looked at the first page of the journal and seemed to recognise the handwriting.

"Where did you get this?" she asked.

"Mortimer gave it to me and…" Danny knew there wasn't time to explain.

"Look, we need to see him. We need to tell him something and we need to give him this book."

As Michelle flicked through the journal again, trying desperately to make sense of everything, Spike now spotted something over her shoulder. There was a black, open-topped car coming down the road and on the front of it were two fluttering Nazi swastika flags. This was an army car and in the back seat sat a Gestapo Officer.

"Danny," Spike said quietly.

Danny ignored him. He was still pleading with Michelle.

Now, as the vehicle drew closer, Spike recognised the Gestapo Officer in the back as the same one who had questioned them earlier on the road into town.

"*Danny!*" Spike said again, more forcefully.

This time Danny looked up. As he did so, he found himself staring into the eyes of the Gestapo Officer - and the officer seemed to have recognised him.

In that instant, Michelle had gone. She had taken one look at the approaching car and quickly slipped away.

"Wait!" Danny shouted - and he was about to take off after her when the army car suddenly pulled up beside them.

"It's the German boy!" the Gestapo Officer shouted, pointing at Danny.

There were three youngsters in the back of the car as well. Two of them were big strong-looking boys, aged about fifteen and sixteen - probably brothers. They were wearing khaki uniforms that Spike recognised as those of the Hitler Youth, a Nazi organisation that all German boys were forced to join from an early age. The third young person in the car was a pretty girl (about Charley's age) with blonde plaited pigtails.

"These are my children," the officer said proudly to Danny. "They are on their way to the greatest rally in the history of the world – the Nazi Party rally in Nuremburg. You are German! You should be going as well!"

"What?" Danny scoffed at the ridiculous suggestion. He was still more interested in following Michelle. "No, I don't think so."

This response seemed to annoy the officer.

"Oh, and why don't you think so?" he asked.

"Why?" Danny scowled. "Because…"

He shrugged. He didn't even want to be having this conversation. This was clearly not good enough for the officer, who now surprised them all by climbing out of the car.

"I'm sorry," growled the officer as he approached Danny. "I didn't quite get that. You don't want to go because…?"

Danny was taken aback. He shook his head.

"Because… I can't!" he replied.

"You *can't*!" the officer howled indignantly.

He glanced at his sons, who immediately sprung out of the car as well. It was the older of the two boys (who seemed particularly serious and arrogant) who now came right up to Danny.

"And why is it that you *can't* go to the greatest rally the world has ever known?" the boy asked.

Although the boy was considerably bigger than him, Danny held his stare.

"Because… I don't want to," he replied.

The boy's eyes flashed angrily at this. It was as though Danny had just slapped him in the face.

"When the Fuhrer, our Great Leader, holds a rally and invites us all to come, we do not refuse! We thank him for inviting us! We are honoured that he has invited us!"

"You, with your German blood, should know that!" said the officer.

He seemed to be enjoying watching this encounter between Danny and his son.

"I'm not German!" snapped Danny.

"But you *are*!" said the officer. "You told me yourself that your uncle was German. Listen to how beautifully you speak the language."

Now the young girl was leaning out of the car.

"Come with us!" she shouted. "It will be the experience of a lifetime!"

Danny looked at them all incredulously. *Were they mad? Did they really expect him to just go along with them?* He shook his head.

"I'm sorry, I have to go!" he said.

As he started to move, the older boy stepped in his way, and then suddenly his brother was also alongside him.

"Get out the way, please," said Danny. "I can't come with you."

"Did you not understand?" the older boy hissed. "Nobody refuses an invitation from the Fuhrer!"

Again Danny tried to move, but now both boys stepped across to block his way. He was now starting to realise just how serious the situation was getting. Suddenly he thought about his *Combat X* program. *Surely it will activate now? This must count as self-defence?*

He concentrated hard on the program, mentally requesting the combat skills he thought he might require. *Judo, karate, kick-boxing? That should do it, but how was he meant to know if the program had activated? He didn't feel any different! There was only one way to find out.* He took a deep breath and imagined the move he was about to make - a reverse round-house kick that should put one brother down then a couple of rapid-fire punches should take care of the other one - then they could all make a run for it.

With a sudden roar Danny leapt into action.

"*Aaaaaaargggghhhhh!*"

He hardly got off the ground. As he started to jump both brothers lunged forwards and latched on to him with such a tight grip that he could barely move! He tried desperately to shake them off, but there was no way he was going to break free. In fact, his attempt to escape had been so weak that he could see the boys grinning at their father.

Danny felt his anger rising. *Another dud program?* He cursed the program and those rip-off artists, Frankie and Glide.

"Bring him along!" the officer said to his boys. "I think he needs a lesson in German honour!"

The next thing Danny knew he was being manhandled towards the car, and there was nothing he could do about it!

"Leave him alone!" Charley screamed, as she and Spike now rushed forwards to help, but the officer held them back while the boys shoved Danny into the back seat and sat on either side of him, still holding his arms. The officer climbed in and shut the door.

Charley rushed up to the car.

"Please! Let him go!" she pleaded.

Now the pretty blonde daughter gave her the biggest of smiles.

"Don't worry, my angel," she said. "We'll bring him back! He is honoured. He is going to see the Fuhrer! Heil Hitler!"

With that, the car took off, leaving Spike and Charley standing in the middle of the road, staring after it in stunned disbelief!

"We need to follow them, Spike!" Charley shrieked, her eyes wide with panic.

She was just about to take off after the car when Spike grabbed her arm.

"Hold on, Charles!" he said, realising that she hadn't quite grasped the full extent of the problem. "They said the Nazi Party rally was in Nuremburg."

Charley shook her head.

"*So?* We need to go there!"

"Charles," Spike said. "Nuremburg is hundreds of miles away - right in the heart of Nazi Germany!"

# Chapter 10

# The Yellow Star People

At about the same time as Charley was choking on the distressing news that Danny was heading for Germany, Maurice was finishing up his morning chores at the farm. He had just fed the cattle and was now walking back to the house for his morning tea. He was casually whistling a tune as he came around the corner of the barn - but that's when the whistling suddenly stopped.

Standing in front of him were two of the most hideous-looking men he had ever laid eyes upon. They were enormous - tall and broad with obscenely scarred faces and freakishly dreadlocked hair. They wore large, black weathered jackets and had some sort of weapons (the likes of which Maurice had never seen before) hanging from their shoulders.

It seemed they had just emerged from the barn, as the door was still open. Maurice glanced quickly into the barn and saw that some of the hay had been swept aside to reveal the machine's metallic exterior. They had clearly found what they were looking for.

Now they started moving towards him. He said a quick prayer and prepared himself for the worst, but they were not interested in him and merely tossed him to one side. They were heading towards the Bordeaux road, walking with purpose, as if guided by some sort of signal.

Maurice picked himself up off the ground. He wasn't to know that these two unpleasant creatures were called 'Hogs', yet it wasn't difficult for him to guess where they had come from and who they were after. Last time it had been the police who had arrived shortly after the machine. Now Maurice found himself wishing that it was the police again. At least they had only arrested Mortimer and sent him back to where he had come from.

He sensed that these two beasts were not interested in arresting anyone. They struck him as nothing less than killing machines.

Maurice now watched as the two giants reached the main road and started in the direction of Bordeaux. He raised his eyes to the heavens and muttered in an angry, trembling voice:

"At least save *these* children! You owe me that!"

*

Spike and Charley had started to run down the road in the direction the car had gone - not because they thought they would catch up with it, but because they didn't know what else to do!

It therefore came as a great surprise when they rounded a corner and saw the black army car parked at the front of what looked like the main train station.

"There!" Charley shouted, suddenly sensing a glimmer of hope.

They crossed the road, ran through the car park and into the station building. The platform was packed full of people. There was a train waiting to leave and it looked like most of the passengers were already on-board. Everyone else was milling around, saying their goodbyes through the train windows. The first thing Spike and Charley noticed were a lot of uniforms! It seemed like there were many German soldiers putting their children on the train - and most of these kids were dressed in Hitler Youth uniforms. There was even a loud, enthusiastic band playing a lively German tune at one end of the platform, and various military banners and flags fluttering from above.

Spike and Charley started to walk along the platform, searching for any sign of Danny - then, about halfway down, Charley spotted the Gestapo Officer. He was chatting to his daughter, who was leaning out of a train window. When they looked farther into the train they saw Danny.

"There he is," said Charley.

Danny was sitting glumly on the far side of the carriage, still flanked by the two brothers. They were trying to talk to him, perhaps trying to cheer him up, but he was just staring ahead, surly and silent, as if they weren't even there.

Then a conductor, standing nearby Spike and Charley, gave a loud blast on his whistle. It made Danny look up and that's when he saw them.

*

Danny had heard very little of what the brothers were saying to him. The only thing on his mind was how to get off the train before it left the station. He had noticed how the arrogant older brother was ordering around the other Hitler Youth, as though he was some kind of leader in the organisation. Unfortunately it was him who was sitting between Danny and the aisle, which was going to make his escape more difficult.

When Danny heard the blast of the conductor's whistle he knew it was now or never. That's when he looked up and saw Charley and Spike through the window. He only saw them for a split second then they disappeared from sight as everyone clambered aboard and the carriage filled up.

As the train began to move and all the youth started to shout their goodbyes, Danny felt the attention had shifted away from him. He decided to make his move.

In a single sudden movement he leapt up, over the legs of the older brother and into the aisle. The boy grabbed the back of his shirt, but it ripped in his hand and Danny suddenly found himself careering down the aisle, barging people out of his way. Shouts and screams filled the carriage as people ducked out of the way or were bowled over. Danny could see the door of the carriage up ahead. It was about to close - if he could just reach it...

Suddenly he came crashing down hard with someone on top of him and all the air was knocked from his lungs. As he lay there, gasping for breath, he realised it was the older brother who had tackled him and now had him pinned down.

"He has spirit, this one!" the boy crowed, grabbing Danny by the collar and hauling him to his feet.

All around him the uniforms were cheering and laughing. Danny, still battling for breath, caught sight of something through the window. It was Charley and Spike, running alongside the carriage.

Now the train began to gather speed and they were gradually left farther and farther behind.

*

Charley and Spike stopped running, and watched as the train accelerated out of the station. Charley had caught a last glimpse of Danny as he was wrenched to his feet with the back of his shirt ripped open. For just a moment he had looked out of the window at them - then he was gone.

Now, as they watched the train disappearing down the track, they were both overcome by a feeling of utter helplessness. Charley started to cry. Spike stood, staring blankly, until the train was out of sight. Eventually he seemed to notice Charley's sniffling and he guided her to a nearby bench where they both slumped down heavily.

"Come on, Charles," Spike said, trying to sound reassuring. "Crying is not going to do us any good."

"Well, do you have any better suggestions?" Charley sniffed, dabbing her nose with a tissue.

At that particular moment in time Spike would have to admit that he didn't, but he was thinking about it. He looked around the platform, which was emptying fast. Some men had started to take down the banners and flags.

"Hold on, let's just think about our situation more clearly," Spike said eventually. "Say we were to go now and find Michelle - and we managed to persuade her and Mortimer not to go to the harbour tomorrow night - then... that would cause the Change to take place, right?"

Charley nodded.

"Once this Change has happened, the whole Time Ripple will take effect - and we'll find ourselves back in the UK. Right?"

Charley nodded again.

"If Uncle Morty's theory is correct, it doesn't matter where Danny is now because once the Change takes place we'll all end up back in the UK anyway!"

Charley thought about this for a while. It *did* seem to make sense.

"So, we've just got to stop Michelle and Mortimer from going to the harbour, and everything will be all right?" she said, sounding more hopeful.

Spike nodded, but Charley could see that he was still thinking hard on the subject and that something was still bothering him. Eventually he sighed and shook his head.

"But we're forgetting something," he said. "Danny has Uncle Morty's journal. If we don't give Mortimer that journal *before* the Change takes place then there will be no chance of them ever building another TIM. That means no chance of Danny trying to save his dad and Catie."

Charley remembered what Uncle Morty had said. He had to receive the journal *before* the Change took place otherwise it would cease to exist. Once the Change happened the Time Ripple would move *forwards* through time, changing everything ahead of it - but, if Uncle Morty *already* had the journal, it would not be affected.

As much as Charley did not want it to be so, she knew that Spike was right again. The glimmer of hope that had appeared so briefly was now extinguished all together.

"We've got no choice," Spike said. "We *have* to go after Danny. We have to bring him and the journal back here, and we've got to do it before tomorrow night."

Charley felt the tears welling up again.

"Spike, you're saying we have to travel to Germany - but *how*? We have no passports, we have no money, we have no ID papers. We don't have anything!"

"I know, I know," Spike replied.

He was trying desperately to think of a plan, but now there was some other activity going on around the station, which was interrupting his thoughts.

Minutes earlier, he had heard the sound of trucks pulling up outside and now he noticed some German soldiers coming out onto the platform. The soldiers, some of whom had rather vicious-looking dogs on leads, started to take up positions along the platform.

Charley did not like the look of them at all.

"Let's get out of here," she suggested.

Spike agreed and they stood up and started walking towards the exit. The problem was that the exit from the platform was also the entrance through which all the soldiers were coming. And now a whole lot of other people also started to stream out onto the platform and it was the sight of these people that made Spike hesitate. There was a baggage storage room right beside them.

"Let's just wait in here for a bit," he said, and they quickly stepped into the darkened doorway.

As much as Charley didn't feel like sticking around, she could see they had little choice. There were now literally hundreds of people streaming out, and what made it worse was that the German soldiers and their barking dogs had positioned themselves on either side of the entrance and were now shouting at everyone to hurry up!

Everybody looked lost and bewildered. They were a real mixture - some young, some old, some wealthy-looking, some poor. There were husbands and wives, children and grandparents. They could see younger people helping the elderly, mothers carrying babies, young children grabbing on to their fathers' trousers, crying because they were afraid of the soldiers and the dogs.

However, there was one thing all the people had in common and that was a yellow star sewn on to the front of their jackets. When Spike saw this he knew instantly what it meant. He remembered that the Nazis had made all Jews wear a yellow Star of David. It was their way of identifying them - so that they could humiliate and persecute them. Suddenly Spike realised what they were witnessing. These were Jews, probably on their way to a concentration camp.

Now the transport arrived in the form of a big steam engine. It came puffing into the station and lurched to a halt with much hissing and clanking. When the smoke and steam had cleared Spike was surprised to see that the train was pulling cattle trucks - high, closed-in trucks with large wooden sliding doors. And it was these doors that the soldiers now began to slide open.

The people on the platform could only stand and stare. *Were they expected to climb into these cattle trucks?* They received their answer. The soldiers now began to shout at them through loudhailers.

"Climb aboard! Choose a carriage! Hurry up!"

As Charley watched the people starting to climb into the cattle trucks, all their own problems seemed to pale into insignificance. She saw a man helping his old mother up into a carriage. She saw a husband passing children up to his wife. She saw an older brother trying to stop his young sister from crying.

Then Charley noticed a father talking to his daughter (who was about the same age as herself) and she could tell immediately that something was going on. Not far away from them was a baggage cart piled with Hitler Youth banners. The father had shown this cart to his daughter and was now telling her to do something, but she didn't seem to like the sound of it because she kept holding on to him - not wanting to leave his side! The father was insistent.

He waited for a nearby guard to turn his back then pushed his daughter towards the cart. The girl ran quickly across the few yards of platform, jumped into the cart and pulled a banner over her head.

"Did you see that?" Charley asked.

"Yup," replied Spike, "but I think that guard did as well."

Charley looked again and, sure enough, it seemed like one of the soldiers had seen something out of the corner of his eye and was now moving towards the cart for a closer look. As the guard approached, the girl's father looked absolutely devastated. He knew his daughter was about to be discovered.

Then, for no apparent reason, the guard suddenly hesitated. He stood beside the cart for a few moments and looked around as though confused. Amazingly, he then turned away and went back to what he was doing by the train.

Charley couldn't believe it. She looked at Spike.

"Was that you?" she asked.

"I think so," Spike replied with a grin.

He had been concentrating all his energy on stopping the guard, and the *Mindbender* program seemed to have worked.

The girl's father looked as though a miracle had just occurred. He was now helping his wife and son into a cattle truck.

It didn't take long for the soldiers to get everyone into the trucks, but it felt like forever for Charley and Spike, who were keeping one eye on the cart with the girl inside. Now the soldiers moved down the train sliding the truck doors closed. For Spike, who had a good idea where these people were being sent to, it was difficult to watch. The expressions of confusion and fear on their faces as the doors were closed was something he knew he would never forget.

Once the train driver had received his signal, the engine began to puff and hiss again and the train slowly pulled out of the station.

Now the soldiers began to leave as well, but for the girl in the cart there was suddenly a new danger. The men who had been taking down the Hitler Youth banners were now returning to wheel away their carts, and one of them was heading straight for the cart with the girl inside!

Charley knew they had to do something. Without even thinking, she left the baggage room and ran out across the platform towards the cart. Spike could do little but follow. Charley arrived at the cart at the same time as the man.

"Don't worry," she said to him in German, "we've got this one."

The man looked surprised.

"Who are you?" he asked.

"Oh…" said Charley, thinking fast. "We work here. We help keep the station clean. We'll take this one."

The man did not look at all sure, but when Charley started to push the cart and then Spike also arrived to help he stood back and let them take it. Charley and Spike aimed the cart for the exit.

To get off the platform they had to go through the station building and it was only now that they saw a few soldiers still hanging around near the exit.

"Oh, nice one!" groaned Spike.

"Just push!" Charley muttered under her breath.

The soldiers were standing around talking and laughing, and didn't pay much attention to Spike and Charley as they came past.

But, moments later, someone suddenly shouted.

"Hey, you!"

Spike looked up – it was a soldier and he was staring directly at him. His immediate thought was that they had spotted the girl under the banners.

"Are you wearing your sister's trousers?" the soldier asked.

This made the other soldiers laugh.

"Has somebody died?" another soldier chipped in. "You seem to be flying half mast!"

The soldiers laughed some more.

Much to Charley's relief she now realised that they were actually joking about Spike's short trousers.

"Just smile and keep pushing," she muttered to Spike.

Spike was not enjoying being the subject of their jokes. At first he bit his tongue and said nothing, but as the soldiers continued to snigger, Charley could see that he was getting more and more irritated. She was just about to say, 'Ignore them' when, to her horror, Spike looked back and shouted in German.

"The fish must drink tea between her trapeze lessons!"

For a second, Charley closed her eyes and cursed silently, then she glanced quickly over at the soldiers and the sight nearly caused her to burst out laughing! Their chatter and jokes had suddenly dried up. Now there were only looks of complete confusion!

Charley tried to look apologetic, tapping the side of her head as if to indicate that Spike was not all there upstairs, then they quickly pushed the cart out through the station exit.

*

Outside, Charley gave Spike a withering look.

"Do you even know what you said?"

Spike shrugged with a smile.

"It shut them up, didn't it?"

Now they noticed that other carts were being pushed towards a nearby truck. This was not where they wanted to go and, instinctively, they guided their cart off in a different direction. They expected to hear shouts from the men by the truck, but none came. Up ahead they spotted a small alleyway leading off the main road. It was the ideal place to hide the cart. They guided it into the alleyway and parked it amongst some dustbins, then Spike lifted up the banner covering the girl and a small frightened face peered up at him.

"Hello," Spike said to her. "Don't worry, we are friends."

There was enormous relief on the girl's face.

"You understand English?" Spike asked as he helped her out of the cart.

"A little," the girl replied, nodding.

*Thank goodness for that!* thought Spike. It was only now that he saw what a dainty little thing she was. She had the most amazing porcelain-white skin and beautiful, long, straight black hair.

"It's rude to stare," Charley muttered to Spike before turning to the girl. "Hi, I'm Charley and this is my brother, Spike. What's your name?"

"Sarah," the girl replied. "Thank you for helping me."

"No problem," said Spike. "The first thing we have to do is get rid of this."

He pulled the yellow star off her jacket and tossed it into a dustbin. Sarah seemed shocked by this, but they could also tell that she was glad to be rid of it.

"OK, listen," said Charley. "We can't hang around here. Sarah, do you know of a safe place where we can go?"

Sarah thought about this for a few seconds then nodded.

"Yes, I know a place," she said.

"Right, let's get out of here," said Spike - and Charley had to smile to herself at how her brother had now suddenly taken charge!

He ran to the alleyway entrance, checked left and right then nodded to the others that it was safe. They slipped out onto the main road and walked briskly away from the station.

\*

A few miles out of town, the two Hogs were walking with grim determination. Apart from the crunch of their large steel-capped boots on the gravel road, they walked in silence. So far they had not encountered anyone else - but now they could hear something. It sounded like some sort of motorised vehicle coming up the road - perhaps a motorbike? They paused for a few moments to listen, then stepped off the road into some trees, and waited.

It wasn't long before two German soldiers, one riding a motorbike and another sitting beside him in a sidecar, came speeding around the corner.

The Hogs waited until the bike was almost upon them and then suddenly stepped out onto the road. With only seconds to react, the rider swerved wildly and the bike went skidding sideways, spraying up a cloud of dust before lurching to a halt in a ditch.

As the soldiers battled to disentangle themselves from the bike, the Hogs strode calmly towards them, simultaneously swinging their sinister-looking weapons (which looked like hi-tech sawn-off shotguns) off their shoulders and into the firing position.

The first blast blew the rider clean off the motorbike and he landed some yards down the road. Seeing this, the other soldier leapt from his tilting sidecar, but a second blast caught him in mid-air and he was blown over a hedge and into a field.

The Hogs walked up to the motorbike and, together, picked it up like it was a child's tricycle. One Hog then wheeled the bike into the adjoining field while the other went and collected the soldier who was lying in the road. He brought him back and laid him down in the field beside his unconscious mate.

The Hogs' similar size (and extreme ugliness!) made it difficult to tell them apart, but perhaps the most obvious difference was that one had a grotesque tattoo of a spider on his neck while the other had the most disgusting set of teeth imaginable!

Once the Hogs had both soldiers positioned near the motorbike, the tattooed one ('Spider Neck') removed a small electronic device from his jacket pocket. It seemed to be some sort of tiny digital video camera because he now pointed it at the motorbike as though he was filming it. He then moved across to the soldiers and filmed them as well. Once he had done this from a couple of different angles he pressed a few more buttons on the device, waited until he received a signal then put it away.

Now it seemed like they had to wait for something because both Hogs went over to a nearby tree and sat down in the shade. They had only been sitting there for a few minutes when the other Hog ('Tooth Rot') spotted a rabbit popping its head up out of a hole. In a flash, he swung his weapon around and let off a single blast. The rabbit was instantly transformed into a blackened crispy mass, covered with frazzled tufts of hair. Looking very pleased with himself, Tooth Rot went over and collected his prize. He then unceremoniously tore it in half and tossed one half to Spider Neck. In no time at all, the only evidence of the rabbit's existence was the grease running off their chins.

After 'lunch', Spider Neck took out his communication device again and had another look. Whatever signal he was waiting for still hadn't come through, which was now starting to annoy him. He kicked angrily at the ground. They sat in silence for a few more minutes then, at last, the device began to beep and both

Hogs were instantly on their feet.

The first thing they did was to scan the vicinity to make sure no one else was around. Then they put on dark glasses, pulled the hoods of their jackets over their heads and crouched down as if they were taking cover from something.

Moments later, it came - a blinding flash accompanied by a deafening crack. Anybody nearby would have mistaken it for thunder and lightning.

The Hogs straightened up again and removed their hoods and glasses. There was now a cloud of smoke hanging over the field, but amongst the smoke there was also something else - something that hadn't been there a few seconds before! The Hogs walked over for a closer inspection.

The newly arrived object was a motorbike and sidecar, almost identical to the one belonging to the soldiers, but bigger. There were also two large German army uniforms draped over the sidecar. Tooth Rot tossed one of the uniforms over to Spider Neck and they began to change out of their clothes.

With the uniforms on (and their dreadlocked hair tucked up into their helmets) the Hogs could easily have passed for two large (battle-scarred!) German soldiers.

Spider Neck had now climbed onto the new motorbike and started it up. The bike may have looked similar to the other one, but as the Hog revved up the engine and took off it soon became clear that it wasn't! At first it motored across the field like a normal bike then Spider Neck pressed a red button beside the throttle and suddenly it began to lift up off the ground! Seconds later, the bike was skimming over the tops of the trees as the Hog did a quick lap of the surrounding forest. When he was satisfied with its performance he brought it down to land in the field again.

Meanwhile, Tooth Rot had put the two soldiers back onto their motorbike and sidecar, and wheeled them out onto the road again. Now, with a single shove from his large boot, he pushed the bike back into the ditch.

He then went over to where Spider Neck was waiting on the bike and climbed into the sidecar. The bike took off towards Bordeaux.

*

Some minutes later, the soldiers on the motorbike in the ditch began to wake up. They appeared to be very drowsy and confused.

"What happened?" asked the rider.

The soldier in the sidecar shook his head and looked around.

"I don't remember," he said. "We must have had an accident. Maybe you weren't concentrating."

"Hey, don't start blaming me!" was the indignant reply. "Maybe we had to swerve to miss an animal or something!"

"Or maybe you fell asleep."

"You were asleep *already*!" countered the rider.

Their argument continued as they struggled to get the bike out of the ditch and on the move again.

*

Sarah had led Spike and Charley on a route that took them directly out of town. Soon they found themselves tramping up a steep rocky path that snaked its way up a hillside above the town. By the time they reached the top they were all out of breath - but the sight that now greeted them suddenly made the effort worthwhile.

"*Wow!*" was all Spike could say when he saw the view.

They were on top of a line of sheer cliffs that dropped way down to the crashing surf below. Farther along the cliff top stood a red and white painted lighthouse.

"There it is!" Sarah announced. "Our lighthouse!"

"*Your* lighthouse!" Spike exclaimed.

"Well, not really," replied Sarah, "but my brother and I call it 'our lighthouse' because... we..." Suddenly it was as if Sarah could no longer talk because the mention of her brother had made the tears well up in her eyes. "Come on," she said, turning away to hide the fact that she was crying.

Following along behind Sarah, Spike's heart went out to her. She had just watched her family being taken away in a cattle truck! She had no idea where they had been sent (which, for now, was probably a very good thing) and she must have been wondering whether she would ever see them again. Spike glanced back at Charley, whom he could tell was also feeling sorry for Sarah.

When they reached the lighthouse Sarah pushed open the door and went inside. Spike and Charley stood at the door peering into the gloom. Soon there was a glow as Sarah returned to the door with two lit candles.

"We'll need these for the way up," she said, handing one of the candles to Spike. She led them over to the bottom of a stone spiral staircase that disappeared up into the darkness. "Watch your step," she said as she started to climb.

Spike and Charley followed behind her - one step after another, around and around in the darkness - until eventually they emerged into daylight once again. They were now on the upper platform of the lighthouse, standing beside the great light that would once have beamed its warning out to the passing ships.

"The light still works," said Sarah. "Before the war we used to sometimes put it on for fun, but now... well... now we wouldn't want to attract any attention. This has become our secret place."

Spike stood at the railing and took in the view. He could just make out the river that snaked its way into the town of Bordeaux. How incredible to think that the British Commandos, who would become known as the 'Cockleshell Heroes', would be canoeing up that river the following night - and that a huge tragedy was going to occur if they didn't do something to stop it! Spike knew they would have to move soon. He also knew they badly needed a plan to get to Germany!

On the upper platform was also a small enclosed room (perhaps where the lighthouse keeper used to sleep), and it was into here that Sarah now led them. They could tell by all the blankets, books and half-used candles scattered around that this was a place where Sarah and her brother had spent a lot of time.

"This is where I'll have to stay for a while," said Sarah, sitting down on a mattress in the corner. "It's not safe for me to go home now. The neighbours will tell the soldiers if they see me."

The tears were now welling up in her eyes again as she thought about the terrible events of that day, and Charley went over to comfort her. After some time, Sarah looked up through her tears, first at Charley then at Spike. With everything that had happened she had not even had time to think about who these people were!

"You are from England?" she asked.

"Yes," Charley replied.

"So… what are you doing here?"

Spike and Charley glanced at each other quickly and seemed to agree that this wasn't the time to tell their story.

"It's actually a bit of a long story," said Charley.

Sarah blew her nose and wiped away the latest tears that were streaming down her cheeks.

"Well, I thank God that you were at the station to help me."

"We were glad to help," said Spike, "but now… we also have to ask for some help."

"From me?" Sarah sounded surprised. "What can *I* do to help you?"

"Well… you see…" Spike began hesitantly, wondering how exactly he was going to say this. Eventually he decided to just blurt it out. "We have to go to Germany."

Sarah sat bolt upright.

"To Germany! Are you crazy? Do you know how dangerous that will be for you?"

"We know, but we have no choice. We have to go, and we have to go *very soon!*"

Sarah spent the next few minutes lecturing them on how foolish they were to even be *thinking* of going to Germany and that it was the worst idea she had ever heard, especially for two *English* children! However, when she saw her arguments were having no effect on either of them, she went quiet for a while. Eventually she spoke up again.

"If you really are so stupid that you want to do this thing - I *may* know someone who can help."

"Really?" said Spike and Charley together, their eyes lighting up.

"I'm not promising anything," Sarah said, "but we can at least go and ask. We'll have to wait until it's dark though. It's not safe to go now."

It would be dark in only a few hours, so a decision was made to rest until then. Charley snoozed on a mattress while Spike showed Sarah his *iPod*. She couldn't stop looking at this amazing object. It was like nothing she had ever seen before! When Spike put the earphones into her ears and pressed the play button, it was as though she was hearing the most beautiful thing in the world!

Spike watched her for a while, happy that he was at least able to take her mind off the day's events then, he too, settled down on the mattress and fell asleep.

\*

It must have been at least an hour later when Spike awoke to find Sarah shaking him vigorously by the arm.

"Spike!" she cried. "There's something wrong with Charley!"

"What?"

Spike floundered around in the semi-darkness until he found Charley. She was still lying on the mattress, but now her whole body was shaking!

"What is it, Charles?" he asked, already fearing the worst.

Charley looked up at him with terrified eyes, but seemed unable to reply.

Something outside in the night sky caught Spike's attention. At first he couldn't quite make out what it was because of the candlelight reflecting in the window, but then he saw it more clearly. Now he couldn't *believe* what he was looking at!

Staring directly through the window at them were two enormous German soldiers, sitting on a motorbike and sidecar - which was *hovering in mid-air*!

Chapter 11

# Heil Hitler!

Within hours of leaving Bordeaux Station the train had already crossed the border into Germany and was now speeding south towards its destination - the City of Nuremberg.

From listening to the conversations around him, Danny had picked up that they would be arriving in Nuremberg in a few hours and going directly to the Nazi Party rally. There was a real buzz of excitement on the train, especially when anyone mentioned the guest of honour at the rally, Adolf Hitler (whom they called *the Fuhrer*, meaning 'The Leader'). Every now and again a group on the train would start to sing a song (usually praising the Fuhrer or Germany or both!) and everyone in the carriage would join in.

Once the train had got underway the brothers had given Danny more space (after all, they were fairly certain he wasn't going to try and dive out of a speeding train!). Nevertheless, Danny still felt he was being watched by the older brother (whose name, he had discovered, was Herman) and this was especially true when his sister, the blonde girl with the pigtails, came over and sat beside him.

"Why the long face?" she asked.

Danny ignored her and continued to look out of the window. The girl tried again.

"Would you like a drink of something? Some tea?"

Danny shook his head.

"What's your name?"

Danny didn't reply.

"My name is Trudy," she said cheerfully.

Now she noticed Herman looking over in their direction and saw how Danny scowled back at him. There was clearly no love lost between them.

"Don't worry about him," Trudy said, smiling. "I don't! He thinks he's the greatest German our nation has ever known! Apart from the Fuhrer, of course!" Trudy laughed then she became a bit more serious. "After the rally he is going to join the army. All these boys are."

Danny looked over at Herman and the other young boys in the carriage. They all looked much too young to join the army. Trudy continued her chatter.

"You know, we really are very honoured to be going to see the Fuhrer - to hear him speak! He may even come and shake our hands. It really is a once-in-a-lifetime opportunity."

Danny was wondering how long she would continue this one-way conversation when he noticed two other girls coming over. They were holding something between them and looking very excited.

"Here it is!" Trudy suddenly announced with a bright smile.

Now Danny saw what the girls were holding. It was a Hitler Youth uniform.

"*Your* uniform!" Trudy said to Danny, as if he was receiving the world's greatest gift. "Put it on!"

"*Nein danke*," said Danny, shaking his head firmly.

"Oh, come on!" pleaded Trudy. "You'll have to wear it for the rally!"

"Well, then I guess I won't be going to the rally!" Danny replied, folding his arms and looking out of the window.

Herman and his mates were also gathering around now.

"Our friend is not acting like a very good German is he?" said Herman, with a sneer.

Quick as a flash, Herman lunged for Danny's rucksack and, before Danny could stop him, he had it in his grasp. Danny flew after it, but Herman quickly tossed it across the carriage to another boy. Again, Danny went after it, but now it was thrown to a boy standing beside an open window, and, when Danny took a step towards him, he suddenly held the rucksack out of the window!

Danny froze on the spot. All he could think about was Uncle Morty's journal inside that rucksack. Losing that journal would mean losing all hope of saving his father and sister.

The boy at the window made as if he was going to drop it.

"*No!*" shouted Danny, and all the boys in the carriage laughed.

"Well then, maybe it's time to put on your uniform?" Herman crowed. "We would hate for you to lose your precious rucksack!"

Danny knew he had no choice. He snatched the uniform from the girls and went into the restroom to change. He looked at himself in the mirror. What would Spike and Charley say if they could see him now? He wondered how they were doing; *what* they were doing. He knew they would probably be trying to find Michelle again; trying to persuade her and Mortimer to stay away from the harbour. This meant that he would have to get back to Bordeaux with the journal before eight o'clock the following night. The consequences of the Change happening before he managed to give the journal to Mortimer were too horrible to even think about!

\*

While Danny was in the restroom changing, Herman had taken his rucksack into a quiet corner and was now starting to rummage through it. Danny had reacted so violently to having it taken away that Herman just *had* to see what was so important inside. A few of his mates also came over to take a look, but he shooed them away.

The first thing Herman pulled out was a small, sleek white box with a wire leading from it and two little bobbles on the end. He had no idea what this strange thing was and even the label on it didn't help him - there was a picture of an apple and underneath it said *iPod*.

Herman put this strange item back and continued to dig around. The next thing he pulled out was a toothbrush. It was multicoloured and all strange and bendy! He had never seen a toothbrush like it before! He studied it for a few moments then threw it back into the bag as well.

Now Herman pulled out a book. He opened it up and discovered that it was some sort of handwritten journal. Every page was crammed with spidery writing, detailed diagrams and mathematical formulae. He couldn't understand a word of it because it was all written in English!

*English!* Why would this German-speaking boy, who was supposedly living in France, be carrying around a book that was written in *English*? Herman's suspicions were growing by the second. From now on he would have to keep an even closer eye on him.

He then noticed one thing in the book that he *could* understand. Written on the inside front cover it said, '*For Daniel*'.

At that moment, a cheer went up at the other end of the carriage and Herman saw that it was for Danny, who had just emerged from the restroom in his uniform. He stuffed the book back into the rucksack and went over to join the group that had already gathered around the boy.

Danny felt like a complete dork! He couldn't remember ever wearing what he had on now - a shirt with long sleeves buttoned at the wrist, long baggy shorts held up by a leather belt and long socks with boots! To make matters worse, Trudy and the other girls were adding other bits and pieces. Trudy put a scarf around his neck and knotted it neatly in the front, one of the other girls wrapped a swastika armband around his upper arm and a third girl tried to start combing his hair into a side parting. That's when Danny snapped!

"Please!" he said sharply, shaking his head - and, thankfully, the girl with the comb backed off.

Danny now saw Herman pushing his way through to the front and the first thing he noticed was the rucksack over his shoulder. Herman came right up close to him and made a big show of inspecting his uniform. He straightened Danny's scarf (which Danny found extremely irritating!) then nodded his approval.

"My rucksack, please," said Danny.

"Don't worry, Daniel," Herman said with a smile. "It is 'Daniel' isn't it?" he asked, enjoying the look of surprise on Danny's face.

As hard as Danny tried he could not help blinking a few times. His mind was suddenly rushing. *How did Herman know his name? The journal? He must have been looking through the journal!*

Herman gave Danny a few moments to digest this then he took the rucksack off his shoulder and tossed it into the waiting hands of his brother, who was standing nearby.

Danny sighed. *Did Herman still want to play this game?*

Herman was now nodding towards his brother.

"Claus is our Master of Stores," he said. "He looks after everyone's personal belongings. He will take good care of your precious bag."

Before Danny could protest, Trudy also joined in.

"We can't carry our own bags at the rally. Not when we have things like flags and drums to carry. Don't worry, it will be well looked after, won't it, Claus?"

Claus nodded and took the rucksack over to a large metal trunk, which he unlocked, tossed the rucksack inside and locked again. Meanwhile, Trudy was asking Herman something.

"Drum, trumpet or flag?" she asked, looking over at Daniel.

Herman grinned.

"I don't think our friend can be trusted with a drum or a trumpet just yet!" he said, and everybody laughed. "I think perhaps some lessons in carrying a flag are in order."

Now, as people ran off to get flags, Herman and his mates sat back to enjoy the show.

It was the 'Danny Marching with a Flag Show'. For the next half an hour, Herman and the others were treated to the sight of Danny marching up and down the aisle with a large flag held out in front of him. Every time he held it incorrectly Herman or one of the instructors would bark an order and Danny would have to lift the flag, tilt it, or straighten it.

As Danny marched back and forth, obeying the orders like a good soldier, Herman and his friends must have thought he had been broken and would now go along with everything they said without question or complaint. How wrong they were! The only reason Danny was playing along now was because he knew this wasn't the right time to resist or rebel, but he also knew that, sooner or later, that time would come, and when it did, he swore he was going to make Herman pay for what he was doing - and pay *hard*!

Once Herman was satisfied that Danny had mastered the art of carrying the flag he shouted to those instructing him.

"And now the salute!"

For this 'lesson' Herman and his friends also stood up and snapped to attention. Following Herman's lead, everyone in the carriage did the straight-arm Nazi salute and all roared in unison:

"*Sieg Heil!*"

The only person who didn't do the salute was Danny. Herman noticed this and headed across towards him. With salutes and 'Sieg Heils' going on all around them, he now leaned close to Danny and spoke in his ear.

"Daniel, if you *ever* want to see your rucksack again - and, oh yes, that special book of yours, I would strongly suggest you do as you are told."

Danny hesitated for a moment then he too started to salute.

He did it silently at first, but gradually joined in with all those around him.

"Sieg Heil! Sieg Heil! Sieg Heil!"

\*

As they disembarked from the train at Nuremberg Station, Danny was given his flag and told to go and wait with the group of flag bearers.

Herman strutted around the platform issuing orders.

"Drummers, collect your drums over there! Trumpet players over here! Flag bearers get lined up! Single file!"

When Herman was satisfied that everyone was ready he gave the order to march, and the entire Hitler Youth brigade moved off down the platform. Danny marched along with the other flag bearers, trying his best not to kick the feet of the boy in front of him. At one point he heard someone say his name and when he looked across he saw Trudy and some of her friends walking along beside them. He had to do a double take because the girls were now wearing pretty dresses and had Alice bands made from flowers in their hair. They were also carrying baskets of flowers.

The sight of the girls made Danny lose his concentration for a second and he clipped the foot of the boy in front of him, nearly sending him sprawling.

"Hey, watch it!" the boy in front snapped at Danny.

"Sorry!" said Danny.

He could hear the girls giggling beside him, but he decided to keep his eyes to the front and concentrate on his marching.

\*

Outside the station, in the fading evening light, they climbed aboard waiting trucks and rumbled out onto the streets of Nuremberg.

As they travelled through the city Danny was surprised to see large areas that had been completely destroyed, obviously by English and American bombing raids. In one area it looked like a whole suburb had been reduced to rubble. They could see the people picking through the ruins of their homes.

He noticed how the sight of these desperate people was influencing the mood on the truck. Trudy and her girlfriends gazed on with sadness and sympathy, while Herman and his mates became increasingly angry and started to mutter bitterly about how they would make the British and Americans pay!

Danny was also affected by what he saw. Yes, the Germans were supposed to be the enemy, but look how the lives of these ordinary people had been ruined. Ruined because a madman like Hitler decided that Germany should be the biggest and greatest nation in Europe! To achieve this goal he had ordered his armies to invade their neighbouring countries, one after the other. As Danny could now see for himself, the only thing that was really being achieved was the destruction of Germany and its people.

*

They knew they had reached their destination when they began to pass line after line of parked trucks. They must have passed a couple of hundred before they parked. Danny was learning very quickly about the enormous scale of this event!

As soon as the truck stopped they all began to clamber off. From the dullness of the parking area, they began to march towards a great glowing light. Danny had half-expected to be going into a stadium, but he couldn't see any towering grandstands up ahead. In fact, with all the swishing flags he couldn't see much at all!

Minutes later they reached the venue and Danny was suddenly treated to one of the most mind-blowing sights he had ever seen!

They had arrived at the top of a vast cascade of steps that led down onto an enormous parade ground. There stood *hundreds of thousands of people* - not all crowded in like people at a music concert, but lined up with military precision! There were different groups wearing different uniforms - soldiers in grey, Nazi storm troopers in brown - and each group stood in its own block with its own flag bearers.

Herman was shown where they should position themselves and he signalled to his brigade to follow him down the steps. Once they reached the bottom they jostled into position again and began the march down the long centre aisle, through the rows and rows of uniforms. They were marching towards a raised podium at the front, behind which hung three giant swastika banners. Danny kept expecting them to be stopped and positioned along the way, but they kept on going - all the way to the front!

At the front, two curved flights of steps led up to the podium and it was on these that Herman now ordered Danny and the other flag bearers to position themselves. Herman followed them up, making sure each flag bearer was positioned correctly. When he got to Danny he leaned close and whispered:

"You are honoured! Now face the front!"

Danny turned to face the front and almost gasped at the sight. Now the thousands of people in uniform were *facing* him and, because of his elevated position, he knew he must be visible to everyone! Down below, he could see that the Hitler Youth drummers and trumpeters had taken up positions alongside a mass of other musicians stretching right across the front of the parade. He could also see Trudy and the other flower girls standing to one side near the bottom of the steps. Once Herman had finished his inspection he strutted self-importantly back down the steps and took up his position beside the others.

Now, as they waited, Danny was struck by just how still and silent this mass of people was. There was barely a movement or sound.

Then something did start to happen. The drummers and trumpeters were ordered to make themselves ready. Danny couldn't see what was going on up on the podium behind him, but he could tell by the growing excitement in everyone's expressions

that something was definitely about to happen.

A command was given and suddenly over one thousand drums and trumpets erupted, filling the night air with a deafening fanfare. At that precise moment, over one hundred giant floodlights, positioned all around the ground, were suddenly turned on. The effect was amazing! It was as if the entire arena was suddenly surrounded by these giant glowing pillars of light.

A voice came booming over the loudspeakers. At first Danny thought it must be Hitler himself, but then he realised it was just somebody introducing the Fuhrer. The speaker whipped up the crowd by singing the praises of their 'most beloved Fuhrer', calling him 'the saviour of Germany' and 'the greatest German ever'! To conclude, he suddenly shouted:

"*Heil Hitler!*"

In response to this, the entire parade ground roared.

"Heil Hitler! Heil Hitler! Heil Hitler!"

Each 'Heil Hitler!' was accompanied by two hundred thousand

# Heil Hitler!

arms thrust forwards together in salute.

Now Danny knew that Hitler must have appeared on the podium because suddenly the whole crowd erupted into wild cheers and rapturous applause. This went on for a couple of minutes then Hitler must have asked for silence because it suddenly died down and, seconds later, you could have heard a pin drop!

Then another voice came crackling over the speakers and Danny knew instantly that this was the Fuhrer. He started quietly, speaking slowly and deliberately in a deep, rasping voice - but as the speech continued, his voice grew louder and more passionate. He spoke of Germany, saying it was destined to rule over Europe in what he called 'the New Order'. He spoke of victory over the enemy, and now the anger grew in his voice as he mentioned the British, the Americans and the Russians.

"They *will* be defeated! Victory is *ours!*" he roared, and the crowd once again burst into spontaneous applause.

As Hitler's voice continued to boom out through the loudspeakers Danny looked down at the people below. They were spellbound, hanging on his every word. He noticed how Herman's eyes were gleaming, particularly when Hitler began to speak about Germany's youth.

"The weak must be chiselled away!" Hitler demanded. "I want young men and women who can suffer pain! A young German must be as swift as a greyhound, as tough as leather and as hard as Krupp's steel!"

Herman looked as though these words were being directed at him alone. His chest swelled with pride and there were tears in his eyes.

Hitler built his speech up to a dramatic climax, demanding that all Germans must be willing to give everything ('even their lives'!) for their nation. As if to show their Fuhrer they were willing to do this, the entire crowd erupted once again into salutes and a thunderous roar of:

"Sieg Heil! Sieg Heil! Sieg Heil!"

Now Danny could sense an even *greater* excitement growing amongst Trudy and the other girls at the bottom of the steps. He dared not turn around to look, but it seemed as if they were now gathering at the bottom to meet someone. He heard voices and footsteps coming down the steps behind him and suddenly a group of men came past so close that they brushed against his flag. In the group were several bulky-looking men who could have been army generals, but right in the middle of them all was a much smaller man whom Danny knew had to be Adolf Hitler.

When Hitler and his entourage reached the bottom of the steps Trudy and the other girls came forwards and presented him with flowers. Danny could see the complete adoration on their faces as they did this. This was undoubtedly the greatest moment of their lives!

As he watched, Danny had to remind himself that this man with the slicked down hair and the big moustache, who was now smiling and chatting to all the youngsters as if he was their favourite uncle, was actually one of the greatest monsters the world has ever known.

\*

By the time the rally had finished it was getting late. Danny and the Hitler Youth brigade were informed that they would be spending the night at an army barracks. This was bad news for Danny. He knew he had to make his bid to escape that night and he didn't like the thought of having soldiers all over the place. He also knew there was no time for delay. He only had tomorrow to find Michelle and Mortimer, and he still had to get all the way back to France!

There was a festive atmosphere at the army barracks when they arrived. It seemed as if everyone was in high spirits after the rally and a lot of the soldiers had been given the night off to relax. Many of them were now gathered in a large courtyard situated in the middle of the barracks. Food was being served and they had been given some beer, so there was plenty of talk and laughter.

Danny and the others were shown to a long dormitory-like room where they were told they would be sleeping. They were also invited to go out into the courtyard for something to eat and drink.

As the others began to file out into the courtyard Danny pretended to be busy tying up his flag. What he was really doing was trying to delay going out, so that he could see where Claus put the trunk containing their personal belongings.

He was undoing and retying his flag for the third time when Trudy came over. "Come on! Let's go and eat!" she said. "Aren't you starving?"

Danny nodded.

"I'll be out shortly."

Trudy was insistent.

"Come on, you can do that later."

Danny could tell that she wasn't leaving without him, so he put his flag to one side. He followed her to the door and was just about to go out into the courtyard when Claus and his mate carried the trunk in and slid it under a bed. Now Danny knew where to find the trunk. The next more worrying problem was going to be trying to get the keys that he knew lived in Claus' pocket!

It was a little intimidating walking out into a party of German soldiers. They went over and collected a plate of food then found a relatively quiet place to sit and eat. Only now did Danny realise how starving he was! He wolfed down his food and was finished before Trudy had had more than a couple of mouthfuls.

"I guess you *were* hungry!" She smiled. "I'm not surprised. What a day! I still can't believe I actually met our Fuhrer! He had such kind eyes. Do you know what he said to me?"

Danny was only half-listening. He had noticed Claus going over to collect his food.

"He said, 'Thank you, my angel'!" Trudy looked at Daniel to make sure he was looking suitably impressed. "That's what he called me - 'my angel'!"

"Really?" said Danny, battling to sound enthusiastic.

Claus was busy eating, and he could now also see Herman trying his best to mingle with the soldiers. Trudy shook her head at the sight of her brother.

"Look at him. He just *cannot wait* to be a soldier!"

Another door opened nearby and the sound of more men enjoying themselves spilled out into the courtyard. Through the open door Danny could see a lot more uniforms inside.

"Officers," said Trudy. "That must be the Officers' Mess."

One of these officers came out into the courtyard. He strolled over towards the soldiers and started to mingle with them. When the soldiers saw who it was, many of them jumped to their feet, but the officer told them to relax and sit.

Now Trudy noticed the excited expression on Herman's face. He was looking over at her and nodding towards the officer, which made her take another look - then she too started to get excited.

"Oh, my goodness," she said. "That's Commander Skorzeny!" She looked at Danny and was amazed to see his blank expression. "You know, *Commander Skorzeny*?" she repeated.

Danny could only shake his head and shrug.

"The war hero? The Fuhrer's favourite commando?"

"Oh, right!" Danny said, suddenly thinking that he'd better pretend to have heard of him.

He looked at the officer again - the respect he commanded from the soldiers was obvious and, as for Herman, he looked like he was ready to bend down and kiss his boots!

Now Danny's attention shifted suddenly because he noticed Claus heading back towards the barrack room. Hopefully he was off to take a shower and go to bed. Danny knew this could be his opportunity.

"I think I'm going to call it a night," said Danny, feigning a yawn. "Really tired!"

"OK," said Trudy. "Goodnight. Sleep well."

At that moment Danny wondered if he would ever see Trudy again. He had decided that she was actually a good person - a good person caught up in an evil situation that she could not possibly understand. He gave her a friendly smile and wished her goodnight.

*

Inside the barrack room Claus did not go and shower immediately. Luckily for Danny most of the Youth were still outside, but there was one other boy hanging around, who chatted with Claus for a bit. This meant that Danny had to try and look busy again, but thankfully it wasn't for long because Claus soon grabbed a towel and headed for the shower room. Danny gave it a few moments then he too made his way to the showers.

When Danny entered the shower room Claus had just stepped into one of the shower cubicles. The door swung closed behind him and Danny heard the shower being turned on. He glanced around and immediately laid eyes on what he was looking for - Claus' clothes dumped in a pile on a bench.

Danny went straight over to the clothes and was just about to delve into a jacket pocket when suddenly the door from the barrack room opened and the other boy came in. Danny had to quickly pretend that he was undressing. He started to take his shirt off while the other boy went to a basin and began brushing his teeth.

Danny undressed as slowly as he could, but still the boy at the basin kept brushing and brushing! If he carried on much longer Claus was going to finish his shower! Eventually, with Danny down to just a towel around his waist, the boy finally finished and left.

There was no time to waste. Danny returned to the clothes on the bench and had just started searching the pockets when he suddenly heard Claus' voice behind him!

"Hey, can you pass me some soap please?"

Danny turned and was relieved to see that Claus had only opened the door enough to put his hand out. Danny quickly grabbed a bar of soap off the basin and put it into Claus' hand.

"Thanks," said Claus, and the hand disappeared again.

Danny skidded back over to the pile of clothes and started to rummage through Claus' jacket pockets again. In the second pocket he found the keys. He knew he was running out of time - Claus would not be in the shower for much longer. With only his towel wrapped around him, Danny rushed out of the shower room - and stepped right into the path of Trudy!

"Hi!" blinked Trudy, clearly surprised by Danny's sudden appearance in just his towel.

"Hi," said Danny, his eyes large.

There was now an awkward pause until Trudy eventually spoke.

"I thought I would also go to bed," she said.

"Oh, right," Danny said, nodding.

He could feel the cold metallic keys digging into his hand.

"So..." said Trudy. "We'll see you tomorrow then? Goodnight."

"Goodnight," Danny replied.

He waited for her to leave the barrack room then, after a quick check to make sure there was no one else around, he went over to Claus' bed and pulled the trunk out from underneath. There were quite a few keys in the bunch, and the faster he tried them in the lock the more uncoordinated he seemed to become! Only on his fourth attempt did the key slide into the lock and it clicked open.

The trunk was packed full of stuff, but Danny's heart leapt

when he saw his rucksack sitting near the top. He took it out, locked the trunk again and pushed it back under the bed. He quickly skidded down to his bed and threw the rucksack under it. Just as he did this a few other boys came in from outside.

Danny walked back to the shower room at a more sedate pace, the keys still concealed in his hand. He pushed the shower room door open and suddenly froze. Claus was standing near the bench drying himself off.

It took Danny a couple of seconds to recover his poise.

"Hello," he said, as casually as possible. "Forgot my clothes!"

Claus was not interested. He turned away and was just about to start dressing when the shower room door opened and some other boys entered. They were obviously friends of his because they now started chatting about the appearance of Captain Skorzeny outside. Danny hovered near the bench, bent down to pick up his clothes and dropped the keys back into Claus' jacket pocket.

Seconds later, Danny was out of there, striding back towards his bed. When he reached the bed, he sat down and nudged the rucksack a little farther out of sight. He lay back, and it was only now that he allowed himself to breathe a little easier.

More and more of the Youth were now drifting in from outside. Danny knew it would still be a while before everyone settled down. He would have to wait until everyone was fast asleep before he even *considered* making his move. Now he started to feel the weariness of his own body. It would probably be a good idea to get some rest before his next journey began. He closed his eyes and gradually drifted off to sleep.

*

It could not have been more than an hour later when Danny found himself being roused from a very deep sleep. At first he had trouble opening his eyes because the lights in the barrack room were still on, but as his eyes gradually got used to the light he was surprised to find Herman standing beside his bed.

It seemed like Herman had been taunting Danny in his sleep because there was an audience of boys sitting on their beds, watching and giggling at his antics.

"Herman?" Danny said, half-sitting up, still blinking.

"Hello, Daniel!" said Herman. "Do you know who I've been talking to out there?"

Danny was still waking up.

"What?"

"I've been talking to Germany's greatest war hero! Commander Skorzeny!"

"Oh, really?" said Danny.

Only now was he starting to notice all the other boys watching.

"And do you know what I thought while I was talking to Commander Skorzeny? Who, by the way, is fluent in five or six languages - including English! I started wondering if he might be interested in seeing your little book. Your precious little book written in English!"

Danny sat up, suddenly *very* awake!

"Why do you think he'd be interested in my book, Herman? It's not that interesting, I promise!"

"There are also those other strange things in your bag!" Herman continued. "Maybe he'd like to see those as well?"

"It's just personal stuff, Herman!" Danny protested. "Didn't anyone ever tell you to keep your nose out of other people's belongings?"

The fact that Danny was getting so riled made Herman chuckle.

"You know what? I wouldn't mind taking another look at that stuff!" He shouted over to Claus. "Hey, Claus! Bring me Daniel's rucksack, will you?"

Danny couldn't believe this was happening.

"Just leave it alone, Herman! It's none of your business!" he growled.

But Claus was already opening up the trunk...

# Chapter 12

# Spike Air

"Let's move!" Spike shouted. "Sarah, help me get Charley down the stairs!"

As they lifted Charley between them, Sarah was shocked at how badly she was shaking.

"What's wrong with her?" she cried.

Spike didn't answer. He was too busy trying to make sense of what he had just seen through the window. *Had he imagined it? Dreamt it?* As they struggled towards the stairs, he tried to get another look. Now he saw it again - two soldiers hovering around the top of the lighthouse on a motorbike!

"Give us a *break*!" Spike muttered.

At that moment it didn't make sense, but the sight of a flying motorbike accompanied by Charley's trembles was reminding him very much of the future - and that meant trouble! His only thought now was to get them off the top platform!

They reached the top of the stairs and started down. It was so dark that they could hardly see the steps in front of them. Spike knew he had a torch in his rucksack, but this was not the time to start digging around for it.

"Careful," he said, feeling for one step at a time in the darkness.

"There's a storeroom a bit farther down," Sarah said. "We could go there?"

"All right," Spike agreed.

At this stage he didn't have a better idea. Carrying Charley all the way to the bottom in the darkness was not an option.

A couple of flights farther down they came across a door.

"In here," said Sarah, pushing it open.

It was obviously another place that Sarah and her brother

knew well, as she immediately began to feel around on a shelf for candles and matches. She found a single, stubby candle that, once lit, provided enough light for Spike to check out the room. It was a small narrow room, full of shelves, probably where the lighthouse keeper used to store his supplies. Spike was pleased to see that the door could be bolted from the inside. They sat Charley down on the floor.

"You all right, Charles?" Spike asked.

Charley's shakes seemed to be easing a bit, but Spike could see by her terrified expression that she was thinking along the same lines as he was.

"Timecops?" she whispered to Spike.

"I don't know," was Spike's honest reply.

Now Spike noticed a small window at the end of the storeroom. He went over to it and carefully stuck his head out, just enough to get a look up towards the top of the lighthouse. The motorbike was still hovering above, but then he saw something even more disturbing - the motorbike pulled in close and the soldier in the sidecar suddenly hopped out onto the platform!

When Spike pulled his head back in, Charley could see by his expression that things were getting worse.

"What is it?" she asked.

"One of them just got off," Spike muttered.

This terrified Sarah.

"They are German soldiers - looking for *me*!" she gasped.

Spike shook his head.

"On a flying motorbike? I don't think so."

Spike was now pacing around, trying to think. He remembered his rucksack on the floor. He crouched down beside it and began to dig around for his torch. He found the torch, switched it on and was just about to put the rucksack to one side when something else caught his eye. It looked like a small gate remote. Only when he picked it up did he realise that it was one of the *Immobilaser*s they had bought from that dodgy shop in the future.

"Do you think it will work?" Charley asked.

"I don't know," said Spike, studying the item more closely, "but if you've got any better ideas…"

Just then they heard the motorbike going past the window. Spike went over for another look. As he watched, the bike landed in an adjoining field and was then driven back and parked at the base of the lighthouse. The second soldier hopped off and entered the lighthouse through the bottom door.

"*Great!*" cursed Spike.

Now they had one soldier above and another below, and they were sitting in the middle, armed with nothing more than a gate remote thingy! Spike knew they couldn't just sit in the room and wait; the bolt on the door wasn't *that* strong! He started towards the door.

"Where are you going?" Charley asked in amazement.

"Bolt the door behind me," Spike said.

"Spike! Are you mad?" Charley couldn't believe what she was seeing! "You can't go out there!"

Spike already had the door open.

"Bolt the door behind me!" he repeated then he slipped out through the doorway into the darkness.

Outside he stood by the door until he heard the bolt being drawn back across - then he started to make his way cautiously up the stairs. Spike's thinking was that it would be better to test out the *Immobilaser* before the two soldiers reached the storeroom. If it didn't work, at least they wouldn't be sitting ducks.

Now he heard footsteps coming down the stone steps from above. He crouched down on the stairs and waited. As the footsteps got closer he could see the soldier's torchlight beginning to flicker on the walls around him. He made sure the *Immobilaser* was ready, his thumb sitting firmly on the button.

"*Please work!*" he whispered to himself.

The soldier's shadow loomed large on the wall in front of him. It seemed enormous! Now Spike saw *why* it was so enormous. It belonged to a giant! For a moment the sheer size of the figure coming around the corner made Spike hesitate, but when the soldier started reaching for his weapon Spike aimed the *Immobilaser* and pressed the button.

The giant froze on the spot.

Spike couldn't believe it! He waited a few seconds to make sure there really was no movement then he looked down at the *Immobilaser* with new found respect! How could something so small stop someone so big?

"You little beauty!" he whispered.

Spike moved tentatively towards the huge man. Although he was tall for his age this man still towered above him. It was a strange feeling approaching someone who you felt might suddenly come back to life and grab you. Spike leaned over and tried to pull the torch out of the soldier's hand, but the grip was tight and he had to wrestle with it before it came free.

Spike then turned the torch back on the soldier. The sight made him gasp and step back. He had seen this horrifically scarred face before - it had been at the window of TIM as they were leaving the future. His worst fears were confirmed - the Hogs had followed them into the past!

There was also *another Hog* coming up the stairs! Spike went over to the railing and looked down into the stairwell. He could not see any sign of a light down there. The other Hog was obviously coming up without a torch!

Spike was just about to turn off his torch when he noticed the weapon in the first Hog's hand. It looked like some kind of hi-tech gun. He wasn't sure he would ever try and use it himself, but he knew he would feel happier if the weapon was no longer in the Hog's possession. He quickly went back over to the giant and tried to pull the weapon out of his hand, but again the Hog's grip was tight.

"Let go, you big oaf!" Spike muttered as he tried to twist the weapon free.

For just a second, Spike thought he saw the Hog's fingers move to get a better grip. He quickly shone the torch up into the Hog's face again, but found the eyes still staring ahead, unblinking.

Spike decided to give the weapon one more try. This time he tugged really hard on it and it was just starting to come free... when suddenly the Hog's hand grabbed at it again! Spike leapt back and shone the torch up into the Hog's face again. To his horror, the giant blinked!

He backed away, quickly feeling around in his pockets for the *Immobilaser*. He tried his jacket pocket then his trousers - w*here had he put the stupid thing?* All the time he could see the Hog slowly coming back to life!

At last he found it in his top pocket. He pulled it out, but was shocked to see the Hog was now coming towards him! He tripped over backwards and the torch went clattering across the stone floor. He pointed the *Immobilaser* up at the towering figure and pressed the button. To his great relief the Hog froze again, but the question now was, *for how long*?

Spike knew the other Hog must have heard the noise and seen the flashing torch. He had to move, and he decided it would be easier to surprise the Hog if he went down to meet him.

Spike slowly started down the steps. He had to let his eyes get used to the dark again. He reached the landing with the door to the storeroom and there was still no sign of the other Hog. He silently went past the doorway and continued down the steps, all the time straining his eyes and ears for any sign of movement.

A little farther down, just as he was starting to wonder where on earth the other Hog could be, he heard something that sounded like somebody breathing. He stopped and sat down slowly on a step. He waited... listened. Yes, it was the sound of breathing -

and it was gradually getting closer. Spike held the *Immobilaser* out in front of him, screwing up his eyes to try and see in the darkness.

Moments later a dark shape came around the corner. Spike took aim and pressed the *Immobilaser* button.

Nothing happened.

He pressed it again, but still the dark figure kept coming! He tried a third time - now the figure froze. Spike allowed himself to breathe again. One thing was becoming clear - the strength of the *Immobilaser* was disappearing at a rapid rate! More shoddy products from Frankie and Glide!

Now Spike knew he had to *really* move! The first thing he had to do was collect the girls! He turned to go back up, but hadn't even taken a step when he heard heavy footsteps coming down the steps again. The other Hog was on his way down!

With the *Immobilaser* seemingly about to die, Spike knew he had no choice but to retreat down the steps. This meant having to push past the enormous frame of the second Hog, which was not a pleasant experience. He slid past, pushing himself up against the wall, and almost choked as he got a whiff of what smelled like rotting teeth!

As soon as he was clear, Spike took off down the steps.

\*

When Spider Neck came bounding around the corner he almost ran straight into Tooth Rot (who was just coming to his senses again). The two Hogs looked at each other for a few seconds and some sort of wordless communication seemed to pass between them.

Next thing, Spider Neck had turned around and was heading back up to look for the others, while Tooth Rot had taken off down the steps after Spike.

\*

Inside the storeroom, Charley and Sarah sat huddled together in a corner. They had heard all sorts of noises outside, but had no idea what was going on.

Charley was beginning to fear the worst - wondering if she would ever see Spike again. She couldn't believe how incredibly brave he had been! Her thoughts were suddenly interrupted by a nudge in the ribs. Sarah was staring at the door.

"Look!" she whispered.

Charley looked - and the sight made the hairs on the back of her neck stand up!

The handle of the storeroom door was slowly moving down.

\*

On the other side of the door Spider Neck was trying the door handle. When he found it locked he put his ear up against the door to listen for any sounds. At first he heard nothing, but as he listened more intently he started to hear a sound that made him grin. It was the sound of whispering voices!

Spider Neck backed up from the door and unleashed a vicious kick. The door splintered and cracked in various places, but the bolt held firm. Annoyed by this, he backed up farther and now charged at the door, flinging himself against it. The door flew off its hinges and crashed to the floor with him on top of it!

In one slick movement Spider Neck rolled onto his back with his weapon at the ready. He was expecting to see someone with one of those annoying *Immobilasers*, but surprisingly there was no one there. He quickly swung around to see who was behind him, but again there was no one. The Hog got to his feet and looked around, confused. The room appeared to be empty!

Spider Neck then noticed the open window. He quickly strode over to it and peered out. The fact that it was a sheer five-storey drop down to the ground below did not make it a likely escape route. He was just about to pull his head back in when he saw something down at the foot of the lighthouse. It was the skinny boy who had *immobilasered* him earlier. He was busy trying to start their motorbike!

\*

Spider Neck's sighting of Spike could not have come at a better time for Charley. If the Hog had put his head farther out and looked up above the window he would have seen the two girls clinging to the outside of the lighthouse.

Although Charley hadn't tried out the *Go Ape!* program since they had tested it at the shop she had known it was their only hope of escape. Sarah thought Charley had gone completely mad when she told her she was going to climb out of the window. When she then suggested that Sarah climb out after her and clamber onto her back, she *really* thought Charley had lost her mind!

However, with the first door-splintering kick, there was suddenly no time for any argument or discussion. At that stage Charley was already halfway out through the window, trying not to think about the terrifying drop below as she tested whether she could grip on to the brickwork with her fingertips.

"Get on my back! *Now*!" she snapped.

Sarah had obeyed - only because she knew the German soldiers were about to come through the doorway to get her! She held on to Charley's shoulders and was amazed when Charley began to pull herself up the wall above the window.

That's when the door had come crashing in.

\*

A few minutes earlier Spike had flown out through the doorway at the bottom of the lighthouse and almost collided with the Hog's motorbike. Up until that moment he hadn't even considered the idea of using the bike, but it then occurred to him that this machine might provide his one and only chance of rescuing the girls. Except that this would mean not only riding the bike, but actually trying to *fly it* as well!

Spike hovered around the machine, not sure what to do, knowing a Hog was probably already on his way down the stairs after him. He glanced up at the lighthouse and saw something way up high above the storeroom window. It took him a couple of seconds to realise that he was looking at Charley and Sarah clinging to the outside of the building!

It was in that heart-stopping moment that Spike knew he would have to give the motorbike a try!

He had ridden a motorbike before, so he managed to kick-start the bike into life. He remembered how important it was to let the clutch out slowly to ensure a smooth take-off - and this is exactly what he was trying to do when suddenly the second Hog came bursting out of the lighthouse! Spike got such a fright that he let go of the clutch all together and the bike took off like a greyhound after a rabbit!

As he whizzed across the field Spike was desperately trying to find the brakes, which meant he didn't see the hedge looming up very quickly in front of him! He ploughed straight through it, emerging with his glasses askew and bits of hedge stuck in his hair. But it was only when he had his glasses back on straight that he saw a much greater danger up ahead - the edge of the cliff!

Suddenly he abandoned his search for the brakes and tried to look for something to make the bike take-off. There was a red button blinking on the handlebars - this surely had to be it. With the cliff edge fast approaching he pressed the red button.

Nothing happened!

"Come on, you stupid piece of junk!" Spike roared, as he frantically looked for anything else that might put the bike into flight mode.

All he could see was the red button. He tried it again - still nothing happened!

They say that before you die your entire life flashes before your eyes. At that moment the only thing flashing before Spike's eyes (apart from the bit of hedge still stuck in his hair) was the image of Charley and Sarah still clinging to the outside of the lighthouse.

The bike arrived at the cliff and reared up over the edge.

"*Nooooooooooo!*" Spike screamed as the bike launched into the darkness.

What he couldn't see (because his eyes were firmly shut!) was that the bike was not actually descending - it was flying level! It took a few moments before he opened his eyes and realised what was happening. Now he discovered that he could make the bike climb or descend by pulling back or pushing forwards on the handlebars.

From feeling like he was plummeting to a nasty death to suddenly be *flying* was an incredible sensation!

"*Whoooohoooo!*" he yelled triumphantly.

Then he glanced down and saw the rocks and the churning white surf *way down below*! He quickly looked up again.

"Looking down - not a good idea!" he shouted to himself.

It was only after he had taken a few deep breaths and calmed himself down a bit that Spike felt ready to face his next big challenge - *how to turn the bike around*!

\*

"Charley, are you OK?" Sarah asked.

Charley didn't reply. There were tears rolling down her cheeks from the effort it was taking to haul herself and Sarah up the sheer wall. Sarah still couldn't believe that Charley was managing to pull them both up! Now, as the platform got nearer, it seemed as though Charley's strength was fading fast and every 'pull-up' was requiring monumental effort!

Sarah noticed that one of the metal struts supporting the platform at the top of the lighthouse was not too far above their heads. She knew if she could grab hold of this it would be a great help to Charley. She stretched her one arm up as far as she could, but the strut was still just out of reach.

"Just a little bit more, Charley!" she urged.

Charley shook her head. She had not one ounce of energy left!

Sarah heard something. It sounded like a motorbike. She looked over her shoulder and saw the soldier's flying motorbike approaching. Her first reaction was to panic – but then she saw who was on the bike!

"It's Spike!" she cried.

Charley slowly lifted her head.

"*What?*"

"It's Spike. He's... he's flying the bike!"

Charley was unable to turn around to look, but this news seemed to give her renewed hope.

"All right. Are you ready to grab that thing?" she said to Sarah.

"I am," Sarah replied.

Charley gritted her teeth – then with one last concerted effort she pulled herself up just a few more bricks. It was enough for Sarah to grab hold of the strut. With Sarah's weight off her back Charley suddenly felt as light and nimble as a monkey again.

"Just hold on there!" she said as she started to climb the last bit.

The platform jutted out over their heads, which required a bit of upside-down climbing.

In the meantime Sarah was left alone, dangling high above the ground, determined not to look down!

Charley pulled herself up onto the platform and climbed over the railings. Lying flat on the platform, she stretched an arm back down through the railings towards Sarah.

"Sarah! Grab hold of my hand!" she shouted.

For Sarah, who was gripping tightly onto the strut with both hands, this was a terrifying thought because it meant she would have to let go with one hand!

"Come on, Sarah!" Charley shouted again.

Now Charley saw something else that set off the alarm bells! The two soldiers were standing at the bottom of the lighthouse, staring up at them! It was as if they had just spotted the girls because they now suddenly both ducked into the lighthouse.

Charley knew they were on their way up!

"Grab hold of my hand *now*!" she screamed at Sarah.

Sarah took a deep breath, let go of the strut with one hand and grabbed hold of Charley's hand. Sarah's sudden unexpected weight pulled Charley up against the railings. It was a strain just to hold on to her! How on earth was she ever going to manage to pull her up?

\*

As Spike approached the lighthouse he could see that Charley was having a problem holding on to Sarah, but he had a problem of his own. He could slow the bike down, but he hadn't worked out how to stop it!

"Hold on there, Charles!" he shouted.

"I can't!" Charley shouted back at him. "Spike! Hurry, *please*!"

Spike pulled on the brakes as hard as he could, but the bike still kept on going.

"What are you doing?" shouted Charley.

"Er… trying to stop this thing," Spike muttered.

"Spike, those soldiers are on their way up!" screamed Charley.

Sarah was also starting to panic.

"Please, don't let me go," she pleaded.

Given the circumstances, Spike knew there was only one thing he could do.

"Charles, I'm going to bring the sidecar under Sarah," he shouted. "When the sidecar is in position I need you to let her go."

"*What*?" Charley screamed. She didn't like the sound of that plan at all! "Can't you just stop the thing?"

"No, Charles, I can't!" Spike shouted back. "*That's* the problem!"

Sarah was now looking really terrified and, to make matters worse, she could feel her hands were starting to slip.

"Just hurry please," she pleaded.

There was no more time for debate. Spike pushed on the handlebars and the bike descended. When he was at a level just below that of Sarah he levelled the bike out and steered it towards her.

"Now listen," he shouted. "As I come underneath I will shout 'now!' and that's when you must let go! Both of you at the same time! All right, Sarah?"

Sarah nodded. She was beyond words. Her hands were now slipping so much that she had to keep readjusting her grip.

Spike aimed the bike so that the sidecar would pass directly under Sarah, trying to slow it down as much as he could.

"OK, hold it... hold it... wait for my signal." As the bike passed beneath them, Spike roared, "*Now!*"

Charley let go first, but Sarah held on just a fraction longer. This meant she missed the seat in the sidecar and instead landed right on the back and would have toppled back over if Spike hadn't grabbed on to her and pulled her into the seat.

Sarah slumped into the seat like an exhausted rag doll while Spike took the bike up higher to collect Charley.

Charley had already climbed over the railings of the platform and was now waiting impatiently for them. She knew she was going to have to leap into the sidecar as it went past. She watched as Spike reached her level then turned the bike around to face her.

"Come on, Spike," she muttered to herself.

Suddenly she heard something behind her. It was the sound of footsteps rushing up the stairs and now, when she looked back, she could see the light from the soldiers' torches flickering on the walls.

"*Spike, they're coming!*" she screamed.

Spike saw the torch lights as well and knew they only had a few seconds. This meant he had to keep the bike moving at a reasonable speed.

"Ready, Charles?" he shouted, trying to steer the sidecar as close to the platform as possible.

As the bike approached, Charley thought it was going much too fast for her to jump, but she also knew she didn't have a choice. Behind her she heard the soldiers emerging from the stairwell. The motorbike glided closer. She jumped.

Charley even surprised herself with the jump. She had only meant to do a small hop into the sidecar, but she had so much extra spring that her hop turned into a leap - and she very nearly jumped *right over* it! Only by throwing out one hand did she manage to just grab hold of the very back.

For a horrible moment both Spike and Sarah thought she had missed it, but then they saw her hand gripping the back of the sidecar.

"Help me pull her up, Sarah!" Spike shouted, as he tried to lean back to grab her.

Even while dangling from the back, Charley could see the soldiers rushing up to the railing and getting their weapons ready.

"Just *go*, Spike!" she screamed.

Spike hesitated for a second then he too saw the danger.

"Hold on!" he shouted as he pushed forwards on the bike and put it into a dive.

The bike dropped like a stone and Charley, her legs flailing out behind her, had to hold on for dear life! She would never have been able to hold on if it wasn't for the *Go Ape!* program, and once again she thanked her lucky stars for it.

The Hogs opened fire - their weapons barking and belching fire like a couple of demon dogs - and suddenly the cliff edge beside them started to erupt. The force of the explosions rocked the bike and showered them all with debris and dirt. They closed their eyes and braced themselves for a crash landing.

Seconds later they had dropped below the level of the cliff - out of sight of the lighthouse - and were in the clear. Only now was Spike able to level the bike out, so that Sarah could lean back and help pull Charley in beside her.

When they were a safe distance from the lighthouse Spike took the bike back up above the cliffs and, brimming with confidence, he announced his new idea.

"Hey, we could go to Germany on this!" he said.

Charley immediately had her doubts. For one thing they didn't even know which direction Germany was in!

"What are we going to do, Spike - stop and ask directions?" she shouted.

Spike didn't answer. He had just noticed another potential problem - the fuel gauge on the bike was very close to 'empty'.

They also had to think about Sarah. She obviously wouldn't be coming to Germany with them, so they would have to drop her off. In the distance they could now see the lights of Bordeaux, so a decision was made that they would first drop Sarah off then decide what to do next.

This sounded easy in theory... Spike may have grasped the basics of flying the bike, like going up and down, but the machine was still very cumbersome in the air. Doing sharp, sudden turns was not an option. Of course, there was also the nagging question regarding how to actually *stop* the machine!

The first scary moment involved a windmill. It appeared suddenly like a ghost out of the darkness.

"*Spike!*" Charley screamed.

Spike shoved the handlebars to one side with all his might and the windmill's big spinning blades slipped past just a few feet away.

After this scare (and with the town fast approaching) Charley urged Spike to land the bike as quickly as possible. He took it lower and tried to slow it down as much as he could while looking for somewhere to land. They had to keep a sharp lookout for trees and telephone poles and, at one point, he had to pull up quickly to get over a stone bridge.

"Can't you just land this thing?" Charley shouted.

"*Where Charles?*" Spike shouted back.

He was frantically looking for a bit of open ground, but because they were now on the outskirts of town, it was becoming more and more built up.

Suddenly they were coming into town! A church spire went past on one side, a double-storey building on the other. And that's when the engine cut out!

Charley looked at Spike.

"Now what?" she asked.

"Uh, I suspect that's the end of the fuel," Spike replied.

"What?" Charley gasped. "You *are* joking?"

It soon became abundantly clear that he wasn't! The bike was now drifting silently along, losing altitude by the second. They found themselves gliding past people sitting on their balconies. At one point Spike even said 'Bonjour' to a couple, who were sitting there, sipping wine by candlelight. He only wished he could have seen the expressions on their faces!

"Concentrate, Spike!" Charley scolded.

In truth, there was not a whole lot Spike could do. The bike would come down wherever it decided to come down! All he could do was try and avoid any large buildings and hope that at least there would be a stretch of road or something on which to land.

Charley and Sarah braced themselves in the sidecar and prepared for the worst.

Spike saw an open cobbled area up ahead, possibly the town square. It looked mostly empty apart from a large statue in the middle and some tables and chairs outside a café. He knew it was their best chance. There was just one more tiled roof to clear before they got there!

They all held their breath as the roof approached. For a moment there was a horrible grating sound as the underside of the bike scraped across the tiles, but then they were in the clear again - and now the cobbled surface of the square came up fast to meet them. The bike hit the ground hard - so hard that they heard something *crack*! Spike applied the brakes vigorously as they rattled over the cobblestones. The bike was vibrating so badly that bits and pieces were starting to fly off in all directions.

Although they were slowing down it was taking too long and now they could see the statue looming up ahead and, beyond that, the outdoor café. Spike tried to steer the bike away from the statue and that's when there was suddenly an almighty cracking sound as the sidecar and motorbike parted company! The bike continued to turn, but the sidecar carried on straight ahead!

All Spike heard was a long drawn-out scream from both the girls as the sidecar slid off in a shower of sparks, narrowly missing the statue, before ploughing through tables and chairs, and coming to rest in the front window of the café.

By the time Spike had managed to stop the bike there were lights coming on all around the square and he could see people coming to their windows to see what all the commotion was about. He dumped the bike and ran over to where the sidecar sat amidst the carnage. The girls were still sitting in it, too stunned to move, covered with fragments of glass from the shattered window.

"Are you OK?" Spike asked.

Both girls nodded vaguely, but didn't move.

"Good," said Spike, who now noticed people coming out onto the square. "I think it would be a very good idea if we got out of here!"

Spike helped the girls out of the sidecar. He could see they were both still in shock, but he knew he had to get them moving.

"This way," he said, guiding them down a small lane beside the café, where they were able to disappear into the shadows.

\*

It took a while for Sarah to find her bearings, but as soon as she started to recognise places, she took the lead and the others followed her through the narrow streets.

Eventually they came to what looked like a shopfront with a large window. It was too dark to see inside, but written on the window they could just make out the words, *Marchand du Vin* (Wine Merchant).

Sarah's attention, however, was on the windows above the shop where there appeared to be some sort of apartment, also in darkness. She went to a door situated beside the shop and rang the bell.

Almost immediately a light came on upstairs and they could hear the voice of a man complaining about the late hour. A window opened and somebody stuck their head out.

"Who is it?" asked the man, grumpily.

"Uncle Bernard," Sarah replied, trying to keep her voice down so as not to wake the neighbours, "it's Sarah."

"Sarah!" the man exclaimed, sounding amazed.

He quickly ducked his head back in - then they could suddenly hear a very excited woman's voice as well. A few moments later a light came on downstairs and the front door was opened. A large burly man in a dressing gown came out and hugged Sarah warmly then he quickly shepherded them all inside and closed the door.

Only when they were inside, under the light, did they realise how absolutely filthy they were! They were all covered in dirt and the girls still had pieces of glass stuck in their hair. Uncle Bernard was holding Sarah by the shoulders and staring at her, as if still trying to believe it was *really her*! He hugged her again.

Now they could hear the woman coming down the stairs.

"Sarah? Sarah?"

As the woman reached the bottom of the stairs Sarah rushed to greet her.

"Aunt Henrietta!" she cried, flying into her open arms.

Like Uncle Bernard, it appeared that Aunt Henrietta couldn't quite believe what she was seeing! As she hugged and kissed the top of Sarah's head she was also wiping away her tears.

"Oh, Lord, we give you thanks!" said the large, friendly-looking woman.

Of course, this and all the other conversation was now being spoken in French, so once again Spike had that frustratingly familiar feeling of being absolutely clueless!

\*

It wasn't long before they all found themselves sitting around the kitchen table, drinking grape juice and eating cheese. Aunt Henrietta had Sarah on her lap, as if she didn't want to let her go.

"We heard they had put you all on a train!" Aunt Henrietta was saying. "Into cattle trucks! Philistines! Barbarians!" She looked heavenwards. "Forgive me, Lord, but I am certain you feel the same way."

Now Sarah told the story of how Charley and Spike had helped her escape from the train station and also from the German soldiers at the lighthouse.

"I owe my life to my new friends here," she said.

Aunt Henrietta now started to say something to Spike and he could sense that her words were full of gratitude, but beyond that... He had to stop her.

"I'm sorry," he said, "but I can't understand you." He pointed to himself and Charley. "We are English!"

Uncle Bernard and Aunt Henrietta looked shocked. It was probably the first time the English language had ever been spoken in their house!

"*Anglais*?" gasped Aunt Henrietta.

"Engleeesh!" exclaimed Uncle Bernard.

"That's right," nodded Spike then, when confronted by their puzzled expressions, he felt the need to add, "it's a long story."

With Aunt Henrietta looking heavenwards again (what a night of miracles and surprises this was turning out to be!) and Uncle Bernard deciding to pour himself a drink, Charley now gave them both another surprise when she started to speak in French.

"I can speak just a little," she said coyly, "and... there is something we needed to ask you."

Charley hesitated, suddenly feeling shy under the gaze of the French couple. Only when Sarah gave her a nod of encouragement did she continue.

"You see... we have a problem," Charley said. "And Sarah said you might be able to help us."

"Yes." Aunt Henrietta was nodding. "We will try and help you in any way we can."

Charley glanced at Spike then decided to just come straight out with it.

"You see... we really need to get to Nuremberg."

There was silence, punctuated only by the clinking of glass as Uncle Bernard poured himself another drink.

Aunt Henrietta leaned forwards. *Had she heard correctly?*

"Nuremberg? In Germany?" she enquired.

Even Spike understood this.

"Yes, Nuremberg. In Germany."

What Charley and Spike witnessed now was a discussion 'French-style' in which everyone spoke (and even shouted) passionately at the same time. Aunt Henrietta wanted to know why on earth anyone would want to go to Germany. Uncle Bernard made it clear that the whole idea was crazy and quite out of the question! Sarah did her best to try and explain that they were desperately searching for a friend and that it was a matter of life and death!

Even when all the shouting had stopped, they appeared to be no closer to any sort of agreement. Aunt Henrietta suggested that Spike and Charley might like to clean themselves up, which gave her the excuse to show them through to the bathroom and, while giving them soap and towels, she looked at them earnestly.

"You *really* need to go to Nuremberg?"

When Charley replied that it was the most important thing they had ever had to do, she nodded thoughtfully. It appeared she had some sort of plan.

*

Freshly washed and feeling much better, Spike and Charley returned to the kitchen and immediately noticed that Aunt Henrietta and Sarah were looking quietly pleased with themselves. Uncle Bernard, on the other hand, was not looking at all happy.

"Apparently the Good Lord has sent you here for a reason," he said, grumpily.

"You know it's true," said Aunt Henrietta. "With the Lord's help these good people have delivered Sarah to safety. Now it is our turn to do the right thing."

"That might be so," Uncle Bernard replied, draining his glass, "but it won't be the Good Lord driving the truck to Germany, will it?"

With that, he stomped out of the kitchen.

It was only then that Aunt Henrietta and Sarah were able to smile openly and nod to the others.

*

Sarah led Spike and Charley through a side door into the adjoining building. It was a wine warehouse filled with huge wooden vats and piles of wine barrels. There was also a truck parked in there, laden with barrels, and it was here they found Uncle Bernard busy strapping the barrels down.

"Look at this," said Sarah, climbing up onto the back of the truck.

She was drawing their attention to a large barrel lying on its side. Much to Spike and Charley's amazement, she suddenly pulled on one end of the barrel and it opened up like a door on hinges. Inside was a mattress and some blankets. Sarah smiled at their stunned reaction.

"Your transport awaits!" she announced. "This is how my brave Uncle Bernard has saved the lives of hundreds of Jews. You see, every time he delivers French wine to Germany he brings something more important back - people!"

"Never taken anyone the other way!" Uncle Bernard muttered as he pulled hard on a rope and tied it to the side of the truck.

Now Sarah jumped off the truck and, despite Uncle Bernard's

protests, she gave him a big hug.

"That's why we call him Saint Bernard," she said, "because he's just like one of those big dogs who save people in trouble!"

All this talk was making Uncle Bernard look embarrassed and he now gruffly changed the subject.

"Where's that aunt of yours?" he grumbled.

"Here I am!" cried Aunt Henrietta as she came through from the house.

She was carrying a basket full of food and drink, which she now placed in the truck.

"All right, time to go," announced Uncle Bernard. "We need to be at the border before it gets light."

Spike and Charley said goodbye to Aunt Henrietta and thanked her for all her help. She gave them both a big hug and told them she had already asked the Good Lord to please pay special attention to their safety.

It was time to say goodbye to Sarah. Much to Spike's embarrassment, she stood on tiptoe and kissed him on both cheeks then did the same to Charley.

"I will never *ever* forget what you did for me," she said to them both, and they could see the tears welling up in her eyes.

The sight of Sarah's tears caused even Spike to start choking up and he diverted attention away from himself by offering Charley a hand-up onto the truck. He climbed up after her and they both crawled into the barrel.

Once they were inside, Sarah also climbed up to close the barrel. Doing her best to smile, she said goodbye again then said something to Spike in French. The barrel closed and suddenly Spike and Charley found themselves in darkness except for a few spots of light coming through small peepholes in the barrel.

"What did she say?" Spike asked.

"I'll tell you later," Charley replied.

The truck started up and, as it reversed, they could see Aunt

Henrietta and Sarah standing together, waving goodbye.

Once out of the warehouse, Uncle Bernard engaged first gear and the truck rumbled off down the road.

*

It was less than two hours later when Aunt Henrietta and Sarah (who had both fallen asleep on the double bed upstairs) were suddenly awakened by an almighty crash!

They sat up and listened. It was coming from downstairs. Somebody was crashing around down there! Now they heard heavy footsteps coming up the stairs. Aunt Henrietta quickly took Sarah over to the wardrobe and shoved her inside. Before closing the door she put a finger to her lips to say, 'Quiet!'.

Standing nervously in the middle of the room, Aunt Henrietta apologised profusely to the Good Lord for bothering Him *yet again* that night!

"Normally I wouldn't be so demanding," she said. "It's just that I have this strong feeling that I'm going to need your help with whatever is about to come through that door!"

The heavy footsteps came clomping down the passage and stopped outside the bedroom door. Suddenly it was flung open and there stood two of the largest and, it has to be said, the *ugliest*, German soldiers she had ever seen!

Chapter 13

# Combat X

The longer Claus took trying to find Danny's rucksack the more impatient and irritated Herman became.

"Hurry it up!" he snarled. "I'd like it preferably before the war is over!"

Claus had emptied almost the entire contents of the trunk onto the barrack room floor and there was still no sign of Danny's bag. Eventually he looked up and shook his head.

"It's not here," he said.

"What are you talking about?" Herman cried. "You *did* lock it in there, didn't you?"

"Of course I did!" Claus snapped back.

Herman was about to go and take a look for himself, but then something must have occurred to him because he stopped suddenly and turned back towards Danny.

"Unless, of course, somebody else has already been in the trunk?" he said.

Suddenly Danny felt like the entire barrack room was looking at him.

"Let's have a look around, shall we?" said Herman, his eyes still fixed firmly on Danny. "Start by looking under *his* bed!"

It only took a few moments before one of the boys was triumphantly clutching Danny's bag. He tossed it to Herman, who couldn't stop grinning.

"Thinking of going somewhere, were we?" he asked.

Danny didn't reply. At that moment all he felt was utter dejection.

"You know," Herman continued, "the more I think about it the more certain I feel that Commander Skorzeny would be very interested in the contents of this bag. Especially the book written in English!"

For a moment it appeared as though Herman was going to show the captain right away, but then he thought better of it.

"Of course, I won't disturb the captain tonight," he said, returning to his bed, "but tomorrow... tomorrow I will show him everything! Until then, *I* will hold on to this!" He then lay down with Danny's rucksack clutched to his chest. "Now, turn off the lights!" he barked.

\*

Danny waited until he was sure that everyone had gone to sleep then waited another half an hour just to be extra sure! Apart from the odd snore and the occasional groan the barrack room was now dead quiet, which meant that he had to move with the greatest of care. Once he had put on his shoes, he got to his feet and walked slowly and silently down towards Herman's bed.

Herman was sleeping on his side, still clutching the rucksack to his chest. Danny leaned over and pulled gently on the bag, but it wouldn't budge. He took a deep breath (telling himself he had nothing to lose!) and then carefully lifted one of Herman's arms off the rucksack. Herman began to stir, grumbling to himself in his sleep. Thinking he was about to wake up, Danny quickly crouched down beside the bed.

Only when Herman's breathing returned to normal did Danny decide to try again. Once more he set about removing the first arm then he managed to successfully remove the second one as well. He then pulled very carefully and very slowly on the rucksack until it came free. When that happened Herman stirred again and started to mumble something.

Danny froze.

Herman still seemed to be asleep, so Danny backed away slowly from the bed, only turning when he felt it was safe to take off down the barrack room. He turned directly into a dark figure standing in his path. It was Claus.

"Going somewhere?" Claus asked in a voice so loud that Herman sat bolt upright like a zombie being raised from the dead!

Danny took off down the barrack room. He knew there was an exit near the showers.

"*Stop him!*" screamed Claus, and almost immediately two or three boys leapt up to block the exit.

Danny changed direction and started vaulting over beds as he headed for the windows.

Now the lights came on and Herman was on his feet, staggering around, still waking up.

"The windows!" he roared.

Boys were now rising from their beds all over the place and the route to the windows was soon blocked as well. Danny changed direction again, but he was running out of options. There were now boys everywhere and they all looked like they wanted to get their hands on him. Soon he realised he was totally surrounded - and now he saw Herman and Claus pushing their way through to claim their prize.

It was at this moment, as Danny defiantly put the rucksack onto his back (and made a pledge to himself that they would not get it off him without a fight), that an amazing feeling of strength and confidence started to grow inside him. He felt himself becoming more and more aware of everything around him, as if everything had slowed down, enabling him to notice even the minutest of details. Considering his situation, he couldn't believe how incredibly calm he was feeling!

Danny took up a fighter's stance; legs bent and apart, hands raised and at the ready. Of course, when he did this all the boys roared. Herman and Claus, who were both so much bigger than Danny, grinned at each other and moved in for the kill.

Rather than wait for them to arrive, Danny attacked! Before Claus even knew what was happening he had received three flat-handed slaps to the face and a kick in the stomach that sent him hurtling over a bed.

A collective '*ooh*!' went up - a clear sign that every boy there felt that Danny had just signed his own death warrant. If anything, Danny seemed to swell in confidence. He leapt up onto a bed and prepared to meet his next attacker - Herman!

Herman came at him like a mad dog possessed, but Danny felt like he had all the time in the world. He stepped out of the way and, as Herman went flying past, he helped him on his way with a well-timed kick in the backside. Herman went sprawling into a line of lockers.

Danny hadn't felt like this since his experience with the ogres in the *BAM* arena! He knew that his *Combat X* had well and truly kicked in!

Suddenly most of the other boys who were circling Danny did not look that keen on mounting an attack. As Herman picked himself up from amongst the fallen lockers, his eyes bulging, his whole body shaking with rage, he screamed at the top of his voice.

"*Get him*! *What are you waiting for?*"

Several boys (deciding on safety in numbers!) now charged Danny together, but again his speed and clarity of vision enabled him to deal with each boy separately and, one by one, they were all jettisoned in different directions.

All the noise in the barrack room had attracted the attention of the soldiers out in the courtyard, who were now gathering outside the doors and windows to see what all the commotion was about. As Danny repelled yet another attack and sent a few more boys packing, the soldiers roared their approval. This was great entertainment!

Commander Skorzeny had also picked his way through the soldiers to see what was going on and he too seemed intrigued by the sight of this boy dealing so efficiently with everything that

was thrown at him. His lightning-fast reactions and the obvious power behind his punches and kicks were truly remarkable!

The fight now spilled out of the barrack room and into the courtyard. The soldiers pushed back to make room for the combatants, and soon a large circle formed around them. With an audience of soldiers (including his hero, Commander Skorzeny!) Herman was now more determined than ever to get the better of Danny. He muttered something to Claus, and the two large boys now launched a joint assault from opposite directions.

Again Commander Skorzeny was utterly amazed to see how this boy dealt with the attack. As the two large boys came at him from different sides he suddenly leapt above them and slammed their heads together with his legs! The two boys crumpled to the ground and the soldiers roared again.

As Danny prepared for the next onslaught he noticed Trudy and the other girls had also come out in their dressing gowns to investigate the commotion. Trudy looked shocked to see that it was her brothers and Danny involved in the fight.

Now Commander Skorzeny called over to a soldier standing nearby and suggested that he should have a go. The soldier, who looked like a born fighter, with a scar on his cheek and a broken boxer's nose, seemed to relish the opportunity. With a broad grin he took off his jacket and stepped out into 'the ring'. The sight of him made the other soldiers cheer, and the boys (including a bloody-nosed Herman) cleared out of the way.

Danny could tell immediately that this man was a far more formidable opponent. He had taken up a boxer's stance with his fists raised and was now edging closer. Danny knew he was going to have to step up his game.

Suddenly the boxer lashed out with a lightning-fast punch that Danny only just managed to avoid. Punches then came in thick and fast, and Danny had to duck and weave, and do everything he could to avoid being hit. The longer the boxer failed to land a punch the more frustrated he became, and Danny decided to just carry on taking evasive action without even trying to throw a punch himself.

Soon the boxer began to tire. He started cursing Danny and demanding that he stand still! Danny continued to bob and weave, just waiting for the right moment. It came - for just a brief second the boxer was distracted by the jeering soldiers. Danny took the opportunity and landed a punch fair and square to his jaw. The boxer shook his head. He didn't know what had hit him. Danny landed a few more and now his opponent was staggering. Danny followed him around the ring and delivered one final bone-crunching punch that laid the boxer flat out on his back - and that's where he stayed.

The soldiers cheered and applauded. They couldn't believe what they were witnessing! Danny couldn't believe it either. As he looked down at his fists he had to admit that he was *loving* this feeling of power!

Commander Skorzeny was also applauding as he stepped out from amongst the soldiers. Danny's first reaction was that someone else was stepping out to fight and he instinctively took up his fighting stance again, but the commander held up his hands in mock-surrender.

"I wouldn't dare!" he said, and all the soldiers laughed. "Anyone else like to have a go?" he asked, looking around.

There were no takers.

The commander now walked up to Danny.

"In all my years of army life I don't think I've ever seen such a fine fighter. May I ask your name?"

Danny was just about to answer when there was suddenly a shout, a scream and a whole lot of disturbance. Somebody was pushing their way through the soldiers. As the figure emerged from the crowd Danny's blood ran cold. It was Herman - and he had a rifle pointed directly at Danny!

Danny knew that no amount of *Combat X* fighting skills were going to protect him from a bullet. The look on Herman's face, with his bloody nose and his wild angry eyes, was truly terrifying. The humiliation of taking a beating in front of everyone had clearly proved too much for him to handle. He was so consumed by rage that Danny could see the rifle was shaking in his hands.

The soldiers behind Danny (who were suddenly in the firing line) began to scatter. The commander, on the other hand, didn't budge. He merely held up his hands and spoke in a calm voice.

"What is going on?" he asked. "Why have you got that weapon?"

"Move out of the way please, Commander," Herman said through gritted teeth, his voice bristling with anger.

The commander still didn't move.

"I ask you again. Why the gun? Put down the gun, please."

Herman shook his head.

"I'm sorry, Commander, but I can't do that. You see, I have

come to realise that there is something not right at all about this boy."

"Because he kicked your butt, fair and square?" asked the commander.

A few soldiers laughed at this and Herman's eyes flashed angrily again.

"No, Commander - because I think he is a spy!"

"A spy?" The commander looked at Danny with raised eyebrows. "And what has led you to this conclusion?"

"He has strange things in his bag. I wanted to show you. Including a book written in English."

"Really? I have many books written in English. Does this mean I am a spy as well?" asked the commander.

Again this caused a ripple of laughter amongst the soldiers, which irritated Herman further.

"No, Commander," Herman snapped, "but he has other strange devices with him as well. I urge you to take a look - and look at the combat training he must have received. No normal person can fight like that."

Now the commander turned his attention to Danny and spoke in English.

"Is this true? Are you an English spy?"

Danny was caught off guard and, for a moment, he didn't know how to reply. Eventually he just shook his head.

"But you *do* speak English?"

Danny decided to tell the story about his great-uncle having lived in England, but when he opened his mouth to speak something very strange happened.

"У меня есть дядя, который живет в Англии," said Danny.

"Russian!" The commander was unable to hide his surprise. "You also speak Russian?"

Danny couldn't believe that Russian had just come out of his mouth. He now concentrated hard on speaking German and tried again, but this time a totally different language came out.

"*Jag har en farbror som bor i England...*"

Danny didn't even know what language it was!

"Swedish!" exclaimed the commander. "Is that Swedish?"

There was now a buzz of excited conversation amongst the soldiers.

Herman looked delighted.

"I told you! You see!" he shouted. "Russian! Swedish! English! Are you telling me he is normal? He's a spy - I'm sure of it!"

It seemed like the commander was starting to agree.

"Bring him to my office," he said, then added, "and let me see this bag of strange devices."

Danny thought about one last ditch attempt at making a run for it, but he could see that Herman was just itching to pull the trigger.

Herman could not have looked more pleased with himself as he marched Danny off at gunpoint towards the commander's office. They had to pass nearby where Trudy and her friends were standing, and Danny could see the confusion on her face. He wished that he could just stop and explain everything to her, but Herman gave him a prod in the back with the rifle barrel and kept him walking.

\*

Danny sat across the desk from the commander, who had tipped the entire contents of the rucksack out onto the desk and was now busy going through everything.

When they had arrived at the office Herman had tried his best to wangle his way inside, but the commander had ordered him to wait outside. As a precaution though (this boy was clearly full of surprises), he had posted two armed guards just inside the door, directly behind Danny.

The first thing that caught the commander's eye was the

*iPod*. He turned it over in his hands several times then looked at Danny.

"What is it?" he asked.

Danny opened his mouth to reply.

"这是一个机器播放音乐."

Danny cupped a hand over his mouth. He had meant to say in German, 'It's just a machine for playing music', but instead some other funny language had come out! It sounded like Chinese!

The commander stared at him. He suspected the boy was just using these different languages to hide behind, yet the shock and disbelief on the boy's face every time he spoke seemed genuine.

Danny was actually starting to panic. It was as if his *Translatormate* program had suddenly gone haywire - just when his *Combat X* had started to work! He concentrated hard on saying something in English.

"Είμαι προσπαθεί να μιλήσει αγγλικά, αλλά κάτι είναι λάθος!"

The commander stared hard at him.

"Greek? Are you playing with me, boy?"

Danny shook his head and the commander could see that there was real distress in his eyes.

The commander pushed the *iPod* to one side and picked up another small item. It was one of the *Immobilasers* from Frankie and Glide's shop. Danny didn't even know if it worked - but if it did he was going to have a lot to explain! When he saw the commander about to press the button on the *Immobilaser* he tried to casually lean out of the way. Luckily it was pointing more towards one of the guards by the door – and what nobody noticed was that the guard froze and unfroze several times before the commander stopped pressing the button.

Still baffled by this item, the commander held it up and asked Danny what it was. For the first time that night Danny prayed that his reply would not come out in German or English. He didn't have to worry.

"*Se trata de un control remoto para la apertura de una puerta de garaje*," he said.

The commander had stopped even looking surprised. He shook his head and moved on to the next item. It was the item Danny had been dreading the most - Uncle Morty's journal. The commander opened the journal and the first thing he saw was the inscription, '*For Daniel*', written on the inside front cover.

"Daniel. You are Daniel?" he asked.

"*Si*," replied Danny, nodding.

Now the commander started to read, and what worried Danny the most was that he didn't just start skimming through the pages, he was actually really *reading* everything and trying to make sense of it all. When he got to the sketches and diagrams he studied them closely, trying his best to work out what they meant. Eventually he looked up at Danny.

"Who wrote this?" he asked.

Danny didn't know how to answer, but he was fairly confident that whatever he said would come out in some strange language that wouldn't be understood anyway.

"*Je ne sais pas*," he said.

Danny had tried to get away with saying 'I don't know', but unfortunately his answer had come out in French and he could tell immediately that the commander had understood him.

For the first time Danny could see that the commander was getting angry. He flipped to the front of the book and pointed at the '*For Daniel*' inscription.

"You don't know?" he growled. "Then why is your name in the book?"

Danny had been caught out and he knew he had to quickly get the commander back on his side.

"All right," Danny continued in French. "My uncle wrote the book."

The commander was now watching him closely for any signs that he may not be telling the truth.

"Where does your uncle live?" he asked.

"In England," Danny replied.

"Really? Tell me - is your uncle a scientist?"

"Commander..." Danny hesitated, trying to think how he could steer the conversation in a different direction. "To be honest with you, my uncle is a little crazy. In fact, some people think he is more than a *little* crazy!"

"*Is he a scientist?*" the commander repeated.

"Yes," Danny replied.

Now Danny was asked the one question he had been dreading the most.

"Tell me, Daniel, what exactly *is* this machine that your uncle is describing? What is it designed to do?"

Danny didn't know what to say. If he lied he knew the commander would be able to tell, and yet there was no way he could just come out with the truth. Eventually he opened his mouth to speak.

"*Você não iria acreditar em mim se eu te disse,*" he said.

"*No!*" the commander roared, slamming his fist down violently on the desk. "I will not allow you to squirm out of answering my questions any longer!"

Danny tried again.

"*Tôi đang cố gắng tốt nhất của tôi!*"

"Speak French, or German, or English! I demand it!" the commander roared.

"*Існує нічого не можу зробити!*," Danny replied, shrugging apologetically.

Once the commander had calmed himself down enough to speak, he picked up the telephone and spoke in German, which Danny was able to understand.

"Was it tomorrow that the scientists were going up to the

Berghof?" the commander asked. He nodded when he heard the reply then continued. "Yes, I thought so... I've got something here that they might find interesting. I think I will take it up there myself tomorrow. Make the arrangements will you? I'll be leaving first thing in the morning. Thank you. Oh yes, and make sure there is also room for a boy and two guards please." He put the phone down then nodded to the guards. "We are taking a little trip tomorrow, Daniel," he said, "to see some very important people. I advise you to get a good night's rest."

With pointed rifles, the guards now indicated to Danny that it was time to leave.

As they left the office Danny glanced back and saw that the commander had gone back to reading Uncle Morty's journal.

*

Danny sat, cold and alone, in a small dark room. It was called the Guard Room, but it was actually just a prison cell. Every now and again a small hatch in the door would slide open and the face of a guard would peer in at him.

Danny had never felt so alone. For the first time in the whole journey he truly wished he had never made the trip to Bosworth Manor. How could things have gone so terribly wrong? Their deadline to stop Mortimer and Michelle was the following night - *and look where he was*!

Now his thoughts were suddenly interrupted by a girl's voice outside the door.

"Daniel?"

The small metal hatch slid to one side and, in the dim light, he could just make out the face. It was Trudy.

"Daniel, I've bought you a blanket and something to eat."

Trudy pushed the blanket and a packet of bread rolls through the hatch.

Danny tried to say, 'thank you', but once again the words came out in a strange foreign language.

"What are they going to do with you?" Trudy asked.

Danny tried to tell her about the commander's phone call and that he had mentioned a place called 'the Berghof'.

Again Trudy couldn't understand - until he said 'the Berghof' then her expression suddenly changed.

"Did you say 'the Berghof'?" she asked.

Danny nodded, wondering why she was suddenly looking so flustered.

"They are taking you to the Berghof?" Trudy asked, blinking in amazement.

She couldn't believe it when Danny just shrugged blankly as if to say, 'So, what's the big deal?'

"Daniel," she said, "the Berghof is the Fuhrer's mountain headquarters! They are taking you to Hitler's residence in the Bavarian mountains!"

Chapter 14

# On the Wine Route

At about the same late hour as Danny was being visited by Trudy, Aunt Henrietta and Sarah were also being paid a visit - of a far less welcome nature!

The Hogs (whom of course Aunt Henrietta considered to be German soldiers searching for Sarah) had appeared at her bedroom door like the Devil's own henchman!

Standing before the two towering soldiers, Aunt Henrietta had asked the Good Lord to please stay close in this time of great need. The Good Lord had worked His wonderful ways on many occasions throughout her life, but what happened next she would later describe as 'His greatest miracle yet'!

The soldiers began to look around the room and Aunt Henrietta's heart sank when one of them ripped open the wardrobe door and discovered Sarah standing there amongst the clothes. At that moment, Aunt Henrietta feared that all was lost, but then - the miracle!

The soldier took a close look at Sarah, saw who it was, merely pushed her to one side and continued his search! When the soldiers failed to find anyone else in the bedroom they left and moved on to the other upstairs rooms.

Aunt Henrietta sat on the bed with her arms around Sarah and listened to the banging and crashing going on in the other rooms. They heard the heavy footsteps going back down the stairs again and, a short time later, it sounded like the soldiers had gone through to the wine warehouse next door.

Aunt Henrietta waited a long time before she felt it was safe to move. She told Sarah to stay in the bedroom then she made her way, slowly and quietly, down the stairs. When she got to the inter-leading door to the warehouse she put her ear up against the door and listened carefully for any sounds.

Suddenly, from within the warehouse, there came an almighty ear-splitting bang, accompanied by a blinding flash that she could see under the door. It was as if there had been a lightning strike and a crack of thunder *inside* the warehouse!

Aunt Henrietta couldn't even begin to imagine what could have caused this, but the next noise she heard was the back door of the warehouse being opened. She hurried through to the kitchen to look out of the back window and was just in time to see the two soldiers riding out of the warehouse on a motorbike and sidecar! They hesitated when they reached the main road, as if waiting to be guided by something. They then turned the same way Bernard had turned earlier. They were also taking the road to Germany.

*

A few hours farther down that same road Spike and Charley were asleep in their 'barrel cabin'. The comfort of the mattress in the darkness and the gentle rocking of the truck had lulled them both to sleep soon after leaving Bordeaux.

It was Charley who awoke first. At first she didn't know where she was, but then she saw the night sky through the peepholes in the barrel.

"Spike? You awake?" she asked.

"I am *now*," Spike replied with a grunt.

"There's something I've been wanting to ask you."

"Mm?"

Spike still sounded half-asleep.

"Those soldiers on the motorbike…"

Spike knew immediately where this conversation was heading.

"What about them?"

"They weren't Timecops were they?"

No answer.

"Spike? They weren't, were they?"

The last thing Spike wanted was for his sister to start panicking.

"I'm not sure," he replied unconvincingly.

"Come on, Spike!" Charley cried. "You *know* what they were!"

"All right, all right. I think they may have been... Hogs."

It confirmed Charley's worst fears.

"They're going to just carry on coming after us, aren't they?" she said. "It's like they always know how to find us!"

Spike tried to sound positive.

"We just need to stay ahead of them. We'll find Danny, get back to Bordeaux and get out of this place!"

"Just like that, eh?" said Charley, not sounding at all convinced.

Spike decided to change the subject. He also had a question he had been meaning to ask.

"So... um... what was it Sarah said as we were leaving?" he asked casually.

Charley leapt at the subject.

"I think you've got an admirer there!" she gushed.

"Charles, don't give me trouble!" Spike whined. "Just tell me what she said."

"How much is it worth?" Charley asked, giggling.

"*Charles!*"

"All right, but don't go getting big-headed now!" Charley warned. "She said that you were her hero and that she hoped to see you again."

"She said that?" asked Spike, trying not to sound *too* pleased!

"Yup, and that you had a completely brilliant sister!"

"Charles! Are you making this up?" Spike shouted.

"No, no, no... OK, only the last bit."

Spike lay back. He had to admit it would be really great to see Sarah again. Just his luck that, if all went to plan, they would be gone by the end of the following day.

Charley hadn't finished on the subject.

"She definitely has a soft spot for you!" she crowed.

Spike decided it was time for revenge.

"You mean she feels the same as you feel towards Danny?"

"*What*?" Charley exploded - this was totally unexpected!

"Come on, Charles." Spike chuckled. "It's obvious!"

"Spike! What are you talking about?" Charley shrieked. She could feel herself starting to blush. "I've never heard anything so stupid!"

"Oh really, so you're telling me you don't have any feelings for Danny?"

Now Charley was all stutters and stammers.

"Look, I think he's a n-nice guy and all that, b-but that's it... I mean I would never..."

"*Nice guy*? Charles, don't give me that! You've got a huge crush on him! I can see it a mile off!"

"*Spike! I have not!*"

Charley was now blushing so much that she felt like her face must be glowing in the dark!

Now (luckily for Charley!) they had to drop the subject because the truck had suddenly started to slow down. Spike peered out through one of the peepholes beside him. For a moment he could see the orange glow of dawn on the horizon – but this now disappeared as the truck pulled into a brightly lit area and came to a halt. They had reached the German border.

Charley was about to say something when Spike quickly shut her up.

"*Shh!*"

It was lucky he did because the next moment a man in uniform came walking past just a few feet away from the barrel. They could hear him talking to Uncle Bernard in German.

Eventually the truck took off again - but it hadn't travelled very far at all before it came to a grinding halt once more. They heard the crunch of footsteps again - then it felt like someone was climbing up onto the truck. Charley gripped Spike's arm. Now the end of the barrel was opening...

A face peered in. It was Uncle Bernard.

"Welcome to Germany," he said. "Should be all right to ride up front now."

\*

It only took a couple more hours to reach Nuremberg. Uncle Bernard seemed to know about the 'great Nazi rally' and it didn't take him long to find the vast, empty parade ground. The only people there now were a few soldiers clearing up after the rally.

Uncle Bernard pulled the truck up next to a soldier and asked where they could find the Hitler Youth brigade. At first the soldier appeared a little suspicious, but he soon changed his tune when Uncle Bernard explained that Spike and Charley were interested in joining up! Suddenly the soldier was full of approving nods as he issued precise directions to the nearby army barracks.

\*

Ten minutes later Uncle Bernard was parking his truck across the road from the entrance to the army barracks.

As soon as they saw the entrance they knew their difficulties were about to begin. There was a boom at the gate, manned by several armed guards who were checking every vehicle that arrived. It clearly wasn't going to be a matter of just driving in there and looking for Danny.

Uncle Bernard turned off the engine and sat back, scratching his stubble as he contemplated their next move. While they sat waiting (for what, they weren't exactly sure), Charley and Spike noticed a café beside them. Every now and again someone would walk out with a cup of coffee or a loaf of bread, and Charley and Spike were finding it difficult not to stare. Eventually Uncle Bernard got the hint.

"Hungry?" he asked. "Breakfast?"

Charley nodded, but couldn't help looking embarrassed because they had no money whatsoever, never mind *deutschemarks* (the German currency). Realising this, Uncle Bernard reached into his pocket for some money.

"Coffee please," he said, handing the money to Charley, "and get something for yourselves."

"Merci!" Charley replied - and she and her brother were out of the truck so fast that Uncle Bernard couldn't help having a quiet chuckle to himself.

It was warm inside the café, and the wonderful aroma of coffee and freshly-baked bread was making their mouths water. Charley gave their order to a *fraulein* behind the counter and it wasn't long before she was handing them steaming cups of hot chocolate and buns - and a coffee for Uncle Bernard.

Just as they were turning to leave, a group of Hitler Youth entered the café, and amongst them they immediately recognised the pretty blonde daughter of the Gestapo Officer.

Charley and Spike concentrated on their cups of hot chocolate and headed for the door! Outside the café, they had almost reached the truck when they heard a girl's voice behind them.

"Excuse me! Hold on a minute!" The girl had followed them out and was now running up to them. "Excuse me!" she said. "Aren't you Daniel's friends?"

As she came up to them Charley couldn't help noticing how tall and pretty she was! Charley felt like a stumpy dwarf beside her!

"Hello, my name is Trudy," she said with a smile. She held out a hand for them to shake, but then laughed when she realised their hands were full. "I'm *so* surprised to see you," she continued. "You've come all the way from France? What are you doing here?" As soon as she asked the question, she seemed to guess the answer. "You've come... looking for Daniel?"

Charley glared at her as if to say, 'Of course we have! What do you think we're doing – taking a vacation?' She couldn't believe how friendly this bubbly blonde girl was trying to be!

"Where is he?" Charley asked bluntly.

Now, for the first time they could see a look of concern sweeping over Trudy's face.

"I'm afraid he's in a bit of trouble," she said.

"Trouble?" Charley's eyes flashed angrily. "What do you mean 'trouble'? Is he all right?"

"Yes… at the moment, but…"

"*But what?*"

Charley felt like grabbing her by the pigtails and shaking the information out of her!

"They think he's a spy!" Trudy suddenly blurted out.

To Charley's amazement, Trudy's eyes began to well up with tears.

"They're taking him to the Berghof!" Trudy continued, tears now rolling down her cheeks. "I'm so worried about him!"

"The Berghof?"

Spike immediately recognised the name. He sounded surprised, and Charley had no idea why.

"The Eagle's Nest?" Spike whispered.

"The Eagle's *what*?" Charley cried, thoroughly confused and frustrated. "What *are* you talking about?"

Before Spike could explain, Trudy suddenly spotted something across the road, which caused her to quickly shepherd the others back behind Uncle Bernard's truck. Now she pointed to a vehicle emerging from the army barracks.

"That's Commander Skorzeny's car," she said, peering over the bonnet of the truck.

"Who?" asked Charley, standing on tiptoe to get a better look.

It was a very smart-looking black car with two small swastika flags on the front.

"Daniel is in that car," Trudy said suddenly.

"*What?*"

Charley was shocked. She took another look at the car, but it was impossible to see who was inside. It had now pulled out onto the road and was starting to head away from them.

"Believe me," Trudy said, "Daniel is in that car!"

Charley didn't know *what* to believe! Now Uncle Bernard had climbed out of his truck and was coming around to find out what was going on.

"So?" he asked, taking his coffee from Spike. "What are we doing?"

Charley glanced at Trudy again - then made a decision.

"Uncle Bernard," she said, "Danny is in that car. We have to follow him."

Uncle Bernard, who was just about to take his first sip of coffee, now realised that she was referring to the large black Nazi car that was disappearing down the road!

"Please, Uncle Bernard!" Charley pleaded. "If we don't go now we're going to lose them!"

Uncle Bernard looked at the car, looked at his coffee then looked at the car again. With a shake of the head and an enormous great sigh, he stomped back around to his side of the truck.

Once they had clambered back in and Uncle Bernard had started up the engine, Charley looked out through her window at Trudy. For just the briefest moment there seemed to be a connection between these two young girls from different worlds. Charley nodded at Trudy through the closed window and mouthed the words, 'Thank you'.

Trudy nodded back, did her best to smile and mouthed the words, 'Good luck'.

The truck lurched forwards and she had gone.

*

Driving out of the city, Spike and Charley were treated to some very colourful French language from Uncle Bernard. He had to drive fast to catch up with the car and he was also trying to hold on to his cup of coffee! After two sharp corners, which resulted in two coffee spills into his lap, the cup was unceremoniously tossed out of the window.

Only when they were out on the open road, with the sleek black car travelling at a safe distance up ahead of them, did Uncle Bernard start to calm down a bit.

"So, can anyone tell me where we are heading now?" he asked grumpily.

Charley looked at Spike.

"What did you say about an 'Eagle's Nest' or something?" she asked him.

Spike seemed a bit cagey about replying, but because they were speaking in English he hoped Uncle Bernard wouldn't be able to understand.

"Um... maybe we shouldn't mention where we're going," he

said.

Charley was about to ask why when Spike gave her a look and spoke slowly and emphatically.

"Trust me on this, Charles. You don't want to say where we are going."

\*

The farther they travelled south the grumpier Uncle Bernard became. They were now in Bavaria, the southernmost part of Germany, but still they continued to go south. If they carried on along this road for too much longer they would be arriving in Austria!

It was beautiful mountainous countryside with thick green forests carpeting the landscape as far as the eye could see. Up ahead, the car they were following peeled off the main road and headed towards the mountains. Uncle Bernard also took the turn-off and, as he did so, they passed a sign that read *Berchtesgaden*. For some reason, this name made Uncle Bernard appear even more agitated. With all the muttering and grumbling coming from Uncle Bernard, Charley felt like she was sitting next to a volcano that was about to erupt!

They continued down the road with the mountains looming ever larger up ahead, and soon found themselves passing through a small village. Here they noticed a lot of military uniforms and vehicles around, which led to increased grumbling from Uncle Bernard, but it was when the car turned again and he saw the next signpost that the volcano *really* erupted!

The sign said *The Berghof* and, as soon as Uncle Bernard saw it, he brought the truck to a screeching halt.

"*The Berghof*! *The Berghof*!" he shouted. "Are you mad? Are you crazy? Have you totally lost your minds?"

He started to turn the truck around. Charley couldn't believe what was happening!

"Please, Uncle Bernard! What are you doing?"

"What am I doing? I'm getting out of here - that's what I'm doing!" he bellowed as he fought with the steering wheel. Once he had the truck pointing back the way they had just come he looked at Charley again. "Do you have any idea who lives at the Berghof?" he asked.

Charley shook her head.

"*Hitler!*" Uncle Bernard roared. "We're about to pay a visit to the Fuhrer!"

This latest bit of information definitely came as a surprise to Charley. She looked at Spike.

"The Eagle's Nest?"

Spike nodded. He had been waiting for this moment to arrive and so far it was going pretty much as expected!

With Uncle Bernard now revving up the truck and about to take off, Charley knew she had to make one last-ditch appeal. Surely they hadn't come all this way just to turn around now?

"Uncle Bernard," she pleaded, "if we don't find Danny and get him back to France by tonight someone is going to die. A beautiful French girl called Michelle, who is engaged to a brave young English soldier and-"

"Girly," Uncle Bernard interrupted, "don't you understand? If you carry on up this road *you'll* be the ones who are going to die! Do you have any idea how tight the security will be up there? How do you expect to get in, never mind get your friend *out*?"

Charley didn't have an answer.

"I don't know," she said, "but we have to try. We can't just leave him!"

"Well, then you'll be trying on your own," Uncle Bernard said, revving the truck again. "If you want to act like imbeciles that's up to you, but I'll have no part in it, so I'm afraid you are on your own now."

Charley couldn't believe that Uncle Bernard was actually going to leave them there. She started to say something, but he had had enough. He now leaned over and opened up the truck door on their side.

"If you want to be mad, get out. If not, let's go home."

For Charley and Spike there was only one option - they both climbed out of the truck. Uncle Bernard gave them a last shake of the head then, as the truck door closed, he put his foot down and roared away.

Spike and Charley could only watch as the truck disappeared down the road. Soon it was out of sight and they found themselves standing alone in the enormous silence of the mountains.

"Well," said Spike, "that went well."

They turned and started to walk up the winding mountain road.

Chapter 15

# The Eagle's Nest

Just a few miles farther up the road from Spike and Charley, Danny was getting his first glimpse of 'The Eagle's Nest'. It wasn't difficult to see why it had earned this name. It was a giant, double-storey chalet perched high up on the side of a sheer mountainside. It looked like there were only two ways to get up there; either you could drive up a steep road that zigzagged its way up through the forest, or you could go directly from the bottom to the top via cable car.

Danny had travelled all the way from Nuremberg sitting beside Commander Skorzeny with the two armed guards sitting directly opposite him. He had spent the entire trip looking for opportunities to escape, but the guards had been keeping a close eye on his every move. Now, as they approached this mountain fortress, passing through one security checkpoint after another, Danny felt his chances of escaping gradually slipping away.

When they reached the foot of the mountain they came across yet another security barrier, but this wasn't just a checkpoint, there seemed to be an entire army barracks stationed here! Commander Skorzeny gave the SS guard at the gate his name and they were instructed to pull over and wait while he sought permission for them to go up.

The driver pulled the car over to one side and Commander Skorzeny suggested they all get out and stretch their legs. Before wandering up the road for a bit of a stroll, he instructed the guards to keep a close eye on Danny.

\*

A little farther down the mountain Charley and Spike were starting to sweat. The sun was now high in the sky and the road was getting steeper and steeper.

"How much farther do you think it is?" Charley asked. She was battling for breath in the thin mountain air.

"Eagle's nests are generally right at the top."

"Great," muttered Charley then added, "it would have been nice of you to mention who actually *lives* at The Eagle's Nest."

"Would it have made a difference?" replied Spike. "Would you have decided not to come if you had known it was Herr Hitler's residence?"

Before Charley could respond they heard the sound of a vehicle coming up the road.

"Quick, off the road!" Spike shouted, and they both bundled themselves into the roadside ditch.

As the vehicle approached they could hear the engine straining on the steep hill. Spike lifted his head up just enough to peer through the grass - then he smiled.

"What is it?" Charley asked.

"You're not going to believe this!" said Spike, who now surprised Charley by standing up!

"What *are* you doing?"

"Take a look," said Spike, who was now climbing out of the ditch.

Tentatively, Charley stood up as well and was amazed to see that the vehicle coming up the road was Uncle Bernard's truck! When he saw the two of them stepping out onto the road he pulled the truck over to one side.

"Uncle Bernard, you came back!" Charley shrieked as she ran over to the truck.

She couldn't believe how much better she suddenly felt.

Uncle Bernard was looking even grumpier than normal, and when Charley started to try and thank him, he quickly shut her up.

"Listen!" he growled as he climbed out of the truck. "I will try once and once only to get you in through the main gates. That is all I can do. After that it is up to you. Do you understand?" Charley nodded and was about to try and thank him again when he snapped, "*Listen!* Don't talk! When we go through the checkpoints I am going to say you are my children. You have just come along for the ride, all the way from France, to deliver special Bordeaux wine to the Fuhrer. Do you understand?"

Charley nodded.

"I will do *all* the talking, all right? You will be quiet! Understood?"

Charley nodded again then Uncle Bernard looked at Spike.

"Like him. Be quiet like him!" Now he went around to the back of the truck. "There is something we must do before we go," he said. "Give me a hand here."

Uncle Bernard was soon up on the back of the truck manhandling the large empty barrel in which they had travelled. When he saw Charley and Spike's quizzical expressions he explained.

"At each checkpoint they will search the truck. What are they going to say when they find this barrel? We'll just leave it in the ditch here and collect it on the way back. Come on, help me. Grab the other side."

Spike and Charley took hold of one end of the barrel. It was very heavy and they had to really strain to lift it. Uncle Bernard clambered down and was just coming to their assistance when the barrel suddenly slipped out of Spike's grip. The weight was too much for Charley and the barrel crashed to the ground, immediately beginning to roll down the steep incline. As it rolled it gathered pace until it ramped over the edge of the mountain and disappeared into the valley below.

Uncle Bernard stood rooted to the spot, staring at the place where he had last seen his precious barrel. Charley and Spike shuffled around nervously, waiting for the inevitable volcano eruption.

"Sorry," Spike said eventually.

He was about to start explaining how his hands had slipped, but Uncle Bernard held up his hand to silence him. It seemed like there was a whole stream of angry words on the verge of exploding out of him, but somehow he kept them bottled up. Instead, he turned his attention to pulling aggressively on the ropes holding the other barrels down.

Charley and Spike took the opportunity to escape to the front of the truck.

"Well, I guess we won't be going back to France in a barrel," said Charley as they climbed up into the cab.

Soon Uncle Bernard joined them.

"What do you have to remember?" he asked Charley sternly.

"To be quiet," Charley replied.

Uncle Bernard gave an exaggerated nod before starting up the truck and pulling away.

*

Danny had found a place to sit in the shade of a tree. The two guards were standing only a stone's throw away, but he was encouraged by the fact that they were now talking to one of the SS guards at the gate. As they chatted and laughed amongst themselves Danny noticed how they would look over in his direction every now and again. He now rested his head back against the tree, closed his eyes and pretended to be going to sleep. The ploy seemed to be working because, through the slits in his eyes, he could see that the guards were definitely paying him less and less attention.

He knew he had to choose exactly the right moment. He waited until one of the guards had launched into a story that seemed to have captured the others' attention then very slowly, inch by inch, he began to edge himself around the tree. When he was most of the way around, he did a quick little shuffle around to the other side then sat there with his heart pounding, listening for any reaction from the guards, but still their conversation continued.

Now he knew he would have to *really* move! Crouching down

low, he scampered off through the trees.

Danny had only gone a short distance into the forest when he heard a sound that made him freeze instantly. It was the sound of a revolver being cocked. Danny slowly straightened up to find Commander Skorzeny standing in front of him. In his hand he held a revolver, which was pointing directly at him.

"What took you so long?" the commander asked, smiling.

\*

Uncle Bernard was brilliant! From the first checkpoint they went through Spike and Charley knew how lucky they were that he had returned for them. They could tell immediately that he had done this kind of thing many times before. When it came to dealing with the guards he was a master. At every checkpoint he acted so naturally, sharing a joke with the guards, telling them that the Fuhrer had ordered only the best, even convincing them to have a taste of the wine.

At first the guards looked a little guilty because they were on duty, but most of them would eventually be persuaded to have a quick glass. They would then happily send the truck on its way, just presuming that the wine had been specifically ordered.

Spike and Charley, sitting *quietly* up front, were completely ignored.

\*

Danny was now locked in Commander Skorzeny's car with the two guards standing directly outside. When the commander marched him out of the forest he had given the guards such a severe dressing down that they were now not letting Danny out of their sight!

From inside the car Danny could see Commander Skorzeny hanging around impatiently outside the guardhouse. Eventually the SS guard came out, and he must have given the commander the permission he had been waiting for because he now saluted the guard and started back towards the vehicle.

It was at this point that Danny noticed a truck loaded with wine barrels arriving at the main gate. He didn't pay too much attention to it and was about to look away again when suddenly his eyes were drawn to the two figures sitting beside the driver in the cab.

Danny blinked. *Were his eyes deceiving him?* He tried to look again, but now the guards were climbing into the car, blocking his view. Once they were seated he managed to sneak another look. He couldn't believe it! It looked like Spike and Charley! With the guards sitting opposite him, Danny had to try and conceal his utter amazement!

Commander Skorzeny climbed in and gave the driver the order to go. They began the steep climb up towards The Eagle's Nest.

\*

Getting through the main gate required Uncle Bernard's best performance yet!

The SS guards at this gate were a lot more thorough, and the first thing they did was check on their list to see if they were expecting a wine delivery. When they found nothing they made a call up to the main house, but a message came back saying that they weren't expecting anything either.

Uncle Bernard threw up his arms in frustration.

"I'm asked to deliver the finest wine *all the way from Bordeaux*! I bring it and nobody wants it!" Anyone who didn't know better would have thought that he was fuming as he stomped back to the truck. Just before he climbed in, he roared, "And it's already been paid for!"

Still muttering and shaking his head, he started up the truck and was just about to begin reversing when a guard came over and tapped on the window. As soon as that happened Uncle Bernard gave Spike and Charley the tiniest of winks then he put on his grumpy face again and turned to the guard.

The guard instructed Uncle Bernard to bring the truck in and park it while they investigated this delivery further. He drove in and parked under the very same tree that Danny had been sitting under just a few minutes earlier.

*

By now, Danny was just reaching the top of the mountain. It was a picture-perfect setting up there with beautiful gardens, lovely rolling lawns and little pathways leading to benches where people could sit and take in the view. What a magnificent view it was! In the distance there was a range of majestic snow-capped mountains, while nestling in the valley below was a picturesque village surrounded by dense forest. The Fuhrer had chosen the site of his residence wisely. From where he lived the whole world looked like something on a tourist postcard!

Now the house came into view. Here it was - the Berghof! The Eagle's Nest! Danny gazed up at the large alpine-style residence. It could have been a small mountain hotel except that there were armed guards standing on the steps ready to greet the guests!

The guards came trotting down the steps to meet the commander's car. As soon as it stopped they opened the back doors and stood to attention.

Stepping out onto the crunchy gravel driveway, Danny was suddenly struck by the reality of his situation. He felt a jab of nerves in the pit of his stomach. He was about to walk into the home of the Fuhrer!

*

Down at the bottom there were now several guards on the back of the truck checking that the barrels were indeed filled with wine.

Spike and Charley had climbed out and wandered a short distance from the truck, as if stretching their legs. What they were really doing was weighing up their options. From the main gate they had seen the car with Danny inside driving off up the long winding road to the top, but the road was full of soldiers and military traffic, so they certainly weren't going to be able to take *that* route.

The next option was the cable car, but this didn't seem to be operating at the moment. It was just parked there at the bottom station. Perhaps it was only used for emergencies?

The only other option, which Charley was now surveying (and Spike wouldn't have considered an option at all!), was the steep, rocky cliff face that rose up all the way from the forest to where the Berghof sat majestically, high above.

When Spike saw what Charley was looking at he gave an amused grunt.

"You're not even *thinking* about that are you?"

Charley looked around to make sure there were no guards within earshot.

"Spike, I could climb that," she said in a low voice.

Spike started to protest, but Charley stopped him.

"No, Spike, I'm serious! This... *Go Ape!* monkey program whatever it is... is *amazing*! I feel like I could climb up anything!"

"All right, Charles, that's all very well, but you're forgetting one thing."

Charley looked at him blankly.

"*Me!*" Spike exclaimed. "I don't have your monkey program! What am *I* meant to do?"

"Let me go up," Charley replied. "You just wait here and I'll-"

"Don't even think about it," said Spike firmly. "There is *no way* I am letting you go up there alone."

Now Charley spotted the rope hanging from the back of the truck, which the guards had undone to check the barrels.

"I could help you," Charley said to Spike. "We could use the rope."

Spike looked back at the cliff face. He didn't like the idea at all, but at this stage there didn't seem to be much choice. He wasn't going to let Charley go up alone.

*

As the commander and Danny (flanked, as usual, by the two guards) entered the grand entrance hall of the Berghof the first thing they saw was a large group of men spilling out into the foyer from another room.

Danny had heard the commander speaking about a group of scientists meeting at the Berghof, so he presumed this must be them. There certainly were a lot of academic-looking men in suits amongst them, but he also noticed quite a number of soldiers - probably generals, judging by all the regalia on their uniforms.

Once again he felt a deep sense of dread in his gut. Were Uncle Morty's secrets about to be revealed to *all these men*?

Danny scanned the crowd for any sign of Hitler, but at that moment he was nowhere to be seen. The commander now instructed him and the guards to wait while he made his way into the crowd. He seemed to be well known to many of the men, particularly the soldiers, who greeted him with salutes and handshakes. The commander was making a beeline for one man in particular - a tall, wiry, serious-looking man with glasses and a bow tie. Danny wasn't to know it then, but the man (whom the commander was now shaking firmly by the hand) was Professor Wolfgang von Heisenberg, probably the most highly respected scientist in Germany.

*

Uncle Bernard was now standing on the back of the truck drinking wine from a mug.

It had suddenly occurred to the guards that the wine might be poisoned or drugged (perhaps part of a sinister plot to immobilise Hitler's elite SS bodyguard), which is why they had insisted that Uncle Bernard should take a drink from each barrel first - then they could watch him closely for any adverse side effects.

Uncle Bernard was now moving from barrel to barrel scooping

up wine and slurping it back. So far, the only side effects that the growing audience of soldiers could notice was that Uncle Bernard was becoming increasingly tipsy and unsteady on his feet!

Spike and Charley took advantage of Uncle Bernard's little wine-tasting show to slip around the back of the truck where they were hidden from the soldiers' view. Here they started to undo the rope and gather it up.

From the top of the truck Uncle Bernard could see what they were up to and he now made an even greater effort to keep the soldiers' attention. With a silly grin on his face he pretended to be even wobblier than he really was, making the soldiers laugh. The soldiers were just starting to realise how lucky they were - twenty barrels of the finest French wine had been delivered to their doorstep and the catering staff up the hill didn't want it!

Once Charley and Spike had a decent length of rope rolled up and slung over Spike's shoulder, they were ready to move. Seeing this, Uncle Bernard dipped his mug into another barrel and gave them a small nod of the head. He then turned back to the soldiers and pretended he couldn't find his mouth with the mug. This made the soldiers laugh again, and Charley and Spike took the opportunity to duck into the forest.

\*

Commander Skorzeny had suggested to the professor that they retreat into the quiet of the Berghof library. As soon as the commander had described the book and the other unusual items, the professor had agreed to take a look.

Now he sat at a table in the library studying Uncle Morty's journal. Danny had been instructed to sit in one corner (with the guards standing nearby) while the commander paced up and down, glancing at the professor from time to time.

Danny was also watching the professor. At first he noticed he was frowning. It was as if he was battling to make sense of what he was reading, but the more he read the more engrossed he seemed to become. For Danny, this was not a good sign!

At one point the professor asked who had written the book. The commander replied that it had been found on this boy (he indicated Danny), but due to 'language difficulties' they only knew that it had been written by 'his uncle in England'.

On hearing this, the professor briefly glanced up at Danny then went straight back to the book. He had now even begun to scribble down notes on a piece of paper.

The suspense was killing the commander and eventually he had to speak up.

"It appeared to me to be describing some sort of machine, Professor. Do you have any idea what sort of machine this might be?" he asked.

Danny prayed that the professor hadn't worked it out yet.

"No." The professor shook his head without taking his eyes off the page. "But the physics and mathematics are remarkable. I've never seen anything like this before." He eventually looked up from the book. "I would very much like to show this to some of my colleagues, if I may?"

"Certainly," the commander said, nodding. And now, to Danny's dismay, he handed the professor his rucksack as well. "There are also a few items in here that you might find of interest."

"Thank you," the professor said, standing to leave.

As Danny watched him walking towards the door he had a terrible feeling that the journal was gradually slipping farther and farther away from him - and with it was going all hope of ever building a second TIM and trying to save his dad and Catie. Danny knew then that he was going to have to try everything - *risk everything* - to get that book back again!

When the professor reached the door he looked back for a moment.

"Well done, Commander," he said. "I have a feeling the Fuhrer will also be very interested in what you have brought us today."

With that, he went back out into the busy foyer.

\*

As they scrambled through the forest towards the cliff face Spike and Charley found the incline gradually getting steeper and steeper. Soon they were having to use their hands to pull themselves up the slope. Suddenly they emerged from the trees and were confronted by the steep, rocky cliff face towering high above them.

Spike looked up... and up... and up - then glanced at Charley as if to say, 'Are we seriously going to do this?'.

But Charley was already getting organised. She had taken the rope from Spike and was now tying one end around her waist. Once this was tight she secured the other end around Spike. Even as the rope was being tied around his waist, Spike couldn't stop looking up at the cliff. Charley saw the expression on his face.

"Look, don't worry about it, all right? I'm going to lead the way. We'll take it at a nice gentle pace. OK? Ready?"

Spike looked *far* from ready, but he nodded anyway.

Charley leapt up onto the rock face. She stuck to it like she had suction pads on her hands!

"Slowly, Charles! All right? *Slowly!*"

They started to climb.

\*

Adolf Hitler sat twiddling the end of his large impressive moustache as he listened to what Professor von Heisenberg was saying down at the other end of the long table. The professor had asked if he could bring in a blackboard to help explain something he felt sure would be of interest to everyone.

Now, as he scribbled a long and complicated mathematical formula on the blackboard (while referring to a book in his hand), the Fuhrer noticed how riveted all the scientists seemed to be. The soldiers, on the other hand (like himself), did not have the slightest idea what the professor was going on about - and this was beginning to test the Fuhrer's patience.

When the professor completed the equation and stepped back the scientists all concentrated intently on the blackboard and, as they did so, an excited buzz of conversation began to grow around the table.

"Professor!" Hitler barked suddenly, which shut the scientists up immediately. "We have interrupted our discussions on the V-2 rocket for your benefit. The least you could do is translate what you have written for those of us with more military backgrounds!"

"Of course, Mein Fuhrer. I apologise," said the professor, trying to think how best he could explain things in layman's terms. "Mein Fuhrer, if the theory of time and space expressed in this equation is to be believed it would mean... Well, it would mean that, theoretically, time travel would be possible."

At the sound of these words the entire table erupted into excited conversation again and even the Fuhrer stopped his moustache twiddling for a moment.

Fat *Reichsmarschall* Goering was the first to stand and speak.

"Mein Fuhrer, the repercussions of this could be astounding! Imagine being able to look ahead and know what the enemy will do in battle then going back and planning accordingly."

Foreign minister von Ribbentrop was the next on his feet.

"*Reichsmarschall*, never mind about your battles, imagine if we knew the outcome of the entire war!"

Another general stood up, but the room was now so abuzz with discussion that his words could hardly be heard.

"*Silence!*" Hitler roared, slamming a hand down on the table. "Professor! You said 'theoretically'. As we all know, having some figures written on a page and managing to achieve something in practice are two very different things. Where did this *theory* come from anyway?"

"Commander Skorzeny discovered this amazing book on a

young boy, Mein Fuhrer," the professor replied. "Along with some other items that I haven't had a chance to look at yet."

"A boy?" The Fuhrer scowled. "Where is this boy?"

"He is here, Mein Fuhrer - waiting outside with the commander. I should warn you, however, that we are having difficulty communicating with him."

"Really?" Hitler smiled. "Professor, I may not have a scientific brain, but I'm told my communication skills are above average."

Everyone laughed at the Fuhrer's modesty.

"Bring in the boy," said Hitler.

\*

Charley and Spike had made good progress on the climb and were now almost halfway up the cliff face. Spike was still climbing very gingerly, but Charley was so confident and at ease on the rock face that his confidence was also starting to grow.

"That's good, Spike," Charley said reassuringly from above. "Just don't look down, OK?"

"Don't worry," Spike muttered, as he strained to pull himself up a bit farther, "I have no intention of looking down."

Charley, on the other hand, was sitting casually on top of a rocky outcrop, looking at the view. She was spending a lot of time waiting for Spike. If she had been climbing alone she would probably have been at the top by now.

"There is one thing that I can't help thinking about, Charles," said Spike from below.

"What's that?"

"Well, I am a lot bigger and heavier than you," Spike said.

"So?"

"So - if I slipped or fell I would pull you down with me."

"I don't know about that!" Charley smiled. "This program is really amazing. I feel strong enough to hold on by my fingertips. Look!"

When Spike looked up he saw that Charley was holding on to

the rock above her with only one hand, her whole body dangling in mid-air!

"*Charles*!" Spike shouted.

Charley laughed and swung back onto the rock again.

"Charles," Spike spluttered, still recovering from the shock. "Don't *ever* do that again!"

\*

When the commander entered the room he snapped his heels together and gave a straight-armed salute.

"Heil Hitler!"

"Commander!" Hitler said from the other end of the table. "As always, it is good to see you!"

"Thank you, Mein Fuhrer."

"Now, where is this boy that I have been hearing about?" Hitler asked.

When the commander stepped aside Danny was suddenly faced with a long table of staring faces, and down at the far end was Hitler.

Hitler raised a hand and beckoned Danny down towards him.

"Come here, boy."

Danny was frozen to the spot and only started moving when the commander gave him a nudge in the back. Now he made the long walk down the room until he was standing before 'The Wolf' himself - the person many believed to be the Devil incarnate.

"Well, at least he's dressed correctly," Hitler said, referring to Danny's Hitler Youth uniform.

Everyone at the table laughed politely at the Fuhrer's joke.

"Where do you come from, boy?" Hitler asked.

Danny could understand what he was being asked in German, but now he had to try and reply in German. He took a deep breath.

"*Ik kom van Frankrijk, Meneer*," he said.

"I believe that's Dutch," said the commander, "yet he says he comes from France."

"You come from France? Well then, speak French!" Hitler demanded.

"*Ik ben, probeer mijn best*," said Danny.

"He says he's trying his best," the commander translated. "Dutch again."

"He's what? Don't be ridiculous! Speak French! I demand it!"

Danny tried again.

"*Именно это я пытался сделать!*"

The commander shrugged.

"Russian I think. I'm afraid I can't help you there, Mein Fuhrer."

"*Russian?*" Hitler was now starting to go purple in the face. "Is this boy playing the fool with me?"

Danny shook his head.

"*Нет я не.*"

Hitler was about to roar again when something occurred to him.

"He seems to understand what I'm saying. If he can *understand* German then surely he can *speak* German!" He turned back to Danny. "I'm going to give you one more chance. Do you understand? Speak to me now in German, or I promise you, you will regret it. Now, tell me where you come from and where you found this book?"

Danny took another deep breath and concentrated hard.

"*El libro fue escrito por mi tío,*" he replied.

The whole table winced.

"I'm sorry." The commander shook his head. "I don't even know what language that is!"

If there was one thing the Fuhrer hated more than anything else it was being the subject of somebody else's joke. Every man at the table knew that to humiliate the Fuhrer in public was generally the last mistake anybody ever made.

There was a terrible silence as the Fuhrer tried to calm himself down enough to speak. Eventually his eyes flashed towards Danny with such an evil intensity that he had to look away.

"So... he can speak many languages yet he refuses to speak in one that we can understand. He is found to be carrying scientific secrets that have originated in Great Britain. Believe it or not, gentleman, I think we have a young spy here."

There was a rumble of agreement around the table.

"What were you trying to do?" Hitler asked Danny. "Sell your secrets to the highest bidder?"

Danny shook his head.

"Well then answer me, boy."

Danny was reluctant to even open his mouth because he didn't know what language would come out.

"Do you know what we do with spies, boy?" Hitler continued.

Again Danny was unable to respond.

Now it was clear that Hitler had had enough.

"Well, you're going to find out. Get him out of here. We've wasted enough time."

The guards responded immediately and Danny was suddenly being frogmarched towards the door. The last thing he saw before being bundled out through the doorway was the professor removing his *iPod* from the rucksack.

\*

Looking up, Charley estimated that they only had about one third of the way to go before they reached the top. As usual she was waiting for Spike to catch up and she now looked down over the edge to see how he was doing.

"You OK, Spike?" she shouted.

As she looked down, a very strange thing happened; she suddenly became aware of just how high they actually were and

# THE EAGLE'S NEST

what a long, *long* way down it was to the bottom! She quickly pulled herself back against the rock face. Now she felt a sensation growing inside her that she hadn't felt the entire climb - it was fear.

She tried to ignore the feeling and looked up to plan her climbing route, but when she tried to move, she couldn't.

"Come on," she whispered, "this is not the time." She tried to move again, but now the panic was rising up inside her. "Charlotte, do not lose it now. Come on - *move*!" She reached up above her, but her confident grip was gone. She no longer felt like she was sticking to the cliff face. Now she became more and more aware of her precarious position - just this tiny ledge then a drop way down into the valley below. "*No!*" she cursed. "*Please, no!*"

"What's that?" Spike's voice came drifting up from below. "You say something?"

Charley was taking deep breaths.

"No," she replied.

A minute later Spike's hand reached up to the ledge where she was sitting then his face appeared over the lip.

"What were you…"

Spike's question dried up. He could tell immediately that something was wrong. Gone was the confident, casual-looking Charley. Now she sat rigid, pushed up against the rock behind her.

"What's wrong?"

Charley had to take a few more deep breaths before she could get the words out.

"My *Go Ape!* program," she whispered breathlessly. "I think it's stopped working."

\*

A long, long way down from where Spike and Charley clung to the rock face, Uncle Bernard was fast becoming the most popular person at the guards' barracks. They had unloaded the wine barrels and rolled them into the storeroom, and now several of the guards (those not on duty) were sampling the wares.

Meanwhile, the guards at the main gate were cursing their luck that they had to be on duty while all the free wine was flowing. They were now sending subtle messages up to the barracks that a few glasses at the gate would be appreciated!

As they waited to see if anything would materialise from the barracks they hardly noticed the two abnormally large soldiers pulling up at the gate on a motorbike and sidecar. The guards opened the gate and waved the soldiers through.

\*

"All right, Charles, just calm down," Spike was saying for the third time.

Even as he said it, he was becoming more and more aware of his *own* position - hanging over a ledge with his legs dangling in mid-air, attached by a rope to someone who looked like they weren't going anywhere!

"OK, Charles, now you *have* to listen to me!" Spike felt like he was talking to calm *himself* down as well. "We have to carry on. Look, I don't have your program and I was managing OK, wasn't I? You can do the same! All right?"

Charley didn't look like she was going anywhere. The terror in her eyes was plain to see and the sweat was now running down her face.

"Charles! We have no choice! We have to move and we have to move *now*!"

Charley closed her eyes, trying desperately to get a grip on herself. She knew Spike was right. She knew they had no choice. She looked up again at the rock face above her.

\*

The two Hogs climbed off the bike and surveyed the scene around them.

Something caught Spider Neck's eye and he tapped Tooth Rot on the arm. With his special in-built vision enhancer Spider Neck had spotted two small figures way up high on the cliff face. Both Hogs now zoomed right in on the figures until they could see the straining faces of Spike and Charley.

\*

From the Fuhrer's meeting room Danny had been taken down several sets of stone steps into the cold dank bowels of the house. Here, carved into the mountain, was a labyrinth of underground passages and rooms probably, Danny thought, where Hitler's bunker was situated - a place where he could take cover should anyone try to bomb the Berghof.

The guards prodded Danny with their rifles to keep him moving along the dimly-lit passage. Soon they came to a room that was partitioned off with metal prison bars. A gate was opened and Danny was shoved inside. The guards locked the gate and left.

Standing behind the prison bars, Danny cursed bitterly to himself at being locked up again. This place was even more horrible than his previous jail. It was cold and dark, and he could hear the echoing tramp of army boots and the sound of gruff voices issuing orders in the adjoining rooms and passages. He then heard other footsteps, closer, coming down the passage towards his cell. When the familiar face of Commander Skorzeny came around the corner he couldn't help feeling a sense of relief.

The commander did not look at all pleased with how things had turned out. He stood up close to the bars and when he spoke his voice was low and serious.

"Listen to me. If there was ever a time for you to speak out, ever a time for you to make us fully understand what your story is - that time is *now*!"

Danny desperately wanted to make the commander understand. He tried to speak, but as usual the words that came out were strange and exotic. This wasn't good enough for the commander, who now spoke forcefully.

"Don't you understand? Don't you realise what is going on down there?"

He was referring to the sounds of the boots and voices coming from the nearby chamber. Danny shook his head.

"They are preparing a firing squad," the commander said.

Danny shook his head again, still not fully understanding what he was saying.

"They are preparing a firing squad *for you*! The Fuhrer has ordered that you be shot as a spy!"

## Chapter 16

# A Close Shave

Out on the cliff face the progress was painstakingly slow, but at least they were moving again. As far as Spike was concerned that was the most important thing - just to keep moving!

Spike was following closely behind Charley, encouraging her to think only about the next handgrip or foothold. That way they could at least not think too much about where they actually were, which definitely meant *not looking down*!

Charley was still feeling extremely nervous (so much so that she could feel her legs shaking), but the more progress they made, the more her confidence returned. It was at that moment that she stood on a rock and the whole thing came loose!

"*Spike!*" she screamed.

Spike looked up just in time to see a rock the size of a football careering towards his head. He ducked and the rock went flying past!

"Hey, Charles! You trying to get rid of me or what?"

"Sorry."

Luckily she had had a good grip with both hands when the rock came loose, or she might have also gone hurtling past Spike. Now her legs were shaking more than ever.

"Nearly there now, Charles," said Spike, trying to sound like the flying rock incident hadn't affected him at all.

\*

*A firing squad! For him!* Danny was still struggling to absorb this shocking news.

Meanwhile, the commander, who had always felt like there was something different about this boy, but hadn't been able to put his finger on what it was, now had an idea. He removed a small notepad and pen from his pocket.

"Write down where you are from," he said, pushing the pad and pen through the bars.

Suddenly, with the pad and pen in his hands, Danny was faced with a big decision. How truthful should he be? But then the reality of his situation hit home. There was a firing squad being prepared next door! What did he have to lose? He wrote down a single number and handed the pad back to the commander.

The commander squinted at the number in the dim light - *2010.*

\*

Charley and Spike knew they were very close to the top now because they could see a stone wall just above them, which they supposed was the front wall of the Berghof's large terrace.

Charley pulled herself up the last bit then slumped at the foot of the wall, panting, not believing she had made it. When Spike appeared a few moments later she was about to say something to him when he quickly put a finger to his lips to silence her. Spike had frozen where he was and Charley could tell by the way he was peering up that there was somebody there.

It was a German guard patrolling the perimeter of the terrace. If the guard had looked directly down at that moment he would have seen them, but thankfully he was looking out over the view. After a few moments he moved on.

As soon as he had gone Spike pulled himself up the last bit and collapsed beside Charley.

It was only now, as they both sat there recovering, that they allowed themselves to look at the view and marvel at how far they had come. However, beneath the exhilaration of having conquered the cliff there lurked a worrying question:

They had reached the top - *now what?*

\*

Commander Skorzeny stared at the number 2010 for a long time before looking back at Danny. It was still unclear whether he had fully grasped the meaning of the number. To make sure he understood, Danny took the pad back from him again and wrote down a second number - *1942*. Now, when he showed this number to the commander, he indicated that 1942 was *now* - then he tapped the 2010 and pointed to himself.

For the commander it was as if his craziest suspicions were now being confirmed.

"Yes," he said, nodding. "I think I understand and yet my logical rational brain does not want to believe it. Ever since I heard the professor mentioning time travel in those equations I began to wonder, but still I find myself battling to accept such a-"

Suddenly the commander was cut short. There was a sound coming down the passage. It was the distinctive sound of marching army boots and, moments later, a stocky no-nonsense-looking sergeant came around the corner. He was followed by a group of six armed SS troops. Danny knew it had to be the firing squad.

The sergeant saluted the commander.

"My apologies, Commander," he said, "but it is time. The prisoner must come with us."

"Wait!" snapped the commander. "The execution must be delayed."

"Again I apologise, Commander," the Sergeant's tone was respectful, but firm, "but our orders have come directly from the Fuhrer himself and we are to carry them out immediately."

"Sergeant!" the Commander growled. "I order you to wait! I have just received some startling new information that I need to tell the Fuhrer at once!"

The sergeant shuffled around uncomfortably. He was in a difficult position.

"Commander, with the greatest respect, I'm afraid I-"

"Sergeant!" the commander stormed again. "If you carry out

this order before the Fuhrer hears this new information, I promise you the consequences will be extremely grave!"

Still the sergeant did not look convinced, but eventually he nodded.

"Commander, we will wait until five o'clock then I'm afraid we must carry out our orders."

The commander looked at his watch. It was twenty past four. He realised this was the best he was going to get from this stubborn bulldog of a soldier. With a brief glance towards Danny he strode out of the prison and down the passage.

Danny had to sit down. The experience of watching somebody arguing to save his life was making his head swim! He felt like he was trapped in a nightmare that was gradually becoming more and more horrific! And in just forty minutes time he was going to find out how the nightmare ended.

*

With guards patrolling the front terrace Spike and Charley's only option was to skirt around the side. They followed a rocky path along the side wall of the terrace, which eventually led around to the side of the house. Here the well-manicured lawns did not offer them much cover, so when they spotted a half-open window on the ground floor of the house, they both had the same thought.

They crossed the lawn, trying to look as casual as possible in case anyone was watching them. At the window Spike kept a lookout while Charley peeked inside for any signs of life. The coast appeared to be clear.

"Come on!" she said, quickly climbing in through the window.

Spike bundled himself in after her. Inside, they found themselves at one end of a luxuriously decorated passage. There was a thick carpet beneath their feet and precious-looking artefacts displayed all the way down one wall. They could also hear the sound of classical music drifting through the house and a woman's voice chatting away in a nearby room.

Spike and Charley swapped nervous glances before starting to make their way cautiously down the passage.

*

When Commander Skorzeny came up from beneath the house he discovered that the meeting had adjourned and all the men (scientists and soldiers) were now gathering for a cocktail party on the terrace.

On seeing him, several of the scientists (including the professor) tried to engage him in conversation, but he was frantically looking for the Fuhrer.

"Excuse me, gentleman," he said, "I need to speak to the Fuhrer most urgently."

However, the Fuhrer was nowhere to be seen. The only person the commander could see was the Fuhrer's assistant, Captain Bormann. He rushed over to him.

"Captain Bormann, I am looking for the Fuhrer. It is very important that I talk to him."

"The Fuhrer is in his residence, Commander, getting ready for the cocktail party."

"Captain, it is a matter of great urgency."

"What do you suggest I do, Commander, interrupt the Fuhrer while he is dressing?"

The commander and the captain locked eyes, neither of them willing to back down. Eventually it was the captain who looked away.

"I will send a message in with the valet, Commander. That is the best I can do."

As the captain headed off towards Hitler's residential wing the commander checked his watch. Five minutes had already passed.

*

Spike and Charley had only gone a short way down the passage when the music and the woman's voice suddenly grew louder. It was as if a door had just been opened and someone was about to step out into the passage!

With only seconds to react, Spike and Charley bundled themselves through the doorway closest to them. Spike closed the door as quietly as possible behind them then they stood dead still, listening.

They could now hear the woman's voice as she came down the passage - as well as another noise that sounded like... yapping dogs? The talking and yapping grew louder and louder. Spike and Charley tensed up, praying that whoever it was would continue past the door, but they didn't - they stopped right outside!

In an instant of wide-eyed panic Spike and Charley glanced at each other and fled from the door. They were in a large bedroom. The first thing they saw was a big four-poster bed - they scrambled under it.

Moments later, the bedroom door opened and a pair of well-heeled woman's feet came striding in. The woman kicked off her shoes then called out.

"*Stasi*! *Negus*!"

Trotting into the room (at exactly the same level as Spike and Charley!) came two well-groomed, fluffy Scottish terriers.

\*

The commander was pacing impatiently outside the entrance to the Fuhrer's residential wing (guarded by two very serious-looking armed soldiers) when the door suddenly opened and Captain Bormann emerged.

"Commander," he said, coming over, "I have left a message with the Fuhrer's valet. That is the best I can do. Now, may I suggest you go and join the others for a drink on the terrace?"

The commander had no intention of doing any such thing. He looked at his watch again. It was four thirty.

\*

When the dogs saw the two strange faces under the bed they

began to yap.

The moment they started, an irate male voice roared from behind an adjoining door.

"Eva! Shut those little mutts up, please!"

The woman tried to quieten them.

"Shh, my babies! Shh!"

The dogs continued to yap, and suddenly the adjoining door flew open and the man's voice yelled again.

"Shut them up, Eva, or *I* will shut them up!"

From beneath the bed Spike and Charley could now see that there was a man standing in the doorway of what looked like the bathroom. All they could see were his slippers and the bottom of his dressing gown.

"Eva! Please!" the man said. "I'm trying to prepare my speech in here!"

"I'm so sorry, my darling," the woman replied. "I don't know what's got into them."

Spike now lowered his head slightly to try and catch a glimpse of the man's face. The moment he saw it he quickly pulled his head back.

Surprised by this reaction, Charley decided to take a look for herself. She too lowered her head until the man's face came into view. The face was smothered in shaving cream, but even so, from the slicked down hair and the big moustache, Charley knew instantly that she was staring at Adolf Hitler!

*

It was now twenty-five minutes to five and still Commander Skorzeny hadn't received any feedback from within the Fuhrer's residence. Eventually he decided to try and go in himself, but as soon as he approached the entrance both guards stepped in his way and raised their weapons.

No one was entering the Fuhrer's wing without special permission.

\*

Charley and Spike were still getting over the fact that they were in Adolf Hitler's bedroom when another serious problem presented itself. It came in the form of a large Alsatian dog that had just come loping into the room.

As soon as the two terriers saw the Alsatian they quickly scampered under the bed as well. They were still nervous of Charley and Spike (and were keeping their distance), but with the Alsatian around, they had obviously decided that the humans under the bed were the lesser of two evils!

Now the Alsatian crouched down near the bed and started to bark.

"Blondi!" Hitler snapped. "Don't *you* start!"

This made Blondi the Alsatian quieten down a bit, but he continued to sit with his head on his paws staring at the four faces under the bed. Any movement was greeted with a low, lip-quivering growl.

Spike and Charley lay absolutely still. *What else could they do*? The woman was now sitting at her dressing table applying her make-up. Spike had guessed that she must be Eva Braun, Hitler's partner. Only in the last days of the war would Hitler marry her. The ceremony would take place in an underground bunker beneath Berlin then the couple would commit suicide together.

Spike was busy wondering how he knew these facts (was it the *Encyclopaedia* program again?) when his thoughts were interrupted by the sound of faint music. The odd thing about the music was that it was a track they knew very well! In fact, it was Green Day's song 'American Idiot' - a song from 2004! How could that be?

Spike took another peek at Hitler, who had gone back to shaving with the bathroom door open, and he now noticed that the Fuhrer had earphones plugged into his ears - and the wire led down into one of his dressing gown pockets. Suddenly Spike knew exactly where the music was coming from. Hitler was listening to Danny's *iPod*!

Just at that moment Hitler sang in a very out-of-tune voice.

"*Don't wannabe an American idiot!*" He then did a little dance at the basin. "American idiots! Yes! Good song!" he said, laughing.

Under the bed Spike and Charley had to bury their heads to stifle the uncontrollable laughter threatening to burst out of them.

As Hitler continued to shave and sing (or rather *croak*!) at the basin Spike suddenly had the urge to put his *Mindbender* program into action. He stared at Hitler and began to concentrate hard. Charley could see that Spike was up to something and she now also looked at the Fuhrer to see what was happening. As she watched, Hitler picked up a pair of scissors and cut off both ends of his large moustache - then he shaved the sides completely until all that was left was a small section under his nose. When he had finished he admired his new look in the mirror.

Once again Spike and Charley buried their heads to muffle their laughter.

"Eva, what do you think?" Hitler asked as he came sauntering through to the bedroom.

Eva was right in the middle of applying her lipstick when she saw his reflection in the mirror.

"Oh, my!" she said, sounding very surprised. "What have you done?"

But Hitler was busy admiring himself and, with the music still blaring in his ears, he hadn't heard what she had said.

"Hm? You like it?" he asked again. "I thought it had an original look to it."

Eva was speechless.

"It's certainly original!" she said under her breath, knowing that he still couldn't hear her - then she put on a smile for the Fuhrer.

*

The commander had had enough of waiting around by the entrance to the Fuhrer's residential quarters and had now decided on a different tactic. He had remembered seeing a telephone in the library and that is where he now returned.

As soon as he picked up the phone in the library a voice came on the other end.

"Switchboard."

"Hello, switchboard, this is Commander Skorzeny speaking. Please could you urgently put me through to the Fuhrer's residence? It is an emergency."

There was a moment's pause on the other end.

"Hold on, please."

Now, as the commander waited, he looked at his watch again. It was already twenty to five!

*

"Have I done the wrong thing?" Hitler asked Eva.

He was now looking slightly concerned about his new little moustache. He had even removed his earphones to hear her reply.

"No, no darling," Eva assured him. "I just have to get used to it, that's all."

Hitler continued to look worried.

"Will they laugh at me?"

"Of course they won't!" Eva replied. "Not at all. In fact, I'm starting to like it already."

"Really?" asked Hitler, perking up a bit.

Eva nodded.

"Someone as special as you needs to have a *special* look."

Hitler clearly liked the sound of that. He stood up straight again and looked at himself front-on then in profile. Eva now gave him a peck on the cheek, went through to the bathroom and closed the door. Hitler was obviously feeling happier because he now put the earphones back into his ears and strutted over to a large walk-in wardrobe to pick out a suit.

With Eva out of the room and Hitler busy in his wardrobe Charley and Spike knew this was their chance. The only problem was Blondi, who seemed to be just *itching* for them to make a move. Charley was busy sizing up how far it was to the bedroom door when something caught her eye. Sitting on top of a chest of drawers was a familiar-looking small, black remote control. It was the other *Immobilaser* that Danny had been carrying in his rucksack.

Charley silently pointed out the *Immobilaser* to Spike. Initially he seemed pleased to see it, but then he started to think the same thing as Charley. Would they make it to the *Immobilaser* before Blondi made it to them? And would the *Immobilaser* do its job when they got to it? They were only going to have one opportunity to find out!

Just then a telephone next to the bed started to ring. Charley and Spike both cursed the phone, thinking it had blown their chances, but when Hitler failed to come out of the walk-in wardrobe, they realised he probably couldn't hear the phone because of Green Day blasting in his ears!

Eva shouted from the bathroom.

"Are you going to get that, my love?"

Hitler didn't seem to hear that either. Charley and Spike knew that they had to move *now*! Spike whispered to Charley.

"You go for the *Immobilaser*. I'll try and... distract the dog." As he turned around to face Blondi he did not have a clue how he was going to achieve this *great idea of his*! "Good little dogs," he said as sweetly as possible to the two little dogs, leaning over to stroke one of them. But the little dog nearest him snapped at his hand and, when that happened, Blondi also tried to get under the bed!

Charley made her move. She scrambled out on the other side of the bed and charged across the room towards the chest of drawers. At the same time Blondi reversed out from under the bed and took off after her.

Charley reached the *Immobilaser,* fumbled with it for a second then turned it on Blondi just as he was about to pounce. The Alsatian froze on the spot.

"Let's go!" Charley hissed.

Spike was not only battling to get himself out from under the bed, he was also trying to shake off the small dog that was now attached to his ankle! He pulled himself out and eventually shook the dog off, but as he got to his feet, he froze! He had suddenly found himself face to face with Hitler!

Hitler, dressed only in a vest and a pair of large white underpants, looked as though he was going to explode.

"What is the meaning of-"

Now it was the Fuhrer who froze. Spike was surprised at first then he looked across at Charley and realised that she had zapped him with the *Immobilaser*. Suddenly he felt a lot more confident. With a huge smirk on his face he now approached the Fuhrer. What an amazing feeling it was to be so close to this monster - and look how short he was!

"Not so high and mighty now, eh, Mr Wolf?" Spike said, chuckling.

"Come on," said Charley, who was already by the door.

"I know we're not meant to alter history," Spike said, as he looked gleefully at Hitler's funny little moustache, "but I thought we should leave a little memento!"

Suddenly Eva's voice came from the bathroom again.

"Darling? Did you say something?"

"Come on, Spike!" Charley hissed again.

She had the door open and was checking out the passage.

# A Close Shave

Now Spike heard something behind him. It was a low growling sound. He slowly turned around to find Blondi staring at him. Spike took a step towards the door. The dog shook its head, still trying to figure out what had just happened. Spike took another small step - but now Blondi had focused on him and the dog's lips curled back in a teeth-baring snarl.

Suddenly Blondi launched himself - and so did Spike! In three giant strides Spike had reached the door. He knocked Charley out into the passage and slammed the door behind him. Blondi thumped up against the other side of the door in a frenzy of growling and scratching.

Spike leaned up against the door, panting, wide-eyed.

"You don't listen, do you?" said Charley, picking herself up off the floor and shaking her head. "Come on. Let's go and find Danny."

They took off down the passage.

\*

In the library the commander was still waiting impatiently on the phone. At last, the switchboard operator came back on the line.

"I'm sorry, Commander, but there is no answer in the Fuhrer's residence."

The commander slammed the phone down in frustration then looked at his watch again. It was now a quarter to five!

\*

Spike and Charley had discovered two guards at the entrance to Hitler's residential wing and realised they wouldn't be able to get into the main house that way. They decided to retrace their footsteps and were soon climbing back out of the same window they had come through earlier.

Once outside, they carried on around to the back of the house where they came across a large vegetable garden. Just as they were picking their way through it a rather severe-looking *fraulein* stood up from picking tomatoes.

"Extra kitchen staff?" she asked them.

"Pardon?" Charley replied.

"Are you the extra kitchen staff?" she repeated impatiently.

Charley glanced quickly at Spike then nodded.

"Yes..."

"About time!" the *fraulein* grumbled. "This way!"

They followed her into the kitchen.

\*

In Hitler's bedroom Blondi had gone over to his master and was nuzzling and licking him, and wondering why he wasn't getting any response.

Now Hitler blinked and started to come around.

"Hello, boy," he said, patting Blondi's head.

He started to look around the room. *Had he imagined seeing two children in his room?* He shook his head. All the medication the doctors had been prescribing him was starting to play tricks on his mind!

As he returned to his wardrobe he put the earphones back into his ears. A new song had started.

"*Don't ya wish ya girlfriend was hot like me?*" he croaked as he selected a suit.

*

Spike and Charley had been given white coats and told to start putting snacks onto trays for the cocktail party. While they were doing this they overheard some of the conversation between the other kitchen staff.

"Shame, he's just a youngster," one of the chefs was saying. "I believe it's going to happen at five o'clock. Reckon the least we could do is take him a meal."

This was setting off alarm bells in Charley's head.

"Sorry, what's happening at five o'clock?" she asked.

"The boy they brought here earlier," another chef replied casually. "He's being shot as a spy."

A wave of horror passed over Spike and Charley. Spike looked at his watch. It was ten to five!

"*We'll* take him a meal!" Charley said quickly.

Everyone looked at the *fraulein*-in-charge, who just shrugged and nodded.

"All right then," she said. "Make him up a tray of something."

As soon as Charley and Spike had the tray of food they headed for the door. Then something suddenly occurred to Charley and she turned to the nearest chef.

"Er... which way is it again?" she asked.

"Down the stone steps at the end of the corridor," the chef replied.

"Thanks!" said Charley as they scuttled out of the kitchen.

*

Down at the guards' barracks near the main gate the party was getting into full swing. Uncle Bernard was amazed to see that one barrel of wine was already close to being finished, but he was quite happy to open another one. He had no idea what was going on up on the hill, but as far as he was concerned the more tipsy soldiers there were, the better!

One very wobbly soldier staggered out of the barracks and went a short way into the forest to answer the call of nature. As he was completing his business he saw something that caused him to rub his eyes in disbelief! Rising up above the trees and continuing to climb up beside the cliff face were two soldiers on a flying motorbike!

The soldier looked at his mug of wine and tossed it aside. He had definitely had enough for one day!

\*

Charley and Spike trotted down the stone steps into the cold dim cellars. At the foot of the steps a guard suddenly stepped out and blocked their way.

"Food and drink for the prisoner," Charley said.

The guard checked the contents of their tray before letting them pass. As they half-walked half-ran down the passageway Charley suddenly felt butterflies in her stomach. It seemed like ages since they had last seen Danny, but in actual fact it had only been since yesterday!

It was a bittersweet moment as they rounded the corner and saw Danny standing behind the iron bars of the prison cell. He looked strange in his Hitler Youth uniform and the stress of his situation was written all over his face – but, as soon as he saw them, his expression turned instantly to one of huge relief.

"You're a couple of nutters, you know that?" he said with a smile.

Now he had even more reason to smile because the words he had just spoken had come out in English!

Spike went over to Danny with a grin.

"You didn't think we'd just desert you, did you?"

Charley had laid the tray of food down and was now hovering a bit awkwardly behind Spike.

"Hi, Charley," Danny said.

"Hi," she replied. She wanted to say more, but suddenly felt shy. Eventually all she said was, "Want something to eat?"

"No thanks," said Danny. He was still trying to absorb the fact that they were standing in front of him. "I can't believe you guys are here. I thought you would just go and stop Mortimer and Michelle."

"We couldn't do that," Spike said, "not without the book. What about your dad and Catie?"

At that moment Danny felt an overwhelming sense of gratitude and affection for these two new friends of his. He couldn't even begin to imagine what they had been through to get here!

Charley was already looking around the cell.

"We have to get you out of here! We heard they were going to..."

She hesitated, suddenly thinking that maybe Danny hadn't heard about the firing squad yet, but he finished the sentence for her.

"Shoot me, I know. They think I'm a spy."

Spike shook the locked gate of the cell in frustration.

"We just *have* to open this thing!"

This got Charley thinking.

"Spike, have you still got the *Immobilaser*?" she asked.

Spike felt in his pocket and pulled it out.

"What about using it on the guard?" Charley suggested. "He should have the keys."

It sounded like a reasonable plan.

"All right," said Spike, "let's give it a try, but if we do get the keys, we're going to have to move fast because these things don't immobilise for long. Believe me, *I* know!"

"Come on, let's do it," said Charley. "It's nearly five

o'clock."

"Υλικό προκαλείς," Danny said.

He had tried to say 'Good luck', but the English had gone again.

*

At the same time as Spike and Charley were heading back to the guard's post Adolf Hitler and Eva Braun were coming out onto the terrace to join the cocktail party.

The first thing everyone noticed was Hitler's new moustache! This caused several looks and quiet comments to pass between the guests, but everyone who greeted the Fuhrer smiled politely and did their best not to stare!

As soon as he spotted Hitler, Commander Skorzeny made a beeline towards him. However, there was a guest of honour at the party. The leader of Italy, Benito Mussolini, had arrived with his delegation and they were now also making their way over to greet Hitler. Captain Bormann suddenly appeared at the commander's side.

"Wait your turn, Commander," he said firmly.

The Italian ambassador came forward first to introduce Mussolini. Like everyone else he seemed surprised by Hitler's appearance, but tried not to show it.

"Mein Fuhrer," he said, saluting Hitler. "May I present Mr Moustacholini... er, I beg your pardon, I mean to say Mr *Mussolini*."

As Hitler greeted Mussolini he glanced at Eva to check if they were making fun of his moustache, but she smiled back, which made him feel better.

The commander tried to push forwards again to get to Hitler, but the Fuhrer and Mussolini were now exchanging pleasantries, and Captain Bormann held him back once more. The commander's patience was now running out. His watch indicated that it was less than two minutes to five!

\*

As Spike and Charley approached the small guard's room at the entrance to the cellars the guard came out to see what they wanted.

Spike had been avoiding speaking German lately because of his *Translatormate* problems, but he decided now might be a good time to try again.

"Marmalade and crafty ambulances welcome pig's trotter delight," said Spike in German.

The guard blinked a few times. *Had he heard correctly?*

"Midnight says hello to the giraffe doctor's spaceship," Spike continued.

He had no idea what he was saying, but he was enjoying the thorough confusion it was causing!

Charley took advantage of this to survey the inside of the guard's room and there she spotted a number of keys hanging on a key rack. She nodded at Spike, who already had the *Immobilaser* in his hand. He pointed it at the guard and pressed the button. To their great relief, the guard froze.

"OK, hurry, Charles!" Spike shouted, as he checked that no one was coming.

In a flash, Charley was inside the guard's room. She decided to just grab all the keys. Seconds later she emerged.

"Let's go!"

Spike decided to zap the guard one more time for good measure then they took off back down the passage towards Danny's cell.

As they neared the cell, they began to hear noises. There was some sort of activity going on and they could hear voices and the clanking of the metal gate. With only one more bend in the passage until they reached the cell they slowed their pace right down then peered around the corner.

They were shocked by the sight! The sergeant and several of his men were escorting Danny from his cell.

"No!" Charley blurted out, without meaning to.

It was loud enough for the sergeant to hear. He looked down the passage towards them and they had to quickly step back into the shadows.

Next time they sneaked a look they saw Danny, hands bound behind his back, being led away down the passage towards the execution chamber.

\*

With only seconds to go before five o'clock the commander felt he had no choice but to interrupt Hitler and Mussolini. He shook off Captain Bormann's arm and walked up to the two leaders.

"Excuse me, Mein Fuhrer, my apologies for interrupting, but I need to speak to you on a matter of the utmost urgency."

Hitler glared at him, not appreciating the interruption.

"What is it, Commander?" he snapped.

"Mein Fuhrer, it concerns the young boy who is about to be shot."

"*About* to be shot!" the Fuhrer exclaimed, his eyes flashing angrily. "I ordered the execution to be carried out immediately!"

"Yes, Mein Fuhrer, but due to a remarkable discovery regarding the boy I asked that the execution be delayed until five o'clock - so that I could ask you to reconsider."

Hitler looked at his watch.

"Commander, it *is* five o'clock, and I have much more important matters to think about. I believe there is no point in continuing this conversation."

With that, Hitler turned his back on the commander.

"My apologies, Il Duce," he said to Mussolini. "Let me show you the view."

As the two leaders walked away to survey the scenery the commander stood dumbstruck for a few moments. He knew there was nothing more he could do. He backtracked out of the party, ignoring all the stares he was receiving, and started to run

# A CLOSE SHAVE

towards the cellar steps.

\*

Danny was taken into a long narrow room. At the far end was a wall of sandbags and a single wooden post. *Is this how the nightmare is going to end?* he thought as they walked him down towards the wooden post. He knew that no one else could save him now. He had been looking for the opportunity to use his *Combat X*, but ever since taking him out of the cell the guards had constantly had their weapons trained on him.

The bulldog sergeant tied his hands tightly to the post as though he had done it a hundred times before. Danny thought he could smell wine on his breath. He looked up to see six soldiers, rifles at the ready, lined up at the other end.

Once Danny was securely tied to the post the sergeant walked back down to the firing squad and took up his position beside them. He checked his watch. It was five o'clock.

"Firing squad ready!" he barked.

The soldiers brought their weapons up to waist height.

Danny struggled to get his hands free; he knew it was his only chance. He then noticed some movement in the passage. It was Charley and Spike in the shadows just outside the entrance. As they came closer to the door he could see the horror on their faces.

"Firing squad aim!"

Danny looked directly into Charley's wide eyes. He could hear his heart pounding.

The soldiers raised their rifles into the firing position...

Chapter 17

# Hogs on the Hill

*Boom! Boom! Boom!*

Everyone heard the three loud blasts at the same time.

The sergeant in charge of the firing squad - who was just about to shout '*Fire!*' - held up his hand suddenly and listened.

Commander Skorzeny, halfway down the stone steps, stopped immediately to listen. The three deep dull thuds sounded like they had come from upstairs. *Was it the sound of gunfire?* There was something different about it!

Danny thought he was dead. He had been struggling right up until the last moment to get his hands free - not wanting to believe that this was how it was all going to end. When the blasts sounded he thought it was the firing squad and instinctively shut his eyes. Now he opened them again. *Had he been shot?* He looked down. It didn't look like it. It didn't feel like it!

There were only two people on that mountain who had heard that strange-sounding gunfire before. Outside in the shadowy passage, Spike and Charley glanced at each other. They were both thinking the same thing - *there were Hogs in the building!*

\*

Moments earlier up on the terrace, Hitler had been pointing out the picturesque town of *Berchtesgaden* to Mussolini, when they were greeted by a sight so strange that it took them all a couple of seconds to register what they were looking at. Two soldiers on a motorbike and sidecar were rising up, slowly and silently, from below the terrace wall then hovering there in front of them - *in mid-air*!

Hitler stopped in mid-sentence, his arm still pointing towards *Berchtesgaden*.

Mussolini started applauding, thinking this must be a display of the latest German technology, and when *he* started clapping the rest of the Italian delegation joined in. The Italians then began to notice the expressions on all the German faces around them and their applause quickly died down.

Hitler's SS bodyguards were the first to react. They quickly ran over to try and escort the Fuhrer and Mussolini to safety, but Hitler was not having any of it. He was too intrigued by this sight to be moved, and he shook the guards off. This gave the guards no option but to form a line in front of the leaders to provide them with cover, and that's when they made their first big mistake - they aimed their machine guns at the flying motorbike.

*Boom! Boom! Boom!*

Three blasts from one of the Hog's strange stubby weapons and three of the guards were blown clear off their feet.

Suddenly there was chaos as the cocktail party scattered.

Hitler and Mussolini were now dragged off by the bodyguards, whether they liked it or not! Even as the Fuhrer was being scrambled towards the house he couldn't help looking back at the incredible flying motorbike. It had now moved over the terrace and was preparing to land.

There was a crush at the doors as most of the crowd tried to get inside. Only a few brave generals had stood their ground and were now taking potshots at the flying bike with their revolvers.

*

Inside the house, the commander had come back up the steps to see what all the commotion was about. With all the panic-stricken scientists rushing in from the terrace he initially wasn't able to see what was causing all the pandemonium, but then he got to a window and was just in time to witness the astonishing sight of a motorbike and sidecar *landing* on the terrace! As he tried to make sense of what he was looking at, the two enormous men on the bike let off a few more blasts from their strange-looking weapons and, to the commander's amazement, a couple of soldiers were literally blown right off the terrace!

More soldiers had now started to arrive, but the two giant men didn't seem particularly worried. They had climbed off the bike, tossed their helmets aside to reveal long, unruly dreadlocked hair and now looked ready to take on anything that was thrown at them.

Watching from the window, the commander was trying to figure out *who on earth these men were*? He could see from their hair and tattoos that they were not German soldiers. Now he was beginning to wonder if they were even human!

\*

From down below it sounded like a full-scale war had erupted upstairs.

"Let's move!" the sergeant shouted to his men.

Suddenly Danny was forgotten as all the soldiers rushed for the door.

Charley and Spike had to step back behind the door to avoid being seen as the soldiers came past. Only when they were sure that everyone had left did they enter the chamber and head straight over to Danny.

"All right, mate?" Spike asked as he went behind the post and started to untie Danny's hands.

Charley was fighting to hold back the tears, but she didn't want Danny to see, so she also went behind him. They were tears of immense relief! Looking through that door a few moments earlier she had been convinced that Danny was about to die.

Danny was also in a state of shock. In those last frenzied seconds, as the firing squad was preparing to fire, he had thought of his mother. *Now she's lost everyone! First dad and Catie - and now me as well!*

They could now hear more blasts coming from upstairs.

"Know what those are?" Spike asked.

Danny shook his head.

"Hogs," said Spike.

Danny took a few seconds to digest this. *Hogs? As in - those horrendous creatures from the future?* He tried to ask Spike how he knew this, but the question came out in a strange language. He cursed. His English had still not returned.

Charley had understood.

"That's what their weapons sound like," she explained.

"Yeah, ask us - we know!" said Spike, as he undid the final knot and Danny's hands came free.

Danny rubbed his wrists and nodded his thanks to Spike.

"No speaka da English, huh?" Spike joked. "Don't worry, I'm also having language issues. Looks like old Monkey Girl here was the only one who got a decent *Translatormate* program, but you should have seen what happened to her out on the cliff!"

Spike!" Charley snapped. "This isn't the time! We have to get out of here! We have to get back to Uncle Bernard's truck!"

This caused Danny to blurt out something else in the strange language. Spike looked to Charley for the translation.

"He says we have to get the book first!" she said.

Spike frowned and looked at his watch.

"Hey, listen! I don't want to be the bearer of bad news or anything, but in less than three hours time Mortimer and Michelle are going down to that harbour. There is *no way* we are going to make it there by then!"

"No! We must! We have to find a way!" Danny said suddenly, his eyes blazing.

The others looked surprised; he had just spoken English.

"It comes and goes," Danny said, shrugging. "The same with my *Combat X*."

"Where's the book?" Charley asked.

"I don't know. Some professor had it up there," Danny said, pointing up to where they could hear all the gunfire.

This news did not fill Spike with joy.

"*Great!*" he muttered. "In the middle of *Hogsville*."

Danny was clearly itching to get moving.

"*Vamos!*" he said as he started for the door.

"He said '*Let's go!*'," said Charley, taking off after him.

"Yes, I got that bit," said Spike, who also followed along – but with slightly less enthusiasm.

\*

The arrival of these strangely ugly, but super-efficient, fighters (on a motorbike that *flew*!) had the commander's mind working overtime. *Where could they possibly have come from? What did they want? They looked like something from the future… From the future… The future! Did they have something to do with the boy downstairs? Oh, no!* Suddenly the commander remembered Danny. He looked at his watch. It was well after five. He then saw the sergeant and his men coming up the stairs. His first thought was, *Too late! They must have shot the boy!*

As the sergeant came rushing over, the commander confronted him.

"Sergeant, the boy? Is he…"

"He's alive, Commander," the Sergeant replied. He was now clearly more interested in the gunfire on the terrace. "Are we under attack?" he shouted.

Before the commander could answer, a huge explosion suddenly ripped through the front door of the house and everyone was blown off their feet.

The commander was deposited on his back in a shower of dust and debris. It took him a few moments to recover, but when he did manage to lift his head and blink through the dust, he was greeted by an ominous sight. The two giants were standing in the exploded doorway, blasting any soldiers who tried to resist.

The commander knew he had to find cover. The entrance to the cellar stairs was probably his best bet, but now the giants were on the move again and they were coming his way! *Were they also heading for the cellar steps? Were they after the boy?*

The commander was a lot closer to the steps than they were. It was now or never! He launched himself towards the steps and, as he did so, one of the giants swung his weapon around.

*Boom!*

The explosion hit the wall and the commander tumbled down the steps with bricks and plaster raining down on top of him. At the bottom of the steps he picked himself up again.

"I'm getting too old for this," he muttered.

He heard somebody shouting.

"Commander!"

Looking up, he saw three youngsters running down the passage towards him. In the front was Daniel, and with him were two others, a boy and a girl, whom he had never seen before.

"Not this way!" the commander shouted.

The three of them kept on coming.

He shouted again.

"Daniel! *Go back!*"

Now he looked back up the steps and saw two sets of enormous boots arriving at the top.

"*Go back!*" he shouted again.

It seemed like the youngsters had also seen the boots because suddenly they were all slamming on brakes and turning around. The commander took off after them and as he ran he kept looking back, knowing that once the Hogs reached the bottom they would be sitting ducks if they stayed in this passage.

"Go down there!" he roared suddenly, pointing to a passage that was coming up on one side.

They all ducked into it and kept running. It was like they were passing through a rabbit's warren of passages and rooms.

Soon they reached a doorway with a thick metal door, and the commander shepherded them all through. The door was so heavy that they all had to help push it closed. The commander tightened a large wheel on the door as if he was locking a safe. With the wheel firmly tightened he started to relax a little.

"That should do it," he said. "Welcome to the Fuhrer's private bunker."

Spike was still eyeing the door.

"I'm not so sure that will stop them," he said.

This annoyed the commander.

"Who are these men?" he growled.

"Hogs," Charley replied.

"Hogs?" the commander enquired, frowning, waiting for an explanation.

But Charley just nodded.

"Yup, Hogs."

Before the commander could ask any more questions Danny stepped in.

"Is there another way out of here, Commander?" he asked. "Where does that door lead to?"

He was pointing to a door at the end of the room.

"So now he can speak English I see," said the commander, clearly thinking that Danny had been tricking him all this time. "You must think I'm a fool?"

"No, Commander, not at all," Danny replied, "but there's no time to explain now."

"Hey!"

Spike suddenly shut them up with a finger to his lips then pointed towards the door. He had heard something on the other side. They all listened. Yes, there was definitely a noise as if someone was trying to open it. Suddenly Danny sensed the danger.

"Get away from the door!" he shouted.

The others fled across the room - but the commander was too slow. Seconds later, the door exploded and he was slammed into the opposite wall. As the smoke and dust cleared they all looked anxiously towards the door. It was severely bent and cracked, but it still seemed to be holding. Then they started to look around for the commander.

For the third time in the last five minutes Commander Skorzeny blinked his way back into consciousness to discover that his bruised and battered body was once again buried in a pile of rubble! This time he wasn't sure he could move! When he looked up he found Danny bending over him, shouting something - but his ears were ringing so much he couldn't hear anything.

"Commander! Are you all right?" Danny shouted again.

He grabbed hold of the commander's arm and was just about to help him up when there was suddenly a scream from behind him.

"*Danny!*"

It was Charley, pointing at the door. Something was glinting through one of the cracks. It was a Hog's eyeball staring directly at her!

"Give us a hand here, Spike!" Danny shouted, and between the two of them they managed to haul the commander to his feet.

"We have to get out of here!" Danny shouted.

They scrambled for the door and burst out into another passage.

"Which way, Commander?" Danny shouted.

"*What?*"

"*Which way do we go?*"

The commander looked both ways then seemed to get his bearings.

"This way!" he shouted.

They all set off down the passage and hadn't gone far when another explosion shook the building.

"There goes the door!" shouted Spike.

At the end of the passage they discovered a lift door. The commander pressed the lift button and now they waited.

"The Fuhrer's private lift!" the commander shouted. "Goes directly up to his residential quarters!"

At this stage the others were more preoccupied with looking down the passage for any sign of the Hogs.

"Come on, lift!" Charley muttered.

*Ping*! The lift arrived, but the door seemed to take an age to open!

Spike glanced down the passage again and now he saw the two large figures lumbering towards them.

"Here they come!" he screeched.

At that moment the lift doors finally opened and everyone piled in. Inside, Danny hit the 'TOP FLOOR' button, but again the doors seemed to take forever to do anything!

"Come on! Come on!" Charley prayed.

They could hear the heavy footsteps coming down the passage.

"*Close, you stupid door!*" Spike growled.

Charley grabbed hold of Danny's arm.

As the door started to close Danny could see the Hogs bounding towards them. They were only a few yards away when the door shut completely, and suddenly there was an almighty crash as they slammed into it. The lift shuddered for a few seconds then started to ascend.

In the sudden silence all they could hear was their own heavy breathing. Charley sheepishly released Danny's arm.

"I told you that door wouldn't stop them," Spike grumbled.

"*What?*" The commander was wiggling his jaw, trying to get his ears to pop. "Who *are* you two anyway?" he shouted.

"I'm Charley and that's my brother, Spike," Charley replied. "Pleased to meet you!"

"*What?*"

"*Pleased to meet you!*"

"Oh, really! Wish I could say the same!"

"Commander!" Danny spoke loudly in his ear. "We are very grateful for all your help, but there is one more thing we need to ask. That book belonging to my uncle! We have to find it before we leave!"

The commander tried to remember.

"Either the professor has it, or it's still in the meeting room!" he shouted.

Danny nodded.

"OK, we'll have to split up. Spike, you go and look in the meeting room. I'll show you where it is. Charley and I will look for the professor."

Now they could feel the lift slowing as it reached the top.

"Just one thing before you go," the commander shouted. "These men monsters that are on our tail… How do we stop them?"

They all glanced at each other, but no one seemed to have an answer.

"I'm sorry," said Danny, shaking his head, "we're not sure."

Now the lift doors opened and Spike suddenly flung his hands up into the air.

"*Whoah! Whoah, please!*"

Outside the lift was a group of soldiers staring down the barrels of their guns at them. The commander quickly stepped forwards and shouted at the officer in charge.

"It's the next lift that arrives you'll want to worry about – and I suggest you increase your manpower and firepower!"

He now set about organising the troops while the others carried on through to the main body of the house.

\*

The house was a scene of chaos and destruction. It looked like several bombs had ripped through the building. People were running everywhere, including a group of panic-stricken scientists, who were being hurriedly escorted to safety. Danny looked hard, but he couldn't see the professor amongst them.

"Spike, see those doors over there on the other side?" Danny said, pointing across the large reception area. "The door on the right is the meeting room. You check in there. We'll look for the professor then meet you by the entrance in about five minutes."

"OK. Now, don't go getting lost! We have to get out of this place!" Spike shouted.

As Spike headed off into the chaos, Danny's attention shifted to the group of scientists being led into an adjoining room.

"Maybe the professor's already in there?" Danny said. "Let's go and take a look."

Danny and Charley picked their way across the room through the smoke and debris. Every now and again they had to get out of the way as soldiers came running through.

When they reached the room Danny peered in through the doorway. The scientists were huddled together in groups, chatting nervously amongst themselves. Danny scanned the room, but there was no sign of the professor.

"He's not in there," Danny said to Charley, and was just about to suggest they look elsewhere when he noticed another group of scientists coming towards them, and amongst them, he now saw the professor.

Danny let some of the group go by then stepped out into the professor's path. The professor couldn't believe his eyes.

"You? I thought… I thought you were…"

"*Dead?*" Danny felt his anger rising. "Sorry to disappoint you, *Prof*! I'm looking for my book!"

The professor shifted uncomfortably, his eyes darting everywhere – then, to Danny's great surprise, he suddenly straightened up and gave a salute.

"*Heil Hitler!*" he roared.

"*Heil* whoever you want!" Danny said with a sneer. "*Just give me back my book!*"

He then heard Charley right beside him, clearing her throat.

"Er... Danny," she said softly.

Danny was not about to be interrupted.

"*Where is it, Prof?*" he raged.

Charley tried again.

"Danny!"

"*What?*" Danny snapped.

"Er... the Fuhrer..." Charley mumbled.

"*What about him?*" Danny asked impatiently.

"He's... um... standing behind you."

\*

Just as Danny's brain was busy processing this latest piece of information, Spike was busy slipping into the meeting room. He had opened the door a little cagily, not at all sure what to expect, but was pleased to discover that the room appeared to be completely deserted.

Stretching down the entire length of the room was a long table littered with documents and empty water glasses. An object right down at the other end immediately caught his eye - Danny's rucksack!

"Yes!" Spike said triumphantly. *At last something was going their way!* He started down the room to collect it, but hadn't got more than halfway when he heard a voice behind him.

"You!"

Spike froze and slowly turned around. As soon as he saw the man, he recognised him. It was Hitler's second in command, *Reichsmarschall* Goering - head of the *Luftwaffe* (the German Air Force). He had obviously been hiding his rather bulky body behind the door. Now his revolver was pointing at Spike, which was not good news because he appeared to be very nervous and jumpy.

"Who are you?" he demanded to know. "What do you want in here?"

He was speaking in German, which worried Spike slightly

because he knew he was going to have to try and reply in German!

"There is a lemon tree on your nose," Spike said, hoping like anything that he had just explained that he was a waiter. "It's the purple donkey's bath time," he added for good measure, indicating all the glasses he had come to collect.

The *Reichsmarschall* stared at Spike for a few seconds then cocked his revolver.

Spike guessed his reply had probably not come out as intended. He knew he needed another plan - *fast*! It was the ideal time to use his *Mindbender* program. He just hoped it was still working!

\*

The first thing Danny noticed when he turned around was Hitler's funny little moustache. It was so odd-looking that he let out an involuntary grunt of amusement, which he managed to quickly turn into a cough and cover up with his hand.

The Fuhrer was sure he had seen a giggle and his dark eyes now darted around to see if anyone else had noticed it or, worse still, if anyone else was laughing at him! He spoke through clenched teeth, his eyes boring deep into Danny's.

"I ordered this boy to be shot!"

Danny stared directly back at him. Suddenly he didn't care any more. He wasn't going to let himself be captured again. He didn't care that it was the Fuhrer standing in front of him. All Danny saw was a self-important little man with a stupid-looking moustache!

When Hitler nodded to the two blond SS brutes standing nearby, Danny's mind was already made up. As the soldiers came forwards to grab him, he lashed out with such a flurry of punches that they were both knocked clean out before they even hit the floor!

It was completely unexpected and everyone stepped back in amazement. Hitler could only blink repeatedly at the sight of the two large soldiers now sprawled at his feet.

When Hitler looked back at Danny, Danny gave him a big smile. He could feel the incredible calm and strength growing inside him. His *Combat X* appeared to be alive and well, and ready for action!

\*

Unfortunately, the same could not be said for Spike's *Mindbender*. He had been concentrating hard, trying to get it to activate, but still nothing was happening. All the time, *Reichsmarschall* Goering was looking more and more threatening. He kept edging closer, the gun still pointing at Spike.

To try and calm the *Reichsmarschall*, Spike decided he needed to keep talking. He wanted to reassure him that he was just an employee doing his job.

"It's the planet with the onion rings," Spike said in a calm tone, pointing to himself. "My feet - they like to be in chocolate mousse."

Instead of calming the *Reichsmarschall*, Spike's talk seemed to be having the opposite effect. He was looking more and more infuriated. His eyes had taken on a strange wild look and the hand clutching the gun was starting to shake uncontrollably.

"Shut up with your nonsense!" he roared – then suddenly the gun went off, and Spike heard the bullet go whizzing past his ear!

In seconds, Spike was underneath the large table. As he watched the *Reichsmarschall's* shiny black boots circling the table, he concentrated with all his might on activating *Mindbender*.

\*

Outside the lift, Commander Skorzeny now had more than fifty heavily-armed soldiers waiting with guns, bazookas, flame-throwers and various other weapons all trained on the lift doors. Everyone was watching the flashing green numbers above the door and when the light stopped on their floor every finger tightened on every trigger.

The lift doors opened and it was as if hell itself had suddenly been unleashed. Machine guns crackled, flame-throwers scorched, bazookas blasted. There was such a barrage of intense noise and firepower that the commander had to shout and wave his arms repeatedly before the firing eventually died down.

Now all eyes peered anxiously towards the lift, which was, for the moment, completely enveloped in thick smoke. Only when the smoke began to clear did it became apparent that the blackened, bullet-hole ridden lift was in fact *empty*!

"They must have back-tracked!" the commander shouted. "Over to the stairs! Let's move!"

The soldiers all gathered up their weapons and set off after him towards the main body of the house, but one soldier was left behind. He was having trouble with his weapon, which had jammed, and he was now so busy trying to get it unjammed that he didn't notice the two large figures swinging down through the trapdoor in the roof of the lift. When he eventually did look up the two enormous men were already towering above him. His first reaction was to shout to the soldiers who were disappearing down the passage, but his shout was drowned out by a single blast of hog-fire.

\*

As expected, more soldiers had come running after Danny had knocked down the first two, but once again he was able to deal with each attacker quickly and effectively, and soon there were another three men laid out on the floor.

Hitler had drawn his revolver and was pointing it at Danny - but he seemed more fascinated than threatened by this boy with the incredible fighting skills.

It was just then that the commander and his men opened fired on the lift, and this almighty outburst of gunfire distracted everyone for a moment.

It was exactly what Danny needed. He suddenly lunged for the professor and managed to haul him around so that he became a protective shield should the Fuhrer decide to shoot. He tried to resist, but there was no way he was going to shake off Danny's powerful grip.

At first Hitler seemed tempted to shoot - then he must have remembered that Professor von Heisenberg was one of Germany's most valuable scientists!

Keeping the professor in front of him, Danny backed away from the Fuhrer. He was trying to move towards the main entrance where they had agreed to meet Spike. He was also trying to see where Charley had got to, and he now noticed that she had quietly slipped away from the Fuhrer's group and was coming around to join him.

"Let go of me!" the professor fumed.

"In a moment, Prof," Danny replied, as he continued to back up. He was really hoping that Spike might arrive to lend him a hand, but so far there was no sign of him. "Come on, Spike," Danny muttered. "Where are you?"

\*

Spike was actually still under the table. He could hear *Reichsmarschall* Goering wheezing and groaning as he struggled to bend down to look for him. Eventually the large soldier had to get down on all fours to continue his search.

Looking at the *Reichsmarschall*, all pink and sweaty, and crawling around on his hands and knees, Spike couldn't help thinking how much he resembled a large pig!

The *Reichsmarschall* was busy hurling abuse at Spike, unleashing a tirade of curses and insults in his direction, but Spike just stared back at him and concentrated his mind - suddenly all the abusive rude language changed from German into snorting piggy noises! Spike could not conceal his delight. All he had done was concentrate hard on one thought - *You are a pig! You are a pig!* - and thankfully his *Mindbender* had done the rest. Suddenly the *Reichsmarschall* seemed to forget about Spike. He went crawling off, as if foraging for food.

Now Spike remembered what he was meant to be doing in there. He quickly climbed out from under the table and rushed over to Danny's rucksack. He pulled everything out of it, but unfortunately there was no sign of Uncle Morty's journal.

*Let's hope Danny and Charley are having better luck,* Spike thought as he repacked the rucksack and slung it over his shoulder.

Before leaving he took a last look at the *Reichsmarschall,* who was now busy chomping on the curtains.

"Good pig!" he shouted as he rushed for the door.

*

When they heard the single blast of hog-fire behind them the commander and his troops came to a screeching halt and looked back down towards the lift. They were greeted by an extremely intimidating sight. The two giants were walking towards them, side by side, their sinister stubby weapons ready at the hip.

"*Take cover!*" the commander screamed and as his men dived in all directions, the terrible brutal hog-fire began.

The commander did all he could to hold them back. He rallied his troops, shouted orders and tried to organise their defence, but the Hogs kept coming. Their weapons were so unbelievably powerful that the soldiers were continually forced to retreat.

Commander Skorzeny soon found himself back in the main body of the house. He tried to mount one last line of defence, but blast after blast of hog-fire ripped through his troops until he suddenly realised that he was literally the last man standing. He knew this was the end. He had run out of ammunition some time ago. There was nothing more he could do but await his fate.

As the two Hogs came striding through into the main reception area the commander stood up, hands by his sides, and prepared for the inevitable. *So this is how my war will end?* he thought, smiling ruefully as the Hogs approached. *I survived the British. I survived the Americans, but who could ever survive these terrible killing machines?* He closed his eyes.

The Hogs just shoved him out of the way. They weren't interested in him. Their in-built tracking devices were guiding them directly across the large reception area - directly towards Danny and Charley!

\*

As these two enormously destructive giants approached, the professor was suddenly acutely aware of the fact that if he didn't remove himself from the scene now one of these beasts was going to do it for him! He reached into his jacket pocket, pulled something out and thrust it at Danny.

To Danny's amazement it was Uncle Morty's journal!

"Here! Take it!" the professor roared. "Just let me go!"

Danny took the book, tossed the professor aside then, to Charley's surprise, he tried to hand her the book!

"Take it and go!" he shouted.

Charley was shocked.

"What? No! What about you?"

"Just take it and try and get it to Mortimer! Please!" Danny pleaded as he now placed the book into her hands.

The Hogs were now halfway across the reception area, but Charley remained rooted to the spot. She could not bring herself to leave Danny's side!

Danny realised what he had to do. If *she* wasn't going to move *he* would have to! His aim was to draw the Hogs' attention away from her. It was her only chance! He walked out to meet the Hogs.

"*Danny! What are you doing?*" Charley screamed.

"Get out of here, Charley! Now!"

The Hogs looked delighted to see one of their targets coming towards them. They brought their weapons up into the firing position and were just about to pull their triggers when suddenly… they froze.

For a second Danny couldn't work it out then he saw Spike rushing towards him.

"Hurry! Get their weapons!" Spike shouted. "It won't last!"

In his hand Spike held the *Immobilaser*. Moments earlier he had emerged from the meeting room to see the Hogs and Danny walking towards each other. That's when he had started to scramble around in his pockets for the *Immobilaser* and, luckily, had found it just in time!

"We have to get rid of their weapons," Spike shouted.

It made sense to Danny, and the two of them now grappled with the weapons and managed to prise them out of the Hogs' hands. Spike then took both weapons out onto the terrace and threw them over the edge of the cliff.

Danny, meanwhile, was getting his first close-up look at an immobilasered Hog - it wasn't a pretty sight! He was looking at the one with the tattooed neck when, out of the corner of his eye, he thought he saw the other one *blink*! He looked again, but saw no movement. He must have imagined it.

Suddenly a shout went up.

"*Get away from me!*"

Danny swung around. It was Charley - the professor was trying to get the journal back from her! She managed to break free and make a run for it, but he was right behind her, and he looked like he was about to catch her when Charley did something remarkable and made it seem like the most natural thing in the world! As she ran she shoved the journal down the front of her blouse then headed straight for one of the enormous heavy velvet curtains that framed the massive high windows. With a single leap she attached herself to the curtain and quickly scurried up and out of the reach of the professor's clutching paws.

"*Go, Monkey Girl!*" Danny exclaimed, smiling.

But his smile disappeared almost immediately. He had suddenly caught a whiff of something rotten. He turned to find himself staring at the Hog with the rotten teeth. The Hog gave him a grotesque smile and nodded as if to say, '*I'm awake now! Let's play!*'.

Danny's reaction was immediate. He punched the Hog so hard that the giant staggered back a few steps and shook his head. Beyond him, Danny could see the other Hog was also coming back to life. He was blinking and looking around for his weapon. Both Hogs seemed to focus on Danny at the same time - now there were no more smiles! They started towards him, forcing Danny back. His mind was racing. *What was his next move?* He was getting backed up into a corner, right beside the curtain that Charley had just climbed. There was nowhere left to go!

As Danny took up his fighting stance, everything seemed to slow down and he became aware of every small detail around him. He even noticed Hitler and his group gathering over to one side like interested spectators at a prize fight. He saw the commander hovering nearby, looking like he wanted to help, but not knowing how.

High up above him he then heard a cracking sound. It was the curtain rod holding the curtain to which Charley was clinging. It was breaking! He looked up, expecting to see her falling - but again she surprised him. As the rod broke, she leapt from the curtain onto a giant chandelier hanging from the ceiling. There she hung as the curtain came cascading down beside Danny.

The first thing that caught Danny's eye was a section of curtain rod that had clattered to the floor beside him. He picked up a length and gave it a few test swipes. It felt a bit long and unwieldy. With lightning-fast speed he delivered two sharp cracks to the head of the nearest Hog. On the second blow he managed to break the end of his rod off.

"That's better!"

Danny swished the rod back and forth. He had even surprised himself with how unbelievably quick he was with the makeshift weapon. Of course, he knew this was *Combat X* coming into play. What he didn't know was that the appearance of the curtain rod had activated one of *Combat X*'s most powerful disciplines. He had just inherited the skills of a Master in the ancient Japanese art of Stick Fighting known as *Kukishin Ryu*.

This fact was not lost on the Hogs. They had fought enough battles to recognise extreme skill when they saw it. They both bent down immediately and also picked up sections of curtain rod. From the fighting stances they now adopted and the practiced manner in which they swished their rods, Danny had a strong feeling they had done this before!

Danny knew he didn't stand a chance while he was boxed into a corner. He had only one option - to attack. He came out swinging so fast and furiously that the Hogs had no choice but to retreat as they fended off the blows raining down on them. Every now and again his stick would penetrate their defenses and he would catch them with a powerful blow.

\*

Charley, whether she liked it or not, had a bird's-eye view of the fight. From her precarious vantage point she could see the blur of flashing sticks as Danny drove them back. It was then the Hogs' turn to attack and they both came at Danny with such ferocity that he was forced to just block and defend. Now he was the one being driven back - except this time he found himself backing out of the main doors onto the terrace.

As the fight moved outside so did many of the spectators, and Charley was left dangling from the chandelier wondering how on earth she was going to get down from there! Then she felt the book starting to slip out of the bottom of her blouse. She tried to grab it with one hand, but it was too late - it fell to the ground.

Like a scavenging vulture, the professor came loping across the room and picked it up.

"Leave it alone!" Charley screamed, but he was already scuttling off with his prize.

*

Out on the terrace, Danny was still being forced to defend and retreat, which was becoming more and more of a problem because there was now the small matter of a cliff edge coming up behind him! Soon he had no choice but to jump up onto the terrace wall, which at least gave him a bit more of a height advantage. A quick glance down confirmed what he had suspected; it was a sheer drop all the way down to the forest below. He also noticed a cable car making its way up towards the house, which looked like it was full of soldiers.

By now Hitler and his group (including Mussolini and the Italian delegation) had also followed the fight out onto the terrace. Nobody knew what on earth was going on, but that didn't prevent them (the Fuhrer, in particular) from being completely spellbound by the whole spectacle - *especially* this young boy with the incredible fighting skills! Now he was on the wall with the two giants going at him hammer and tongs. Surely it was only a matter of time before they knocked him off, but still (somehow!) he managed to keep fending off their blows as he retreated down the wall.

Mussolini leant over and nodded his approval to the Fuhrer.

"Hitler Youth! Bravo!"

*

Inside, Commander Skorzeny had ordered his men to hold a large tablecloth beneath where Charley was hanging.

"Just let go! We'll catch you!" he shouted.

Charley looked down. She wasn't at all sure about this plan, but there were not a lot of alternatives! She closed her eyes, let go and the next moment she was bouncing around in the big white tablecloth.

"Thanks," Charley said to the commander as she struggled to get out of the tablecloth with at least an ounce of dignity still intact. "Did you see where the professor went?" she asked. "He's got the book."

"We'll find him," replied the commander. "Come on, let's go and take a look."

\*

The cable car was getting closer. Danny knew this because he could hear the soldiers... *singing*?

He was still blocking, jumping and ducking, but was now very aware of the fact that he was running out of terrace wall. The only thing after that was a three hundred feet drop into oblivion!

Just below the terrace the cable car was now docking at the station. Danny could see soldiers hanging out of the windows, singing their hearts out! Some of them were slurping out of mugs. Were they *drunk*?

\*

The commander led Charley directly to the library and, sure enough, they found the professor sitting at a desk, poring over the book. When he saw them he clutched it to his chest.

The commander approached him.

"Hand it over, Professor."

The professor was shocked.

"Commander! Do you have any idea how valuable the knowledge in this book is?"

"Yes, I think I do."

"Valuable to Germany, Commander! To our cause!"

"No, I think it's of far more value to these people, and what's more - it belongs to *them*! Now, hand it over!"

What the commander did not have time to explain was that he had recently been hearing rumours regarding all sorts of terrible atrocities being carried out under orders from Hitler and some of his top army staff. So the thought of giving these men the capability of time travel did not strike him as the best idea in the world!

"If I could just have a few hours to copy down some of the-"

The commander was running out of patience. He came a step closer and held out his hand.

"I won't ask again, Professor."

The professor surprised them all by suddenly jumping up and rushing over to the fireplace. He held the book over the fire.

"I'm sorry, Commander! I must insist you give me a few more hours with this book, or I'm afraid it goes into the fire."

Charley was horrified.

"No, please don't!" she screeched.

\*

Danny was also screaming (but to himself) - '*No! Please! Not now!*'.

With the looming cliff edge behind him and nowhere else to go he had known his only choice was to launch another assault on the Hogs, but when he had lashed out with his stick, Spider Neck had blocked him easily. He tried again, but once more the Hog fended off the blow almost casually.

The horrible reality dawned on him at the same time as it dawned on the Hogs. He had lost his *Combat X*! The Hogs exchanged glances and moved in for the kill.

Danny did the only thing he could do - he turned and jumped down onto the roof of the cable car.

Having just deposited its load of rowdy soldiers, the cable car was pulling out of its docking station again. The only soldier on board now was a young corporal taking the car back down. When Danny landed on the roof the corporal stuck his head out of the window to see what was going on. He couldn't see Danny, but what he did see (and it was a sight he would never forget!) was an enormously ugly, tattooed man leaping off the terrace wall

# Hogs On The Hill

towards his cable car!

When Spider Neck landed on the roof the whole cable car rocked so precariously that the corporal inside immediately pulled the lever to stop it. Danny had to quickly grab on to something to stop himself from toppling over the edge!

When he recovered, he found Spider Neck inching towards him. As usual, the Hog spoke no words, but the grin on his face seemed to say, '*Where you going to run to now, boy*?'.

*

Standing on the terrace wall, Tooth Rot was also considering jumping down onto the cable car when something else on the terrace caught his eye. It was the other boy (the irritating skinny one!) trying to start their motorbike - *again*!

When Spike had run out earlier to dispose of the Hogs' weapons he had spotted the hog-bike and immediately thought it would be the ideal way to get them off the mountain, especially as he was already an experienced flyer!

The only problem was that he couldn't get the bike to lift off.

He had managed to get it started, but no matter what he tried, it wouldn't budge. Now, when he looked up his heart nearly jumped into his mouth. Tooth Rot was striding across the terrace towards him! For the first time in ages, he started to pray.

"God, give us a break here will you... *please?*" He pressed another button - nothing. "I promise I'll be nice to my sister! I'll never forget her birthday again!"

Tooth Rot was now getting close. He had started to swing his rod menacingly.

"I'll do anything she wants me to do - *anything*!"

Still nothing happened then, in frustration, Spike slammed his foot down and it seemed to accidentally release some sort of brake. Suddenly the bike started lifting off the ground.

When Tooth Rot saw this he started to run.

Now Spike remembered how you had to pull back on the handlebars then accelerate. The bike climbed up and away from the terrace.

"It's like riding a bike!" Spike whooped.

\*

"Don't be a fool, Professor," the commander said as he took a step closer.

Charley was holding her breath as she watched the book dangling over the flames.

"Not another step, Commander!" the professor warned. "I *will* drop it!"

He looked like he actually would! In fact, with the fire reflecting in his bulging eyes he looked a little crazy!

The commander stepped back and held up his hands in mock-surrender.

"All right, Professor. We'll give you an hour to make some notes. How does that sound?"

The professor stared at him intently, trying to work out whether he was bluffing or not.

"Move back then!" he shouted. "Right back!"

Keeping his hands raised, the commander turned and started to move away.

Charley was thinking, *An hour! We can't wait that long!* She then saw the look in the commander's eyes and she knew he was up to something. As the professor stood up from the fire the commander suddenly spun around and launched himself. It was a tackle any rugby player would have been proud of and it knocked the professor flat on his back! But even from that position he was still able to hurl the book in the direction of the fireplace.

Charley watched in horror as the book somersaulted through the air and landed directly in the fire. In a flash she was there, fishing the book out of the flames. It was burning on one side! She beat it on the carpet until it was out.

Charley stared down at the precious journal. It was looking slightly charred down one side - but at least it had survived!

\*

Danny looked behind him. One more step back and he knew he would be skydiving off the cable car without a parachute!

As Spider Neck edged closer he was deliberately rocking the car, enjoying the way it was making the boy lose his balance. Danny crouched down to steady himself and was now surprised to hear a voice just below him. It was the corporal sticking his head out of a window.

"Hey! What are you doing up there?" he shouted. "You want to kill us all?"

As angry as the corporal looked, Danny considered him a much safer bet than the approaching Hog. He climbed down the side of the cable car and dangled there, trying to get his legs in through the window. Inside the car, the corporal didn't want any company, thank you very much, so every time Danny got his legs in through the window, he shoved them out again!

Danny looked up and found Spider Neck with one raised boot

about to stamp on his fingers! He had to quickly release with one hand to avoid the boot as it slammed down then the Hog went for his other hand and Danny had to quickly switch hands.

"Enough!" Danny roared as he kicked out violently at the corporal inside, and he must have connected because finally he was able to swing in through the window.

The kick had sent the corporal reeling backwards, but he was now grappling for his rifle and soon had it pointed at Danny.

"Hey! I'm not the one to be worrying about!" Danny said, pointing towards the stomping on the roof.

He saw the expression on the corporal's face suddenly change. Spider Neck had just swung down behind Danny and was now trying to get his legs in through the window!

"Shoot *him*!" Danny screamed, pointing at the Hog.

It was too much for the corporal, who had frozen, wide-eyed. Danny tried to get the rifle from him, but he clung on for dear life.

"Suit yourself!" Danny said – and the next time the corporal looked he was surprised to see Danny climbing back out through a window on the other side of the car.

When Spider Neck burst into the car only to see Danny disappearing back out onto the roof again he became very angry. He ripped the rifle away from the corporal and started blasting holes in the roof.

\*

It was a strange sight that greeted Spike as he guided the bike back in towards the house. He could see Danny on top of the cable car. He was hopping and jumping around like he was doing some kind of strange dance!

Only when Spike got closer did he see the Hog firing shots through the roof! He brought the bike down to the cable car's level and tried to slow it down as he approached.

\*

When Tooth Rot saw the bike coming in below the level of the terrace he knew what he had to do. He waited until it drew closer then he started to run as fast as he could towards the edge of the terrace. He launched himself off the wall in one enormous leap towards the bike.

Spike, still concentrating on the cable car in front of him, was shocked (to say the least!) when he suddenly saw the Hog leaping out towards him, but there was no time to do anything!

*Boom!*

Suddenly a huge blast rocked the bike, Tooth Rot crumpled in mid-air and dropped silently away into the valley below.

The shot had come from Commander Skorzeny. On his way back out to the terrace with Charley he had armed himself with a powerful bazooka – and it was lucky he did because the first thing he saw was Tooth Rot running to make his leap. With Spike and the bike so close it was a dangerous shot, but the commander had had no choice but to take it.

*Boom!*

\*

The impact of the bazooka blast so close to the bike had thrown Spike off course and he had missed the cable car all together. Now he was turning around to make another pass. He could see Danny urging him to hurry up. It seemed like the firing had stopped for the meantime – and now he saw why! The Hog (with the rifle now slung over his shoulder) was climbing back out onto the roof!

Danny had also seen the Hog's head popping up over the edge on the other side.

"Hurry, Spike!" he shouted.

As Spike approached, Danny moved right to the edge.

"Ready to jump?" Spike shouted.

"Can't you slow it down a bit more?" Danny shouted back.

"Er... not really," Spike muttered, trying to apply the brakes again.

Danny glanced over and saw that Spider Neck was now on his feet and coming across the roof towards him. He knew they only had one shot at this. He readied himself for the jump, trying not to think about the sheer drop that awaited him if he got it wrong!

As the bike came past - Danny jumped.

He landed half-in and half-out of the sidecar, and hung there for a few moments with his legs dangling, before managing to pull himself in headfirst. The sight of Danny upside-down in the sidecar with his feet sticking up in the air made Spike laugh.

"Welcome aboard!" he roared.

By the time Danny had got himself upright Spike had made another turn and was now guiding the bike back towards the terrace to collect Charley. They could see her standing beside the commander, waving furiously.

Danny was amazed at how Spike was handling the bike.

"How do you know how to fly this thing?"

"Long story," Spike replied, "and one day I'm going to tell you every gory detail!"

As the bike approached, the commander lifted Charley up onto the terrace wall.

"You ready?" he asked her.

Charley nodded. She had Uncle Morty's journal clutched firmly to her chest.

"Thanks for everything, we'll never forget you."

"Good," he replied, "and when you get back to wherever you've come from, try and stay out of trouble! OK?"

"OK!" Charley said, smiling.

The bike was now close and she could see Danny leaning out of the sidecar getting ready to grab her. It was nerve-racking standing on that wall overlooking the cliff, and she was glad to at least have the commander by her side.

But then suddenly he had gone!

The commander had just spotted something that made him

grab for the bazooka again. It was the Hog on the top of the cable car. He was lying on his stomach with his rifle trained on the incoming motorbike!

\*

Spider Neck was tracking the motorbike in his sights, waiting for the crucial moment before firing. He knew this was his chance to get rid of all three targets with a single shot. He was just waiting for the third one to be collected from the terrace wall.

\*

Spike slowed the bike down as much as he could. Now it was up to Danny.

"Just stand still, Charley!" Danny shouted. "I'll grab hold of you!"

Charley closed her eyes and the next moment she felt Danny's hands grabbing hold of her and hauling her into the sidecar.

It was the moment Spider Neck had been waiting for - he fired.

A second later the commander also let rip with his bazooka. There was a massive explosion on the top of the cable car and the Hog was blown clean off the roof!

The commander looked at the motorbike and realised he had been a fraction of a second too slow. The bike was out of control. It was scraping along the terrace wall!

"Spike!" Charley screamed. "Get away from the wall!"

Charley and Danny were getting showered by sparks and banged around in the sidecar as it crashed up against the terrace wall. It was only when Danny managed to lean across and push on the handlebars that the bike moved clear - that's when he saw Spike.

"*Spike!*" he screamed.

Spike was slumped forwards on the handlebars.

\*

Back on the terrace, the commander watched as the bike climbed rather unsteadily away from the Berghof.

"Come on, come on," he muttered to himself, half-expecting it to come crashing down at any moment.

He then heard a disturbingly familiar voice shouting at him from across the terrace.

"Commander! *Commander!*"

It was the Fuhrer. He was striding over towards him, his little moustache bristling, his face white with rage.

*

With one hand on the handlebars to keep the bike on course Danny pulled Spike back. It was the sight he had been dreading - a blood stain was appearing through Spike's shirt. He had been shot.

"What's the matter with him?" Charley was shouting from behind Danny.

"Help me get him into the sidecar!" Danny shouted back.

As they struggled to get Spike off the bike Charley now also saw the growing blood stain. Suddenly she started to panic.

"*What's happened? Spike! Spike!*"

Danny turned on her harshly.

"*Charley! This is not the time to freak out! Help me!*"

Charley tried to calm herself down as she helped get Spike into the sidecar. Once he was lying down Danny took his place on the bike.

"Charley, you need to bandage him! Tear something up!"

Charley looked around for something to rip up. She saw Danny's rucksack and pulled out one of his old shirts. As she ripped it up Spike opened his eyes. He winced when he felt the wound.

"What happened?" he asked.

"You've been shot," Charley said bluntly, biting her lip, trying to appear strong.

"You hang in there, buddy," Danny said.

Only now did Spike see that Danny was flying the bike.

"Hey, you need some lessons up there?" he croaked.

Danny smiled.

"Actually, maybe I do. How do you make this thing go up and down?"

"Just push or pull on the handlebars."

Danny tried it out and it worked.

"OK, good, thanks. Now we just have to work out which direction to go in!"

\*

Back on the mountain, the Fuhrer had been screaming repeatedly in the commander's face, demanding an explanation for all the chaos that was going on. All the commander could do was keep repeating the same thing.

"My apologies, Mein Fuhrer, but... I was trying to tell you earlier that there was something extraordinary about that boy."

This only made Hitler angrier – and his mood deteriorated further when a group of soldiers now appeared on the terrace - singing a drinking song!

"*What is the meaning of this?*" Hitler screamed across at them. "*One more song and I'll have you all shot!*"

The soldiers quickly shut up and disappeared. Hitler turned his attention back to the motorbike, which was now almost out of sight.

"We can't let them get away!" he fumed. "We need the air force! Where is *Reichsmarschall* Goering?"

The question caused the commander to shuffle around a bit, and Hitler could see that he was reluctant to answer.

"*Commander!*" Hitler raged. "I said *where is Goering?*"

"Um... Mein Fuhrer... I believe that is the *Reichsmarschall* over there."

Hitler looked over to where the commander was pointing. There he saw a large man on all fours digging around in a flowerpot... with his nose!

"*Goering!*" Hitler screamed.

The *Reichsmarschall*'s head came shooting up at the sound of his name. With his face covered in mud, he looked over at the Fuhrer as if to say, 'What can I do for you?' then he gave a couple of good grunts and returned to his foraging.

Hitler began to stamp his foot like a child having a tantrum.

The commander had to turn away because he didn't think that he could keep a straight face any longer. He was happy to see that the motorbike was now out of sight.

*

On the bike Charley was doing her best to clean up Spike's wound, but the sight of the blood was making her feel ill.

"You wouldn't make a very good nurse, would you?" Spike said, joking. He was trying to make light of the situation, but his grey complexion told a different story. Now he took a look at the wound himself. "Just a flesh wound," he said. "Doesn't look too serious."

Danny and Charley weren't so sure. While Charley wrapped her bandage strips as tightly as possible around Spike, Danny was trying to work out in which direction they should be going. The sun was just starting to set, which was helpful because he knew it always went down in the west. He also knew that to get to the west coast of France they would have to head in a north-westerly direction, but how would he stay on that course, especially when it got dark?

Suddenly Danny remembered the few items that Uncle Morty had given him on his departure.

"Hey, Charley! Look in my rucksack will you? Wasn't there a compass in there?"

Charley fished around in the rucksack and, sure enough, she found Uncle Morty's antique-looking brass compass.

"Excellent!" said Danny, taking the compass from her. "OK, now we know which direction we're going in. What time is it?"

Charley looked at her watch.

"Five thirty."

"Right, that means we only have two and a half hours before all hell breaks loose at Bordeaux harbour. Hold on tight, guys - let's see how fast this baby can go!"

Chapter 18

# Running Out of Time

A couple of hundred miles away in Bordeaux, Madame du Pont was just finishing off her dinner (although, as she later explained over the phone to Monsieur Ballac at the local Nazi office, calling it 'dinner' was a bit of an exaggeration! One egg and half a tomato! Sometimes she wondered if she would ever eat meat again!).

As usual, Madame du Pont ate her 'dinner' at a small table beside the window *with the lights turned off*. The reason for this (she also explained to Monsieur Ballac) was simply that she could no longer afford the lighting bills. The fact that she was also able to see everything that was going on outside - *without being seen herself* - was purely coincidental!

It was precisely 6.45pm when she saw the first young man slipping in through the side gate of the Borges' house. She couldn't help but notice this, as their house was situated directly across the street from her. The second man arrived at 6.56pm and the third at 7.01pm. The reason she could be so precise about these times was because she had happened to have a notebook and pen handy on the table, which enabled her to jot down certain details.

"Excuse me, Madame du Pont, but three men arriving at a house is not a crime," Monsieur Ballac had pointed out to her with all the shortsightedness expected of a junior government official.

"Monsieur Ballac," Madame du Pont replied, trying to be patient, "I am familiar with the comings and goings at the Borges' house; after all I have lived opposite them for the past ten years! I did not recognise these three men, Monsieur. Furthermore, if these men were paying a purely social visit then why did they feel the need to slip in through the side gate and not just walk up to the front door? Perhaps you could explain *that*, Monsieur?"

It was at that point that Monsieur Ballac let out a great sigh and confessed that he was not able to explain this strange phenomenon. He would, however, make a note of it and should Madame notice anything else suspicious she should please give him another call.

Madame du Pont assured him she would, before putting the phone down. She returned to her table at the window and made a note in her book: *First call to Monsieur Ballac - 7.07pm.*

\*

Across the street at the Borges' house, Michelle had spent most of the evening pacing around impatiently, waiting for Mortimer to arrive.

Tommy Mitchell and Roger Jakes (Mortimer's two Special Ops colleagues) had arrived first, and Michelle's brother, Christian, had come through to greet them. He shook their hands before leading them to the kitchen. As Roger passed Michelle (now sitting expectantly on the stairs in the passage) he smiled.

"Don't worry, he's right behind us."

"*Merci*," Michelle said, doing her best to smile back at him.

She was trying not to show her nerves, but she had a lot on her mind. Not only did they have the extremely important mission at the harbour tonight, but there was also the strange incident with the English boy at the market, which she hadn't had a chance to tell Mortimer about yet. She began to pace again. *Why was Mortimer always the last one to arrive?* She then heard the familiar gentle tap on the side door and the next moment Mortimer stuck his head through. He beamed when he saw her.

"Bonjour!"

Michelle rushed over to him and Mortimer hugged her tightly. He presented her with a battered bunch of wild flowers, obviously picked in a field on his way over.

"For me?" Michelle said in English (she had been trying to

practise her English!).

"Just a little something I picked up at the local florist," Mortimer joked.

"You shouldn't have!"

"Why not? French wild flowers for *my* French wild flower."

"You are sweet."

"And you are beautiful." Mortimer now noticed that she was looking worried about something. "What's wrong?"

They sat down on the stairs in the passage. She wanted to tell him this before they went through and joined the others in the kitchen.

"Something strange happened to me in the market yesterday," she explained.

"Yes?"

"A young boy came up to me. He said he was English. He had a book that he said he had to give to you. Some sort of journal."

Mortimer wasn't sure he had understood correctly.

"A book to give to *me*? You mean he asked for me *by name*?"

"Yes, he said it was very important that he saw you - that it was a matter of life and death."

Mortimer shook his head, battling to think of any possible explanation.

"It was very strange," she continued, "then a Gestapo car arrived and that's when I ran!"

"*Gestapo?*"

Michelle nodded.

"Do you know what the strangest thing of all was?" she continued. "The writing in this journal - it looked like *your writing*!"

Mortimer took off his cap and scratched his head.

"There must be a simple explanation," he muttered.

*What could it be? No one even knew he was in France, and why had they come to Michelle? That was the most worrying* part of it. It meant that, somehow, someone had discovered a connection between the two of them.

"All right," he said eventually. "We can't worry about it now. Tonight's mission is happening whether we like it or not."

But even now, as they went through to join the others in the kitchen, Michelle could see that Mortimer was still trying to make sense of the strange incident.

\*

Danny and the others had been flying for almost an hour and a half when they saw the first plane.

It was just a flickering light far off in the night sky, but as a precaution Danny turned off the bike's solitary headlight. This meant he had to slow the bike down while his eyes grew accustomed to the dark.

Up until then they had been making good progress. The bike could certainly move and, thanks to the compass, they had been able to stick rigidly to their north-westerly course. Along the way they had passed over several towns and villages, and Danny was now beginning to wonder if they were still flying over Germany or whether they had crossed into France.

It was also starting to get very cold. They had put on every layer of clothing they could find, but Danny could see that Charley was still freezing. He was also worried about Spike, who now looked like he had fallen asleep.

"How's he doing?" Danny asked, not for the first time.

"I'm not sure," Charley replied. "He feels hot and he doesn't sound too good."

Danny leaned down close to Spike and felt his forehead. It was true - he was warm to touch, as if he might be running a temperature, and his breathing had definitely become more laboured. He knew they should probably stop for a break, but he also knew they were running out of time. If they could just make it to Bordeaux in time to intercept Mortimer and Michelle then (if his uncle was correct!) *everything* would change. Once that happened (and the Time Ripple caught up) it would mean they wouldn't even be here in 1942, so Spike wouldn't have got shot in the first place!

Danny was busy trying to get his head around this bizarre thought when something else began to creep into his mind space. It was a sound - still quite distant, but definitely growing louder all the time. It sounded like an aircraft engine!

"Hear that?" Danny asked, looking around.

"Yup."

Charley nodded, scanning the night sky, but couldn't see anything. The sound continued to grow. It was no longer a distant drone. It was now starting to sound *a lot* closer! She twisted herself around in the cramped sidecar, so that she could look directly behind them – and that's when she screamed.

"*There! Behind us!*"

Without even looking, Danny pushed down hard on the handlebars and the bike went into a dive. It was lucky it did because, seconds later, the plane roared over their heads. It was so loud that even Spike was shaken violently from his sleep.

"*Messerschmitt!*" he blurted out, looking around disoriented - then he laid his head back down and drifted off again.

*Messerschmitt.* Yes, Danny remembered the name. That's what this type of German fighter plane was called. He could also just make out the German black cross insignia on the plane's wings as it banked away from them. The question now was - *had the pilot spotted them?*

Keeping a close eye on the plane, Danny pulled back on the handlebars and levelled the bike out again. He felt like they were already flying too low for comfort. His tired eyes were beginning to see all sorts of imaginary trees and mountains looming out of the darkness towards them.

The plane continued to bank away, but thankfully it did not

appear to be turning around to come back. It seemed like this time they had been lucky.

Danny checked the compass and corrected their course. He glanced at his watch. It was 7.15pm. In less than an hour Mortimer and Michelle would be running into trouble at the harbour. There was no time for a break. He started to accelerate again.

*

Everyone was now seated around the kitchen table at the Borges' house. There were the three British soldiers (dressed as civilians), Michelle (sitting close to Mortimer and holding his hand under the table), her brother, Christian, and her father, Dr Borges. The only person not seated was Mrs Borges, who was hovering around preparing coffee and a snack for the guests.

There was nervous tension in the room, everyone well aware of the danger that lay ahead tonight, but as usual it was Roger who was trying to lighten the mood and take their minds off the mission. He liked to joke with Michelle and Mortimer, whom he called the 'lovebirds'.

"So, do you think we're going to be invited to the wedding, Tommy?" asked Roger with a grin.

"I sincerely hope so," Tommy replied. "I've already bought my hat!"

They all laughed at this then Mortimer pretended to look serious.

"Sorry, lads, we were only planning on inviting a couple of hundred people - so I'm not sure there'll be room for you two!"

Everyone laughed again, knowing that Mortimer was only pulling their legs. In fact, after the war, he planned to ask Roger to be his best man and Tommy to be his groomsman.

Dr Borges tried to get his wife to join them at the table, but it seemed like she preferred to be doing something. She now placed a pot of coffee and some snacks on the table, for which they all thanked her.

"So the only person we are waiting for now is Henri," said Dr Borges.

"He'll be here soon," said Christian, looking at his watch.

It was 7.25pm.

\*

"*Dannnny!*"

Charley's shrill scream awoke Danny with a jerk. He had fallen asleep while flying the bike, and in his sleep he must have slumped forward because the bike was now going down! It had been this feeling of rapid descent that had awakened Charley and made her scream. Danny pulled back hard on the handlebars, but the terrifying dark shapes of treetops were already closing in fast.

"Hold on!" Danny roared as the bike barrelled its way through the branches of a tree.

He had to cling on for dear life to prevent himself being swept off the bike! As they burst through the first tree a second even bigger one was waiting for them. Charley ducked right down, her eyes firmly shut. The bike crashed through the second tree - branches clawing like scraggy fingers at their undercarriage. Danny leant back hard, pulling the bike up with all his might - then suddenly they broke free and were in the clear again.

Danny looked down at Charley, who was only now daring to peek.

"You all right?"

"That was *close*!" she replied, not sounding at all happy.

"Sorry about that," Danny mumbled, tugging on a bit of branch stuck in the front wheel.

"We need to stop for a rest," Charley moaned. "I can't feel my legs any more."

Danny shook his head and started accelerating again.

"We can't. We haven't got time. How's Spike?"

Charley took another look at her brother. He was stirring, but still seemed half-asleep. She tried to rouse him.

"Spike, you OK?"

Spike just groaned and turned over. Danny knew this wasn't a good sign. He was getting worse, probably from loss of blood.

As calm as Danny may have appeared on the outside there was now an awful gut-churning sense of desperation starting to play havoc with his insides. *Should they stop and tend to Spike's wound? Was he dying? What would happen if he died before they found Mortimer and Michelle?* Danny took another look at him. He knew he had this boy's life in his hands! A huge and terrible responsibility!

"All right," he said, finally, "let's…"

Danny didn't have time to finish his sentence because suddenly Charley sat bolt upright.

"Hey! Can you smell that?"

Danny sniffed the air. Yes, he could smell it! It was such a distinct smell! Surely - it had to be… They both peered up ahead into the darkness then they saw the first sign - a shimmer of moonlight dancing on a flat glassy surface.

"It's the sea!" Danny cried.

As the bike sped out over the beaches and cliffs both Danny and Charley threw their heads back and let out great whoops of excitement.

It was only as they circled back in towards the coast that Charley asked the question that was already doing the rounds in Danny's own head.

"OK, so now which way is Bordeaux?"

Danny looked at his compass, but quickly realised that this wasn't going to help because he had no idea of their current position. The question was whether they turned left down the coast, or right up the coast. Bordeaux could just as easily be in either direction. As Danny tried to make a decision he looked at his watch and saw that it was coming up for 7.30pm. They only had half an hour. A wrong decision now would be a disaster.

"Why don't we ask someone?" suggested Charley.

At first Danny thought she must be joking, but then he noticed that she was looking down at a small light on the beach below. He had wanted to try and avoid contact with anyone if possible, but at this stage, with so much riding on one decision, he decided it was worth the risk. He pushed the nose of the bike down and they started to descend.

\*

On the beach an old fisherman sat beside a paraffin lamp, untangling his nets. He was so engrossed in his work that he didn't notice the bike coming in silently out of the darkness. Danny slowed the bike down as much as he could.

"*Bonjour!*" shouted Charley as they passed over the fisherman's head.

The old man was up on his feet in a flash, knife in hand, ready for action! He looked around for the source of the voice, but could see no one!

Danny turned the bike around and they came in for another pass.

"*Excusez-moi!*" Charley shouted.

The fisherman now saw the dark shape approaching. He readied himself for an attack, but the voice came again - and it sounded like a young girl!

"*Excusez-moi! Ou se toruve t'on Bordeaux?*"

The old man stared hard as the dark shape passed by. *Could this be an angel?* He rubbed his old eyes. *What else could it be? He hadn't even had a drink that night! But could an angel be lost? Lost - and looking for Bordeaux?*

When Danny and Charley came back past for the third time they found the old man on his knees, his hands clasped together as if in prayer.

When Charley shouted again, '*Bordeaux? S'il vous plaiit?*' he merely extended an arm and pointed in the direction they should go.

"*Merci!*" the lost angel shouted as she drifted off into the night sky.

\*

Madame du Pont was just putting away her single dinner plate when something else caught her eye across the street. She moved over to the window for a closer look.

Yet *another* man was arriving at the Borges' house, but unlike those who had sneaked in earlier, this man had walked straight up to the front door where he now knocked and waited. He looked familiar to Madame du Pont. She had seen him before, hanging around with that wild and unruly Borges boy; the one they called '*Christian*' of all things!

The door opened and this latest visitor was let inside.

"Quite the gathering tonight," Madame du Pont mumbled as she made another note in her book: *Friend of Christian arrives - 7.33pm.*

\*

"It's time to get moving," said Christian, and everyone rose from the kitchen table and started to gather up their things.

Christian was standing with the new arrival, his friend, Henri. He looked at his watch.

"It's 7.35 now. We must make sure we are all at the harbour before eight o'clock. That is when the canoes are expected to arrive. We should start leaving in pairs. Roger and I will leave first then, five minutes later, Henri and Tommy will follow. After another five minutes, Michelle and Mortimer. Does that sound OK?"

Everyone nodded.

"All right, let's be careful out there," Christian warned. "There are soldiers *everywhere!*"

Poor Madame Borges was still producing plates of food, as

if this was somehow going to delay their departure. She made a point of not watching as Christian and Michelle kissed each other and said goodbye.

"See you at the harbour," Christian said.

"Be careful," Michelle said, nodding.

"Right," Christian said to Roger, "let's move."

\*

When Madame du Pont saw Christian and one of the strangers leaving together she was convinced something was going on. When Christian's friend and *another* one of the mysterious men left five minutes later she had no choice but to phone Monsieur Ballac.

"Monsieur Ballac," she said in a grave voice. "I have something very serious to report."

"Is that so, Madame?" Monsieur Ballac replied.

He was flicking through the latest edition of his favourite newspaper, *Action Français*.

"Yes, that *is* so, Monsieur. In fact, I think it would be better if I spoke to one of your superiors."

Monsieur Ballac had to suppress a smile as he flipped to the next page.

"Madame, I'm afraid my superiors are not in the office at this time of night, and neither is anybody else! What would you like to report, please?"

Madame sighed. It seemed she was lumbered with this irritating little man. Aware, however, that the telephone lines were not safe from eavesdroppers, she chose her next words very carefully.

"The chickens are flying the coop," she said.

"The chickens?"

Monsieur Ballac sounded confused.

"Yes, the chickens."

There was silence on the other end of the phone.

"*The chickens* I spoke of earlier!" Madame du Pont said

impatiently.

"Ah, *those* chickens!"

"I suggest you inform the Eagle," Madame du Pont said next.

"The Eagle?"

Madame du Pont felt like she was going to explode with impatience.

"The *German* Eagle!" she snapped.

"Oh, I see! Tell the Eagle about the chickens."

"Precisely."

"I'll be sure to do that, Madame. Thank you very much for your assistance."

Monsieur Ballac had to put the phone down quickly, so that she didn't hear his snorts of laughter.

"The chickens!" he sniggered, shaking his head - then he made a few clucking noises, which set him off giggling again.

*

On the bike, frustration and anger were turning to despair.

They only had twenty minutes left to find Bordeaux and they still had no idea how far away it was. For all they knew the fisherman on the beach could have sent them off in the wrong direction! Now, to make matters worse, a thick fog had started to drift in off the sea, making it increasingly difficult for Danny to follow the coastline. He had already slowed the bike right down and was afraid to go too much lower in case he ran into one of the cliffs along the coast.

He was also starting to *really* worry about Spike. A little earlier Charley had tried to wake him up to give him a drink, but he had just mumbled incoherently without even opening his eyes. Danny could see how much this had distressed Charley. She was now just staring ahead like a zombie, as if she had already given up hope.

Now the fog was getting thicker and closing in all around them. Looking down, Danny could no longer see any of the lights he had been using to follow the coastline. He knew, despite the danger, that they were going to have to go lower. At this rate they could fly past Bordeaux and never even know!

Danny took the bike down, straining his eyes for any signs of cliffs up ahead, but thankfully, as they descended the fog started to thin out until eventually they were in the clear again.

What they saw now came as a terrible shock to both of them! Charley looked one way then the other. All around them, in every direction, there was nothing but *sea*!

"Where's the land, Danny?" Charley shrieked. "*Where is the land?*"

\*

It was now almost time for Mortimer and Michelle to leave. Dr Borges sat with them, puffing pensively on his pipe. He had given up trying to get his wife to sit down.

Although Madame Borges was still hovering around her kitchen she had been able to watch Michelle and Mortimer sitting together, and it was at least of some comfort to her to see how obviously in love they were. Now, quite out of the blue, she unhooked the necklace she was wearing and placed it around Michelle's neck.

When Michelle looked down and saw what it was she was speechless. She knew how much this necklace meant to her mother. It had been given to her as a child by her grandmother.

"I can't take this, Mama," Michelle protested.

Her mother merely kissed the top of her head.

"For good luck," she said.

Mortimer now glanced at his watch. It was 7.45pm.

"Time for us to go I'm afraid," he said quietly to Michelle.

Although Madame Borges did not understand Mortimer's English she knew it was time to say goodbye.

\*

Danny scoured the horizon, but like Charley he could see no sign of land. While travelling blind in the fog they must have been straying farther and farther out to sea!

Below them the water looked cold and inhospitable. There was a strong wind whipping up the waves and every now and again the bike would be pelted by a shower of icy spray.

Charley was in tears and Danny could see that she was now really starting to fall apart. With her head bowed she kept repeating the same thing, as if willing the nightmare to be over.

"Please, please, please."

All Danny could think was - w*hich direction? Which direction was the land?* Suddenly he remembered - *the compass*! He felt around in his pocket and pulled it out. He tried to hold it steady, flat in the palm of his hand, but just then a massive wave crashed beneath them and the force of the spray made the whole bike lurch. Danny had to grip the handlebars with both hands and, in that instant, the compass was gone.

"*No!*" Danny screamed as he watched Uncle Morty's compass disappearing into the turbulent surf below.

Charley didn't even look up. She was beyond caring.

Suddenly Danny felt very alone. He tried to take the bike up a bit beyond the icy sea spray, but he couldn't go too high because then the fog began to close in again. He had to keep the bike moving, but he didn't know in which direction they should be going. For all he knew they could be heading farther and farther out to sea!

Danny then saw something. At first he thought it might be a flash of lightning way off in the fog, but a few moments later it flashed again, then again. It was a powerful light, flashing at regular intervals. Without saying anything to Charley, Danny steered the bike in the direction of the light.

\*

At the front door Dr Borges shook hands firmly with Mortimer.

"Good luck," he said.

"Thank you, we'll see you soon."

To Mortimer's surprise, Madame Borges came over and hugged him. Whilst doing so, she said something in his ear. It was in French, but he understood.

"Look after her," she whispered. "I have a bad feeling about tonight. Keep her safe."

"I will," Mortimer promised.

She then hugged Michelle and it was as if she didn't want to let her go. Only when her husband opened the front door and said, 'It's getting late' did she quickly kiss Michelle and turn away.

Mortimer and Michelle stepped out into the night.

\*

The light grew stronger and brighter. Every few seconds it came around, its powerful beam penetrating through the fog. Danny was about to call down to Charley, but a glint of light had already caught her eye. She looked up.

"What is it?" she asked.

Danny shook his head and muttered more to himself than Charley.

"I don't know, but whatever it is - I hope it's on land!"

The light was now so bright that it blinded them, but they still couldn't see where it was coming from. Then, all of a sudden, the fog began to melt away and there it was, standing proudly on a cliff-edge - a red and white conical tower with a revolving flashing beacon.

"A lighthouse," Danny whispered.

"It's Sarah's lighthouse!" cried Charley.

Danny looked confused.

"Who's Sarah?" he asked.

Charley just pointed.

"Look! There she is!"

Sure enough, as they drew closer they saw the small figure of a young girl running up to the railing on the platform below the light.

"*Sarah!*" Charley screamed, but Sarah had already seen them and was standing at the railing, waving madly.

\*

As Madame du Pont's voice grew louder, Monsieur Ballac had to hold the telephone away from his ear.

"Now the daughter has left with the third stranger!" she was saying. "Does this not strike you as odd, Monsieur?"

"Perhaps they are all going to a party?" he suggested.

"A party down at the harbour?" scoffed Madame du Pont.

For the first time that night Monsieur Ballac actually stopped reading his newspaper.

"The harbour?"

"That's right, Monsieur. They all turned down the harbour road."

Monsieur Ballac nibbled on his thumbnail as he digested this latest bit of information. There had been all sorts of rumours flying around about how the merchant fleet in the harbour was a possible target for attack. Suddenly he was considering Madame du Pont's observations in a new light.

"All right, thank you, Madame," he said quickly. "I will get someone to take a look."

"Monsieur, if anything does come of this, you won't forget where the information originated from, will you?"

"How could I ever forget, Madame?" he said, putting the phone down. He then picked it up again immediately and dialled. "Army headquarters? Is Captain Strieber available please? Yes, I will hold."

\*

By the time Danny had landed the bike and they had bumped across the field to the lighthouse, Sarah had run all the way down to the bottom. As they pulled up she came bursting out of the doorway.

"Bonjour!" she shouted. "I'm so happy to see you! I've been so worried!"

Charley was battling to get out of the sidecar. Both her legs had gone to sleep and she was having a severe attack of pins and needles.

Sarah came running over to greet them, but gasped when she saw Spike lying in the sidecar.

"What's wrong with him?"

"He's been shot," said Danny.

Sarah looked shocked.

"*Shot*? Is he all right?"

"No." Charley shook her head. "He's not."

Danny knew there wasn't time for explanations or discussions.

"Sarah," he said. "There's something we need to go and do right now - very urgently. Would it be OK to leave Spike here with you?"

"Of course," Sarah replied.

Between the three of them they managed to lift Spike out of the sidecar and carry him towards the lighthouse.

"Your lighthouse saved our lives," Danny said to Sarah.

"I'm so glad," she said. "It was the strangest thing - when I saw the fog I knew I had to turn the light on. Something kept telling me I had to!"

"Well, thank goodness you did, that's all I can say!" said Charley.

They were now taking Spike in through the lighthouse doorway. Sarah spread out a blanket and they laid him down. He stirred and opened his eyes for a few seconds, but it wasn't clear whether he recognised them.

"We'll see you later, Spike," Charley whispered.

At that moment she had a horrible thought. *Would they see him later? Would they ever see him again?* None of them knew what was about to happen! Suddenly she didn't want to leave him. Danny sensed this.

"We'll see him back in England," he said, trying to sound confident. "Come on, Charley. We have to go. It's ten to eight."

As torn as Charley felt, she knew the importance of what they were about to try and do. She gave Sarah a quick hug.

"Look after him," she said.

She then followed Danny out through the doorway.

*

At army headquarters Captain Strieber was in a rush to get off the phone.

"I understand. Thank you for the call, Monsieur Ballac," he said. Monsieur Ballac was still talking on the other end, but he put the phone down anyway. He then opened up his desk drawer and removed his handgun. "*Muller!*" he roared.

Moments later, Sergeant Muller came rushing into his office and snapped to attention.

"Yes, Captain!"

"Get the men ready. We are going down to the harbour."

"Yes, Captain! How many men will you require?" the sergeant asked.

"All of them," the Captain replied as he stood and holstered his weapon.

*

Danny and Charley swooped down over Bordeaux. They were looking out for the road where Michelle lived, but from the air all they could see were row upon row of rooftops all looking the same.

"You'll have to go lower!" Charley shouted in frustration.

Danny took the bike down. People would see them, but he couldn't worry about that now. He went lower and lower until he was weaving in and out between the buildings. One thing was certain, with all this practice, he was definitely getting the hang of flying the bike!

They crossed over the market square where they had first encountered Michelle, and Charley now started to get her bearings.

"That way!" she shouted, pointing.

"You sure?"

"Yes!"

Danny followed her directions, remembering that she had spent more time in Bordeaux than he had.

"It's the next one," said Charley. "On the right!"

Danny took the bike down to street level, slowing it down as much as he could as the ground rushed up to meet them. The bike rattled and bounced as it hit the cobbled street and Danny had to apply the brakes vigorously so that they were able to turn the fast approaching corner. As soon as they turned Danny recognised the street and the Borges' house. He pulled up outside.

"Just go and check, Charley! We might be too late!"

Charley jumped out of the sidecar and ran up to the front door. She beat on it with her fist.

Moments later, Dr Borges opened the door.

"Yes?" he said, looking down quizzically at the diminutive figure of Charley.

"Is Michelle here, please?" Charley asked, breathless and impatient.

The doctor blinked then he looked over her head and saw the German army motorbike parked at the gate. The person sitting on it looked like he was wearing a Hitler Youth uniform!

"No," he said quickly. "She's out. Who shall I say called?"

"Has she already left with Mortimer?" Charley asked.

This really took the doctor by surprise. He looked like he didn't know what to say.

"Please! We are friends! They are in danger!" Charley pleaded.

Still the doctor didn't know how to answer and eventually he just shook his head.

Charley knew she couldn't waste any more time. She ran back to the bike.

"I think they've gone!" she shouted, climbing back into the sidecar.

Danny cursed to himself. He had just looked at his watch and it was already five to eight. In just a few minutes it would be too late. Danny pulled away abruptly and did a quick U-turn in the street. As they came back past the Borges' house, Charley noticed the lace curtains twitching in the house across the street. She was willing to bet that this was the house of Madame du Pont.

Just then Danny decided it was too bumpy and uncomfortable rattling over the cobblestones, so he pulled back on the handlebars and the bike lifted off.

Charley smiled to herself. *That will give Madame du Pont something to talk about!*

\*

Michelle and Mortimer had been walking hand in hand down the road towards the harbour, looking like any normal couple out for an evening stroll, but when they saw the harbour lights, they slipped down a side road they knew was a back route into the harbour area. Soon they were scurrying between warehouses and cranes until they arrived at the agreed meeting place amongst some packing crates on the wharf.

"Any sign of them yet?" Mortimer whispered to Christian. Christian shook his head and continued to peer out into the inky darkness.

Across the way they could see the line of merchant ships moored along the wharf. They could also hear a couple of the guards talking on the ships and, every now and again, the glow of a cigarette would reveal the guards' positions.

Just then Christian nudged Mortimer. He had seen something

in the water. "There!" he whispered.

They all looked. Now they saw it as well - two dark shapes sliding through the water towards the ships. Michelle squeezed Mortimer's arm. It was the British Commandos - just as planned! The German Army in occupied France was about to suffer a major blow! It was difficult for them all to contain their excitement.

At that moment one of the guards on the ships suddenly stopped talking. He then asked his mate if he had seen something in the water. Now there was a dreadful silence as the two guards peered down into the harbour. The commandos in the canoes stopped paddling. Next thing, they heard one of the guards saying he was going off to find a torch!

The time to do something had arrived. Before Mortimer even knew what was happening, Michelle was up and running down the wharf towards the ships.

Mortimer leapt up and followed her.

*

It was Danny who saw Mortimer first. His heart leapt. *We're not too late!*

Moments earlier he had decided to land the bike and they had come bumping down onto the main road into the harbour. They rode down onto the quay and were trundling along beside the large merchant ships when Danny saw the figure of a man running towards them.

At first they couldn't be sure who it was, but as they drew closer Danny realised that he *recognised* this man! It was a face he remembered from old black and white photographs in his father's family album. Suddenly the enormity (and sheer... *weirdness*!) of what was about to happen began to hit home, and Danny couldn't help but feel overwhelmed! He had tried to imagine this moment many times! *He was about to meet his great uncle as a young man! He didn't even know what he was going to say!*

Now Charley diverted his attention.

"Look!" she said. She was pointing up at the nearest ship. "It's Michelle!"

Sure enough, there was Michelle standing near the railings of the ship, talking to a guard.

Danny remembered from Mortimer's story how she had ended up on the ship. To get the guard's attention away from the commandos in the canoes, Michelle had rushed along the wharf, shouting at Mortimer, creating a scene, pretending they were having a lovers' quarrel. Then, much to the guard's surprise, she had rushed up the gangway of the ship and asked the guard for a cigarette. Now she was keeping the guard distracted, so that the commandos could go about their business of attaching their mines to the ships.

Mortimer had stopped beside the ship's gangway. He could see Michelle up by the railing and all he wanted to do was get her off there! But now there was a German army bike coming towards him and it looked like it was being ridden by a member of the Hitler Youth! He suddenly pulled out his revolver and pointed it at the approaching bike.

"*No!*" Danny roared, throwing up his arms as the bike ground to a halt. "We are here to help you! There are soldiers coming!"

Mortimer couldn't believe what he was hearing. Not only had the words been spoken in English, but this boy even *sounded* English!

"Who are you?" he demanded.

Danny didn't know how to answer. His mind was in a spin! It was Charley who spoke up.

"It doesn't matter who we are!" she said from the sidecar. "There are soldiers coming! You have to get out of here!"

Mortimer was stunned to hear another young English voice coming from the sidecar, but now there was someone else coming up behind him. He turned to see Christian approaching cautiously, also armed with a revolver.

"Who are these people?" Christian asked.

Mortimer shook his head.

"I don't know."

"We are friends…" Danny started to say.

That was as far as he got. Suddenly up the road behind them they heard a shout. They looked back and now they saw them coming - soldiers, many soldiers running down the hill towards them.

"It's a trap!" Christian shouted, immediately pointing his gun at Danny! "It's this Hitler Youth boy!"

"No!" Danny shouted. "It was your neighbour who betrayed you - Madame du Pont!"

Christian hesitated, his finger on the trigger. *The boy sounded English!*

Danny knew he had to keep talking!

"Michelle is in danger!" he blurted out. "You must get her off the ship!"

The mention of Michelle's name seemed to snap Mortimer's attention back to the ship, but when he looked, Michelle was no longer standing at the railings.

Suddenly there came the crackle of gunfire. The soldiers had started to shoot at them. Mortimer leapt up onto the gangway of the ship.

"Get back to the others!" he screamed to Christian as he started up the steps.

Christian took off down the wharf, heading for the safety of the packing crates, and Danny knew they also had to find cover. He revved up the bike and took off after Christian, catching him up in no time.

"Jump on!' he shouted.

At first Christian kept running, but then, as the bullets began to rip through the air around them, he leapt onto the back of the bike.

"Hold on!" Danny shouted, opening up the throttle and powering the bike down the wharf to the cargo yard.

There they found Roger, Tommy and Henri taking cover behind a row of packing crates, preparing themselves for the attack. Danny skidded to a halt behind the crates and Christian leapt off the bike.

"*Merci*," he said, nodding to Danny.

"No problem," Danny replied.

Now Christian joined the other men.

"Who are they?" Roger and Tommy asked, but all Christian could do was shake his head.

"I don't know, but I think they're English!"

Tommy and Roger glanced back briefly - but now the bullets were beginning to thud into the crates all around them.

"Here they come!" Roger announced, and they all opened fire on the advancing soldiers.

Danny, meanwhile, had climbed off the bike and was taking a peek around the edge of a large packing crate. It was a terrifying sight! There were soldiers skirmishing down the wharf towards them - pausing to fire their weapons then advancing. He could also see soldiers running up the gangway onto the ship where they had last seen Michelle and Mortimer. He strained his eyes, searching the ship's deck for any sign of them, but it was too dark and too far away. He also looked down into the water for any sign of the commandos - he couldn't see them either. *Had they already finished attaching their mines? Were the ships about to blow?*

Danny knew he had to do something. He ran back to the bike where Charley was still nestled down in the sidecar, too scared to move!

"Charley, get out!" he barked as he climbed back onto the bike.

"Why?" Charley cried. "What are you doing?"

She sounded terrified.

"I'm going to fetch them," Danny said, kicking the bike into life. "Now get out, please!"

Charley climbed out.

"Are you sure about this?" she shouted above the revving engine.

Danny glanced at her, his eyes blazing.

"Charley," he shouted back, "this is why we came!"

Before she could reply, he opened up the bike's throttle to maximum power and suddenly took off.

"Be careful!" Charley shouted after him.

When Christian and the others looked back and saw Danny roaring towards the quayside they must have thought he was about to plunge straight into the harbour! When the bike launched itself over the water and began to climb into the night sky, all they could do is gawk in amazement!

\*

Once Danny had reached a decent height he turned the bike towards the ship. Over on the wharf he could see some of the German soldiers doing a double take on seeing the flying bike.

Danny kept the bike high as he approached the ship. He wanted a bird's-eye view to try and see exactly where Mortimer and Michelle were. As it turned out he was able to spot their position almost immediately because of the flashes coming from Mortimer's revolver. There was a serious gunfight taking place on the ship's deck. The soldiers were moving down the ship, their machine guns spitting fire as they gradually advanced. Farther down the deck he could see the occasional flash from a revolver, which he knew must be Mortimer firing off the odd shot as he and Michelle retreated. The problem was - they were running out of deck! Soon they would be at the bow of the ship with nowhere left to go!

Danny knew he had to get the bike down there fast. He pushed down on the handlebars and the bike swooped in towards the ship.

*

Down on the ship's deck Captain Strieber was shouting orders to his men, urging them forwards, when he spotted the bike in the sky. He could not explain this bizarre flying motorbike, but he recognised it as the same one that had just helped one of the enemy escape down the wharf.

"Bring me the bazooka!" Captain Strieber bellowed.

*

As Danny came in towards the ship he could see that Mortimer and Michelle were now pinned down behind a lifeboat near the bow. There was a bit of open deck fairly close to them, which was where he was going to have to try and land. It was going to be *very tight,* but it wasn't like he had a choice!

Danny slowed the bike right down and prepared for what he suspected was going to be a very hairy landing! That's when he saw the soldier step out onto the open deck. He had a long cylindrical object on his shoulder and it was pointing directly at the bike!

*Bazooka!* was Danny's first thought.

At that moment the bazooka roared and there was suddenly an angry fireball speeding directly towards him! Danny banked sharply to one side and the fiery shell fizzed past so close he could feel the heat!

"Reload!" the captain screamed, and a soldier came running with another shell.

Although rattled by the near miss, Danny knew there was no time to waste. He turned the bike around and aimed for the ship again. He could tell that Mortimer and Michelle's situation was getting even more desperate. They were no longer firing, so had probably run out of ammo. It was now just a matter of time before the soldiers overran them.

Mortimer and Michelle must have realised this as well because Danny suddenly saw them leaping to their feet and rushing

towards the railing. It looked like they were going to jump!

"Yes!" Danny muttered. "Get off! *Jump!*"

They reached the railing and started to climb over. Mortimer was giving Michelle a hand - when suddenly she fell back!

*Had she slipped?* Danny couldn't be sure. Now he could see Mortimer trying to haul Michelle to her feet again, but she was flopping around like a rag doll! *Had she been shot?* Danny didn't want to believe what he was seeing! *Surely it couldn't end like this again? Had they failed to change anything?*

The soldiers were getting closer, still firing their weapons, and Mortimer had no choice but to drag Michelle back behind the lifeboat again.

"*No!*" Danny roared.

*He would not let it end like this!* He took the bike in towards the ship again. There was now machine gun fire coming in his direction as well. He could hear the bullets pinging off the undercarriage. He had to get down fast!

He then saw the German officer lifting the bazooka to his shoulder again and realised he was a sitting duck. The situation required drastic action and he only had a couple of seconds to make a decision. He wound the bike's accelerator up to full power and aimed it directly at the officer with the bazooka. He waited until the bike was just passing over the ship's railings then he jumped!

\*

Looking through the bazooka sights, the captain's eyes grew large as he saw the bike hurtling towards him! He fired off a shell and there was a massive explosion!

\*

Danny landed hard and tumbled across the deck. He had to cover up his head as a giant orange fireball lit up the ship's deck. He could feel the intense heat sweeping over him - so hot that he thought his hair and shirt had caught fire!

When the fireball began to subside Danny looked up. Apart from the burning wreckage of the bike there was not much else left standing! The explosion had flattened most of the soldiers in the advance group and there was definitely no sign of the captain!

Farther back through the smoke, Danny could already see a second wave of soldiers coming down the deck towards them. It was time to move. Using the billowing smoke from the bike wreckage as cover he dashed over to where Mortimer and Michelle were huddled behind the lifeboat.

The scene that greeted him was shocking! Mortimer was crouching over Michelle, ripping up his shirt to make bandages. She was looking up at him, wide-eyed, in shock. She was alive, but there was a pool of blood spreading out on the deck beneath her.

"The boat's going to blow!" Danny shouted. "We have to get off!"

Suddenly a burst of gunfire ricocheted off the railings behind them, and when Danny looked over the lifeboat he was shocked to see how close the approaching soldiers were!

"You need to get yourself and Michelle off *now*!" he barked at Mortimer then, to Mortimer's surprise, this young boy pulled an oar off the side of the lifeboat.

Mortimer lifted Michelle up in his arms and took her to the railing. When he looked back he was astonished to see how calmly the boy was preparing to meet the soldiers, armed with nothing but an oar!

As the first soldier came around the side of the lifeboat Danny whacked him hard with the oar. The soldier landed flat on his back, out cold on the deck. Danny glanced back and saw that Mortimer had now climbed over the railing, but was still hesitating!

"*Jump!*" Danny screamed.

Mortimer looked back at Danny one more time and seemed to

give him a nod of thanks then he and Michelle disappeared over the side.

Danny turned back and got the fright of his life - a soldier was rushing at him with a bayonet fixed to his rifle. Danny stepped aside and hit him so hard on the back of the helmet that he did an impressive forwards somersault over the railing and into the harbour. There were now dozens more soldiers close behind and Danny knew he had to get off as well. He started towards the railing, but another soldier grabbed him from behind. In one fluid movement Danny executed the perfect judo throw and his assailant was catapulted, howling, over the edge.

Now there was another soldier on him then another! He tried to fight them off, but he was getting overwhelmed! As they grappled he noticed he was getting forced back towards the railing. He knew this was his only chance. Instead of trying to push the soldiers away Danny suddenly pulled at them. They all tottered backwards and flipped over the railing.

As Danny hit the icy water one of the soldiers was still holding on to him. He struggled to break free, but he wouldn't let go and the two of them sunk deeper and deeper into the icy darkness. For just a second Danny had a flash of those last dreadful moments with his sister in the sea off Australia, but somehow this image gave him renewed strength. With one last desperate effort he managed to wriggle out of the soldier's clutches and fight his way to the surface.

Danny broke the surface, gasping for air. He was very close to the ship's hull and the first thing he saw, sticking to the ship like some deadly shellfish, was a limpet mine. He knew it could blow at any moment! He started to swim away from the ship, at the same time trying to look out for any sign of Mortimer and Michelle.

"Mortimer!" he shouted, as he swam. "*Mortimer!*"

Suddenly someone grabbed him roughly by the collar. His first thought was that it was a German soldier attacking him again, and he was about to lash out, but he then felt the side of a canoe bumping up against him and now, when he looked up, he saw the blackened face of a commando staring down at him.

"English?" the commando growled, and Danny nodded.

There was a second commando in the canoe, who now began to paddle, and suddenly Danny was being pulled along through the water away from the ship.

"We need to find Mortimer!" Danny spluttered, gasping for air.

"Quiet!" the first commando snapped. "Hold on to the side."

Clinging to the side of the canoe, Danny knew by the way both commandos were now really digging in their paddles that the ship was about to blow. All he could imagine was that Mortimer and Michelle were still in the water somewhere near the ship.

Suddenly the harbour erupted!

Danny felt the force of the first blast through the water. Now there were explosions going off everywhere - blasts ripping through ships all around the harbour. A wave of intense heat swept over them, forcing Danny to turn his head away. When he looked again there were huge billowing fires raging on the ships, lighting up the harbour.

And in this light he now saw another canoe. It wasn't too far from them and beside it he could see two heads bobbing in the water. It had to be Mortimer and Michelle!

One of the commandos now nudged his mate; he had seen something speeding across the harbour towards them. It was a harbour patrol speedboat. They put down their paddles and picked up their machine guns.

Danny cursed and sank down into the water again. He knew if a gun battle broke out now he was going to have to dive!

As the speedboat swept in towards them, they recognised the two figures standing up front. Tommy was at the controls with Roger standing beside him. The relief was enormous. The commandos laid down their weapons again and Danny said a quiet prayer of thanks.

Tommy sped over to the other canoe first. He pulled the speedboat up beside them and, as Roger helped everyone aboard, Danny saw that it was definitely Mortimer and Michelle, but he was disturbed to see how limp and lifeless Michelle looked.

The boat then roared over to their canoe and the next thing Danny felt was Roger's huge hands grabbing him by the shirt and plucking him out of the water. He was deposited on the floor of the boat where he lay, panting for breath. He could hear the boat's engines being revved to the full as Tommy floored the accelerator and powered the boat out of the harbour.

He felt someone at his side. It was Charley!

"Hi," she said with a smile. "You OK?"

Danny nodded. For a moment he was speechless; he was so pleased to see her!

"I've got some good news." Charley smiled. "Michelle is going to be OK. It's just her arm that's been hit."

Charley's words filled Danny with such an overpowering sense of relief that he didn't know whether to laugh or cry. Suddenly everything they had been through - all the terror, all the tension, all the bruises and battles - seemed worthwhile. A smile appeared on Danny's face, and it crossed Charley's mind that this was probably the first time she had seen him *really smile*!

"We did it," said Danny. "We made the Change."

But now his smile began to fade. It was as though something else had just occurred to him. Suddenly he sat bolt upright.

"What's wrong?" Charley asked, shocked by the sudden change.

"Charley! Where's the rucksack?" Danny demanded.

Charley looked around, trying to remember where she had put it.

"Um... I think it's over there. Why?"

"Charley!" Danny was now sounding frantic. "The Change has happened! The Time Ripple will be coming! We have to give Mortimer the book! Now... w*here is the rucksack?*"

Charley blinked a couple of times as she tried to digest this - then suddenly she seemed to understand the urgency of the situation.

"OK, I'll find it," she said, and she quickly went off looking.

Danny went to the back of the boat where Roger was tending to Michelle's wound. Mortimer was sitting with her head in his lap. When he saw Danny he called to him, his voice raw with emotion.

"We owe you our lives," he said, "and we don't even know who you are."

Now Michelle stretched out her good arm towards Danny and took his hand. "*Merci*," she said softly. "*Merci beaucoup!*"

"Please," said Mortimer, "you must tell us who you are."

"It doesn't matter now," Danny replied. He was looking around to see where Charley had got to. "One day you'll find out, but now there's something I have to give you. It's a very important book. You must look after it."

"A book?" Mortimer sounded confused. "What sort of book?"

"I can't explain now. There's a letter inside that you must read. One day you'll understand."

Danny turned again and was about to shout impatiently to Charley when thankfully she appeared with the rucksack in her hand. He took it from her and removed Mortimer's journal. Even in the dark he could tell how tattered and scorched it was. He handed it to Mortimer.

"Please look after it," Danny said. "It's the most important book you or I will ever have in our lives."

"Of course I will," Mortimer replied. "Thank you." He

placed the book safely in his jacket pocket. "Thank you for everything."

At last Danny could breathe. It was as if a huge weight of responsibility had been lifted from his shoulders. He went and sat on one side of the boat and Charley came and sat beside him.

"Now what?" she asked.

Danny shook his head.

"I don't know," he replied.

He really didn't know. They were all just going on Mortimer's theory that, after the Change had happened, time would catch up and they would suddenly find themselves back in England - back in the present. *Was the Time Ripple on its way now? Had it launched itself out of the 1940s? Was it now speeding through the 50s, the 60s, the 70s? Was it blasting through the 80s at that very moment, or perhaps the 90s? Had it gone past his date of birth yet? Entered the new millennium? Was there even such a thing as a Time Ripple? How did Mortimer really know?*

"I wonder how Spike's doing," said Charley, suddenly sounding on the verge of tears. "I wonder if we'll ever see him again?"

"Of course we will," Danny said confidently, putting an arm around Charley's shoulders to comfort her.

Although he wouldn't dare let Charley know, Danny had also been having some doubts and worries about Spike. *What if he died? Surely if someone was dead they were dead - no matter what time frame it happened in?*

They now sat quietly together with their thoughts. The sound of gunfire was fading as the boat powered its way down the River Gironde towards the ocean. Danny thought about Christian and Henri, and the other members of the French Resistance who were still fighting the German soldiers. He prayed that they would all survive that night.

As they reached the mouth of the river the wind picked up and Charley snuggled up closer to Danny. He had to admit he liked the feeling of having her beside him - then out of the blue he was struck by a disturbing thought. What if, after this whole Time Ripple thing caught up, he never saw her again? The Change that had just happened might lead to a chain of events that none of them could predict - in which they never met!

"Hey, Charley, listen to me for a sec will you?" he said. "On the off chance that things change in such a way that we don't get to meet again…"

"*What?*"

Charley sounded alarmed. She didn't even want to entertain the idea!

"Well, we don't know, do we?" Danny continued. "I mean it *might* happen. Anyway, I just wanted to say that I'm… well, I'm really glad I met you."

"I'm glad I met you too."

There was now a bit of an awkward silence. Danny wanted to say more - he just had to work up the courage to say it! He took a deep breath.

"And… well… the other thing I wanted to say is… I actually… well, I actually really like…"

\*

When the sun rose the next morning in Bordeaux very few people in the town had slept. The huge explosions down at the harbour had awakened everyone then a gun battle had raged for quite some time after that.

However, the news was good. Five German merchant navy ships lay at the bottom of the harbour and it seemed the commandos (and those who had helped them) had all managed to escape.

Even though Madame du Pont had not ventured out that morning she knew that something was very wrong! Everyone who walked past her house seemed to stare towards it in a most unfriendly manner. It was as if they knew something! Perhaps her telephone calls to Monsieur Ballac had become public knowledge?

What Madame du Pont could not see from inside were the giant Nazi swastikas someone had painted all over her house during the night.

# Chapter 19

# The Birthday

Danny awoke to the sound of his mother singing.

"Happy birthday to you, happy birthday to you..."

"Ah, Mum!" he groaned, turning over. "It's too early!"

The singing continued and Danny was forced to open one eye and take a peek. His mother was standing at his bedroom door wearing a silly party hat and holding a cake with thirteen candles on it.

"Chocolate cake - your favourite!" she said, coming in and sitting on his bed. "We'd better eat it before we get any visitors, but blow out the candles first!"

Danny sat up, still half-asleep.

"Bit early for cake isn't it, Mum?"

"Rubbish! It's your birthday!" she replied. "Come on, blow and make a wish!"

Danny blew out the candles. His mother then produced two forks and they started to tuck into the cake.

"Oh, and here's another little something," his mum said suddenly with her mouth full.

She pulled out a small wrapped present and handed it to her son. Danny made a meal of studying, rattling (and even sniffing!) the gift before eventually unwrapping it. It was the latest *iPod*.

"Wow!" he raved, clearly impressed. "Thanks, Mum - this is very cool!"

As Danny stared down at the *iPod*, he suddenly had the weirdest of images flash through his mind. For some bizarre reason he suddenly pictured Adolf Hitler with an *iPod*!

"What's wrong?" his mother asked.

But Danny was now off in his own world. This one strange thought had triggered another - of a flying motorbike! He was then thinking about shopping with Charley and Spike in *a futuristic London!* Next he was imagining grotesque creatures called Hogs, which...

"Daniel!" his mother said.

This jolted him out of it and he looked at her.

"Huh?"

"What's wrong?"

"Oh... I... nothing." Danny shook his head. "I think I was just remembering a dream."

"A good dream I hope?"

"Um..."

Danny's mind took off again. Suddenly his head was being flooded by more incredibly vivid, lifelike images - amazing fights where he dominated because of something called *Combat X!* A machine called TIM! Uncle Morty with no legs! He tried to remember how the dream ended. A boat? Charley?

Eventually he nodded to his mum.

"Yes, I think it was a good dream."

"Oh well, that's the main thing," she said, smiling. Just as she was about to stand up, she noticed a mark on Danny's hand. "What have you done to yourself there?" she asked.

Danny stared down at his hand for a few moments. What he suddenly felt like saying was, 'It's where we had our *BAM* chips inserted', instead he just shook his head and said:

"I don't know."

His mother looked at him sideways.

"You OK?"

"Of course," Danny replied, nodding quickly.

His mother thought he was acting strangely, but decided it must be a teenage thing.

"Right, my friend!" she said, getting up to go. "Time for you to rise and shine! I have a feeling today is going to be a big day!"

Once his mother had left the room Danny climbed out of bed

and went over to the window. He stared out at the view - the rolling lawns, the beautiful gardens with the forest beyond. Over the treetops he could just see the roof of Bosworth Manor.

Even this familiar view brought with it a whole host of bizarre inexplicable images. He suddenly felt like he had seen the grounds before when everything *wasn't* looking so pristine and well kept. In fact, he remembered walking through the property when it was looking decidedly overgrown and uncared for! He had been with Charley, Spike and Uncle Morty, and the really weird thing was that his uncle had been *in a wheelchair*!

*Was he going mad?* Where were all these thoughts coming from? They were so vivid and real - not vague and fuzzy like dreams, but clear and detailed like *memories*!

Danny dressed quickly and rushed outside. Even when he looked back at the house he was suddenly struck by a memory of it looking derelict and overgrown. How could that be? The summer house had always looked as beautiful as it did today - ever since Uncle Morty had insisted they come and stay there after the tragedy in Australia.

Danny ran off through the gardens and soon reached the Great Pond. As usual it was a hive of activity with all the resident ducks and swans swimming amongst the water lilies - yet he had a clear memory of it as an overgrown mud-hole!

And then he was suddenly thinking about *monkey cages*! As far as he remembered they were situated just on the other side of this hedge. He ran through the beautifully manicured arch in the hedge, but instead of monkey cages he found a giant rose garden. Of course, he thought, what did you expect? It was Aunt Michelle's famous rose garden, which he had walked through a hundred times!

He then heard a voice.

"Hi."

It was Charley. She was sitting on a bench overlooking the

rose garden.

"Hi," Danny replied. He went over to her and could tell immediately that she was also suffering from an extreme case of confusion! "What are you doing down here so early?"

Charley looked like she couldn't even *begin* to explain!

Danny sat down beside her.

"You weren't checking for monkey cages by any chance were you?" he asked.

Charley looked at Danny.

"Yes!" she said. The relief on her face was immense. "Where Adam and Eve lived! Do you *also* remember that?" When Danny nodded, Charley looked like she could have hugged him! "Oh, thank you!" she said, staring heavenwards. "I really thought I was going mad!" She looked at Danny again, suddenly serious. "Did all that stuff really happen? I feel like it *did*!"

"I don't know," said Danny. "I think it must have."

"I thought it was all just an amazing dream," said Charley.

"So did I," Danny said, nodding, "but we couldn't have both had the same dream!"

They sat in silence for a moment, trying to get their minds around what had actually happened. Eventually Danny tried to put his thoughts into words.

"The theory was that once the Change had happened and the Time Ripple had caught up we would find ourselves back here in the present as if nothing had happened. Well, that *is* what seems to have happened... except for one thing... the memories are still with us." Suddenly he had a thought that made him sit bolt upright. "Hey, Charley! Where's Spike?"

"Spike? Oh, he must be... um..." The more Charley thought about it the wider her eyes became. She had been so caught up in her own 'dream' that she hadn't even thought about her brother! "I don't know," she replied. "I haven't seen him today!"

Now they were both thinking the same thing.

"Do you think he…"

"I don't know," Danny replied, "but we'd better go and look!"

\*

By the time they reached the Barnes' cottage they were both panting. Charley led the way through the house then stopped at Spike's bedroom door and took a deep breath.

"What if he's not here?" she whispered.

"He will be," said Danny, trying to sound positive. "He *has* to be! Open it!"

Charley opened the door. The first thing she saw was Spike's empty bed. They went inside then a voice from the corner startled them.

"What's wrong, guys? You think I might be lying dead in a lighthouse somewhere?" Spike was sitting at his computer. He couldn't help grinning when he saw the looks on their faces. "You didn't think you'd get rid of me that easily, did you?"

"*Spike!*" Charley shrieked. She didn't know whether to laugh or cry! "How could you scare us like that, you big creep?"

"What did I do?" Spike protested then he stood up and came over to shake Danny's hand.

"Happy birthday, mate."

"Oh!" Charley cupped a hand to her mouth. "I forgot! Happy birthday, Danny! Sorry!" she said, looking really embarrassed.

"Thanks," Danny replied, "don't worry about it."

"Quite mind-blowing this whole thing isn't it?" Spike said, returning to his desk. "Actually I *might* have been lying dead in a lighthouse if it hadn't been for Sarah and, of course, you guys - to whom I'm eternally grateful! Come and check this out."

Spike was referring to something on his computer. The others went over for a closer look.

"I googled Sarah's name," Spike said, "and look what I found. She only died a few years ago. It sounds like she became an important person. She moved to Israel and spent her life campaigning for peace. She even wrote a few books."

Charley and Danny looked at the pictures on the screen. They were of an elderly, well-educated looking lady. How incredible to think that this was the young girl in the lighthouse. The girl they had pushed to safety in a baggage cart.

Now Spike was moving on to something else.

"OK," he said, clicking his mouse. "Now if either of you still wants proof that all this really did happen then check *this* out!"

A whole lot of images of Adolf Hitler started to pop up on the screen and in every picture he was sporting his funny little narrow moustache.

"Check out Mr Wolf's whiskers," Spike said with a satisfied grin. "We were definitely there!"

At that moment Mrs Barnes suddenly appeared at the bedroom door.

"Oh, there you are," she said. "Happy birthday, Daniel."

"Thanks, Mrs Barnes," Danny mumbled.

"Your uncle has asked if you could please meet him down at the pavilion. In fact, he asked if *all three* of you could go down there. Don't ask me why!"

"OK, thanks, Mum," said Charley.

\*

The three friends made their way down through the gardens towards the pavilion.

"Hey, do you think our programs still work?" Charley asked.

Spike smiled.

"Good question, Monkey Girl. Let's test them and see. Ask me a question that only the *Encyclopaedia* program could possibly know."

Danny had a question. Just moments before, he had been thinking about what a perfect summer's day it was - beautiful sunshine and a moderate temperature. How different to the hot, muggy, extremely wet conditions they had experienced in the future.

"OK," he said to Spike. "Here's one for you. Tell us what the average temperature in England will be in Year 2200."

Spike thought about it for a moment.

"Thirty-two degrees Celsius! Wow - that's double what it is today!"

"Yes, remember how hot it was," said Charley, "and all the water and the floods? Do you think people have any idea how bad it's going to get?"

"Probably not," said Danny. "Most people only care about what happens in *their* lifetime - not what's going to happen to the Earth in the future."

"It's disgusting," said Charley. "We've got to somehow let people know - so they can start doing something *now*!"

"OK, so my program seems to be working," said Spike. "What about yours, Monkey Girl?"

Charley gave him a withering look.

"Well, what do you want me to do, Genius?"

"I don't know. Why don't you go and climb a tree or something?"

"Hold on," said Danny. They were now getting near the pavilion. "We have to be careful. We'd have a tough time explaining if anyone saw us. I'm pretty certain we all still have our programs because look - we still have our *BAM* chips."

They all checked their hands and saw the marks.

"Maybe it's because we received them in the future?" Danny said. "So the Time Ripple hasn't reached there yet. It's like what happened to us in the future hasn't changed."

Charley screwed up her face.

"I still don't get this Time Ripple stuff," she said.

"Shh!" said Danny.

They were now approaching the pavilion. They could see two

figures sitting in the neat raised structure with its white wooden roof and open sides.

When Mortimer and Michelle saw the three of them approaching they rose to their feet. Despite their advancing years (they were both in their eighties now!) Danny still considered them the most sprightly, elegant elderly couple he had ever laid eyes upon. They told everyone that they kept each other young!

"Greetings!" Mortimer exclaimed, beaming as Danny and the others climbed the pavilion steps.

As his uncle walked towards him, with his hand outstretched, Danny had a sudden flash of a dishevelled, wheelchair-bound Mortimer.

"Hi, Uncle Morty," Danny said shyly.

"Happy birthday, lad," his uncle said, shaking his hand vigorously. "I've waited so long for this day!"

Now Michelle came over to him.

"Happy birthday, Daniel," she said, kissing him on both cheeks like she always did.

"Thanks, Aunt Michelle," Danny said, blushing.

Now Mortimer turned to the others.

"Michael, Charlotte, how very good to see you! What a day this is!"

Michelle kissed them both as well then Mortimer indicated the chairs that had been put out for them.

"Come on - sit, sit, sit," he said. "Daniel, I want you right here please."

Uncle Morty patted the chair beside him and waited until everyone was settled before leaning down and removing something from a leather case on the floor beside him. He then turned to Danny with the item in his hands.

"I've been waiting over sixty years to give you this," he said.

Danny looked at what Mortimer was holding. It was the journal - burned and tattered, and even more worn-looking than the last

# THE BIRTHDAY

time they had seen it.

"For over sixty years, my beautiful wife here and I have been waiting to say thank you to the three of you. Of course, on that night in Bordeaux when you helped us escape, we had no idea who you were or where you had come from! I must confess my curiosity regarding that incident and this book got the better of me a long time ago. As I read this book and the letter in it (that I had written to myself!) I slowly began to realise the enormity of the secret contained in these pages."

Mortimer looked down at the book again. He held it like it was his most prized possession. When he looked up again his eyes were gleaming in a way Danny had never seen before.

"My instruction to myself was to bring this book to you, Daniel, on your thirteenth birthday then together we would embark on the project of building another machine - a 'TIM 2' if you like. Well, I'm afraid, to a certain extent, I've ignored the instructions I gave myself at the beginning of this book."

This announcement made Charley and Spike glance over at Danny. *Ignoring the instructions in the book?* This was not what they wanted to hear!

"You see," Mortimer continued "I realised if I waited until now to do anything I would be way too old. So the truth is I've spent most of my life studying this book and following its instructions. Unfortunately some of the pages containing important information were burned, so I have had to try and work out some things again. I won't lie to you - it hasn't been easy. In fact it has been a lifetime of work, but at least I am able to say to you now that... well, that 'TIM 2' already exists."

"What?" Danny gasped - trying to register what he was hearing! "You've already built another machine?"

Mortimer smiled.

"Already? I suppose to you it must seem like 'already', but it's actually been over forty years of hard work! The missing information from the burned pages has given us some real headaches and, in fact, it was only fairly recently that we started to really see the light at the end of the tunnel. We are now in the process of conducting final tests, but we feel we are on the verge of success." Now he spoke directly to Danny. "What I'm saying, Daniel, is I think we are almost ready for the next journey, and we know where that journey will be to, don't we?

"Australia," whispered Spike, barely able to contain his excitement.

When Danny looked up there were tears in his eyes. He tried to fight them back, but they were soon rolling down his cheeks. Hearing these words was just too much for him to handle. He was going to be given the chance to change the single most devastating event in his life.

"Thank you," he said.

Michelle leaned over and took Danny's hand.

"Daniel. You have given us *our lives*! What a gift! It is us who must thank *you* - and we do so from the very bottom of our hearts! Hopefully it will soon be your turn to receive a miracle."

Mortimer suddenly clapped his hands together.

"But all this talk is for another day!" he said, and there was a mischievous sparkle in his eyes. "Today it is Daniel's birthday and we've organised a little something to celebrate, so, off you go up to the main house. We will see you up there!"

*

Another surprise! To add to everything else! As the three of them walked away from the pavilion the excitement was crackling around them like electricity.

"You OK?" Charley asked Danny.

"Yeah, fine. It's all just… a bit much to take in!"

"We're going on another trip!" Spike raved.

He was doing a little dance he was so excited!

Danny shook his head.

# THE BIRTHDAY

"Guys - I *really* think I should do this next trip on my own."

Spike and Charley looked at him for a few seconds then they both burst out laughing.

"That's a good one!" Spike roared. "Hey, Charles! On his own!"

"Danny!" Charley giggled. "Do you *really* think we'd let you go without us?"

Danny shook his head again and let out an exaggerated sigh.

"You guys have such short memories, you know that? What about small matters such as Hogs and Timecops?"

"We've done it once - we'll do it again," said Spike. "Anyway, this one will just be a quick trip. We nip back to Australia two years ago - change the course of events on that day - then come straight home!"

"Just like that, eh?"

Danny smiled.

"Just like that!" said Spike, nodding.

Now, as they got closer to the main house, they could hear music drifting through the trees.

"Hey! Green Day! Cool!" said Charley, as she recognised the song. "Where's it coming from?"

They emerged from the trees and were treated to the amazing sight of Bosworth Manor gleaming magnificently in the sunshine. A far cry from how they remembered it looking before! The music seemed to be coming from the other side of the manor house, so they made their way around the house and were surprised to find several large white marquees set up on the lawn. Inside, catering staff were adding the final touches to long tables laden with food and refreshments.

Spike looked at the others then gave Danny a vigorous shake.

"Looks like we're having a party, my boy!"

Danny couldn't believe what he was seeing. *Was all this for him?*

But it was the stage beyond the marquees that was really pulling at Danny like a magnet. It was a large stage, decked out with lights and speakers, and from the speakers boomed the sound of his favourite band, Green Day. Now they saw that there was actually a band playing on the stage. They moved up for a closer look.

"Hey, those guys look just like Green Day!" said Charley.

They walked even closer and Charley looked at Danny with wide eyes.

"Danny! That *is Green Day*!" she screeched.

Danny could do nothing but stare in dumbfounded amazement!

And now behind them there was a sudden commotion. They turned to see loads of young people pouring around the corner and rushing up towards the stage. Danny recognised many of them - they were his mates from school! It was then that the band really kicked in with a powerful beat and suddenly Danny, Charley and Spike found themselves surrounded by a sea of laughing, dancing, jumping people.

\*

Mortimer, Michelle and Danny's mum stood far back beyond the marquees and watched everything from a safe distance. A waiter had just presented them with three glasses of champagne.

"My goodness," Danny's mum said. "I know the two of you have always had a soft spot for Daniel, but... all this? For a thirteenth birthday!"

"Margaret - even this is not enough!" Mortimer beamed. "That boy of yours has helped us in ways that you could never imagine!"

"Really?" Danny's mum looked surprised. "I can't get him to make his bed!"

Mortimer let out a hoot of laughter.

"One day, my dear! One day he's going to change your life as well! Just you wait and see!"

Danny's mum still didn't look too convinced, but she raised her glass in a toast. "Well, to unexpected surprises then!"

"Cheers!" said Mortimer.

"Salute!" said Michelle.

\*

Danny and Charley had been dancing so energetically that they were both flushed and out of breath. They decided to take a breather. He led her a little away from the party and they shared a bottle of water as they watched the dance floor.

"Hey, there's something I've been meaning to ask you," said Charley.

"Oh, yes - and what's that?"

"Remember on the boat... you were saying something to me, but... I don't think you quite finished."

Danny smiled, suddenly feeling very self-conscious.

"On the boat? I don't remember that!"

"You liar!" squealed Charley.

"I don't know what you're talking about!" Danny said,

laughing.

"You little liar!"

Then, quite unexpectedly, Charley gave Danny a kiss - right on the lips!

For a second, Danny was shocked, but then he remembered Spike and the mischief he was capable of with his *Mindbender* program. He looked around for Spike.

"Very amusing, Spike! Where are you?"

Spike was actually leaping around in the middle of the dance floor, not paying them even the slightest bit of attention.

Danny turned back to Charley.

"Charley, I..."

But she wasn't standing there any more! She was heading back towards the dance floor, and he was just about to call after her when she stopped and looked back.

"Hey, Danny Piper!" she said, laughing. "Happy birthday!"

Please visit us at:
www.dannypiper.com

We have a whole lot more to talk about -
including a sneak preview of our next adventure!